D0027565

POKéMON

ADVENTURES

EMERALD

™

Pokémon ADVENTURES
Emerald
Volume 26
Perfect Square Edition

Story by HIDENORI KUSAKA
Art by SATOSHI YAMAMOTO

© 2015 Pokémon.
© 1995–2015 Nintendo/Creatures Inc./GAME FREAK inc.
TM, ®, and character names are trademarks of Nintendo.
POCKET MONSTERS SPECIAL Vol. 26
by Hidenori KUSAKA, Satoshi YAMAMOTO
© 1997 Hidenori KUSAKA, Satoshi YAMAMOTO
All rights reserved.
Original Japanese edition published by SHOGAKUKAN.
English translation rights in the United States of America,
Canada, the United Kingdom, Ireland, Australia and
New Zealand arranged with SHOGAKUKAN.

English Adaptation/Bryant Turnage
Translation/Tetsuichiro Miyaki
Touch-up & Lettering/Annaliese Christman
Design/Shawn Carrico
Editor/Annette Roman

The stories, characters and incidents mentioned
in this publication are entirely fictional.

No portion of this book may be reproduced or transmitted in
any form or by any means without written permission from
the copyright holders.

Printed in the U.S.A.

Published by VIZ Media, LLC
P.O. Box 77010
San Francisco, CA 94107

10 9 8 7 6 5 4 3 2 1
First printing, January 2015

PARENTAL ADVISORY
POKÉMON ADVENTURES
is rated A and is suitable
for readers of all ages.
ratings.viz.com

www.perfectsquare.com   www.viz.com

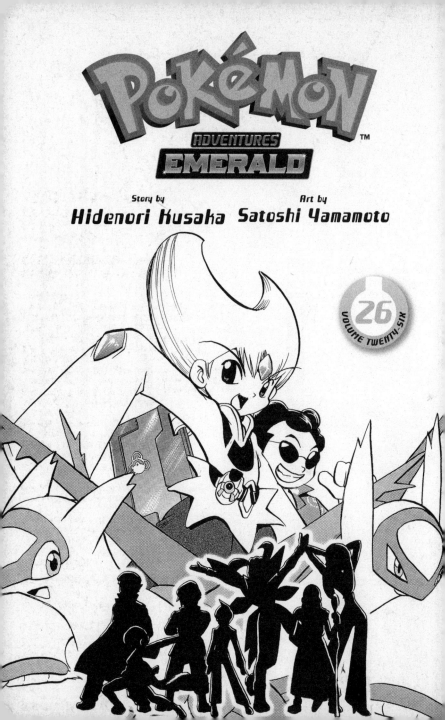

SPECIAL OBJECT

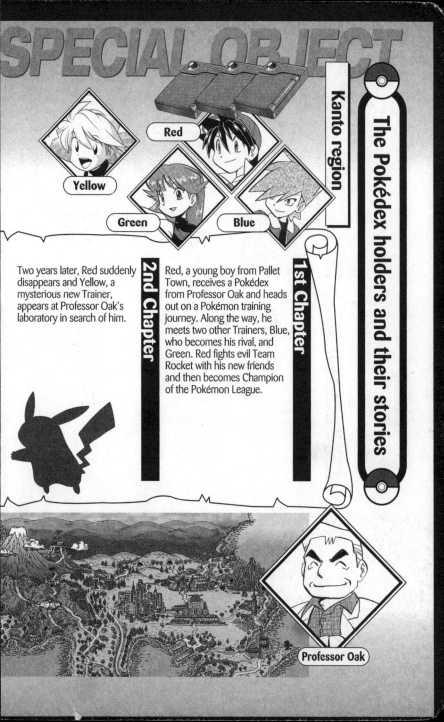

The Pokédex holders and their stories

Kanto region

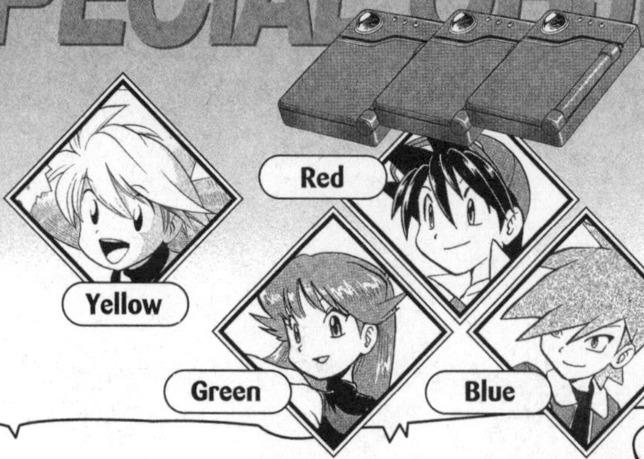
Red
Yellow
Green
Blue

1st Chapter

Red, a young boy from Pallet Town, receives a Pokédex from Professor Oak and heads out on a Pokémon training journey. Along the way, he meets two other Trainers, Blue, who becomes his rival, and Green. Red fights evil Team Rocket with his new friends and then becomes Champion of the Pokémon League.

2nd Chapter

Two years later, Red suddenly disappears and Yellow, a mysterious new Trainer, appears at Professor Oak's laboratory in search of him.

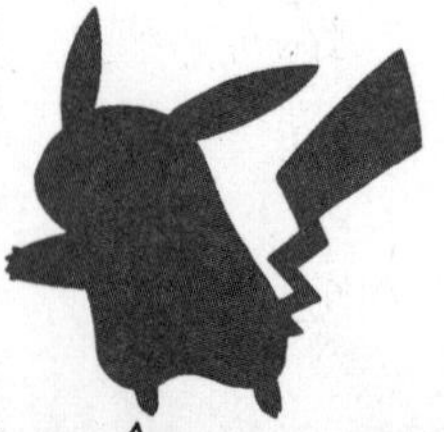

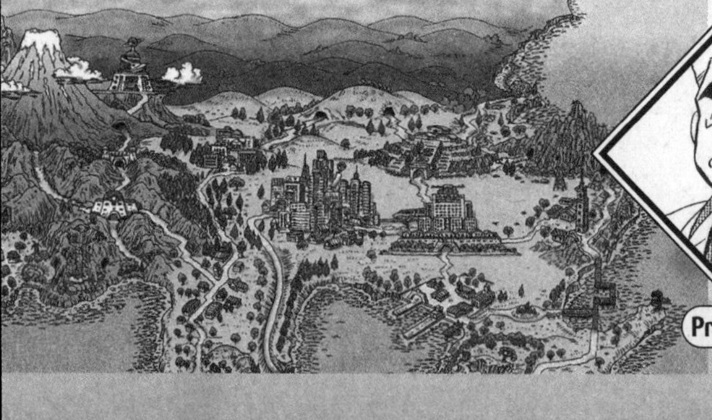

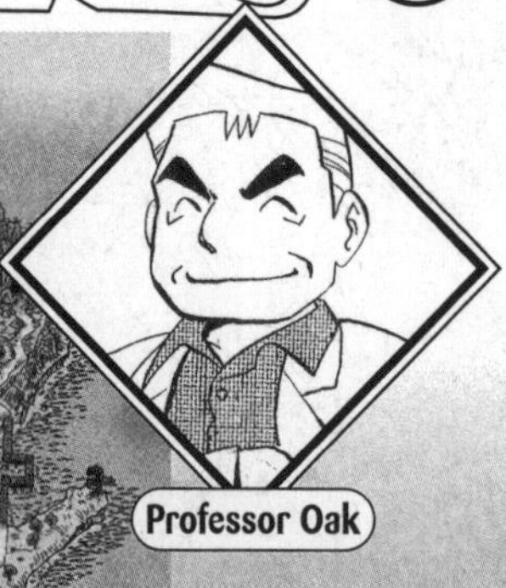
Professor Oak

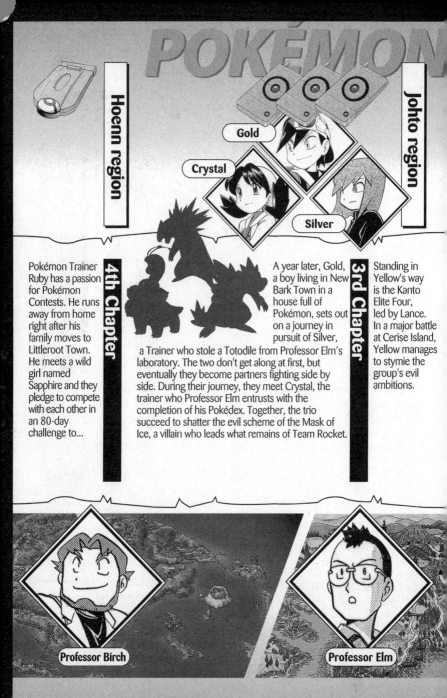

POKÉMON

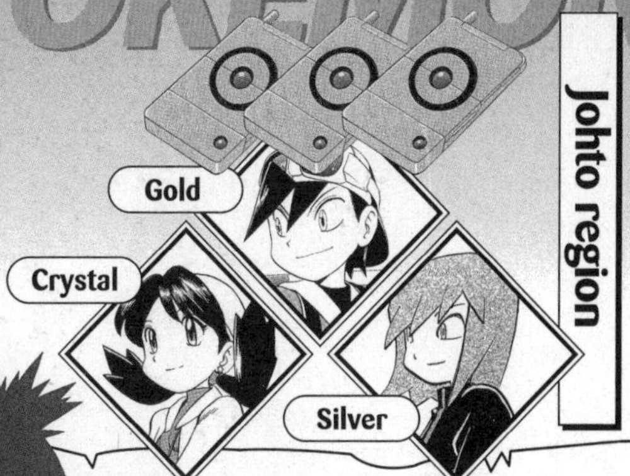
Johto region
Gold
Crystal
Silver

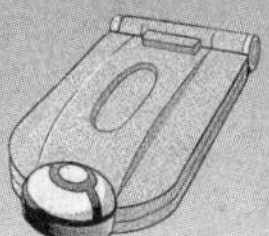
Hoenn region

Standing in Yellow's way is the Kanto Elite Four, led by Lance. In a major battle at Cerise Island, Yellow manages to stymie the group's evil ambitions.

3rd Chapter

A year later, Gold, a boy living in New Bark Town in a house full of Pokémon, sets out on a journey in pursuit of Silver, a Trainer who stole a Totodile from Professor Elm's laboratory. The two don't get along at first, but eventually they become partners fighting side by side. During their journey, they meet Crystal, the trainer who Professor Elm entrusts with the completion of his Pokédex. Together, the trio succeed to shatter the evil scheme of the Mask of Ice, a villain who leads what remains of Team Rocket.

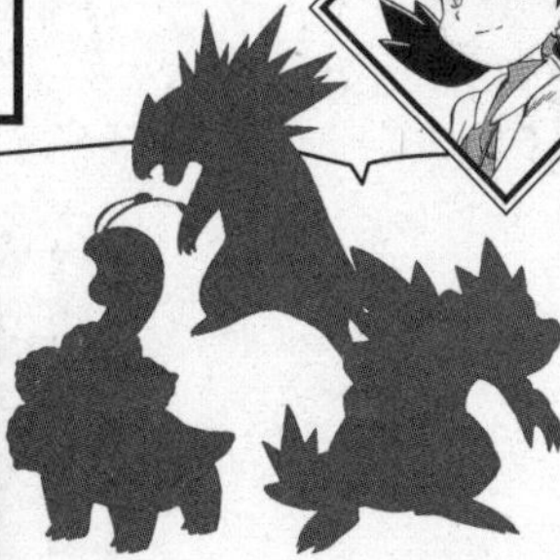

4th Chapter

Pokémon Trainer Ruby has a passion for Pokémon Contests. He runs away from home right after his family moves to Littleroot Town. He meets a wild girl named Sapphire and they pledge to compete with each other in an 80-day challenge to...

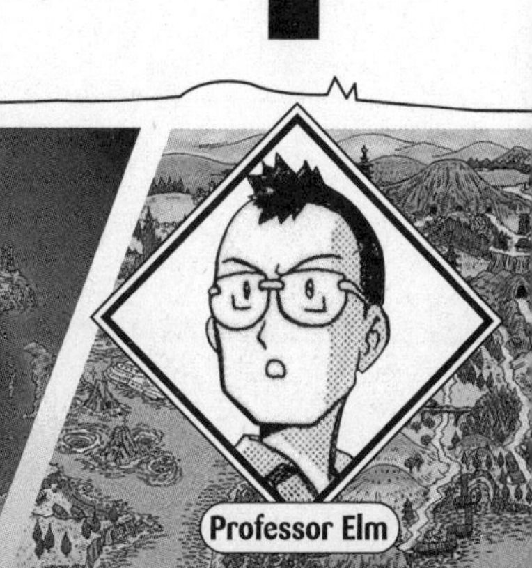
Professor Elm

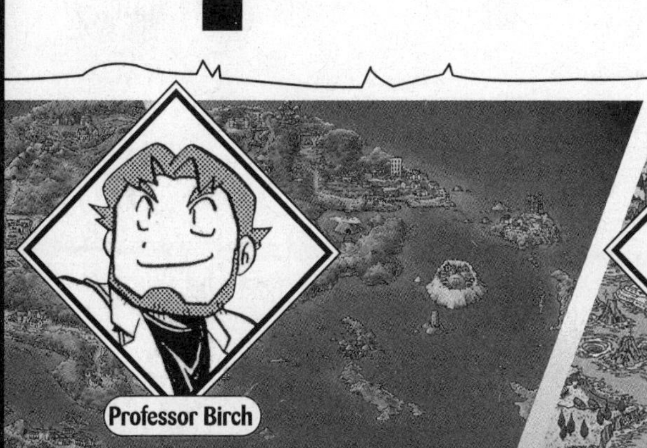
Professor Birch

SPECIAL OBJECT

Kanto region

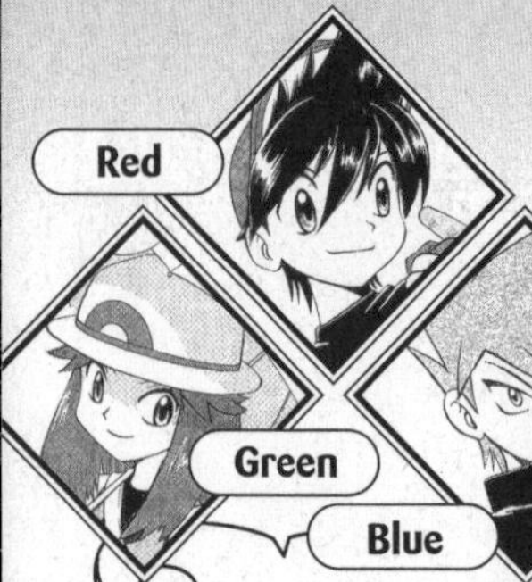
Red
Green
Blue

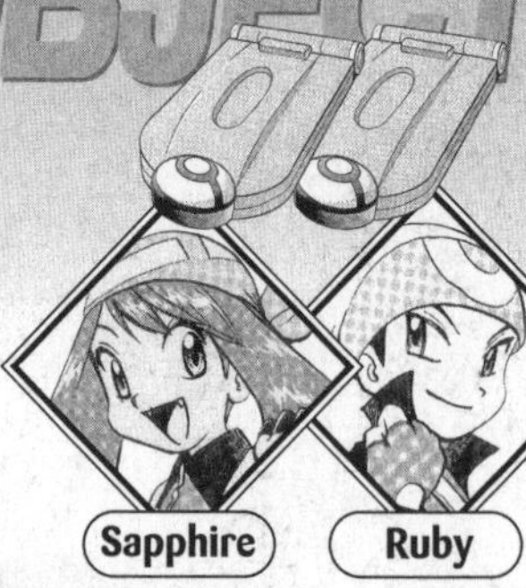
Sapphire
Ruby

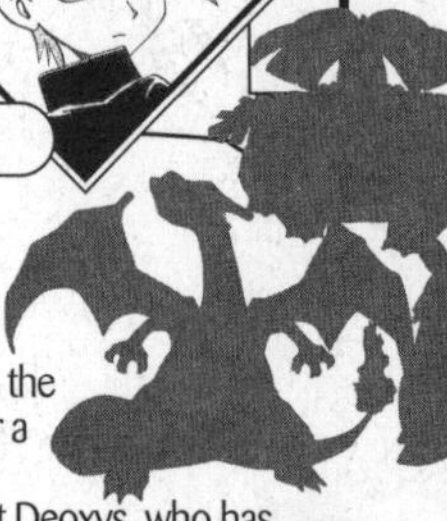

5th Chapter

Six months later, a new adventure unfolds for Red and his friends on the Sevii Islands. After a deadly battle, Red manages to defeat Deoxys, who has fallen into the hands of Giovanni. Silver, in search of his true identity, is faced with the shocking truth that Giovanni is his father. Red and his friends manage to safely land the Team Rocket airship, which was flying out of control thanks to Carr, one of the Three Beasts, who betrayed Team Rocket. But then another of the Three Beasts, Sird, appears, and in a mysterious flash of light the five Pokédex holders–Red, Blue, Green, Yellow and Silver–are petrified. Literally!

...win every Pokémon Contest and every Pokémon Gym Battle, respectively. Meanwhile, in the Hoenn region, Team Aqua and Team Magma set their evil plot in motion. As a result, Legendary Pokémon Groudon and Kyogre are awakened and inflict catastrophic climate changes on Hoenn. In the end, thanks to Ruby and Sapphire's heroic efforts, the two legendary Pokémon go back into hibernation.

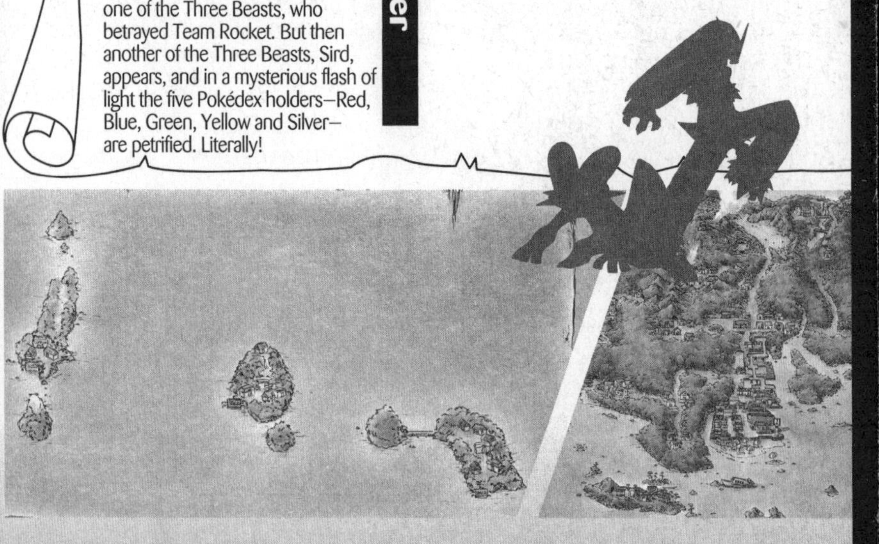

POKÉMON ADVENTURES™ EMERALD

VOLUME TWENTY-SIX 26

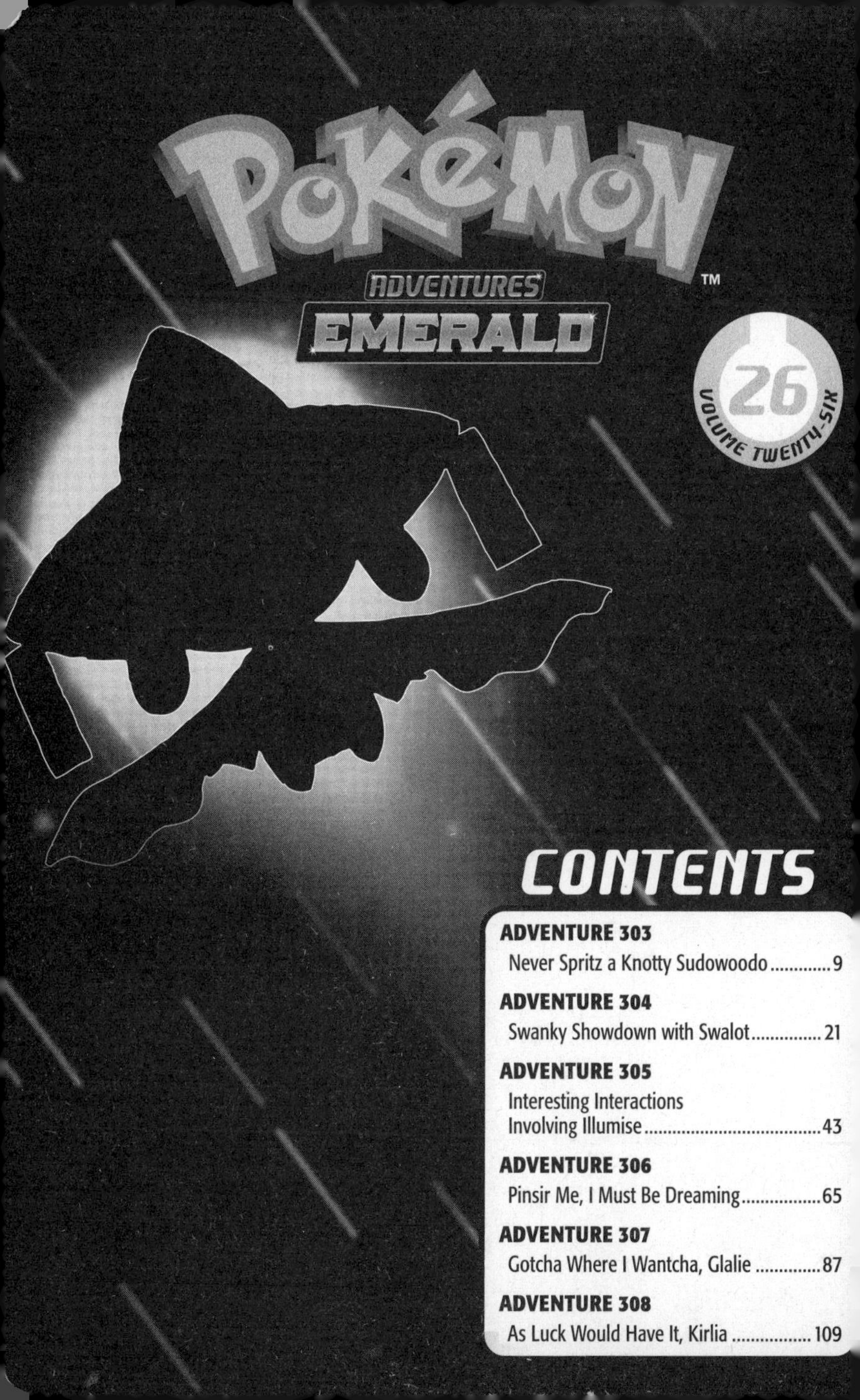

CONTENTS

Emerald

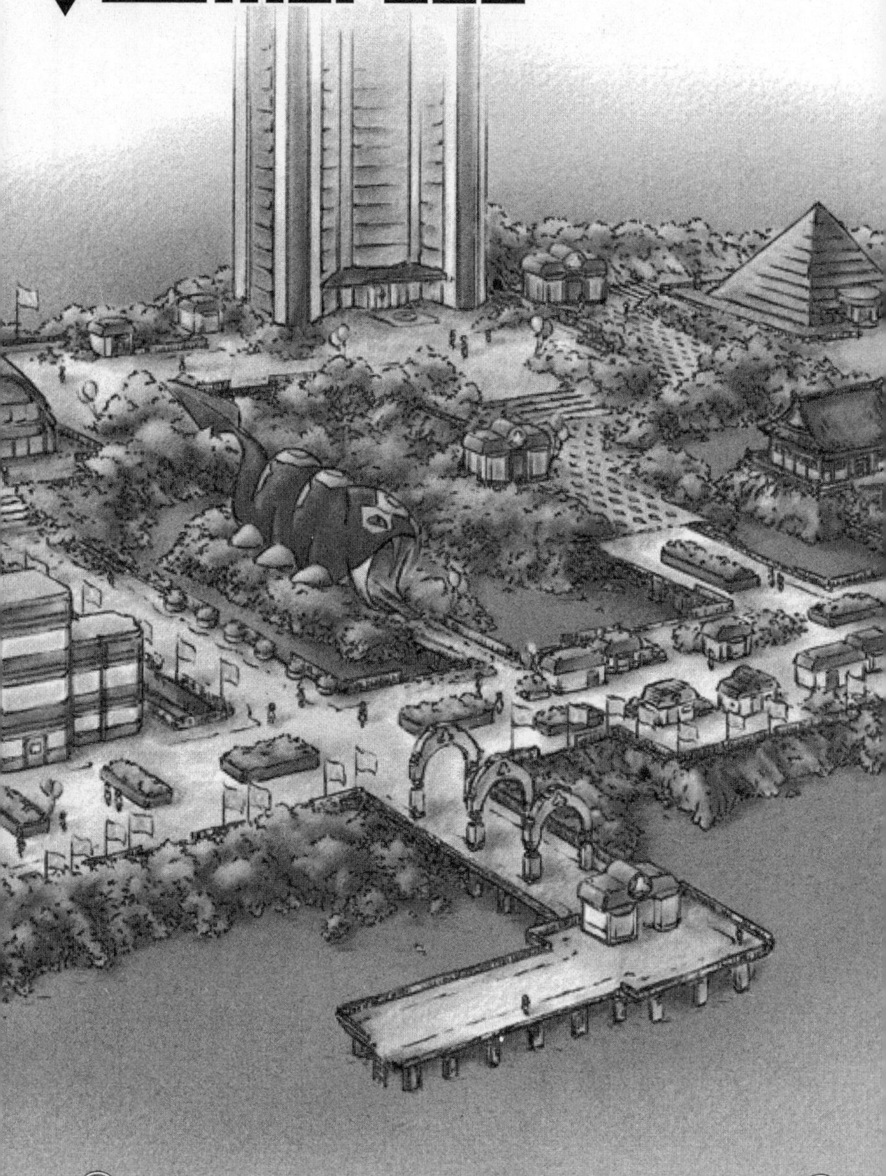

The Sixth Chapter

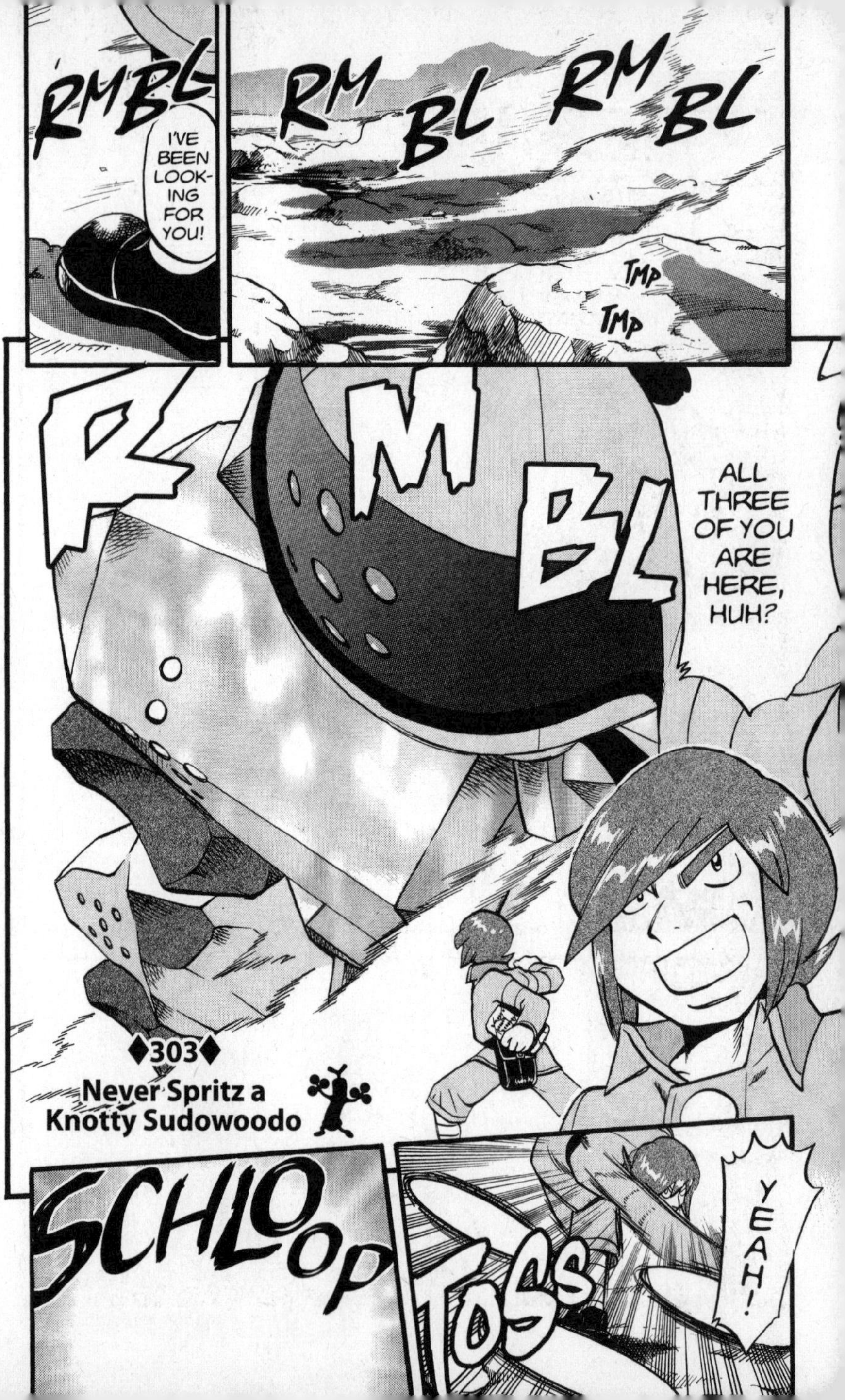
RM BL RM BL
TMP TMP
RMBL
I'VE BEEN LOOKING FOR YOU!
RMBL
ALL THREE OF YOU ARE HERE, HUH?
◆303◆
Never Spritz a Knotty Sudowoodo
TOSS
YEAH!
SCHLOOP

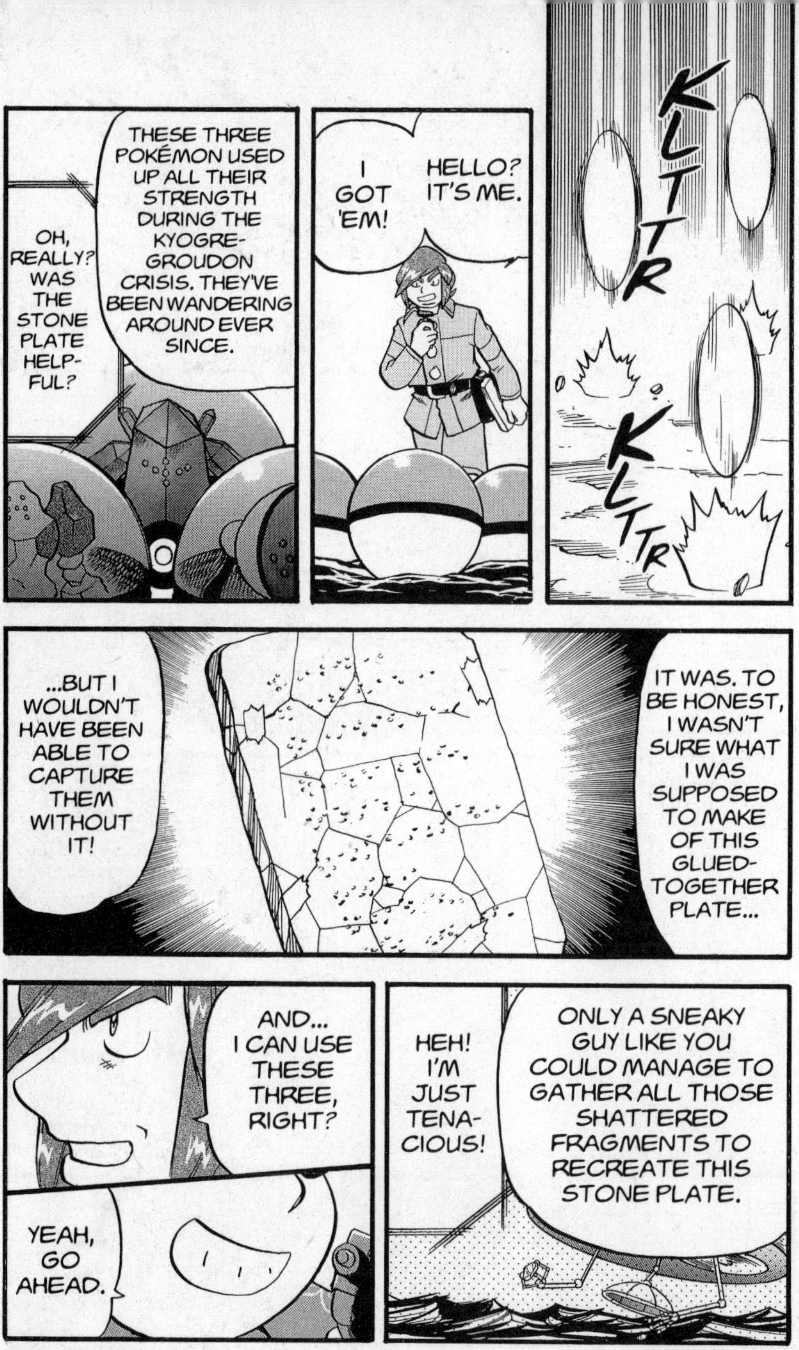
KLTTR
KLTTR
HELLO? IT'S ME.
I GOT 'EM!
THESE THREE POKÉMON USED UP ALL THEIR STRENGTH DURING THE KYOGRE-GROUDON CRISIS. THEY'VE BEEN WANDERING AROUND EVER SINCE.
OH, REALLY? WAS THE STONE PLATE HELPFUL?
IT WAS. TO BE HONEST, I WASN'T SURE WHAT I WAS SUPPOSED TO MAKE OF THIS GLUED-TOGETHER PLATE...
...BUT I WOULDN'T HAVE BEEN ABLE TO CAPTURE THEM WITHOUT IT!
ONLY A SNEAKY GUY LIKE YOU COULD MANAGE TO GATHER ALL THOSE SHATTERED FRAGMENTS TO RECREATE THIS STONE PLATE.
HEH! I'M JUST TENACIOUS!
AND... I CAN USE THESE THREE, RIGHT?
YEAH, GO AHEAD.

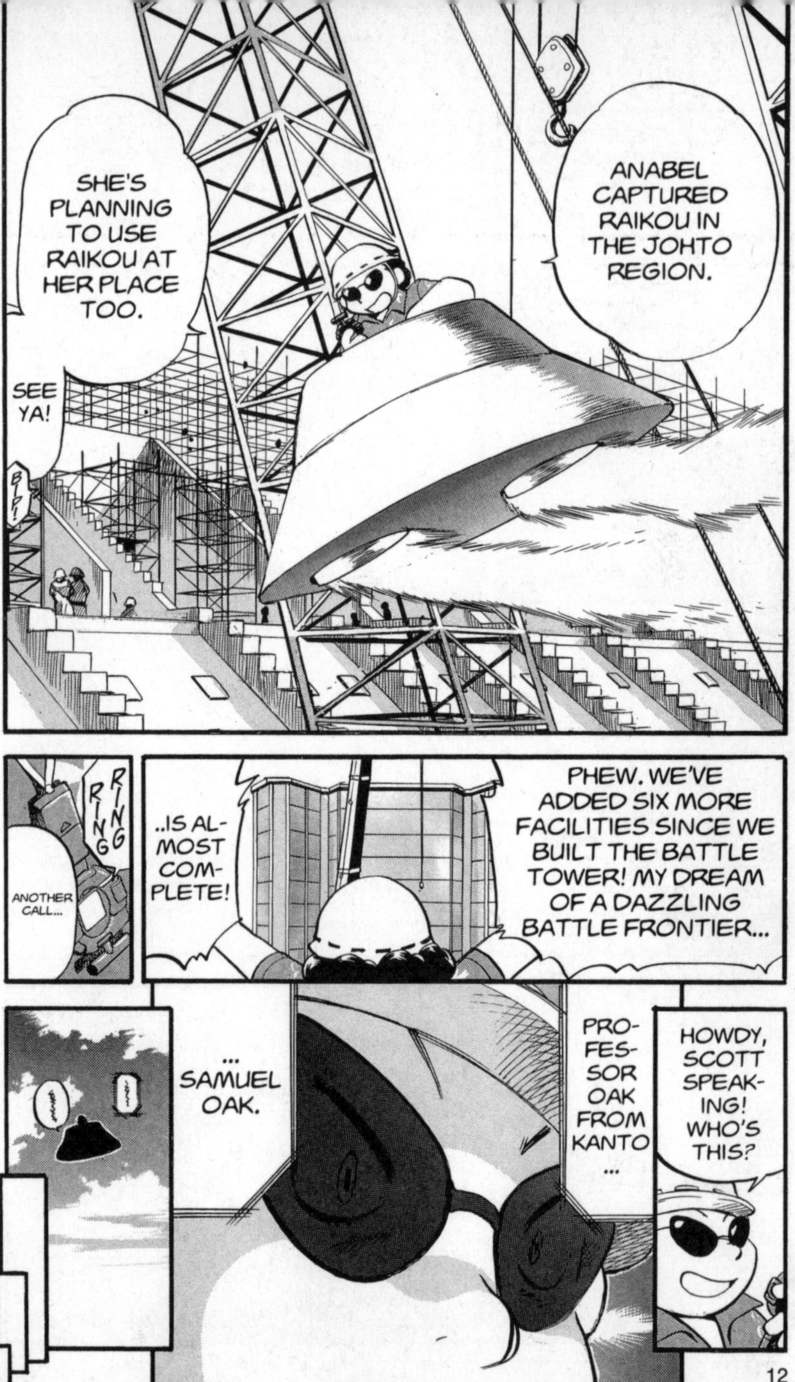
ANABEL CAPTURED RAIKOU IN THE JOHTO REGION.
SHE'S PLANNING TO USE RAIKOU AT HER PLACE TOO.
SEE YA!
BIP!
PHEW. WE'VE ADDED SIX MORE FACILITIES SINCE WE BUILT THE BATTLE TOWER! MY DREAM OF A DAZZLING BATTLE FRONTIER...
..IS AL-MOST COM-PLETE!
RING RING
ANOTHER CALL...
HOWDY, SCOTT SPEAK-ING! WHO'S THIS?
PRO-FES-SOR OAK FROM KANTO ...
... SAMUEL OAK.

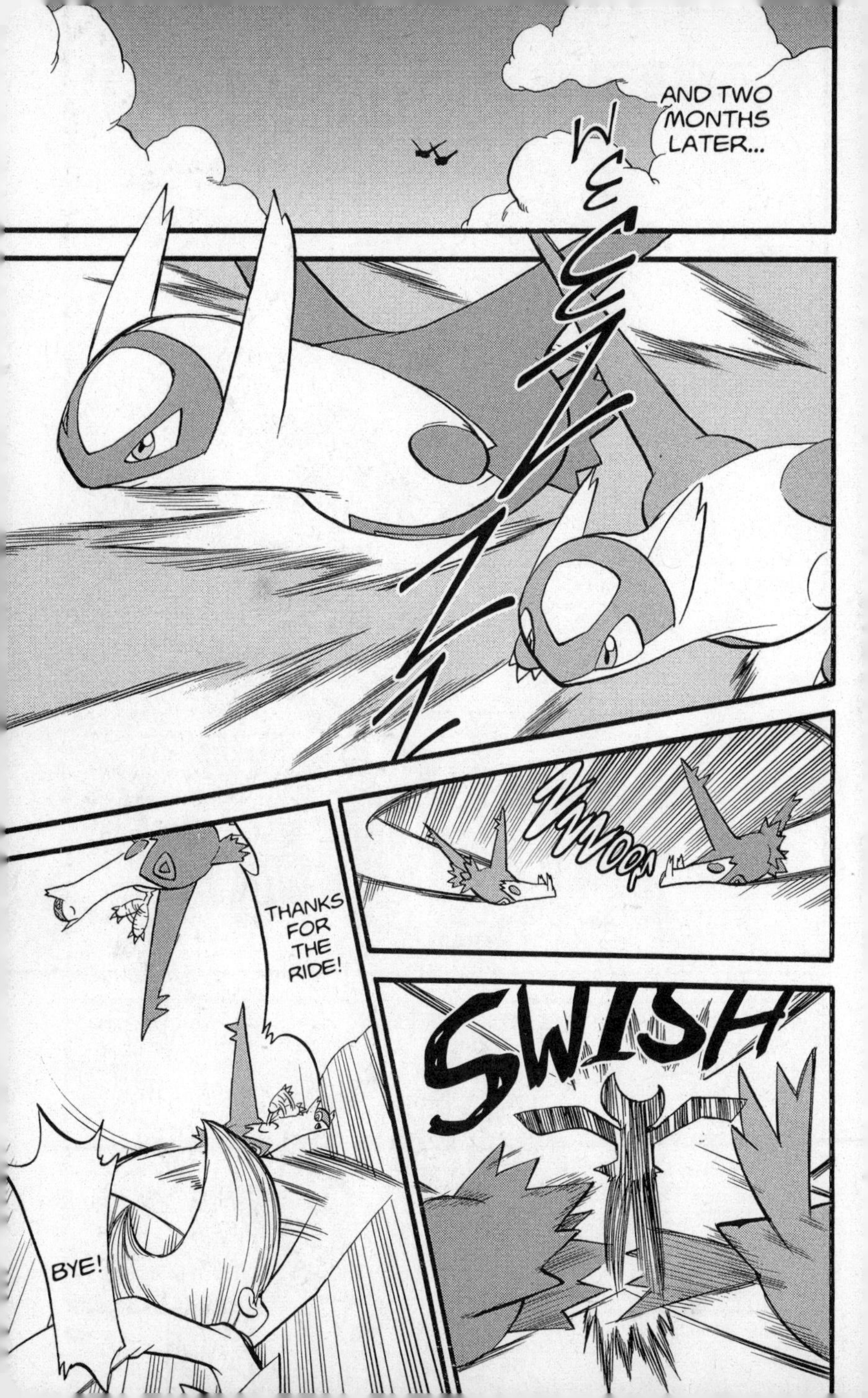
AND TWO MONTHS LATER...
SWISH
THANKS FOR THE RIDE!
BYE!

◆303◆

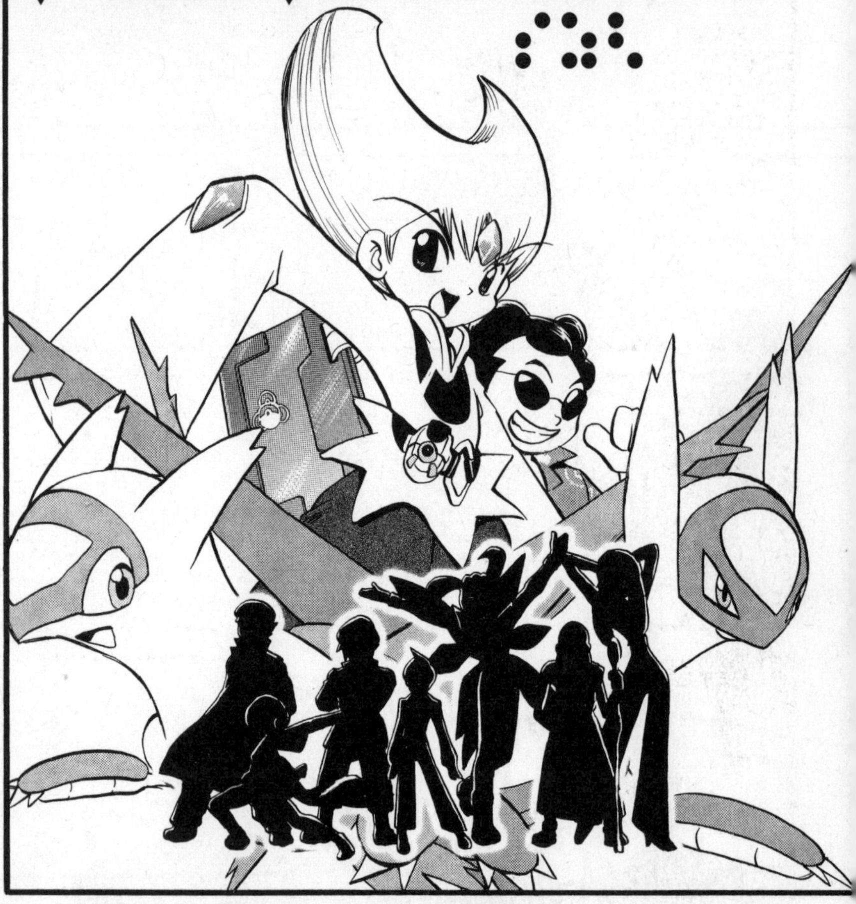

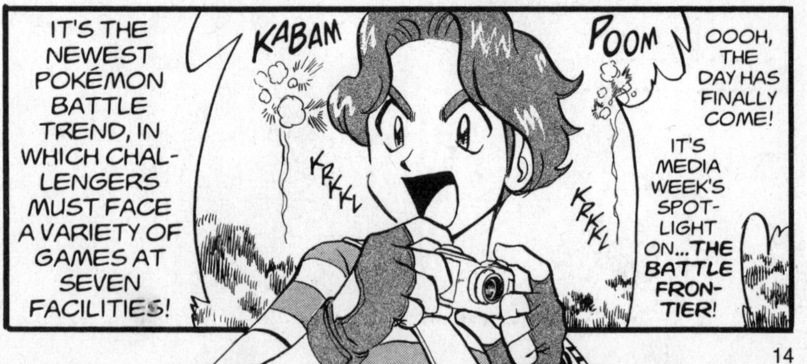

POOM
OOOH, THE DAY HAS FINALLY COME!
IT'S MEDIA WEEK'S SPOTLIGHT ON... THE BATTLE FRONTIER!
KRKKL
KABAM
KRKKL
IT'S THE NEWEST POKÉMON BATTLE TREND, IN WHICH CHALLENGERS MUST FACE A VARIETY OF GAMES AT SEVEN FACILITIES!

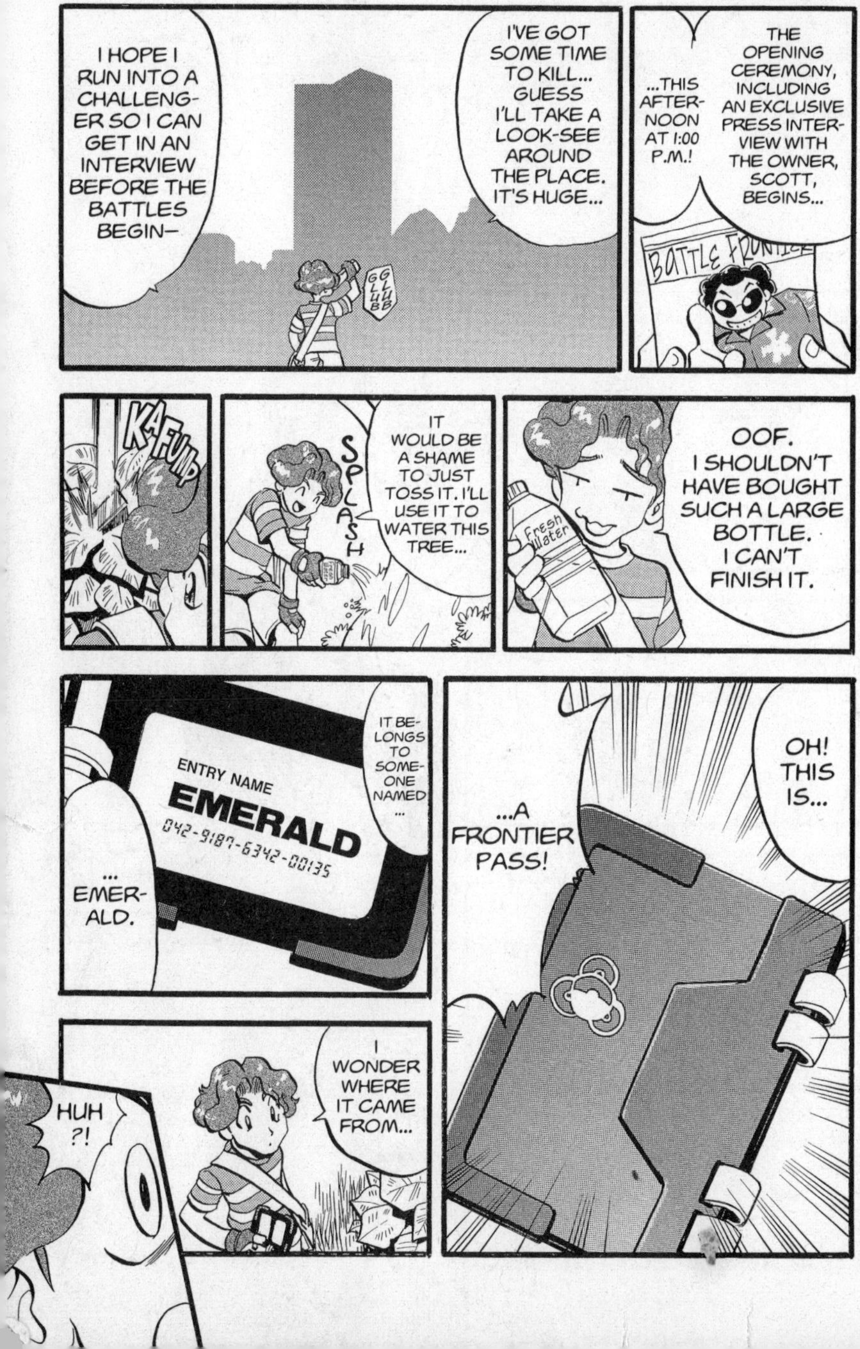
THE OPENING CEREMONY, INCLUDING AN EXCLUSIVE PRESS INTERVIEW WITH THE OWNER, SCOTT, BEGINS...
...THIS AFTERNOON AT 1:00 P.M.!
BATTLE FRONTIER
I'VE GOT SOME TIME TO KILL... GUESS I'LL TAKE A LOOK-SEE AROUND THE PLACE. IT'S HUGE...
I HOPE I RUN INTO A CHALLENGER SO I CAN GET IN AN INTERVIEW BEFORE THE BATTLES BEGIN—
GGLUBB GGLUBB
OOF. I SHOULDN'T HAVE BOUGHT SUCH A LARGE BOTTLE. I CAN'T FINISH IT.
Fresh Water
IT WOULD BE A SHAME TO JUST TOSS IT. I'LL USE IT TO WATER THIS TREE...
SPLASH
KAFUMP
OH! THIS IS...
...A FRONTIER PASS!
IT BELONGS TO SOMEONE NAMED...
ENTRY NAME
EMERALD
042-9187-6342-00135
...EMERALD.
I WONDER WHERE IT CAME FROM...
HUH?!

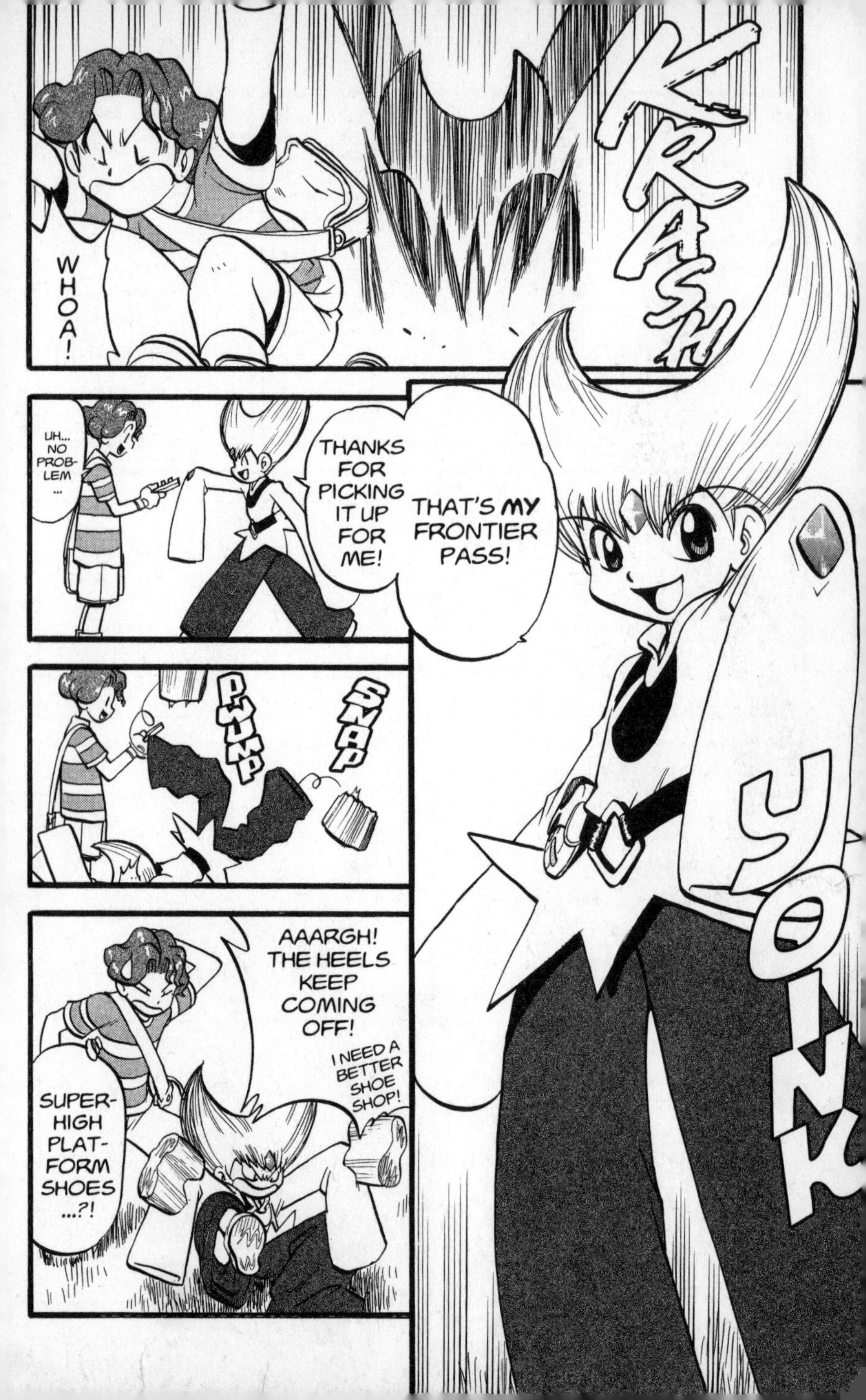
KRASH
WHOA!
THAT'S **MY** FRONTIER PASS!
YOINK
THANKS FOR PICKING IT UP FOR ME!
UH... NO PROB-LEM ...
SNAP
PWUMP
AAARGH! THE HEELS KEEP COMING OFF!
I NEED A BETTER SHOE SHOP!
SUPER-HIGH PLAT-FORM SHOES ...?!

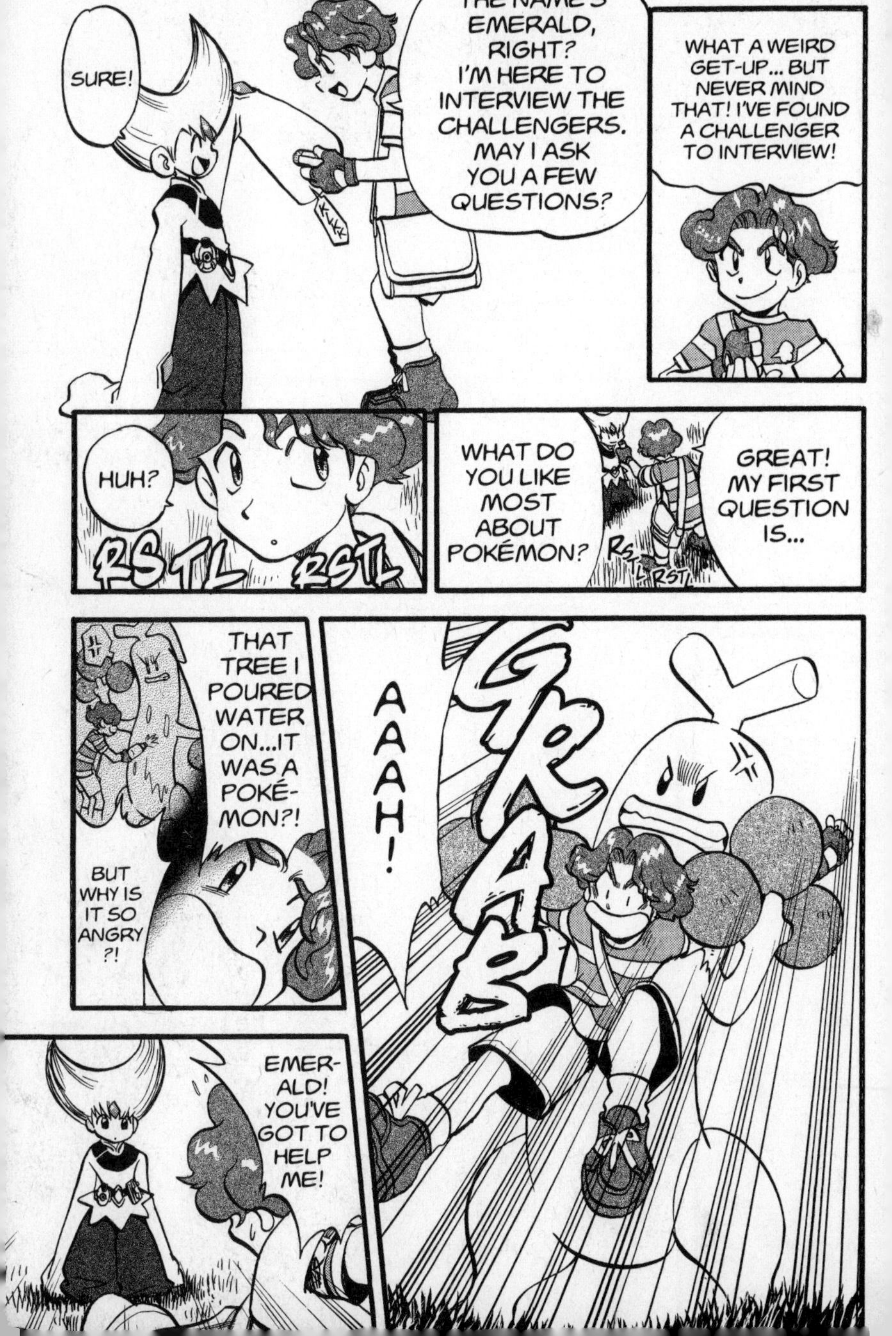
WHAT A WEIRD GET-UP... BUT NEVER MIND THAT! I'VE FOUND A CHALLENGER TO INTERVIEW!
THE NAME'S EMERALD, RIGHT? I'M HERE TO INTERVIEW THE CHALLENGERS. MAY I ASK YOU A FEW QUESTIONS?
SURE!
GREAT! MY FIRST QUESTION IS...
WHAT DO YOU LIKE MOST ABOUT POKÉMON?
RSTL
RSTL
HUH?
RSTL
RSTL
GRAB
AAAAH!
THAT TREE I POURED WATER ON...IT WAS A POKÉMON?!
BUT WHY IS IT SO ANGRY?!
EMERALD! YOU'VE GOT TO HELP ME!

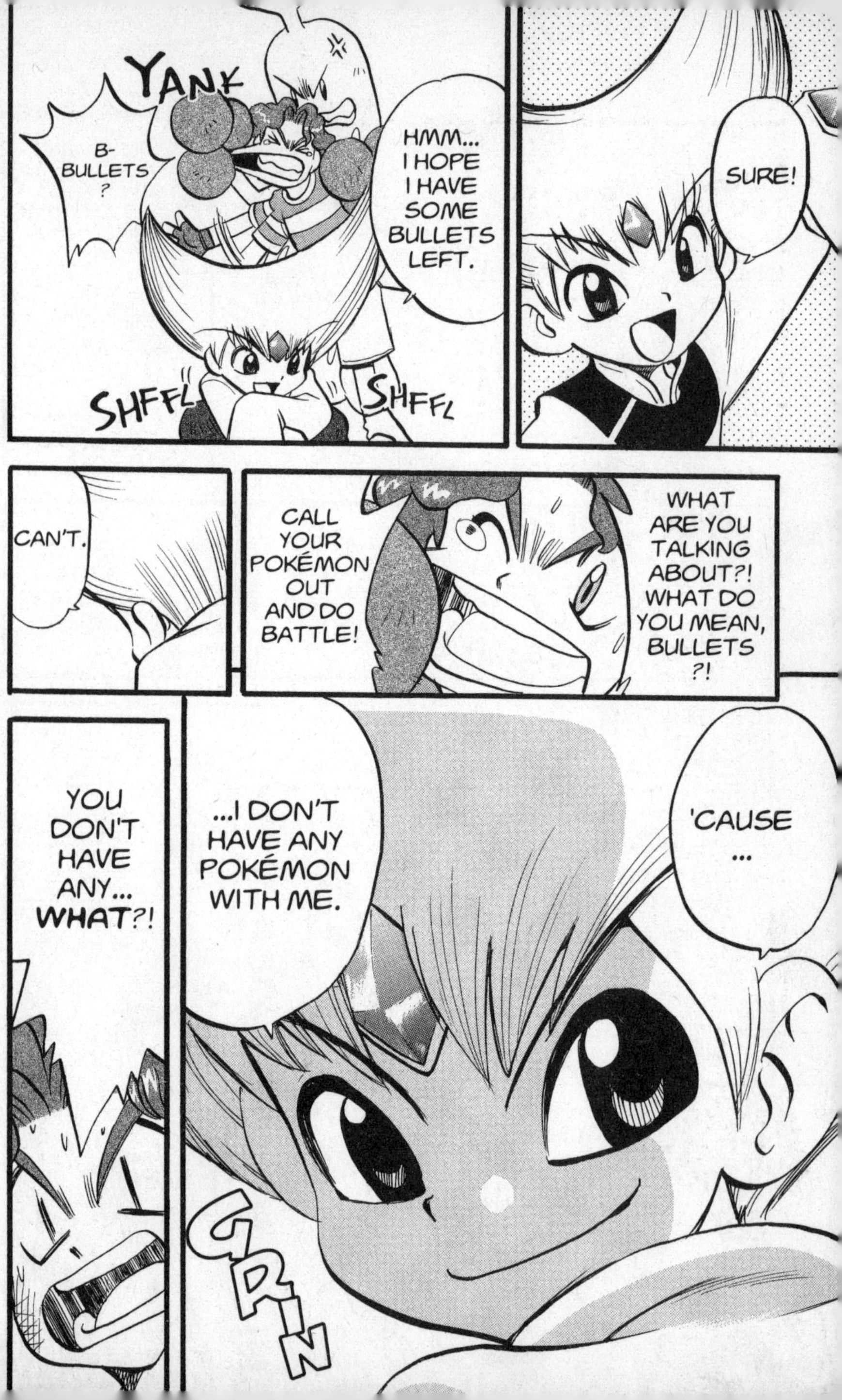
SURE!
HMM... I HOPE I HAVE SOME BULLETS LEFT.
YANK
B-BULLETS?
SHFFL
SHFFL
WHAT ARE YOU TALKING ABOUT?! WHAT DO YOU MEAN, BULLETS?!
CALL YOUR POKÉMON OUT AND DO BATTLE!
CAN'T.
'CAUSE ...
...I DON'T HAVE ANY POKÉMON WITH ME.
GRIN
YOU DON'T HAVE ANY... WHAT?!

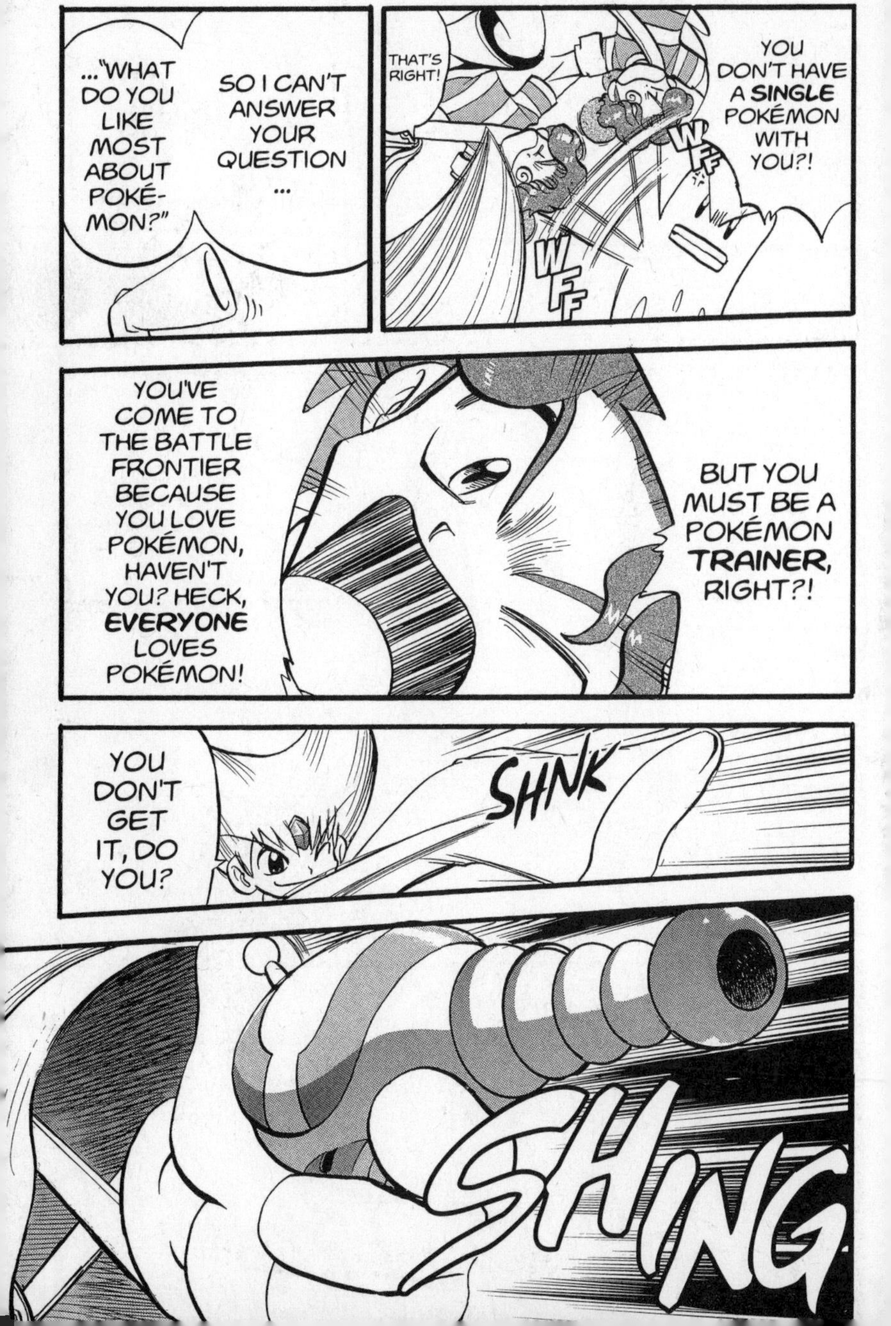
YOU DON'T HAVE A **SINGLE** POKÉMON WITH YOU?!
WFF
WFF
THAT'S RIGHT!
..."WHAT DO YOU LIKE MOST ABOUT POKÉ-MON?" SO I CAN'T ANSWER YOUR QUESTION ...
BUT YOU MUST BE A POKÉMON **TRAINER**, RIGHT?!
YOU'VE COME TO THE BATTLE FRONTIER BECAUSE YOU LOVE POKÉMON, HAVEN'T YOU? HECK, **EVERYONE** LOVES POKÉMON!
SHNK
YOU DON'T GET IT, DO YOU?
SHING

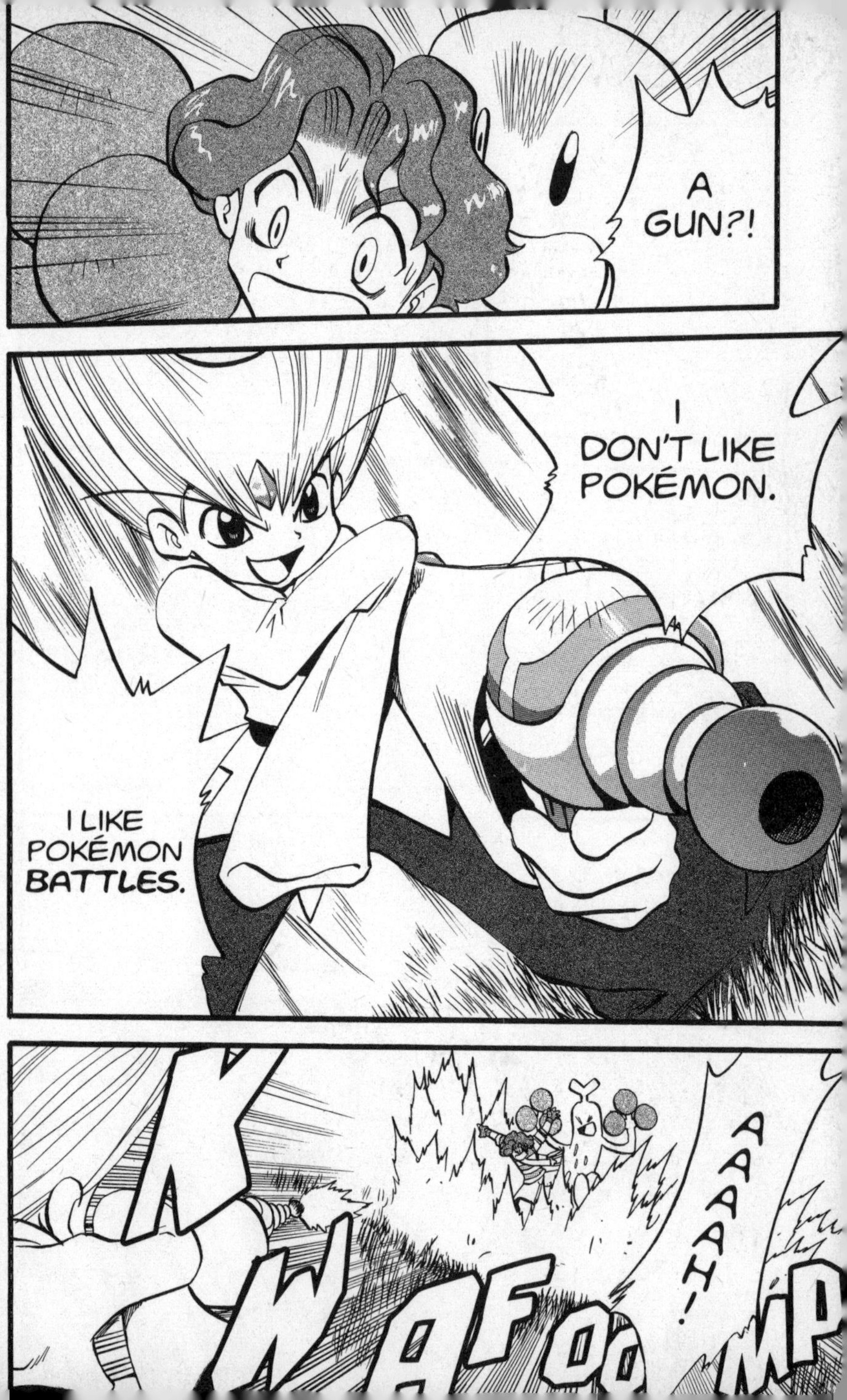
A GUN?!
I DON'T LIKE POKÉMON.
I LIKE POKÉMON BATTLES.
AAAAAH!
KWAFOOMP

TO THE PRESS...

Thank you so much for attending this press conference at the Battle Frontier today. I've spent a fortune creating this facility to offer Trainers the opportunity to participate in cutting-edge Pokémon Battles. We offer a variety of styles of battle at our facilities. Enjoy!

OWNER: SCOTT

▓ PRE-OPENING EVENT ▓ FOR THE PRESS

The pre-opening Media Week starts tomorrow. The Battle Frontier will officially open to the public the following week.

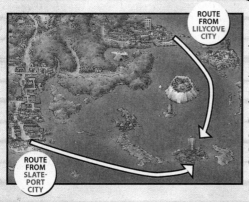

ROUTE FROM LILYCOVE CITY

ROUTE FROM SLATE-PORT CITY

LOCATION/ ▓ TRANSPORTATION ▓

The Battle Frontier is located on an island in the Hoenn region, in between Pacifidlog Town and Ever Grande City. Enjoy a pleasant cruise there via ferry departing from Slateport City or Lilycove City.

Swanky Showdown with Swalot

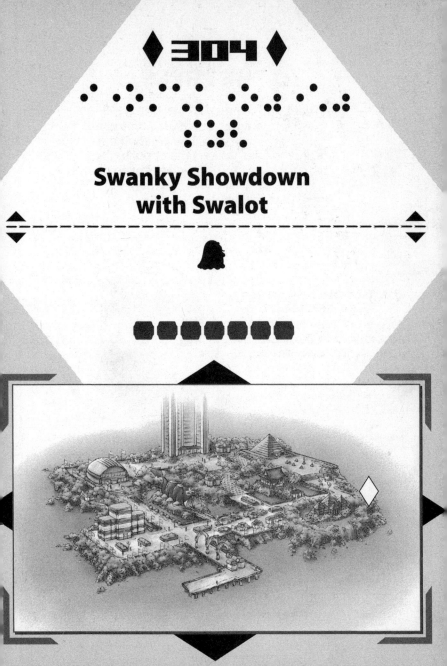

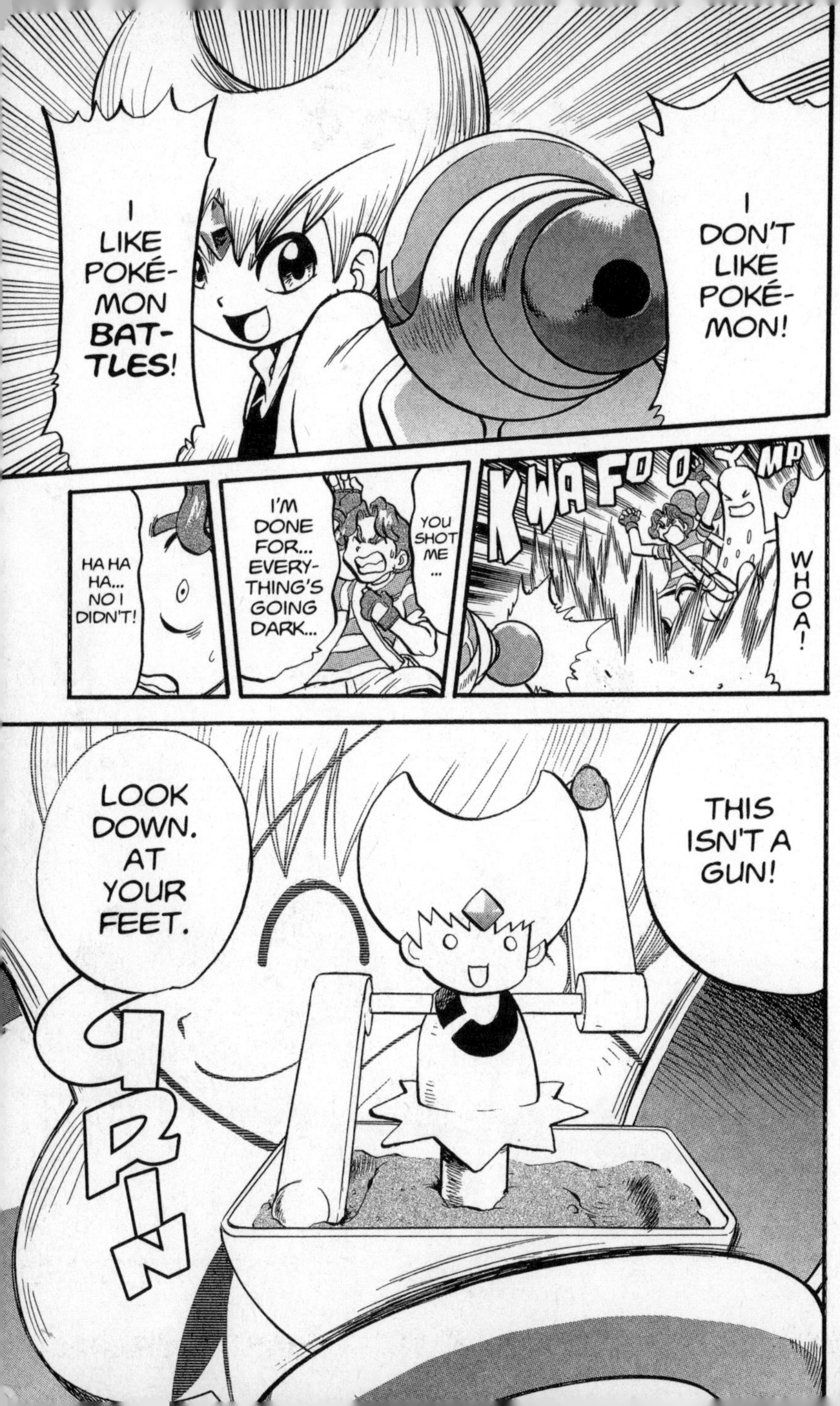
I DON'T LIKE POKÉMON!
I LIKE POKÉMON BATTLES!
KWAFOOMP
WHOA!
YOU SHOT ME...
I'M DONE FOR... EVERYTHING'S GOING DARK...
HA HA HA... NO I DIDN'T!
THIS ISN'T A GUN!
LOOK DOWN. AT YOUR FEET.
GRIN

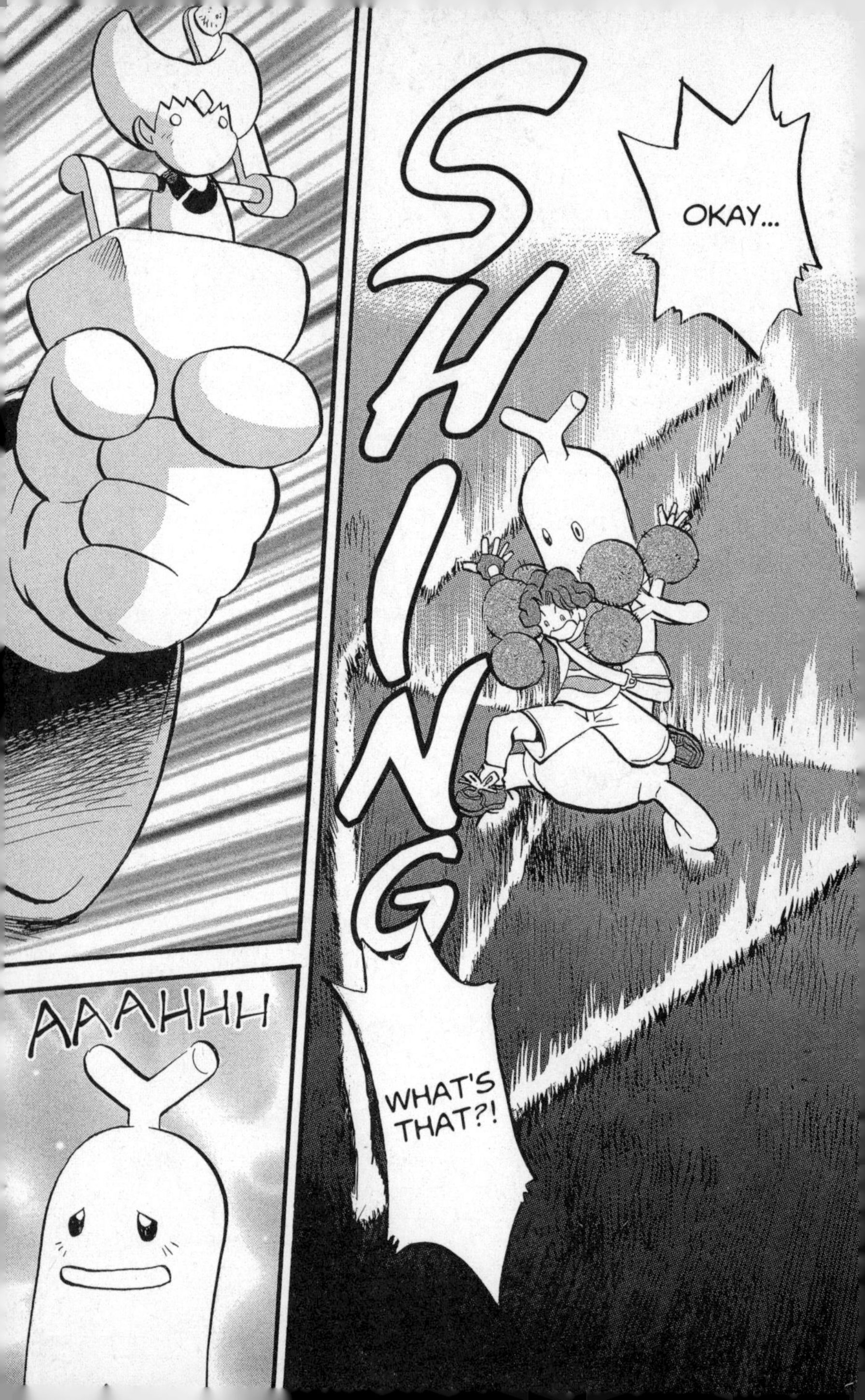
OKAY...
SHING
WHAT'S THAT?!
AAAHHH

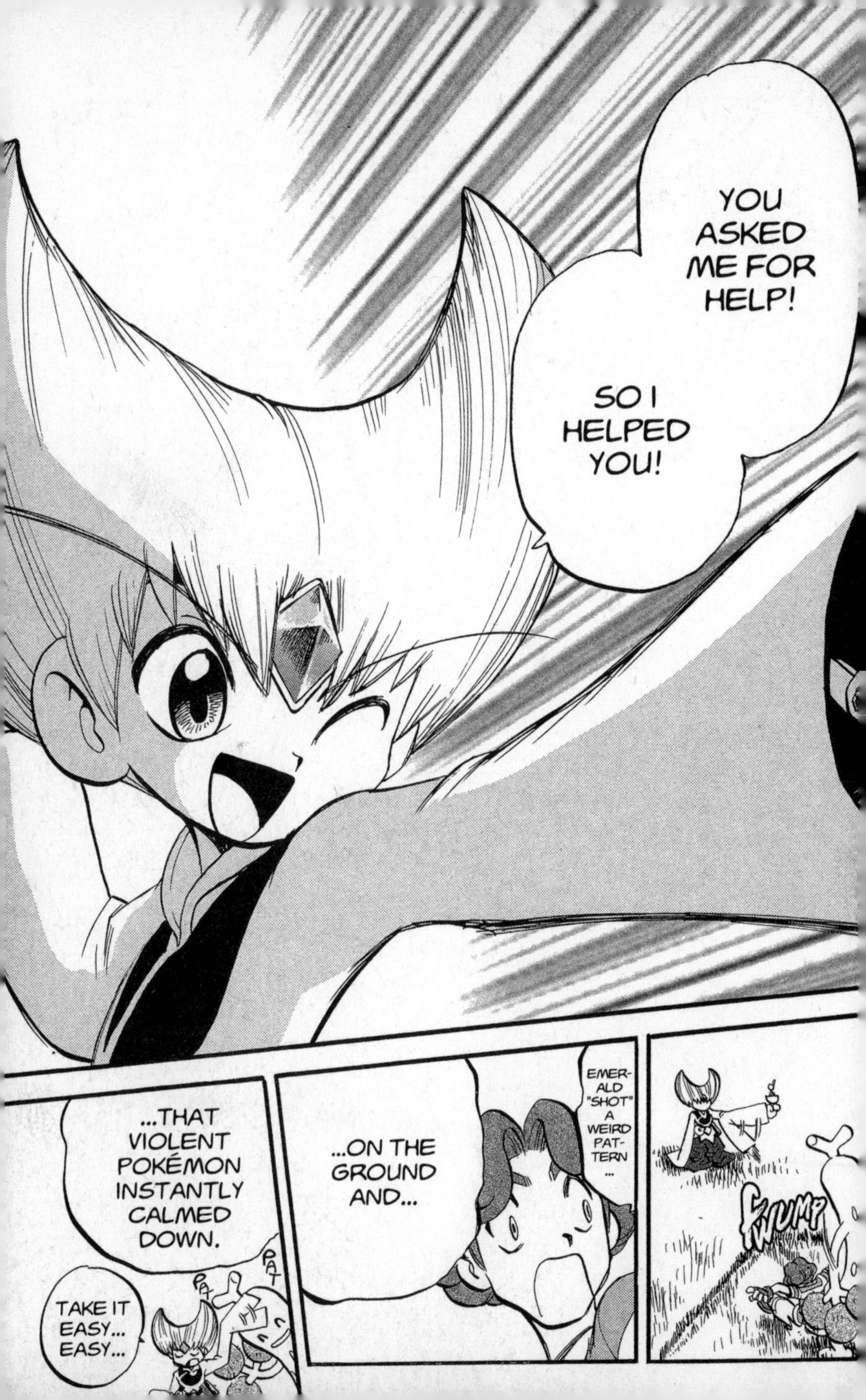
YOU ASKED ME FOR HELP!
SO I HELPED YOU!
FWUMP
EMERALD "SHOT" A WEIRD PATTERN...
...ON THE GROUND AND...
...THAT VIOLENT POKÉMON INSTANTLY CALMED DOWN.
PAT PAT
TAKE IT EASY... EASY...

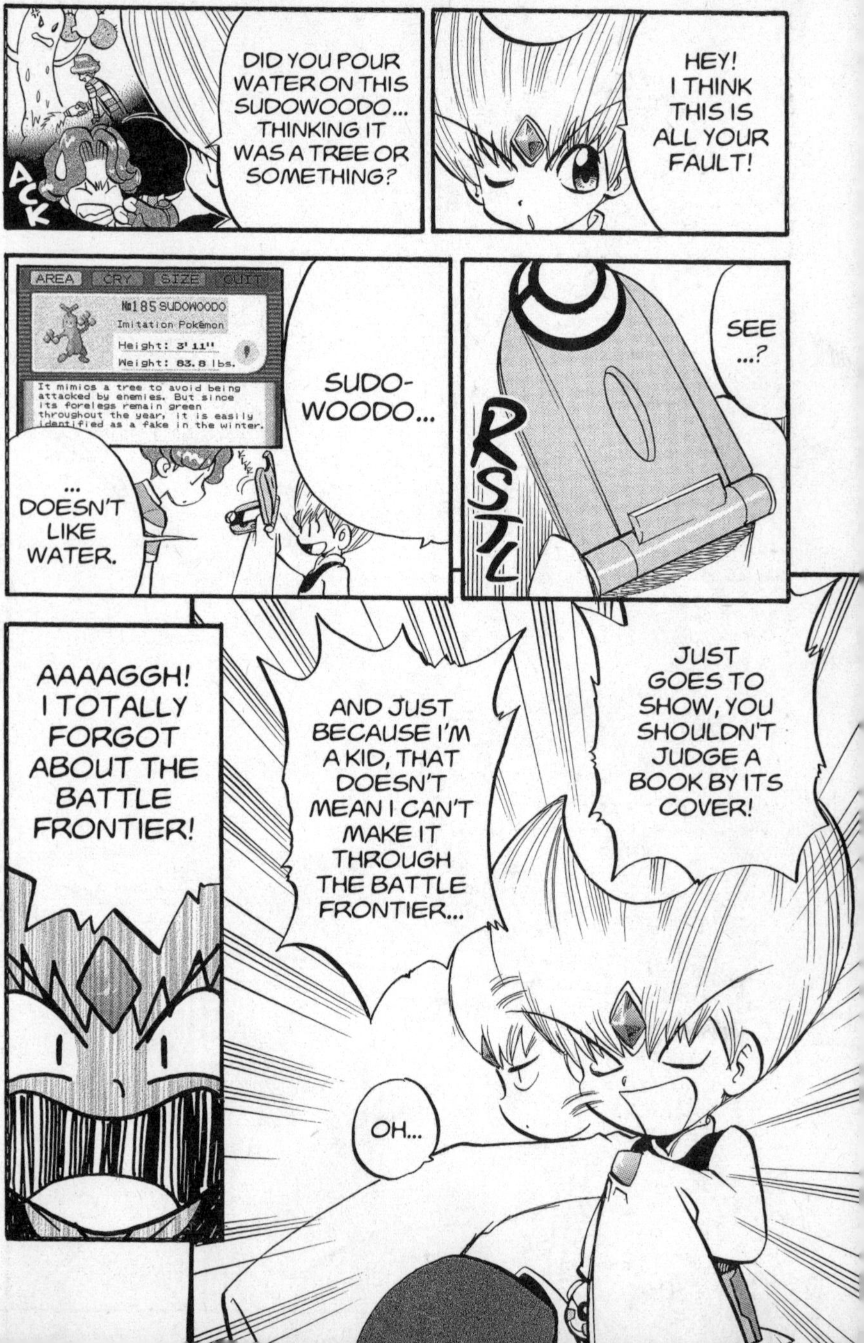
HEY! I THINK THIS IS ALL YOUR FAULT!
DID YOU POUR WATER ON THIS SUDOWOODO... THINKING IT WAS A TREE OR SOMETHING?
ACK
SEE ...?
RSTL
SUDO-WOODO...
AREA CRY SIZE QUIT
№185 SUDOWOODO
Imitation Pokémon
Height: 3'11"
Weight: 83.8 lbs.
It mimics a tree to avoid being attacked by enemies. But since its forelegs remain green throughout the year, it is easily identified as a fake in the winter.
... DOESN'T LIKE WATER.
JUST GOES TO SHOW, YOU SHOULDN'T JUDGE A BOOK BY ITS COVER!
AND JUST BECAUSE I'M A KID, THAT DOESN'T MEAN I CAN'T MAKE IT THROUGH THE BATTLE FRONTIER...
OH...
AAAAGGH! I TOTALLY FORGOT ABOUT THE BATTLE FRONTIER!

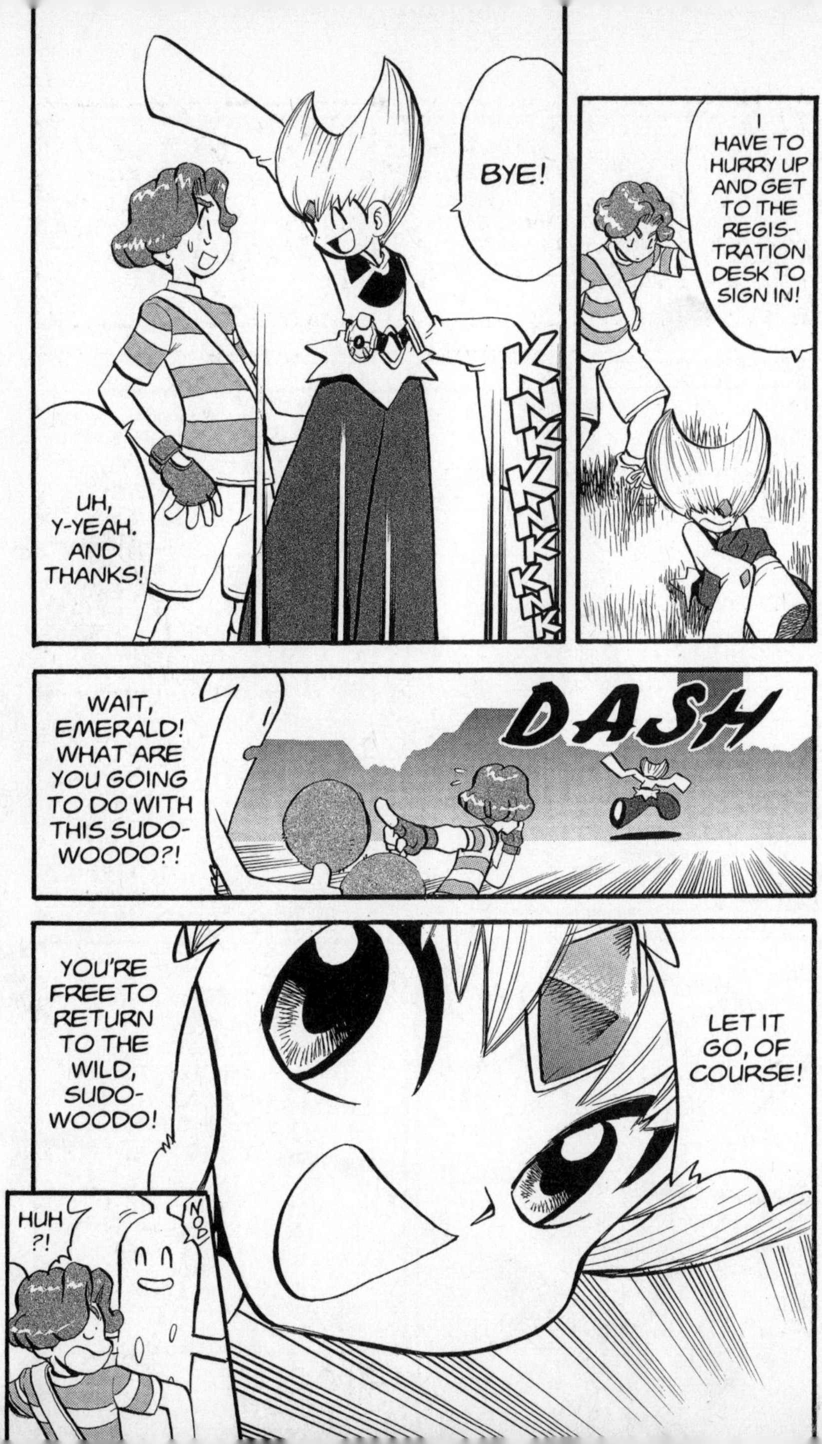
I HAVE TO HURRY UP AND GET TO THE REGIS-TRATION DESK TO SIGN IN!
BYE!
KNKKNKKNK
UH, Y-YEAH. AND THANKS!
DASH
WAIT, EMERALD! WHAT ARE YOU GOING TO DO WITH THIS SUDO-WOODO?!
LET IT GO, OF COURSE!
YOU'RE FREE TO RETURN TO THE WILD, SUDO-WOODO!
NOD
HUH ?!

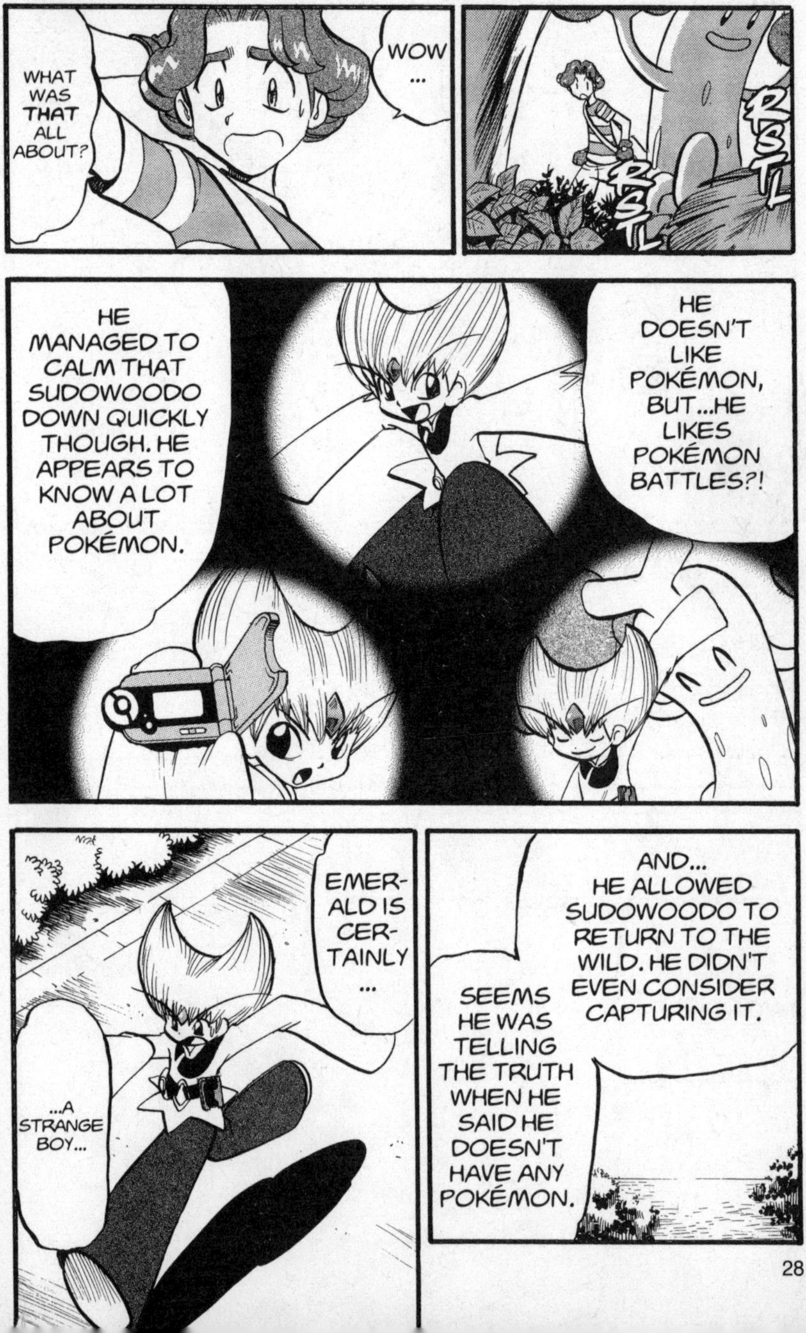
RSTL
RSTL
WOW ...
WHAT WAS THAT ALL ABOUT?
HE DOESN'T LIKE POKÉMON, BUT...HE LIKES POKÉMON BATTLES?!
HE MANAGED TO CALM THAT SUDOWOODO DOWN QUICKLY THOUGH. HE APPEARS TO KNOW A LOT ABOUT POKÉMON.
AND... HE ALLOWED SUDOWOODO TO RETURN TO THE WILD. HE DIDN'T EVEN CONSIDER CAPTURING IT.
SEEMS HE WAS TELLING THE TRUTH WHEN HE SAID HE DOESN'T HAVE ANY POKÉMON.
EMER-ALD IS CER-TAINLY ...
...A STRANGE BOY...

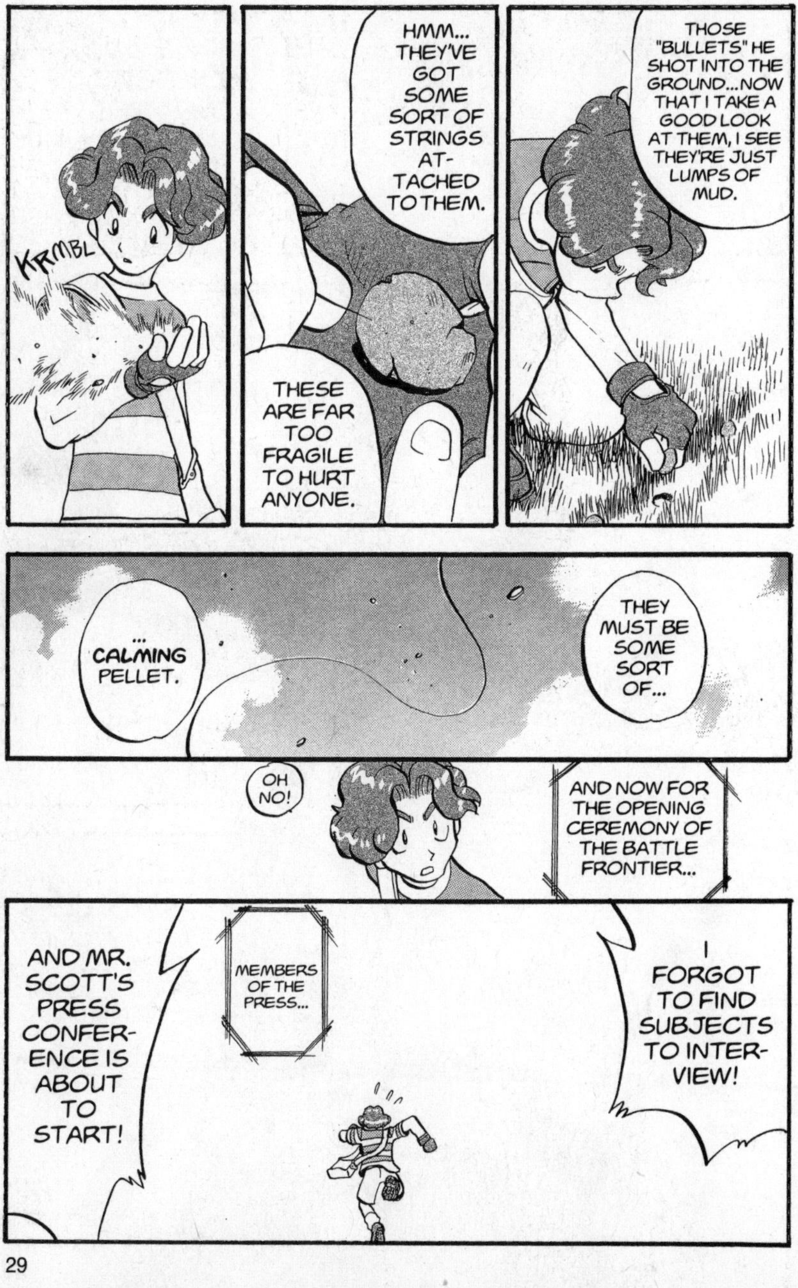
THOSE "BULLETS" HE SHOT INTO THE GROUND...NOW THAT I TAKE A GOOD LOOK AT THEM, I SEE THEY'RE JUST LUMPS OF MUD.
HMM... THEY'VE GOT SOME SORT OF STRINGS AT-TACHED TO THEM.
THESE ARE FAR TOO FRAGILE TO HURT ANYONE.
KRMBL
THEY MUST BE SOME SORT OF...
...CALMING PELLET.
AND NOW FOR THE OPENING CEREMONY OF THE BATTLE FRONTIER...
OH NO!
I FORGOT TO FIND SUBJECTS TO INTER-VIEW!
MEMBERS OF THE PRESS...
AND MR. SCOTT'S PRESS CONFER-ENCE IS ABOUT TO START!

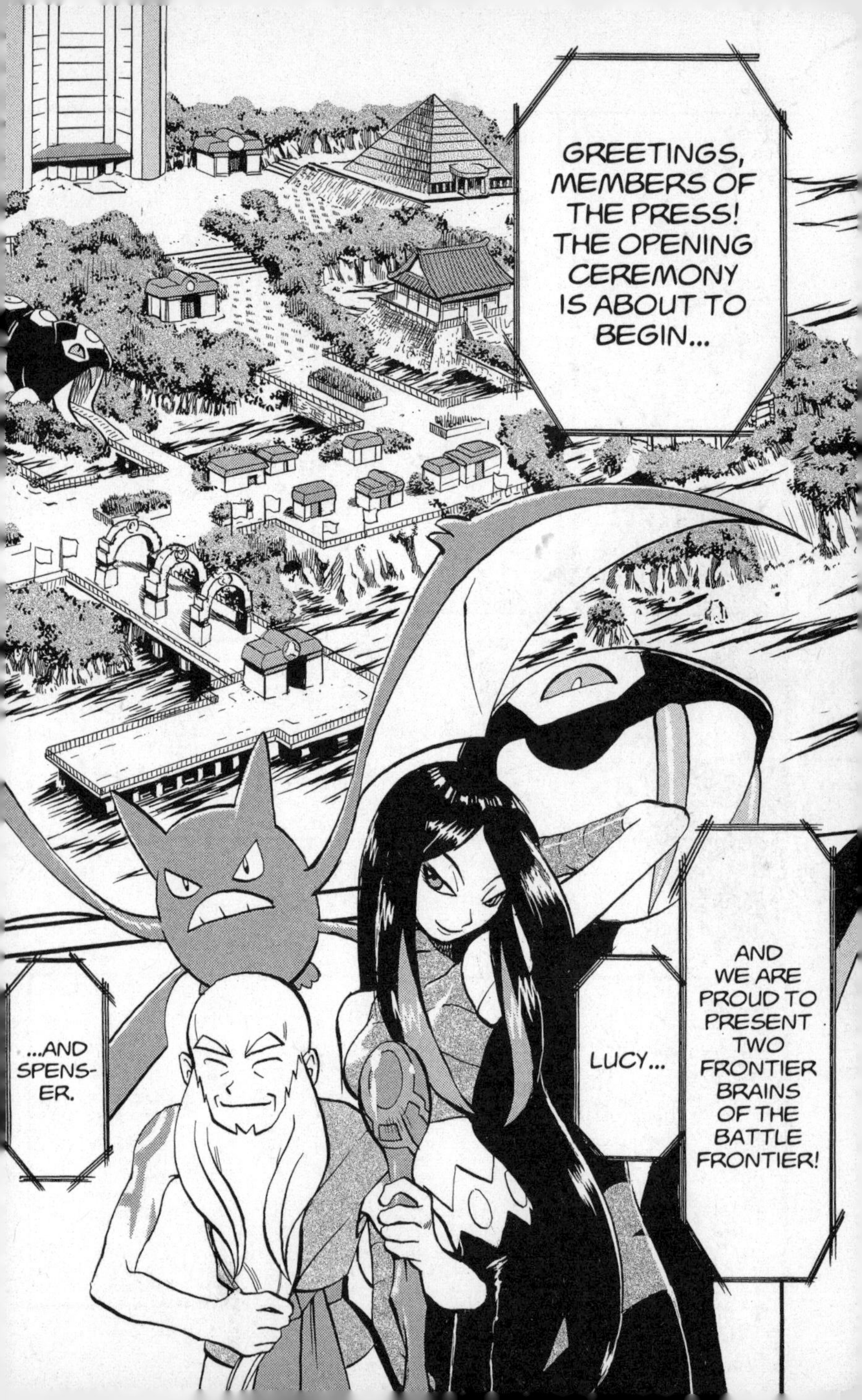
GREETINGS, MEMBERS OF THE PRESS! THE OPENING CEREMONY IS ABOUT TO BEGIN...
AND WE ARE PROUD TO PRESENT TWO FRONTIER BRAINS OF THE BATTLE FRONTIER!
LUCY...
...AND SPENS-ER.

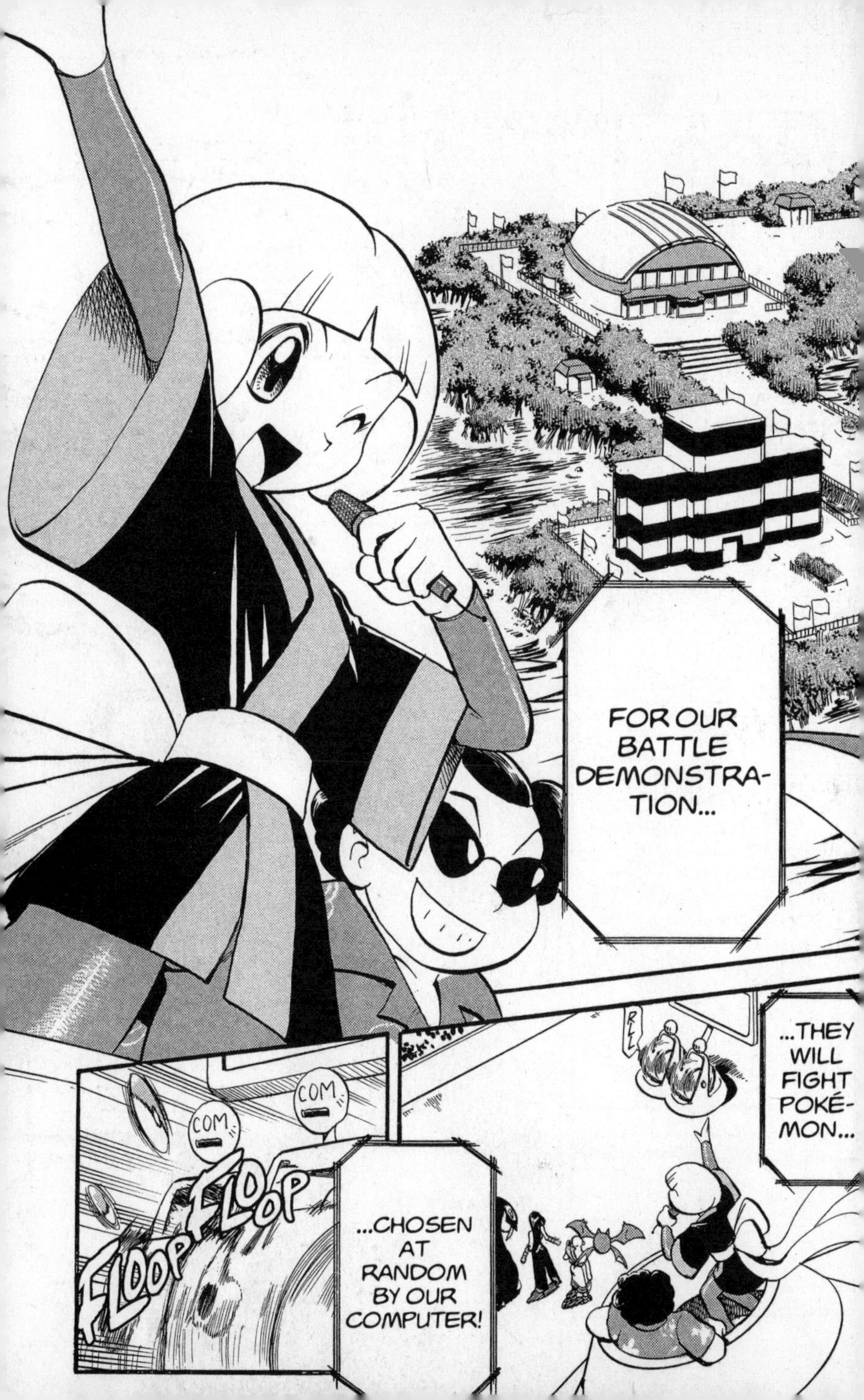
FOR OUR BATTLE DEMONSTRA-TION...
...THEY WILL FIGHT POKÉ-MON...
...CHOSEN AT RANDOM BY OUR COMPUTER!
COM
COM
FLOOP FLOOP

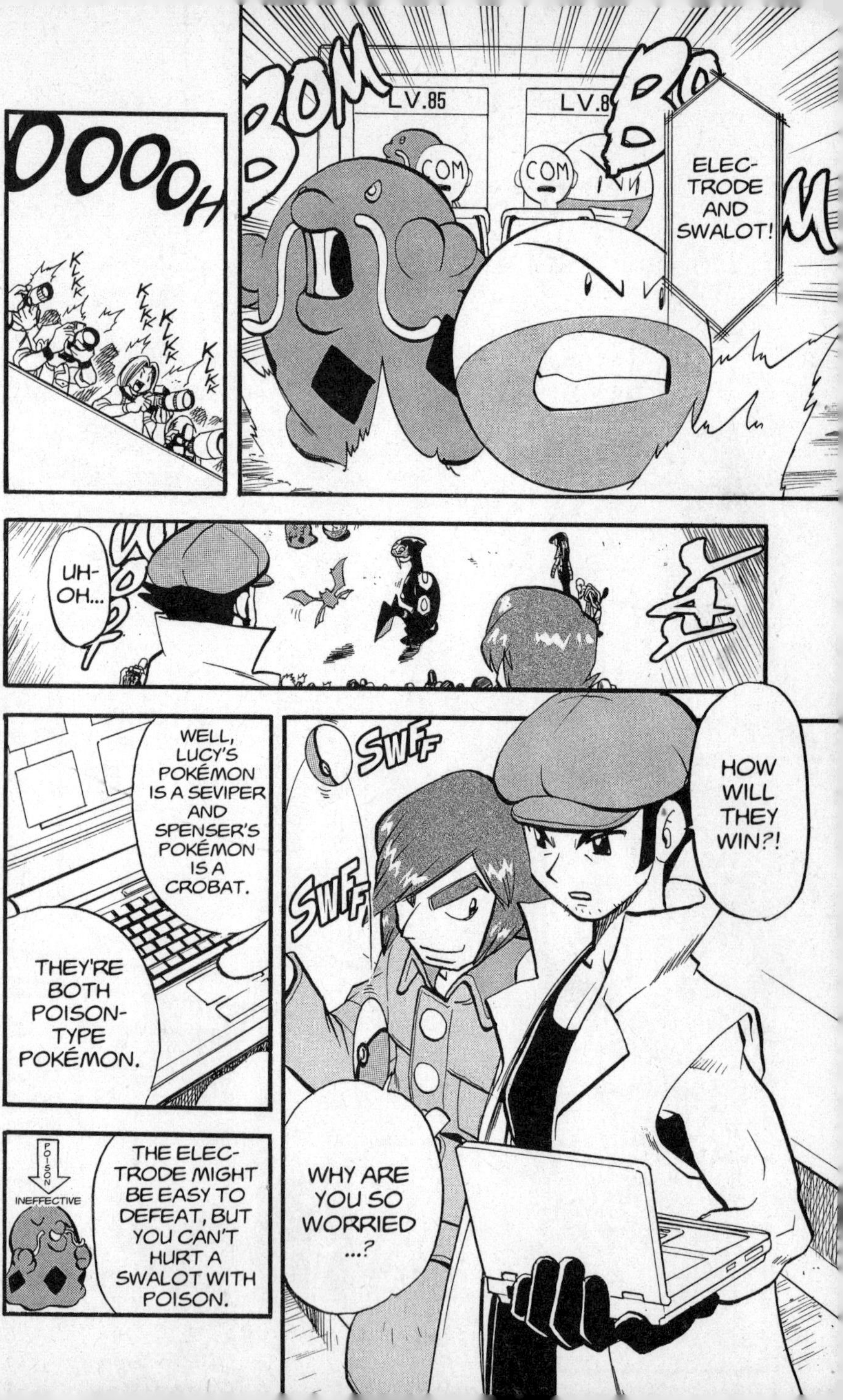

BOOM
LV.85
LV.8
COM
COM
BOOM
ELEC-TRODE AND SWALOT!
OOOOOH
KLKK
KLKK
KLKK
KLKK
UH-OH...
HOW WILL THEY WIN?!
SWFF
SWFF
WHY ARE YOU SO WORRIED ...?
WELL, LUCY'S POKÉMON IS A SEVIPER AND SPENSER'S POKÉMON IS A CROBAT.
THEY'RE BOTH POISON-TYPE POKÉMON.
POISON
INEFFECTIVE
THE ELEC-TRODE MIGHT BE EASY TO DEFEAT, BUT YOU CAN'T HURT A SWALOT WITH POISON.

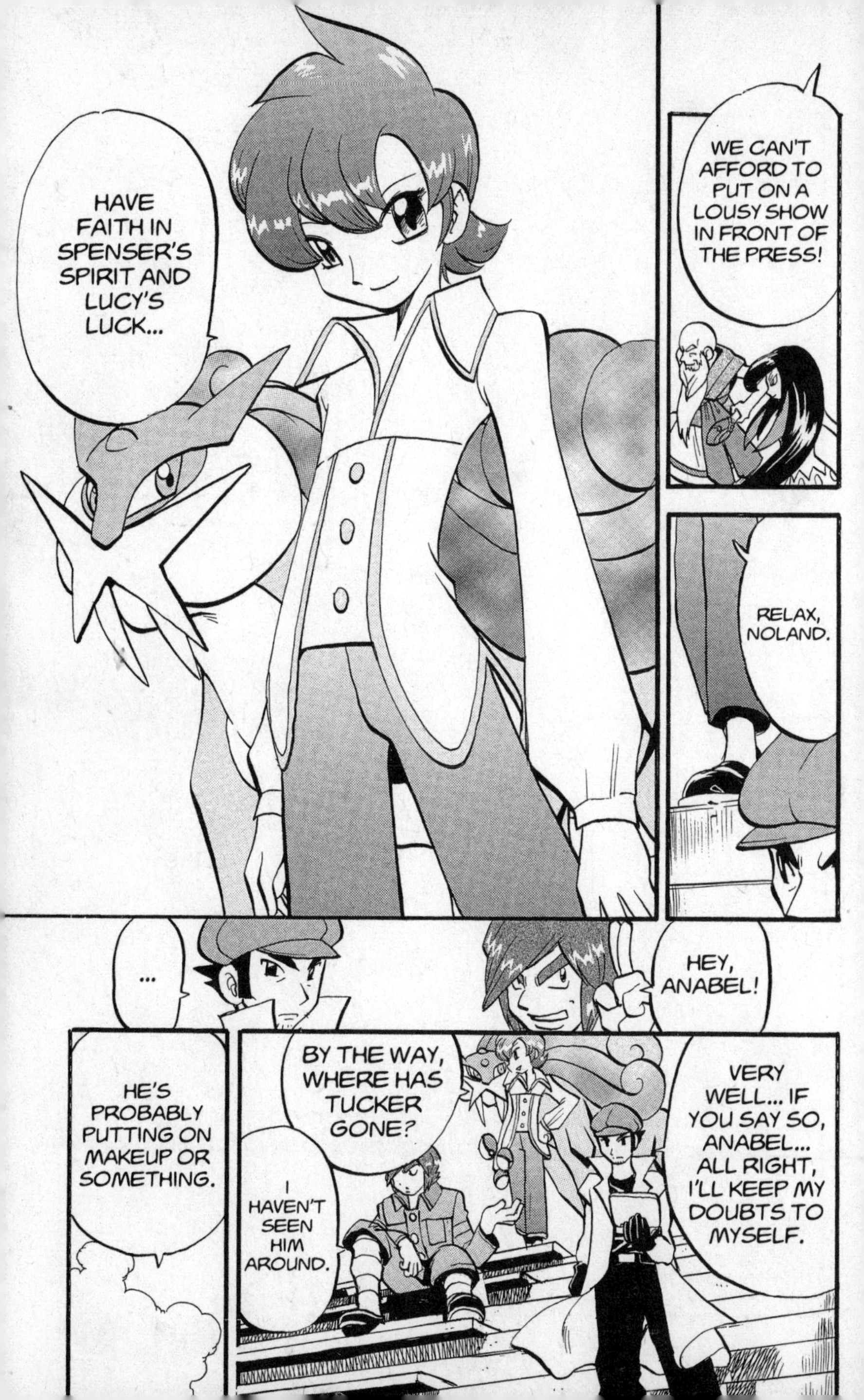
WE CAN'T AFFORD TO PUT ON A LOUSY SHOW IN FRONT OF THE PRESS!
RELAX, NOLAND.
HAVE FAITH IN SPENSER'S SPIRIT AND LUCY'S LUCK...
HEY, ANABEL!
...
VERY WELL... IF YOU SAY SO, ANABEL... ALL RIGHT, I'LL KEEP MY DOUBTS TO MYSELF.
BY THE WAY, WHERE HAS TUCKER GONE?
I HAVEN'T SEEN HIM AROUND.
HE'S PROBABLY PUTTING ON MAKEUP OR SOMETHING.

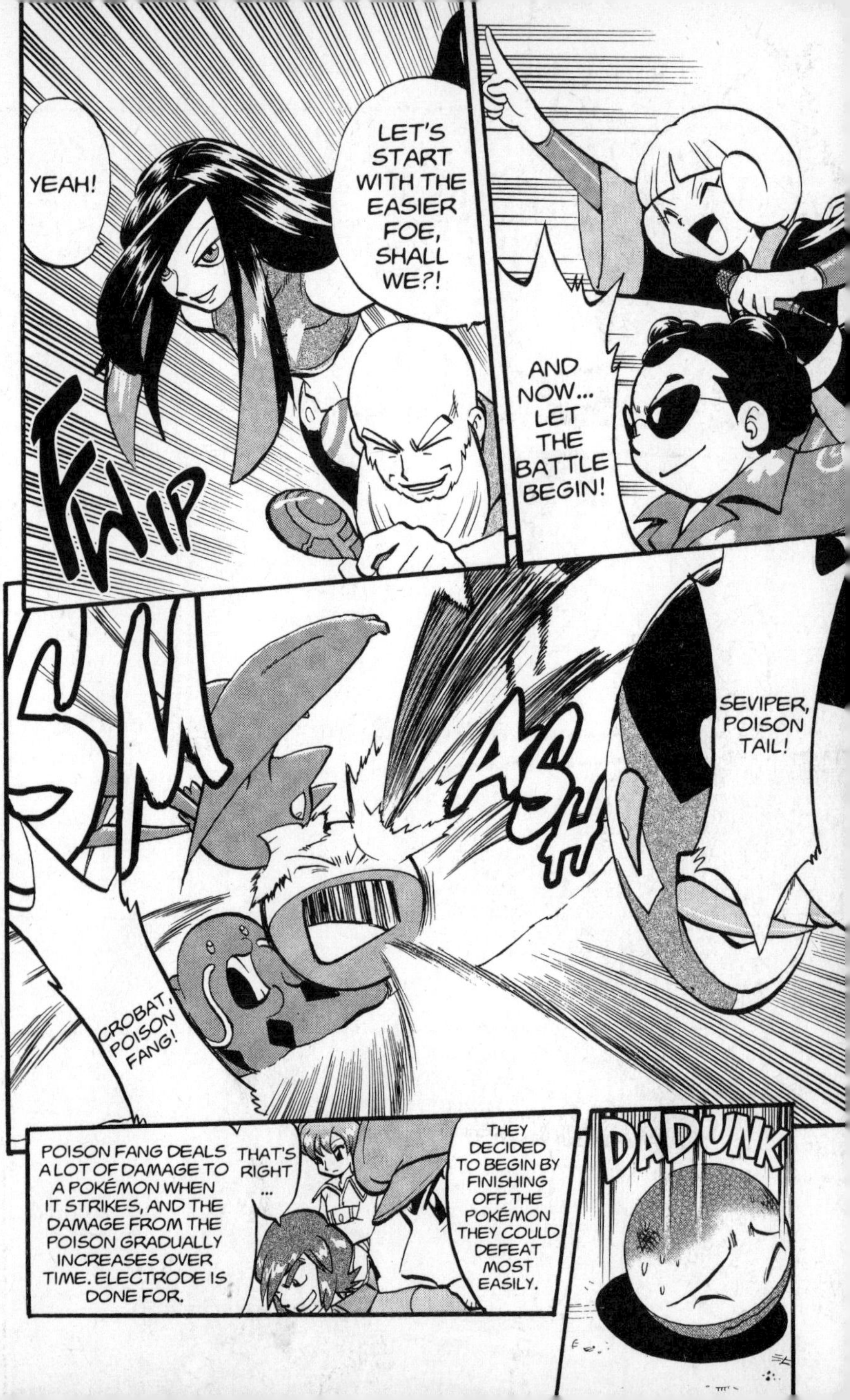
AND NOW... LET THE BATTLE BEGIN!
LET'S START WITH THE EASIER FOE, SHALL WE?!
YEAH!
FWIP
SEVIPER, POISON TAIL!
SM
ASH
CROBAT, POISON FANG!
DADUNK
THEY DECIDED TO BEGIN BY FINISHING OFF THE POKÉMON THEY COULD DEFEAT MOST EASILY.
THAT'S RIGHT...
POISON FANG DEALS A LOT OF DAMAGE TO A POKÉMON WHEN IT STRIKES, AND THE DAMAGE FROM THE POISON GRADUALLY INCREASES OVER TIME. ELECTRODE IS DONE FOR.

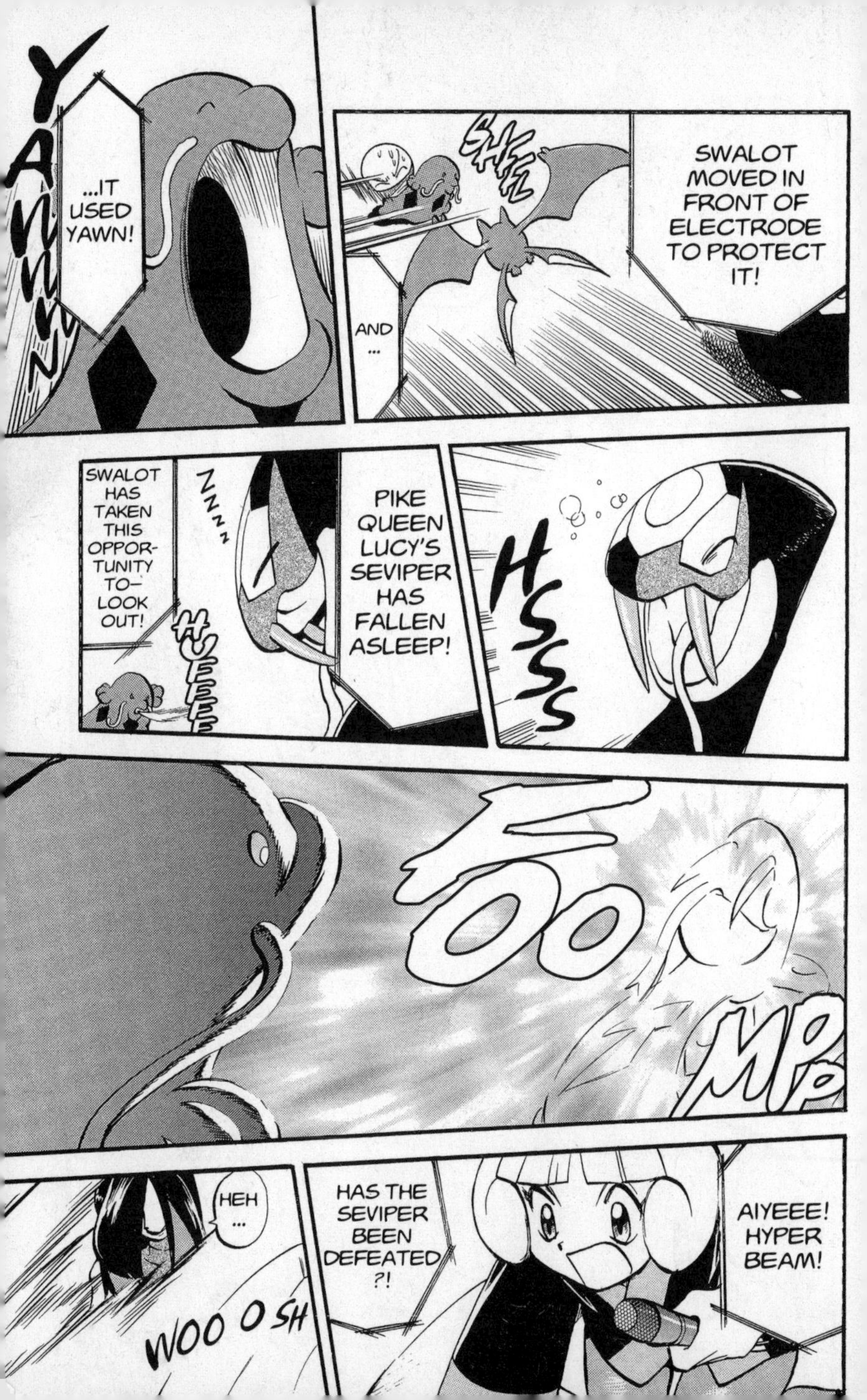
SWALOT MOVED IN FRONT OF ELECTRODE TO PROTECT IT!
AND ...
...IT USED YAWN!
HSSS
PIKE QUEEN LUCY'S SEVIPER HAS FALLEN ASLEEP!
ZZZZ
SWALOT HAS TAKEN THIS OPPORTUNITY TO— LOOK OUT!
AIYEEE! HYPER BEAM!
HAS THE SEVIPER BEEN DEFEATED?!
HEH ...
WOOOSH

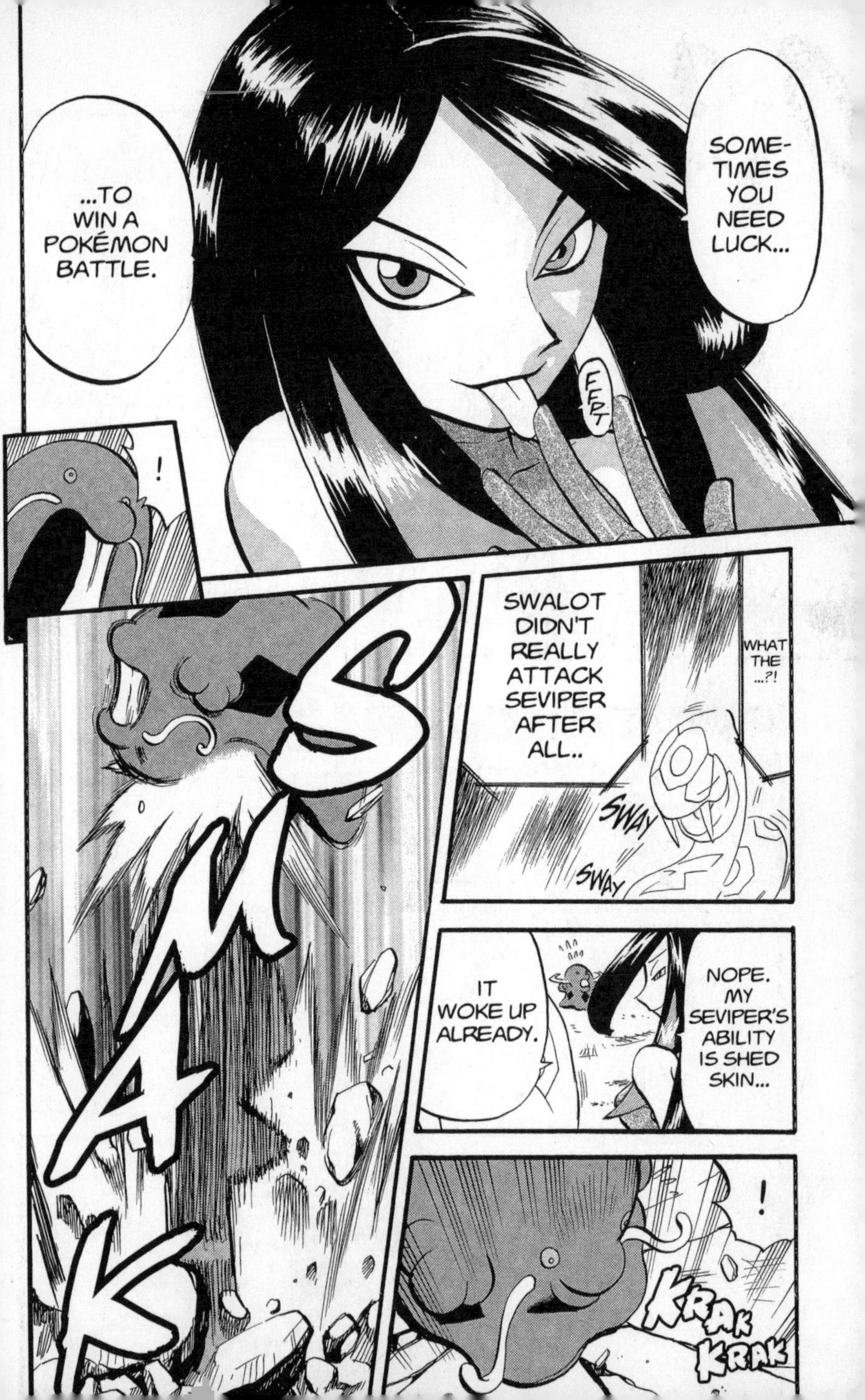
SOME-TIMES YOU NEED LUCK...
...TO WIN A POKÉMON BATTLE.
FFPT
!
WHAT THE ...?!
SWALOT DIDN'T REALLY ATTACK SEVIPER AFTER ALL..
SWAY
SWAY
NOPE. MY SEVIPER'S ABILITY IS SHED SKIN...
IT WOKE UP ALREADY.
!
KRAK KRAK
SMAK

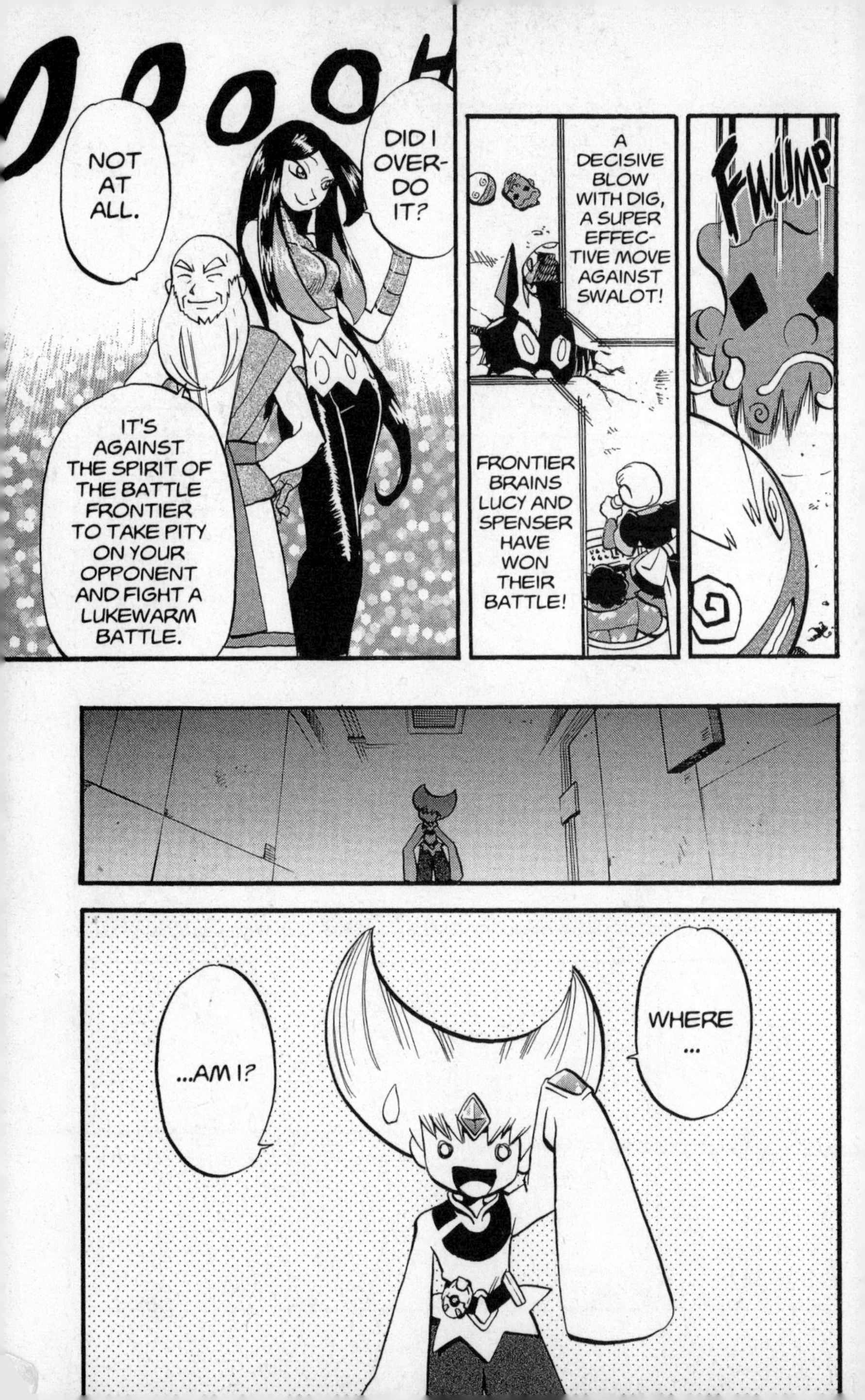
FWUMP
A DECISIVE BLOW WITH DIG, A SUPER EFFECTIVE MOVE AGAINST SWALOT!
FRONTIER BRAINS LUCY AND SPENSER HAVE WON THEIR BATTLE!
OOOOH
DID I OVER-DO IT?
NOT AT ALL.
IT'S AGAINST THE SPIRIT OF THE BATTLE FRONTIER TO TAKE PITY ON YOUR OPPONENT AND FIGHT A LUKEWARM BATTLE.
WHERE ...
...AM I?

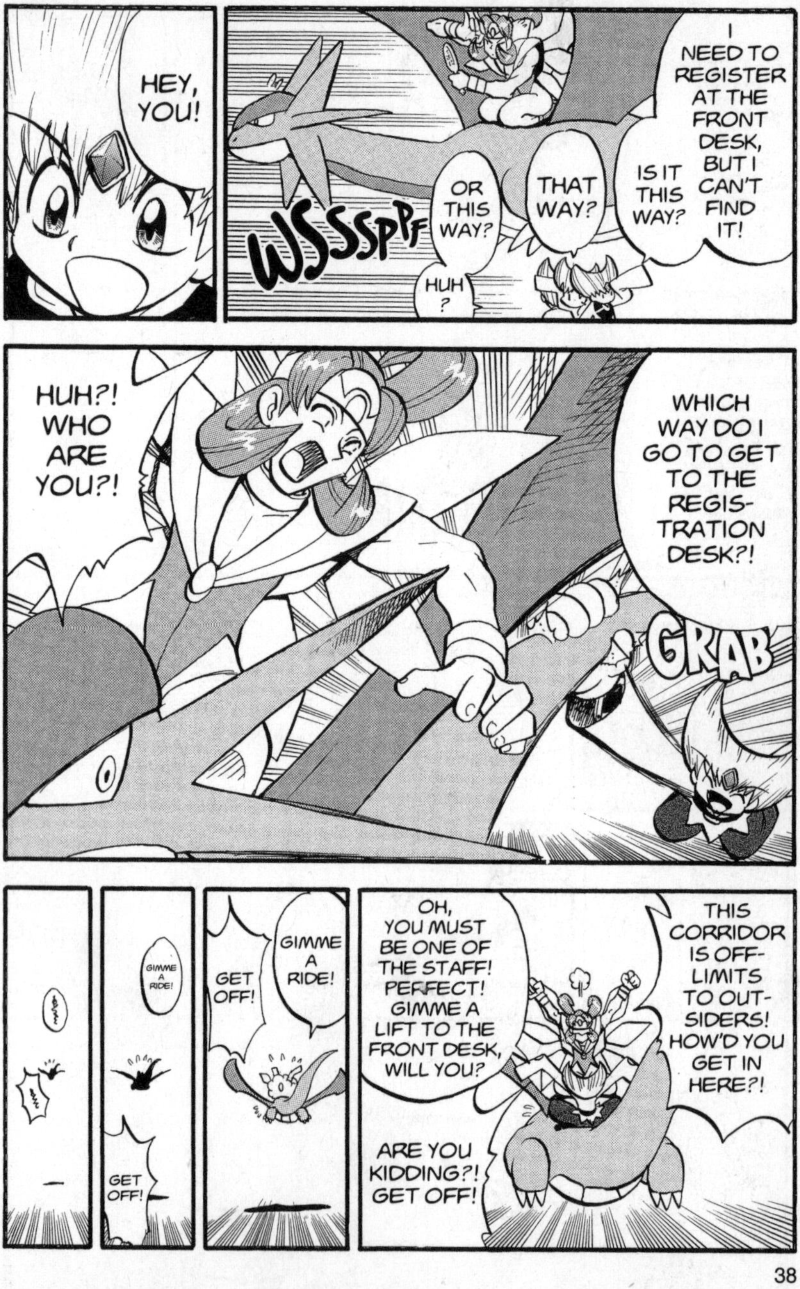
I NEED TO REGISTER AT THE FRONT DESK, BUT I CAN'T FIND IT!
IS IT THIS WAY?
THAT WAY?
OR THIS WAY?
WSSSPPF
HUH?
HEY, YOU!
WHICH WAY DO I GO TO GET TO THE REGIS-TRATION DESK?!
HUH?! WHO ARE YOU?!
GRAB
THIS CORRIDOR IS OFF-LIMITS TO OUT-SIDERS! HOW'D YOU GET IN HERE?!
OH, YOU MUST BE ONE OF THE STAFF! PERFECT! GIMME A LIFT TO THE FRONT DESK, WILL YOU?
ARE YOU KIDDING?! GET OFF!
GIMME A RIDE!
GET OFF!
GIMME A RIDE!
GET OFF!

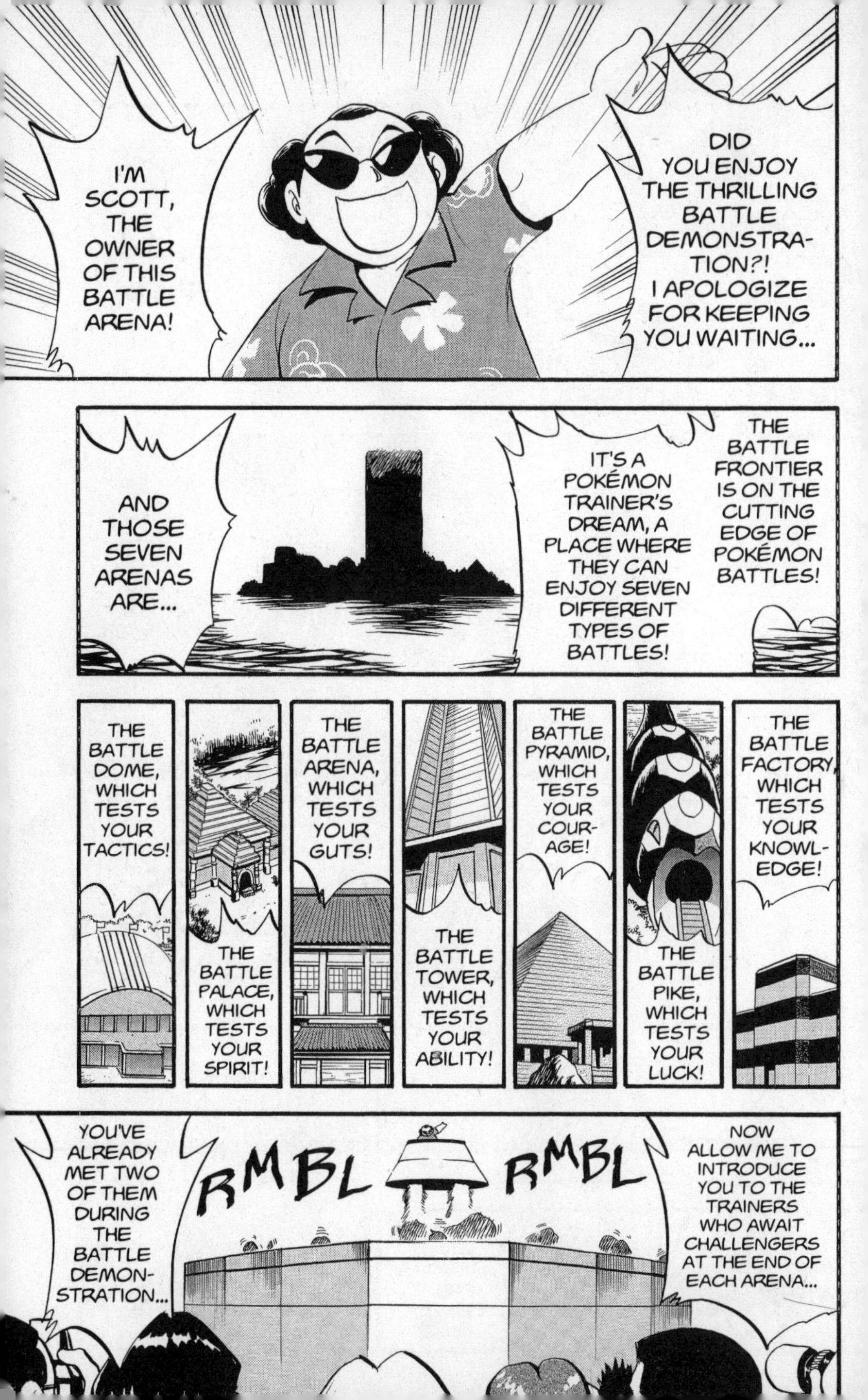
DID YOU ENJOY THE THRILLING BATTLE DEMONSTRATION?! I APOLOGIZE FOR KEEPING YOU WAITING...
I'M SCOTT, THE OWNER OF THIS BATTLE ARENA!
THE BATTLE FRONTIER IS ON THE CUTTING EDGE OF POKÉMON BATTLES!
IT'S A POKÉMON TRAINER'S DREAM, A PLACE WHERE THEY CAN ENJOY SEVEN DIFFERENT TYPES OF BATTLES!
AND THOSE SEVEN ARENAS ARE...
THE BATTLE FACTORY, WHICH TESTS YOUR KNOWLEDGE!
THE BATTLE PIKE, WHICH TESTS YOUR LUCK!
THE BATTLE PYRAMID, WHICH TESTS YOUR COURAGE!
THE BATTLE TOWER, WHICH TESTS YOUR ABILITY!
THE BATTLE ARENA, WHICH TESTS YOUR GUTS!
THE BATTLE PALACE, WHICH TESTS YOUR SPIRIT!
THE BATTLE DOME, WHICH TESTS YOUR TACTICS!
NOW ALLOW ME TO INTRODUCE YOU TO THE TRAINERS WHO AWAIT CHALLENGERS AT THE END OF EACH ARENA...
RMBL
RMBL
YOU'VE ALREADY MET TWO OF THEM DURING THE BATTLE DEMONSTRATION...

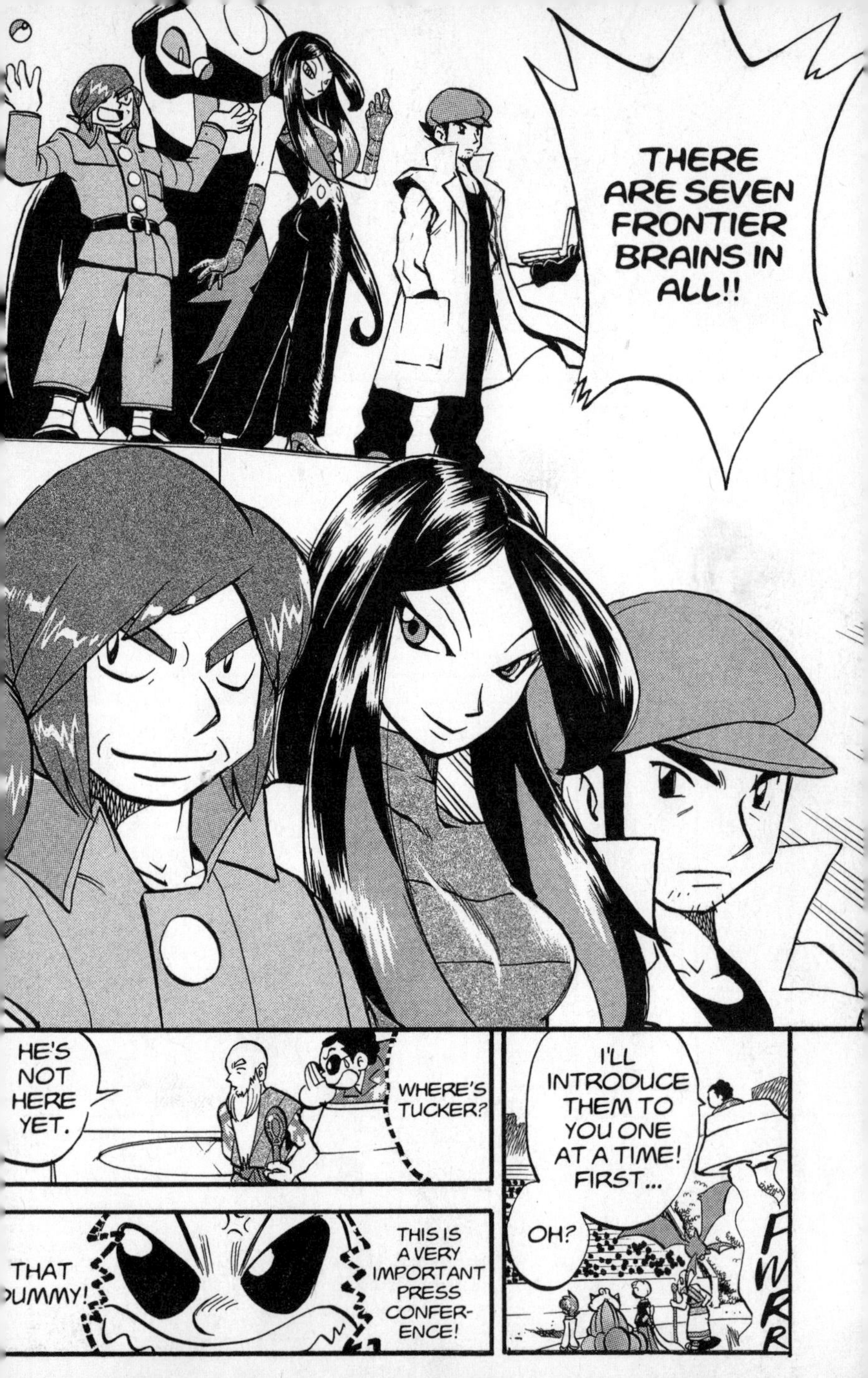
THERE ARE SEVEN FRONTIER BRAINS IN ALL!!
I'LL INTRODUCE THEM TO YOU ONE AT A TIME! FIRST...
OH?
FWRR
WHERE'S TUCKER?
HE'S NOT HERE YET.
THIS IS A VERY IMPORTANT PRESS CONFERENCE!
THAT DUMMY!

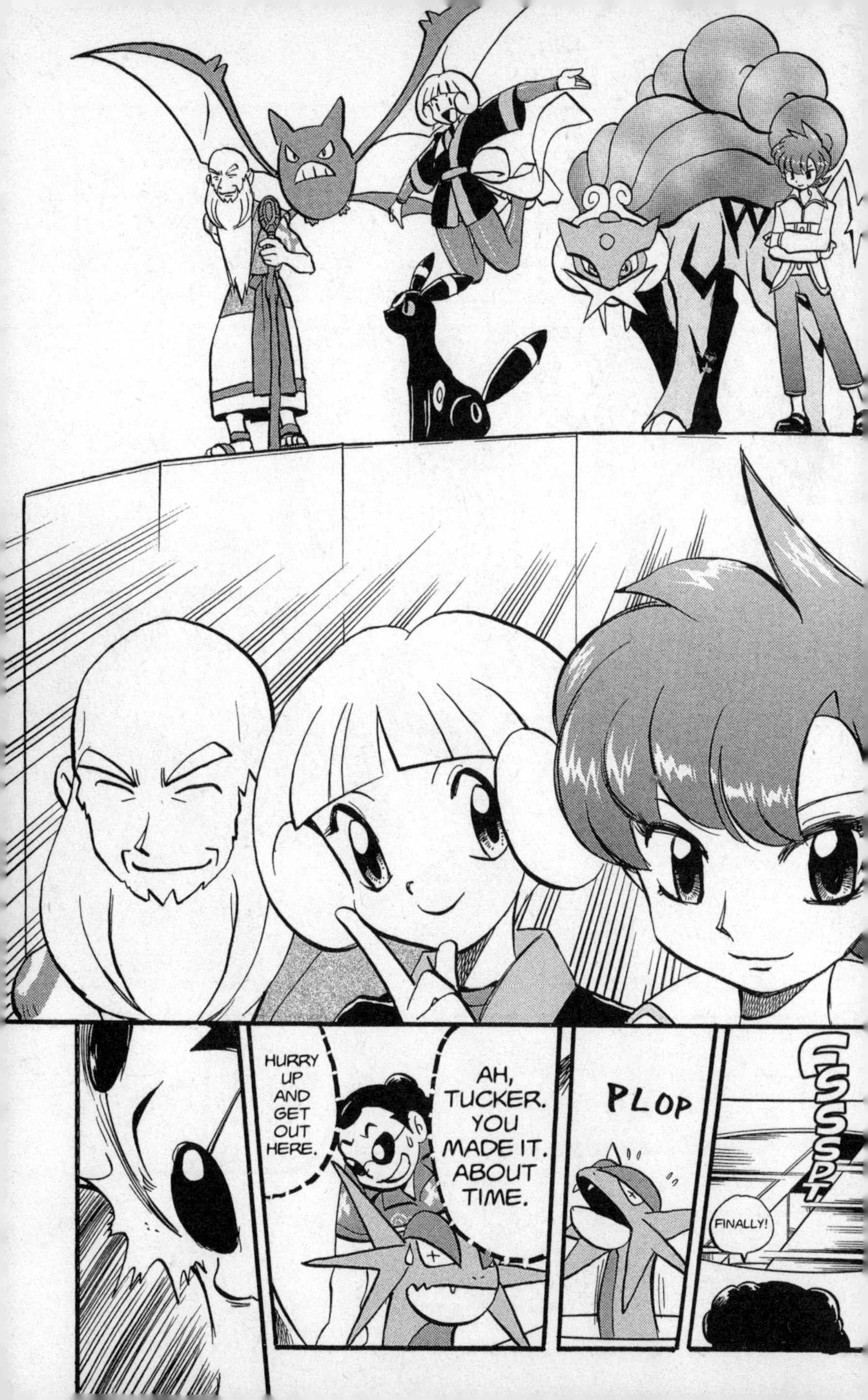
FSSSPT
FINALLY!
PLOP
AH, TUCKER. YOU MADE IT. ABOUT TIME.
HURRY UP AND GET OUT HERE.

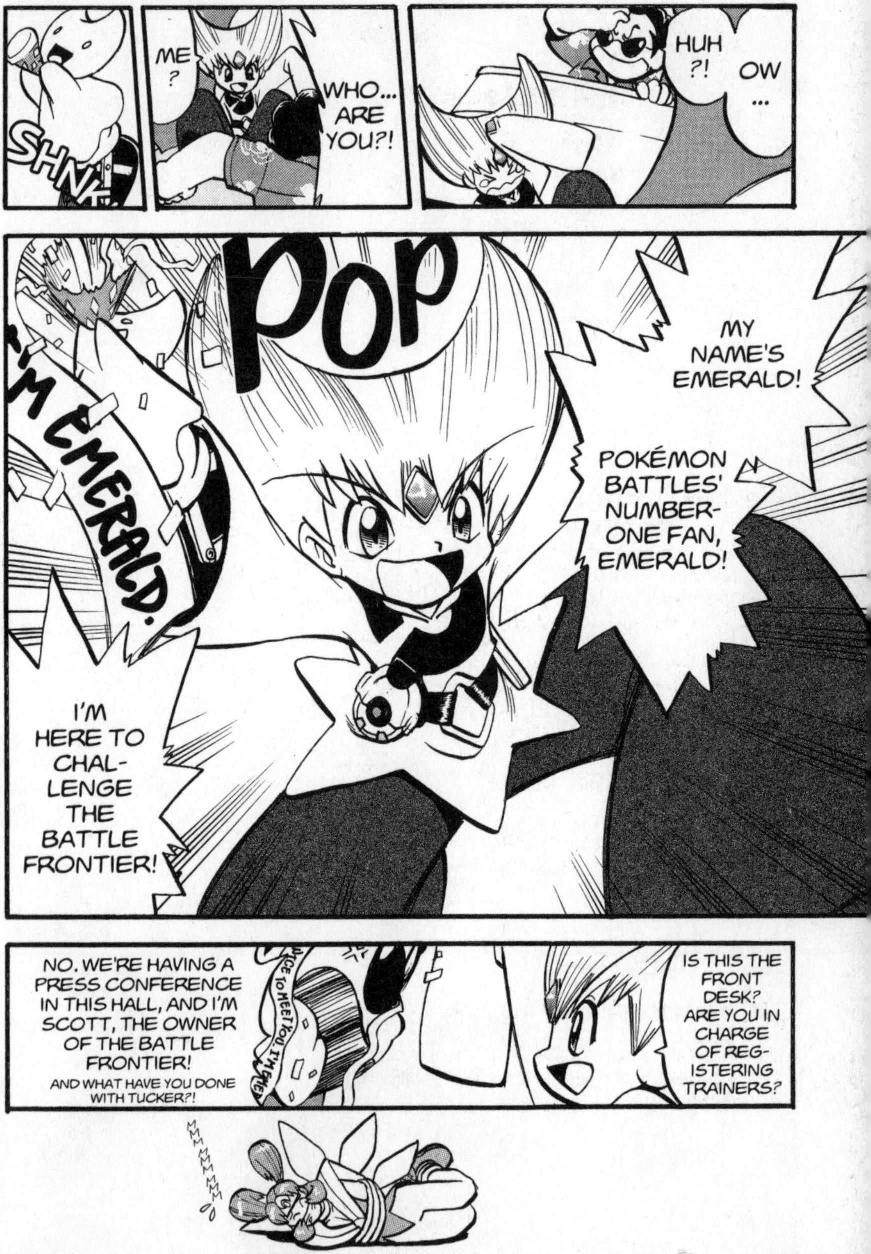
HUH?!
OW...
WHO... ARE YOU?!
ME?
SHNK
POP
MY NAME'S EMERALD!
POKÉMON BATTLES' NUMBER-ONE FAN, EMERALD!
I'M EMERALD!
I'M HERE TO CHALLENGE THE BATTLE FRONTIER!
IS THIS THE FRONT DESK? ARE YOU IN CHARGE OF REGISTERING TRAINERS?
NO. WE'RE HAVING A PRESS CONFERENCE IN THIS HALL, AND I'M SCOTT, THE OWNER OF THE BATTLE FRONTIER!
AND WHAT HAVE YOU DONE WITH TUCKER?!
MMMMMMMM

DEAR MEMBERS OF THE PRESS...

Thank you so much for coming to my
Battle Frontier today. Allow me to take
this opportunity to explain the rules for
Pokémon Battles here...

■ LIMITED POKÉMON ■
USAGE

You may not enter two of the same
Pokémon into a battle.
*Prior permission must be obtained to
participate with an Egg or Legendary
Pokémon.
*Your challenge might not be accepted.
*On the other hand, there is a possibility
that our Frontier Brains will use **your**
Pokémon in battle.

■ ITEM USAGE ■

Apart from certain exceptions, Trainers
are not allowed to use items during
challenges. But Pokémon may hold
an item before battle.

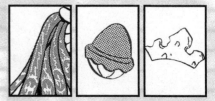

■ NUMBER OF MOVES PERMITTED ■

Each Pokémon is only allowed four moves during a
battle. These moves must be registered before the
battle. No other moves are permitted.

◆ 305 ◆

Interesting Interactions Involving Illumise

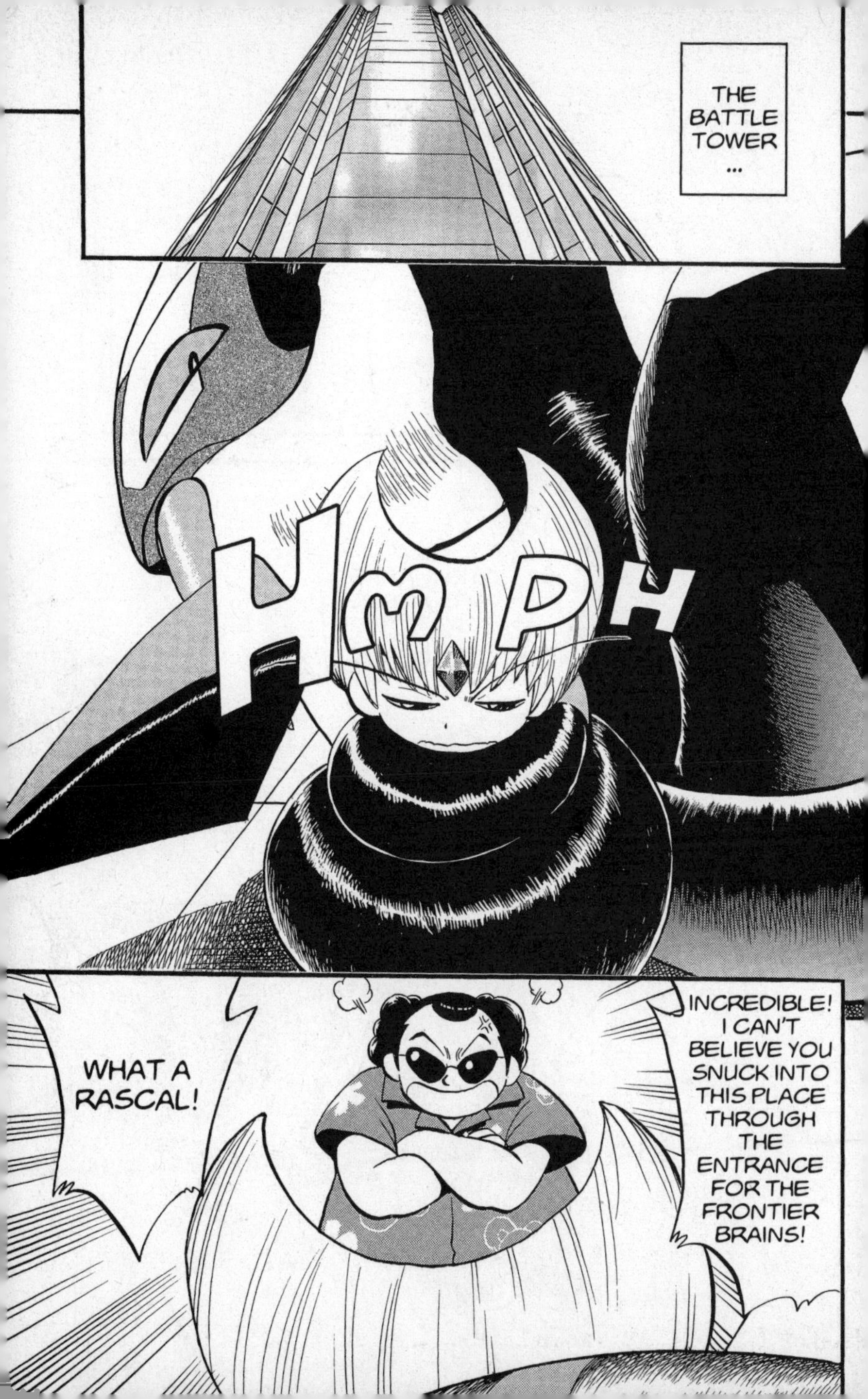
THE BATTLE TOWER ...
HMPH
INCREDIBLE! I CAN'T BELIEVE YOU SNUCK INTO THIS PLACE THROUGH THE ENTRANCE FOR THE FRONTIER BRAINS!
WHAT A RASCAL!

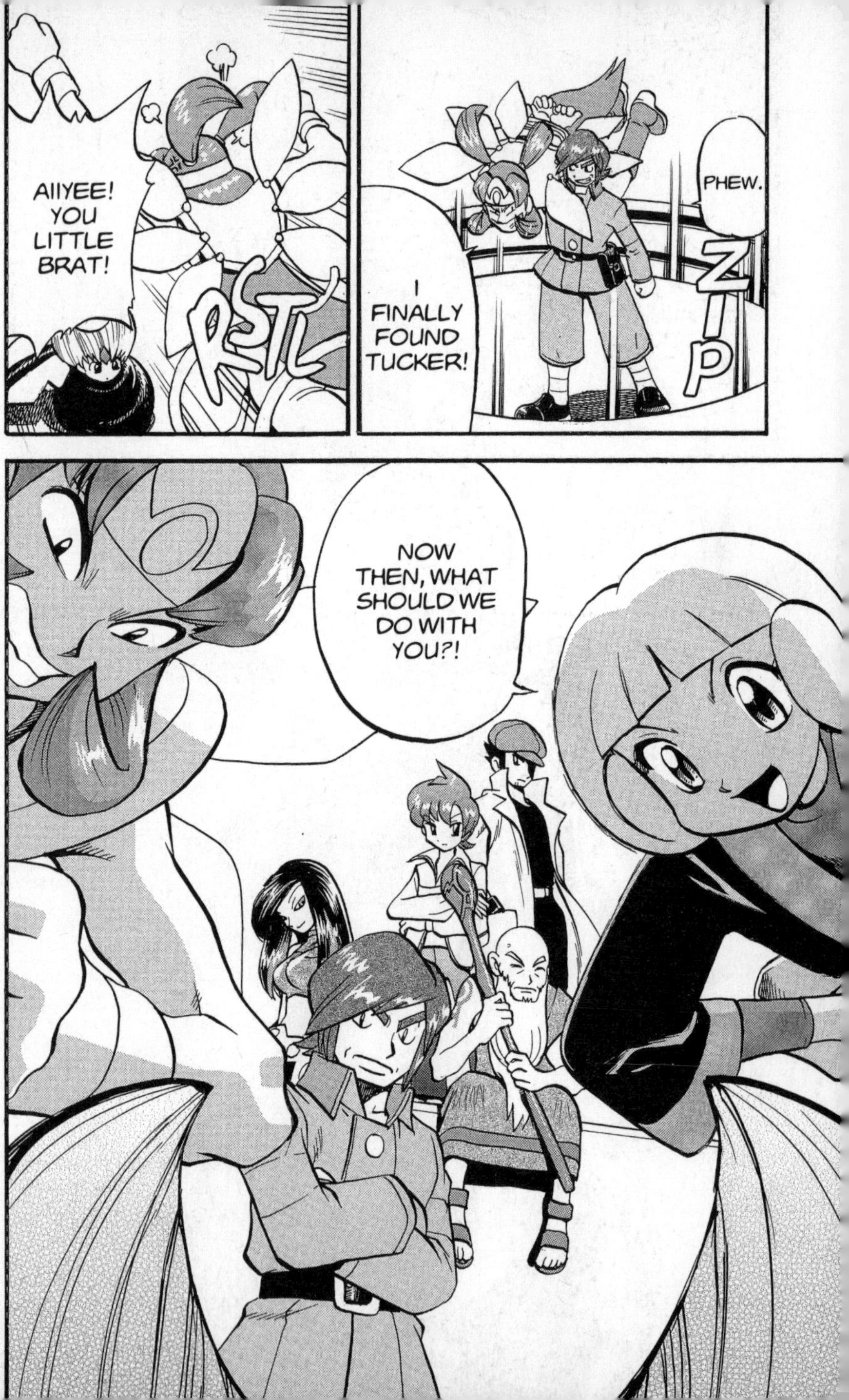
PHEW.
ZIP
I FINALLY FOUND TUCKER!
AIIYEE! YOU LITTLE BRAT!
RSTL
NOW THEN, WHAT SHOULD WE DO WITH YOU?!

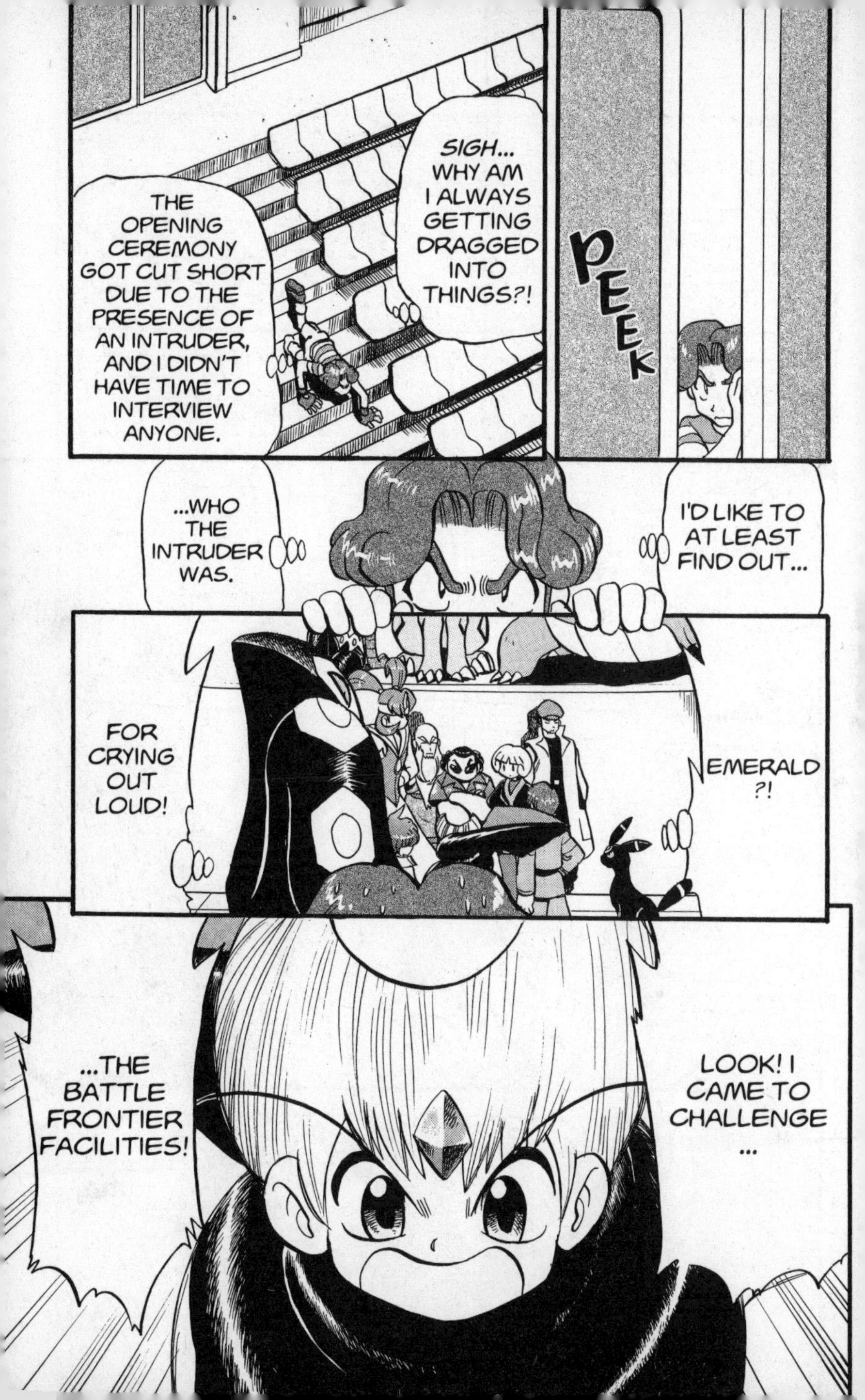
PEEK
SIGH... WHY AM I ALWAYS GETTING DRAGGED INTO THINGS?!
THE OPENING CEREMONY GOT CUT SHORT DUE TO THE PRESENCE OF AN INTRUDER, AND I DIDN'T HAVE TIME TO INTERVIEW ANYONE.
I'D LIKE TO AT LEAST FIND OUT...
...WHO THE INTRUDER WAS.
EMERALD ?!
FOR CRYING OUT LOUD!
LOOK! I CAME TO CHALLENGE ...
...THE BATTLE FRONTIER FACILITIES!

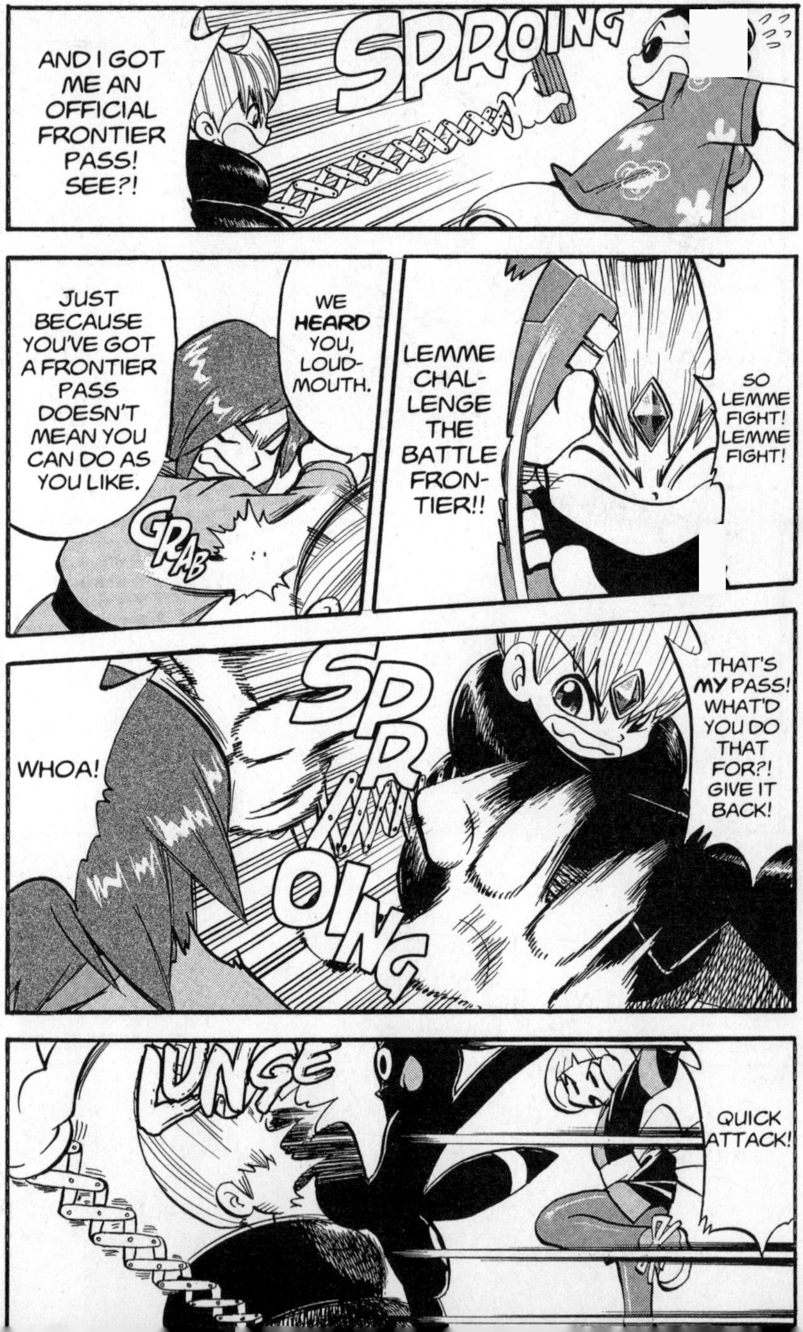
SPROING
AND I GOT ME AN OFFICIAL FRONTIER PASS! SEE?!
SO LEMME FIGHT! LEMME FIGHT!
LEMME CHALLENGE THE BATTLE FRONTIER!!
WE **HEARD** YOU, LOUDMOUTH.
JUST BECAUSE YOU'VE GOT A FRONTIER PASS DOESN'T MEAN YOU CAN DO AS YOU LIKE.
GRAB
THAT'S **MY** PASS! WHAT'D YOU DO THAT FOR?! GIVE IT BACK!
SPROING
WHOA!
QUICK ATTACK!
LUNGE

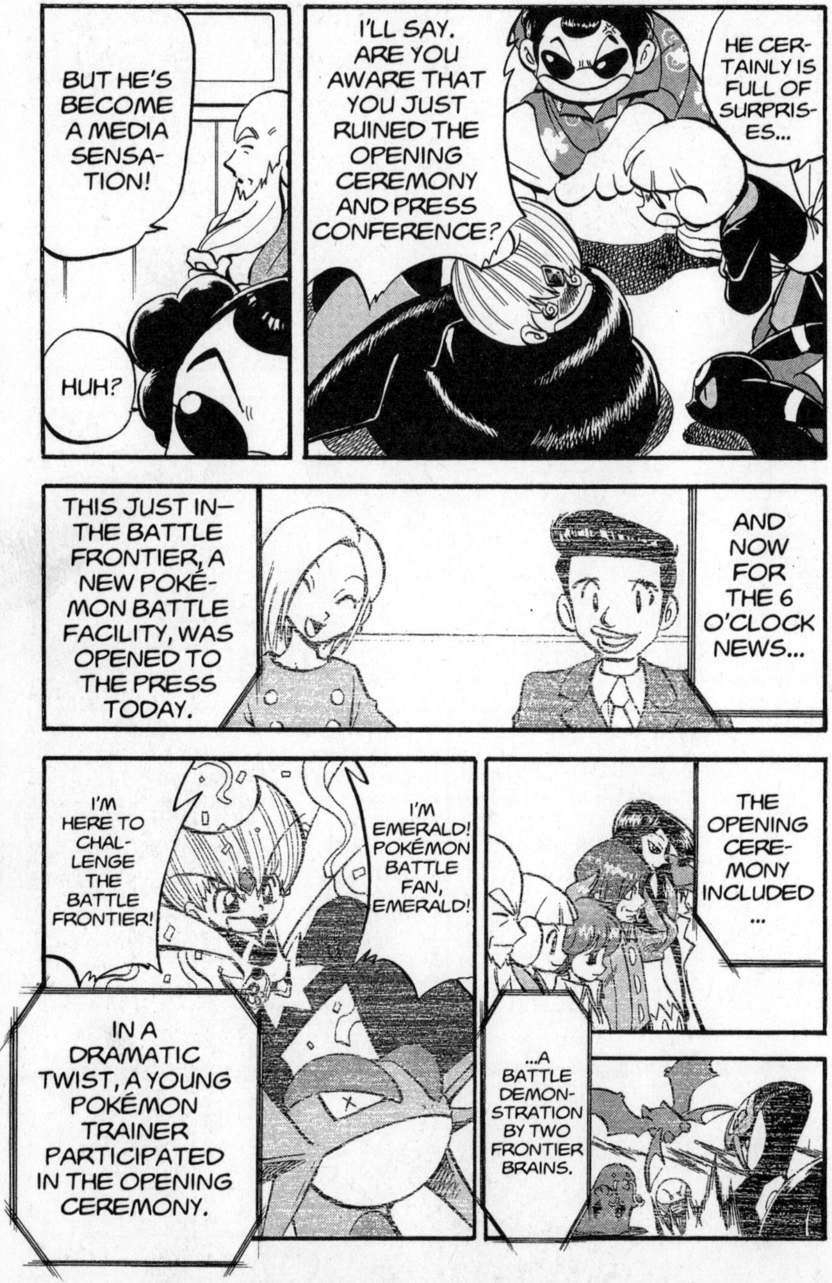
HE CERTAINLY IS FULL OF SURPRISES...
I'LL SAY. ARE YOU AWARE THAT YOU JUST RUINED THE OPENING CEREMONY AND PRESS CONFERENCE?
BUT HE'S BECOME A MEDIA SENSATION!
HUH?
AND NOW FOR THE 6 O'CLOCK NEWS...
THIS JUST IN—THE BATTLE FRONTIER, A NEW POKÉMON BATTLE FACILITY, WAS OPENED TO THE PRESS TODAY.
THE OPENING CEREMONY INCLUDED...
...A BATTLE DEMONSTRATION BY TWO FRONTIER BRAINS.
I'M EMERALD! POKÉMON BATTLE FAN, EMERALD!
I'M HERE TO CHALLENGE THE BATTLE FRONTIER!
IN A DRAMATIC TWIST, A YOUNG POKÉMON TRAINER PARTICIPATED IN THE OPENING CEREMONY.

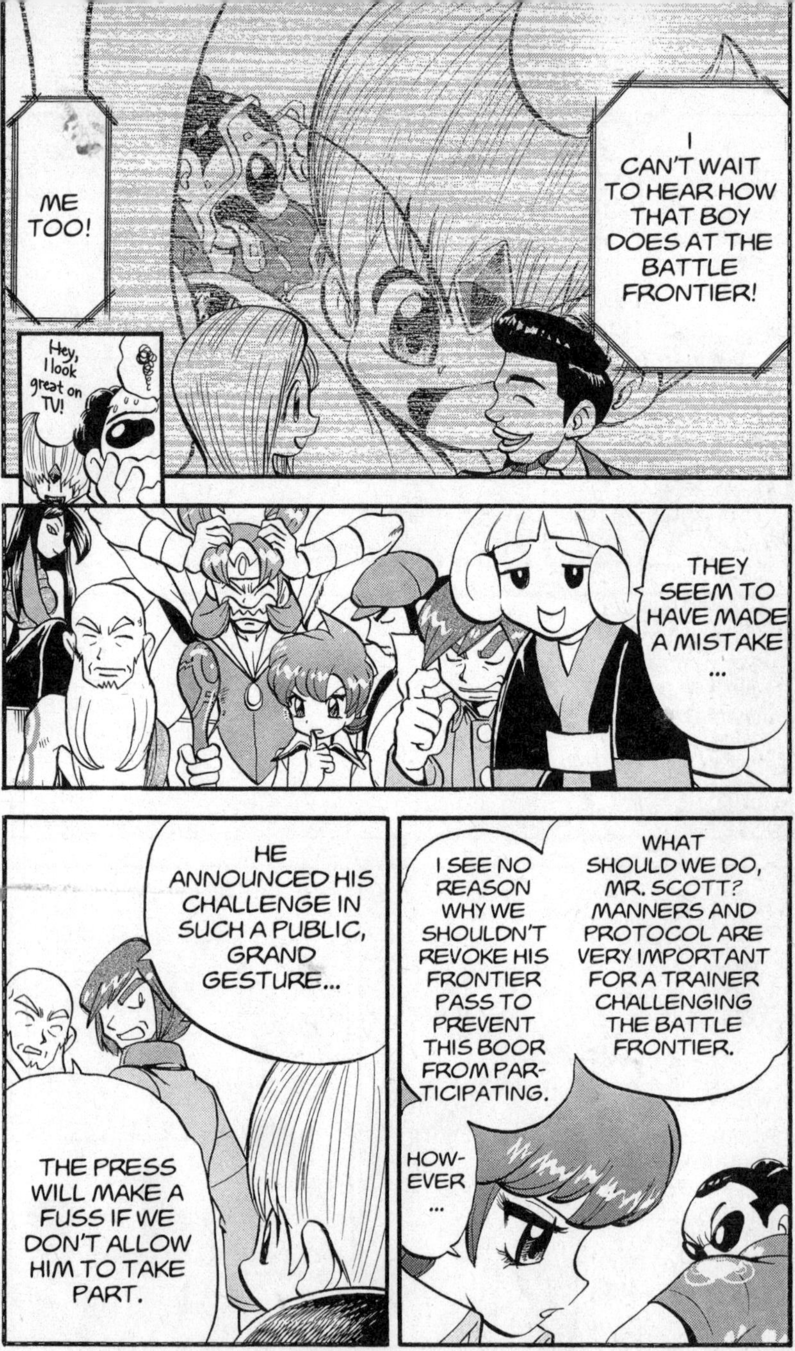
I CAN'T WAIT TO HEAR HOW THAT BOY DOES AT THE BATTLE FRONTIER!
ME TOO!
Hey, I look great on TV!
THEY SEEM TO HAVE MADE A MISTAKE...
WHAT SHOULD WE DO, MR. SCOTT? MANNERS AND PROTOCOL ARE VERY IMPORTANT FOR A TRAINER CHALLENGING THE BATTLE FRONTIER.
I SEE NO REASON WHY WE SHOULDN'T REVOKE HIS FRONTIER PASS TO PREVENT THIS BOOR FROM PARTICIPATING.
HOW-EVER...
HE ANNOUNCED HIS CHALLENGE IN SUCH A PUBLIC, GRAND GESTURE...
THE PRESS WILL MAKE A FUSS IF WE DON'T ALLOW HIM TO TAKE PART.

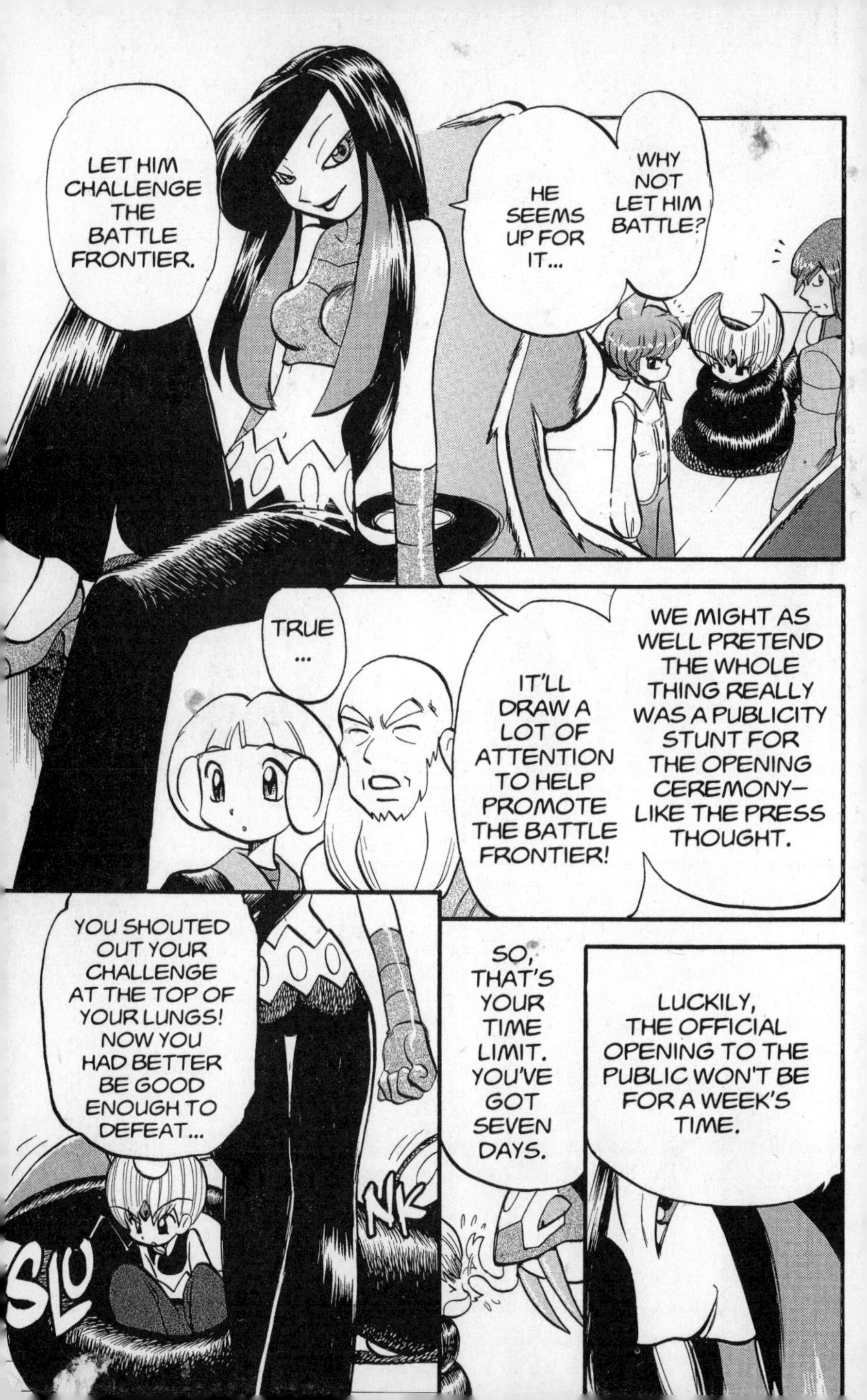
WHY NOT LET HIM BATTLE?
HE SEEMS UP FOR IT...
LET HIM CHALLENGE THE BATTLE FRONTIER.
WE MIGHT AS WELL PRETEND THE WHOLE THING REALLY WAS A PUBLICITY STUNT FOR THE OPENING CEREMONY—LIKE THE PRESS THOUGHT.
IT'LL DRAW A LOT OF ATTENTION TO HELP PROMOTE THE BATTLE FRONTIER!
TRUE ...
LUCKILY, THE OFFICIAL OPENING TO THE PUBLIC WON'T BE FOR A WEEK'S TIME.
SO, THAT'S YOUR TIME LIMIT. YOU'VE GOT SEVEN DAYS.
NK
YOU SHOUTED OUT YOUR CHALLENGE AT THE TOP OF YOUR LUNGS! NOW YOU HAD BETTER BE GOOD ENOUGH TO DEFEAT...
SLU

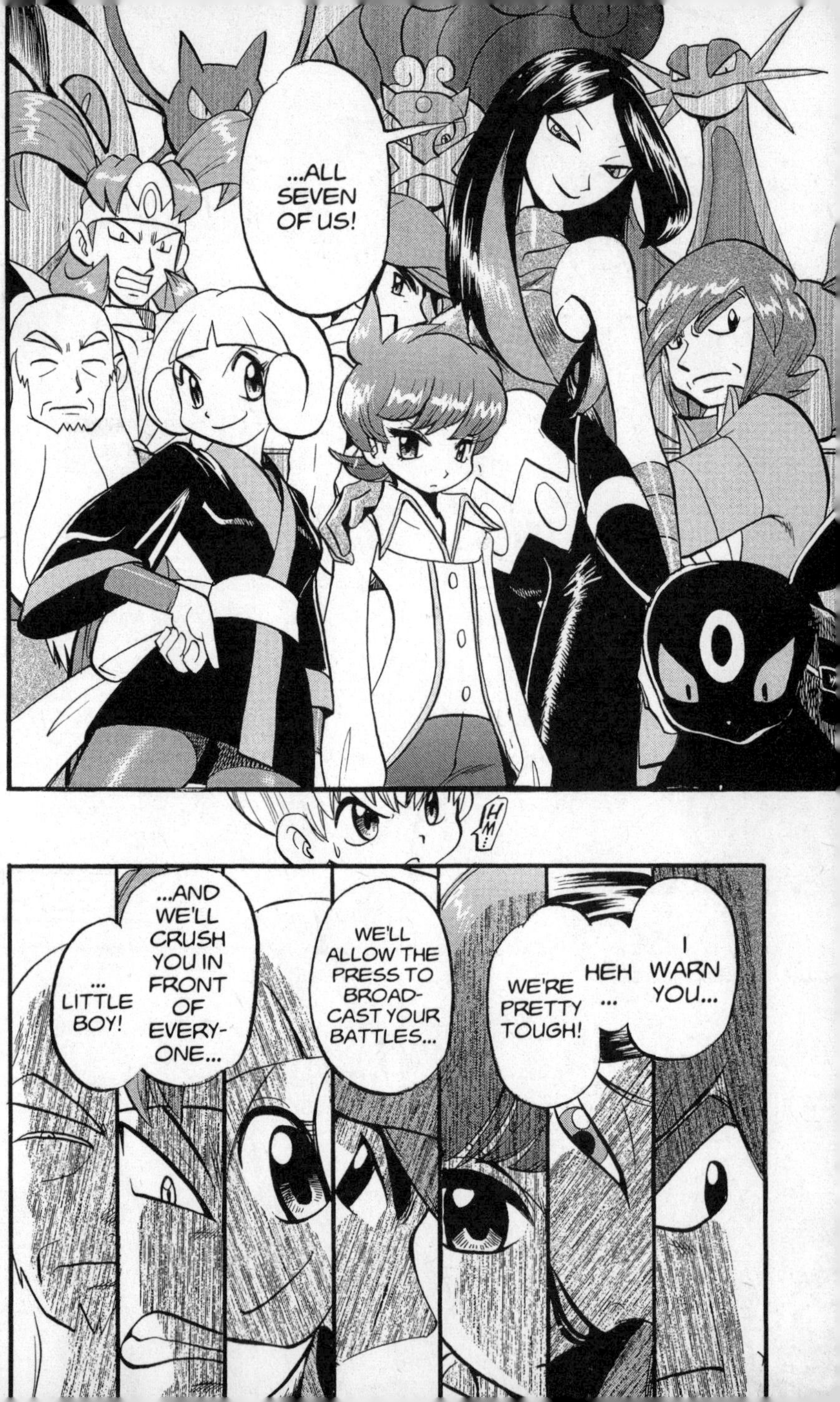
...ALL SEVEN OF US!
HM...
I WARN YOU...
HEH...
WE'RE PRETTY TOUGH!
WE'LL ALLOW THE PRESS TO BROADCAST YOUR BATTLES...
...AND WE'LL CRUSH YOU IN FRONT OF EVERYONE...
...LITTLE BOY!

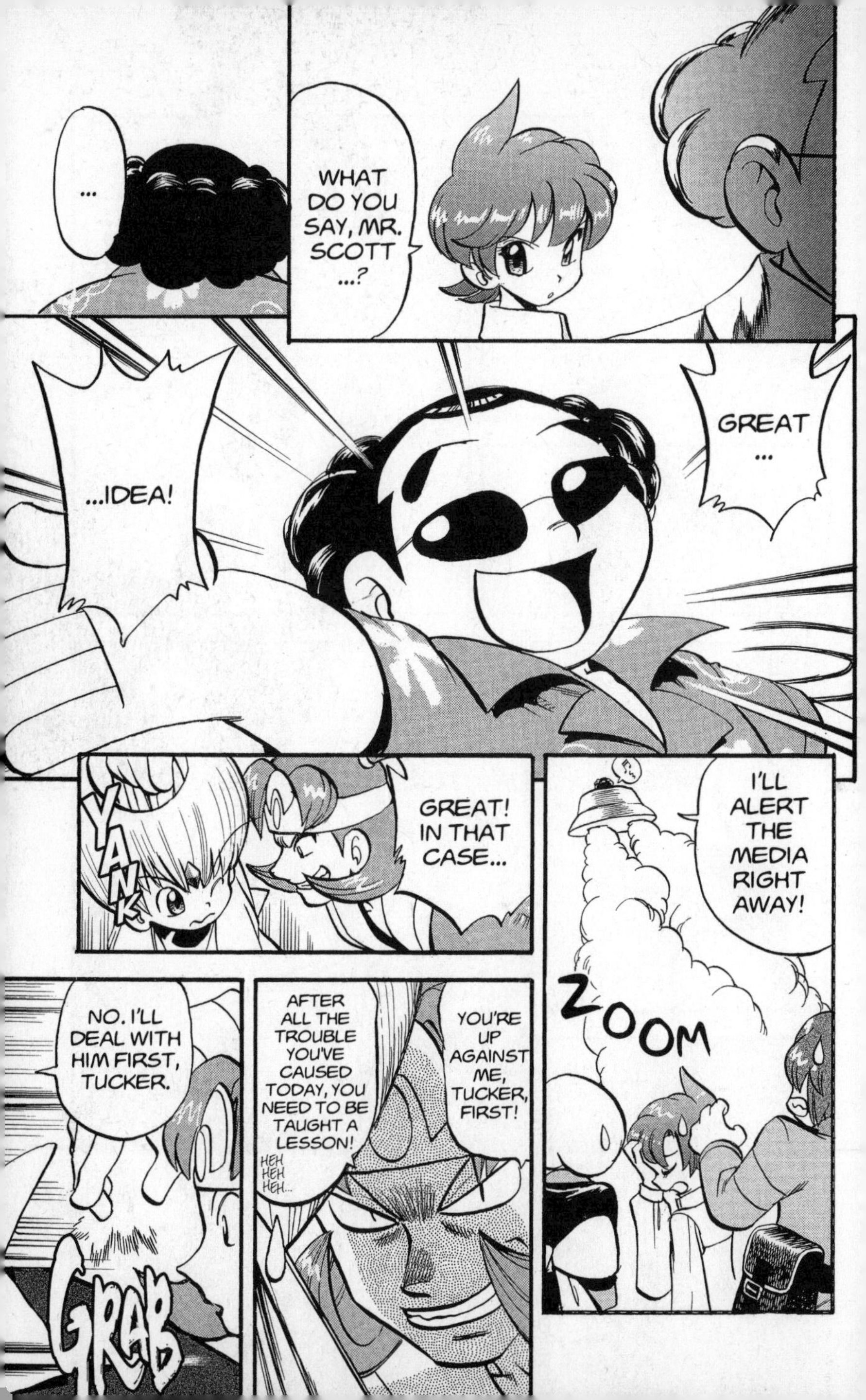
WHAT DO YOU SAY, MR. SCOTT ...?
...
GREAT ...
...IDEA!
I'LL ALERT THE MEDIA RIGHT AWAY!
ZOOM
GREAT! IN THAT CASE...
YANK
YOU'RE UP AGAINST ME, TUCKER, FIRST!
AFTER ALL THE TROUBLE YOU'VE CAUSED TODAY, YOU NEED TO BE TAUGHT A LESSON!
HEH HEH HEH...
NO. I'LL DEAL WITH HIM FIRST, TUCKER.
GRAB

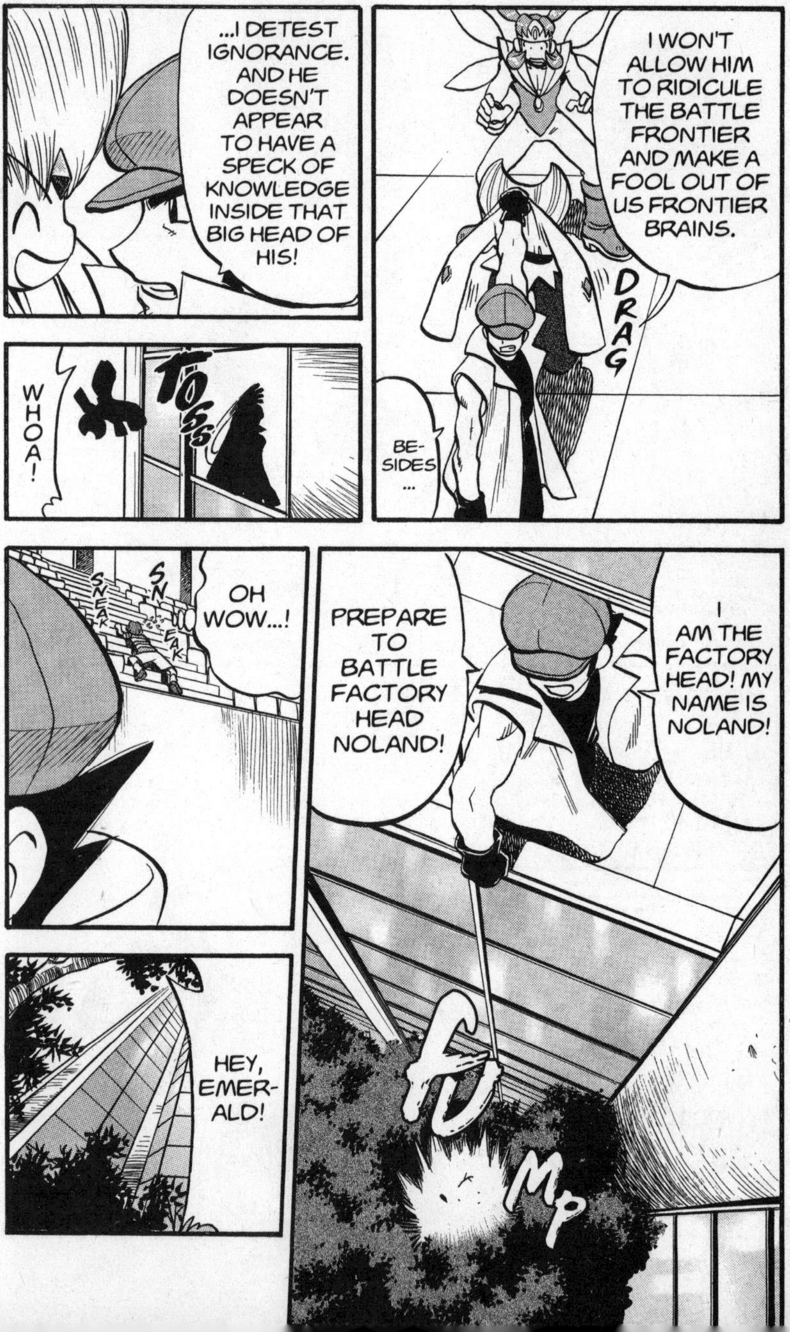

I WON'T ALLOW HIM TO RIDICULE THE BATTLE FRONTIER AND MAKE A FOOL OUT OF US FRONTIER BRAINS.
DRAG
BE-SIDES...
...I DETEST IGNORANCE. AND HE DOESN'T APPEAR TO HAVE A SPECK OF KNOWLEDGE INSIDE THAT BIG HEAD OF HIS!
TOSS
WHOA!
I AM THE FACTORY HEAD! MY NAME IS NOLAND!
PREPARE TO BATTLE FACTORY HEAD NOLAND!
Mp
OH WOW...!
SNEAK
SNEAK
HEY, EMER-ALD!

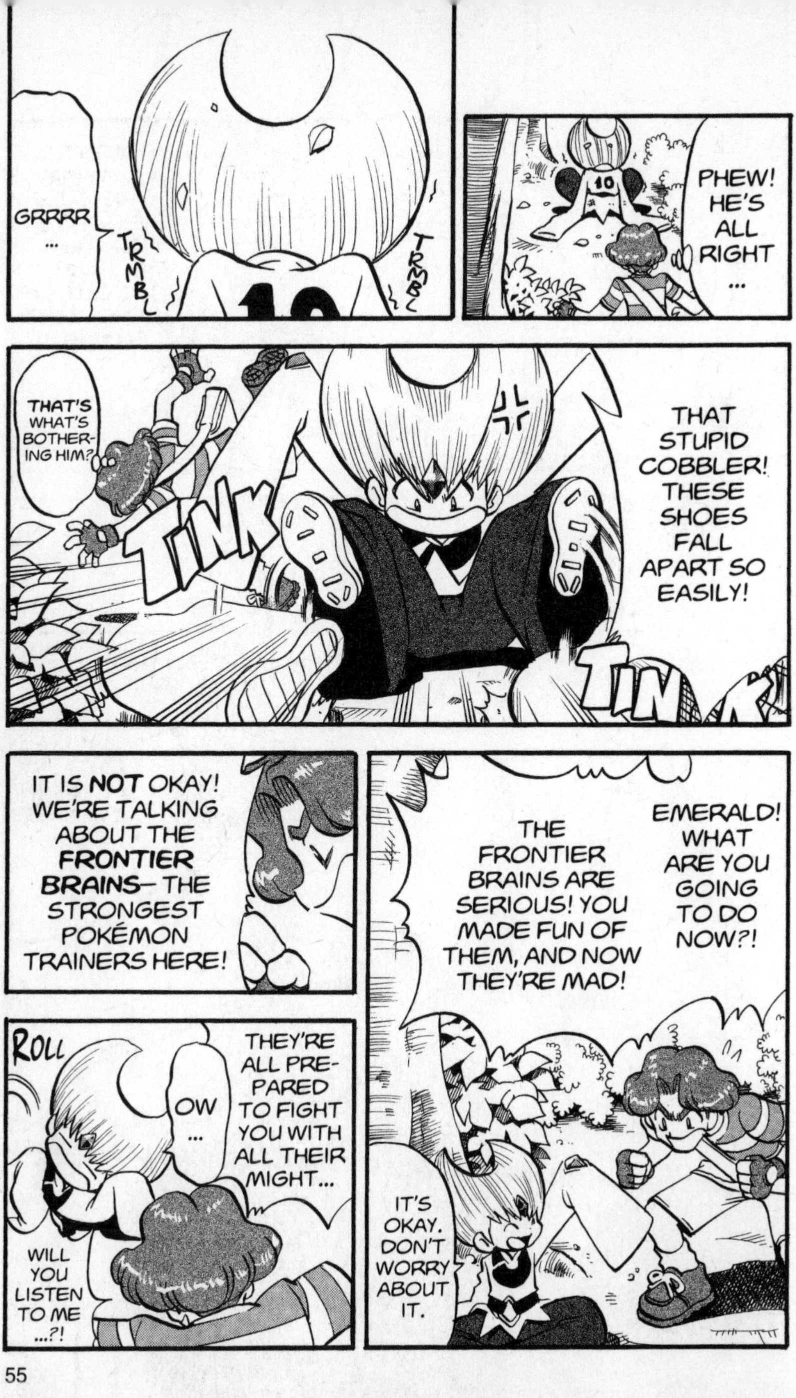
PHEW! HE'S ALL RIGHT ...
GRRRR ...
TRMBL
TRMBL
THAT STUPID COBBLER! THESE SHOES FALL APART SO EASILY!
THAT'S WHAT'S BOTHERING HIM?
TINK
TINK
EMERALD! WHAT ARE YOU GOING TO DO NOW?!
THE FRONTIER BRAINS ARE SERIOUS! YOU MADE FUN OF THEM, AND NOW THEY'RE MAD!
IT'S OKAY. DON'T WORRY ABOUT IT.
IT IS NOT OKAY! WE'RE TALKING ABOUT THE FRONTIER BRAINS— THE STRONGEST POKÉMON TRAINERS HERE!
THEY'RE ALL PREPARED TO FIGHT YOU WITH ALL THEIR MIGHT...
OW ...
ROLL
WILL YOU LISTEN TO ME ...?!

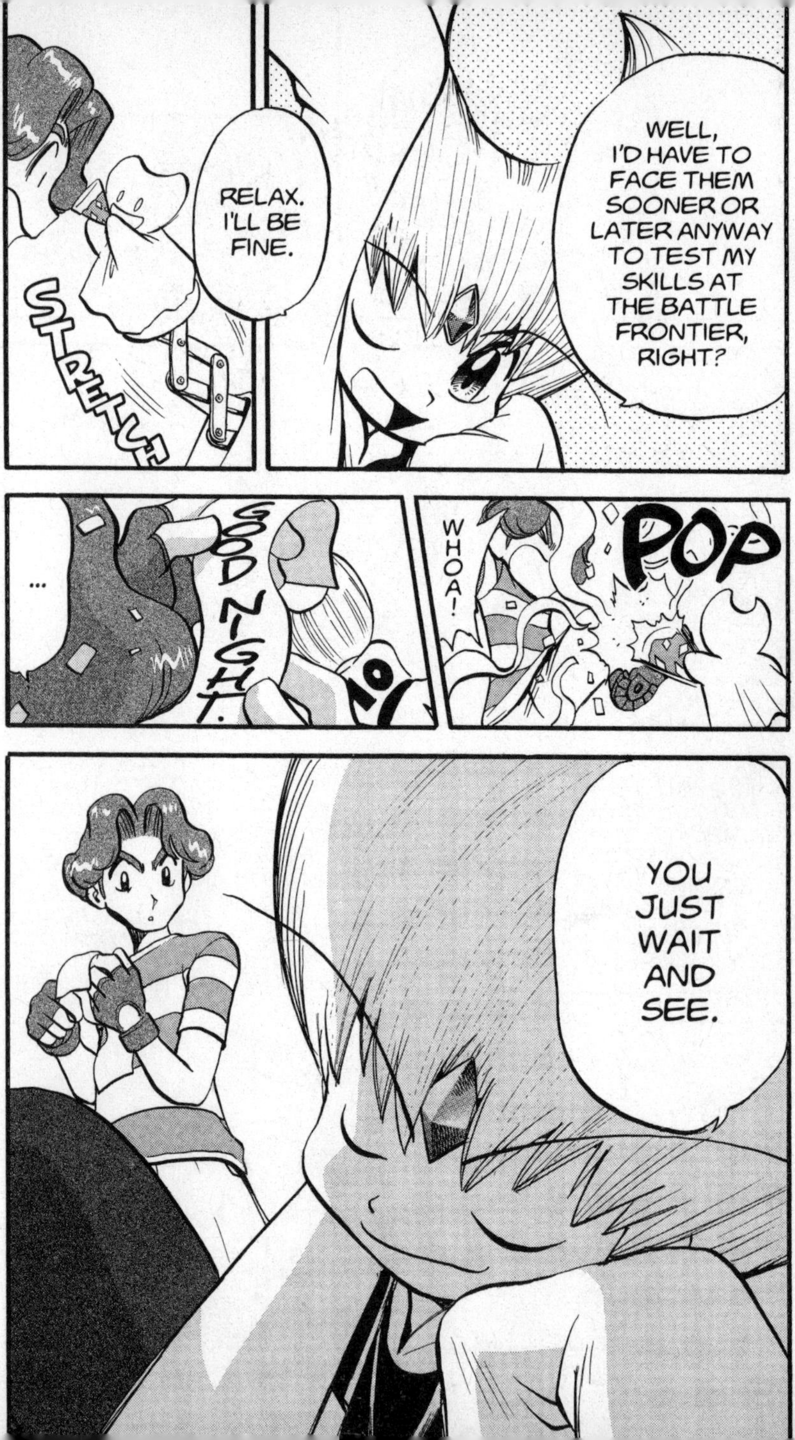
WELL, I'D HAVE TO FACE THEM SOONER OR LATER ANYWAY TO TEST MY SKILLS AT THE BATTLE FRONTIER, RIGHT?
RELAX. I'LL BE FINE.
STRETCH
POP
WHOA!
GOOD NIGHT.
...
YOU JUST WAIT AND SEE.

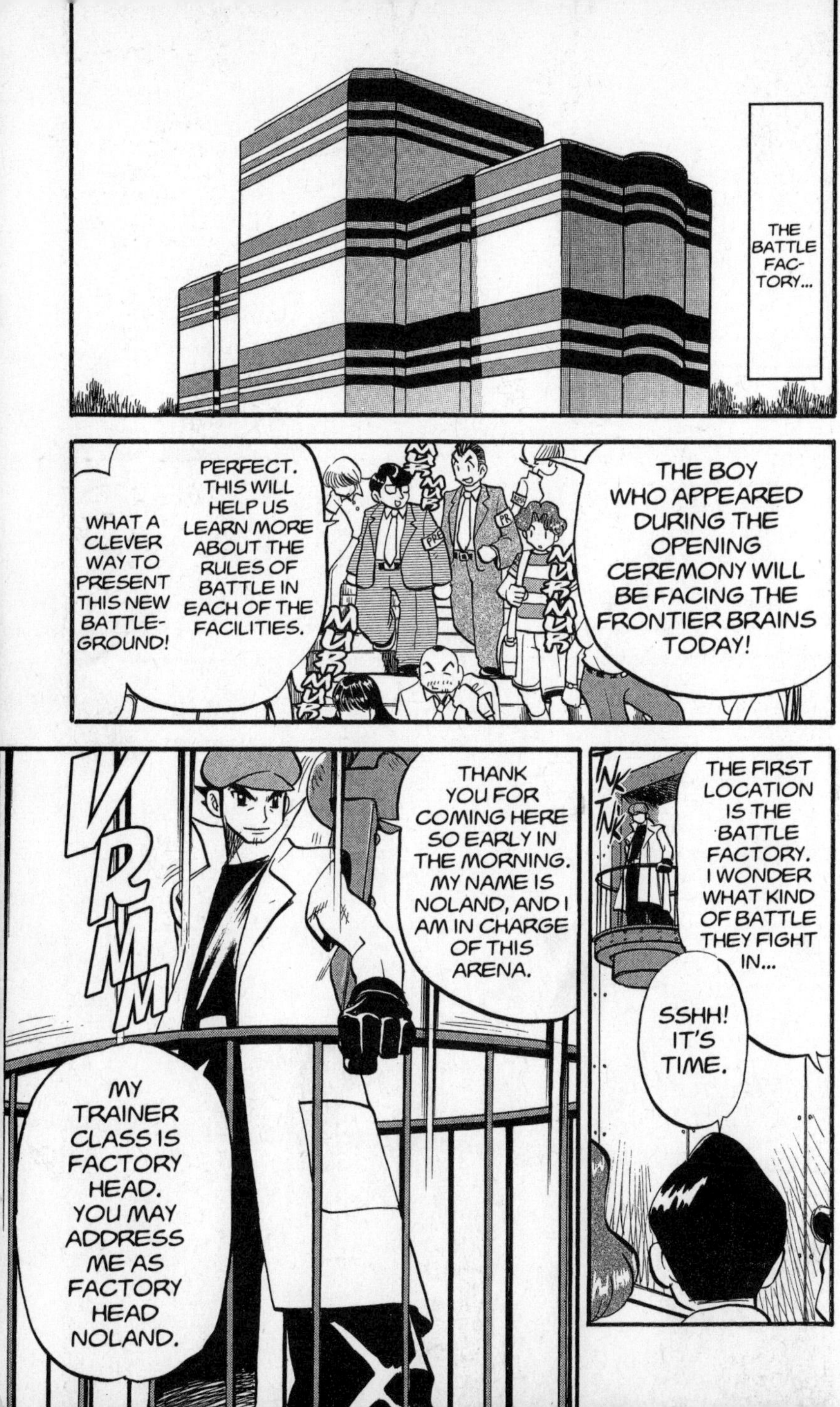
THE BATTLE FACTORY...
THE BOY WHO APPEARED DURING THE OPENING CEREMONY WILL BE FACING THE FRONTIER BRAINS TODAY!
MURMUR
PERFECT. THIS WILL HELP US LEARN MORE ABOUT THE RULES OF BATTLE IN EACH OF THE FACILITIES.
MURMUR
MURMUR
WHAT A CLEVER WAY TO PRESENT THIS NEW BATTLE-GROUND!
TNK TNK
THE FIRST LOCATION IS THE BATTLE FACTORY. I WONDER WHAT KIND OF BATTLE THEY FIGHT IN...
SSHH! IT'S TIME.
VRMM
THANK YOU FOR COMING HERE SO EARLY IN THE MORNING. MY NAME IS NOLAND, AND I AM IN CHARGE OF THIS ARENA.
MY TRAINER CLASS IS FACTORY HEAD. YOU MAY ADDRESS ME AS FACTORY HEAD NOLAND.

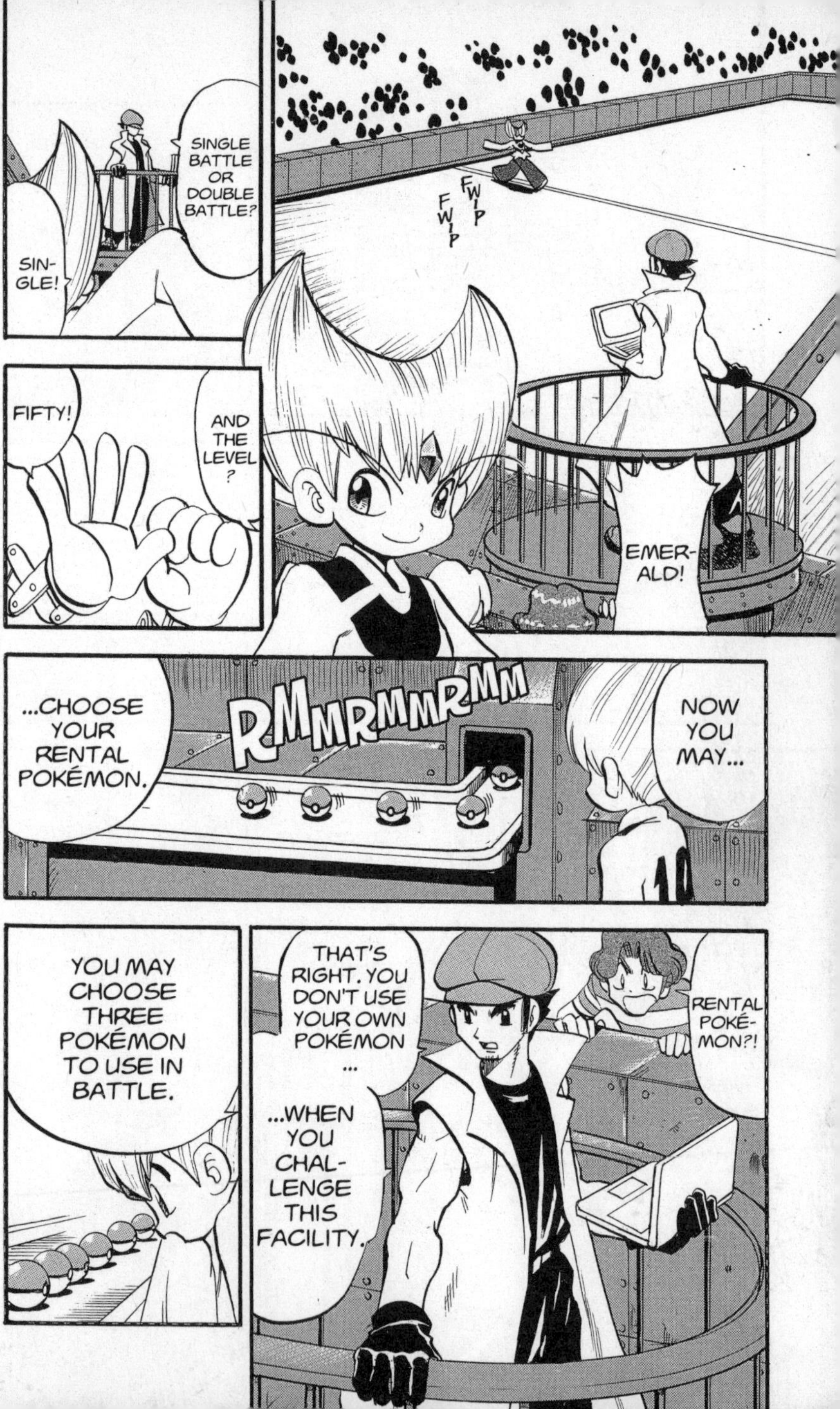
FWIP
FWIP
EMER-ALD!
SINGLE BATTLE OR DOUBLE BATTLE?
SIN-GLE!
AND THE LEVEL?
FIFTY!
NOW YOU MAY...
RMMRMMMRMMM
...CHOOSE YOUR RENTAL POKÉMON.
RENTAL POKÉ-MON?!
THAT'S RIGHT. YOU DON'T USE YOUR OWN POKÉMON ...
...WHEN YOU CHAL-LENGE THIS FACILITY.
YOU MAY CHOOSE THREE POKÉMON TO USE IN BATTLE.

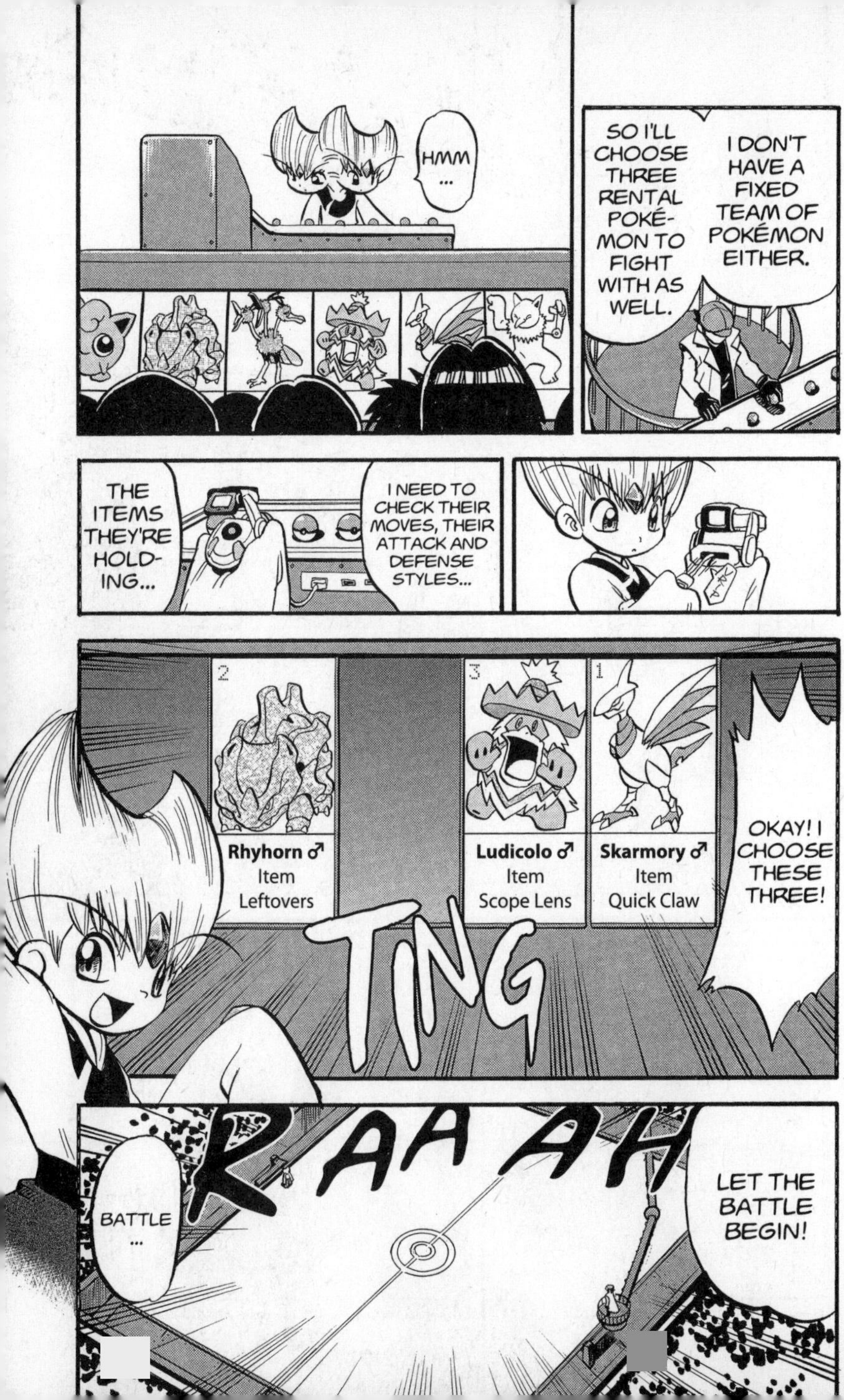

I DON'T HAVE A FIXED TEAM OF POKÉMON EITHER.
SO I'LL CHOOSE THREE RENTAL POKÉMON TO FIGHT WITH AS WELL.
HMM ...
I NEED TO CHECK THEIR MOVES, THEIR ATTACK AND DEFENSE STYLES...
THE ITEMS THEY'RE HOLDING...
OKAY! I CHOOSE THESE THREE!
1
Skarmory ♂
Item
Quick Claw
3
Ludicolo ♂
Item
Scope Lens
2
Rhyhorn ♂
Item
Leftovers
TING
LET THE BATTLE BEGIN!
RAAAH
BATTLE ...

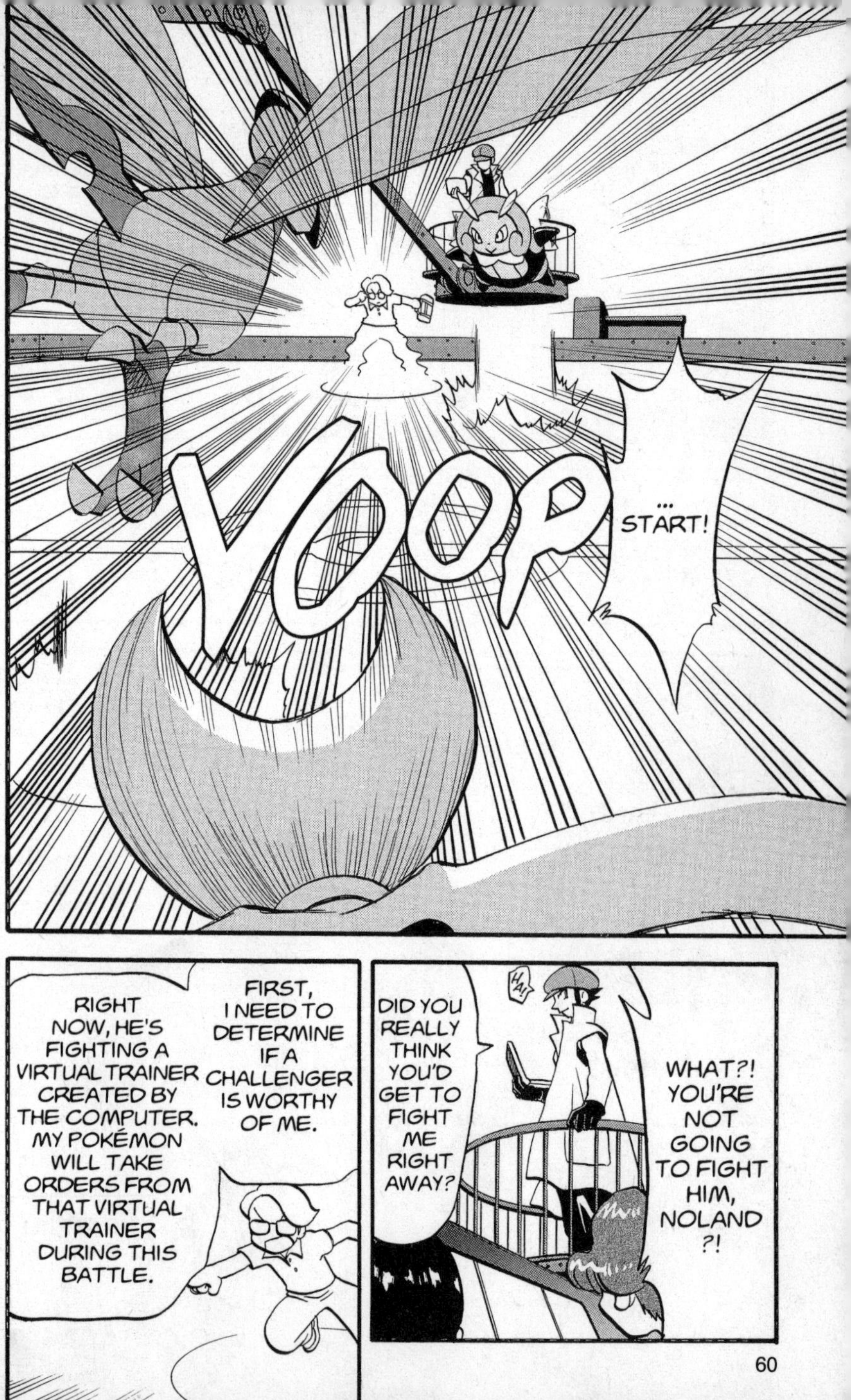
VOOP
...START!
WHAT?! YOU'RE NOT GOING TO FIGHT HIM, NOLAND?!
HA!
DID YOU REALLY THINK YOU'D GET TO FIGHT ME RIGHT AWAY?
FIRST, I NEED TO DETERMINE IF A CHALLENGER IS WORTHY OF ME.
RIGHT NOW, HE'S FIGHTING A VIRTUAL TRAINER CREATED BY THE COMPUTER. MY POKÉMON WILL TAKE ORDERS FROM THAT VIRTUAL TRAINER DURING THIS BATTLE.

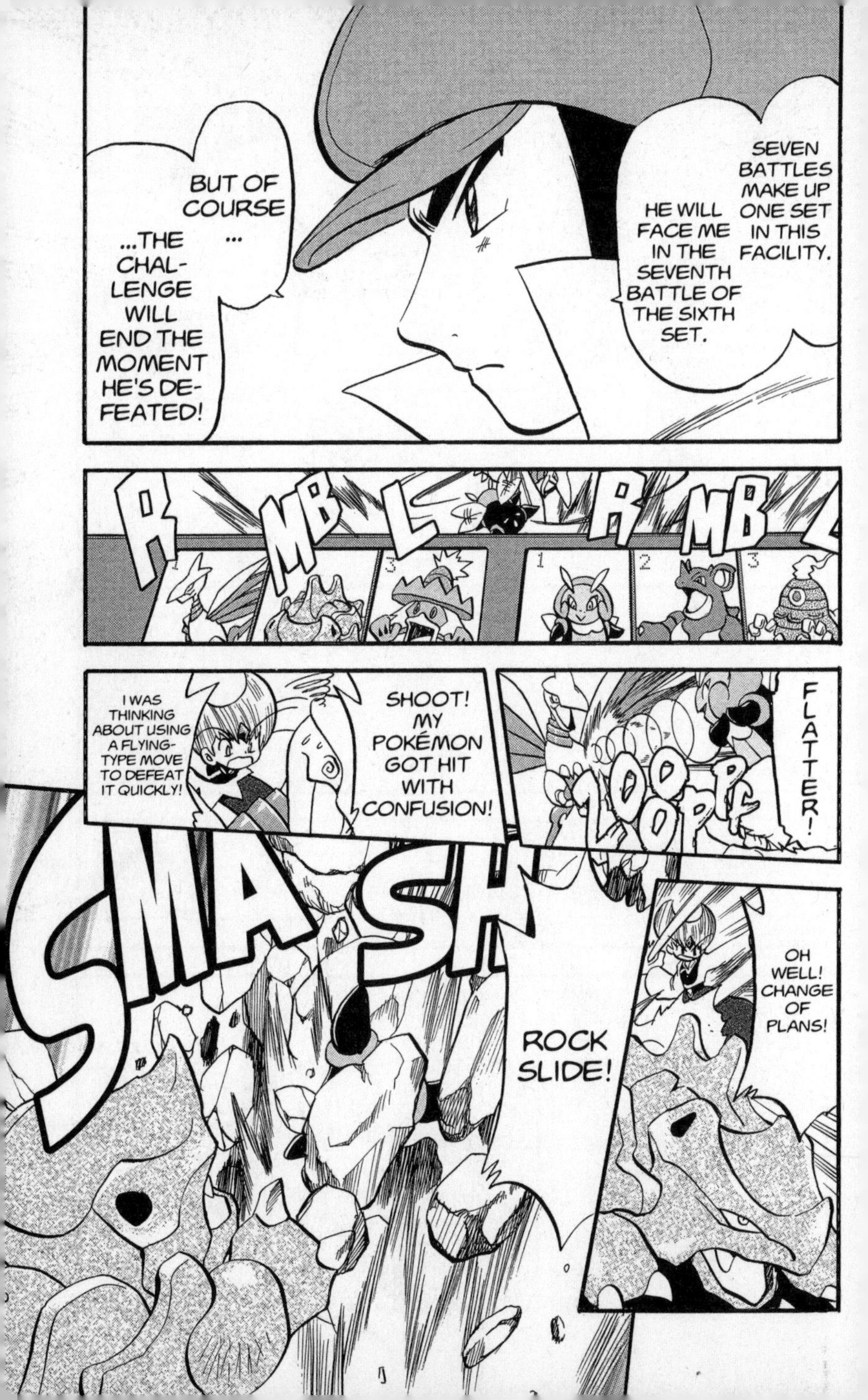
SEVEN BATTLES MAKE UP ONE SET IN THIS FACILITY.
HE WILL FACE ME IN THE SEVENTH BATTLE OF THE SIXTH SET.
BUT OF COURSE ...
...THE CHAL-LENGE WILL END THE MOMENT HE'S DE-FEATED!
FLATTER!
LOOP LOOP
SHOOT! MY POKÉMON GOT HIT WITH CONFUSION!
I WAS THINKING ABOUT USING A FLYING-TYPE MOVE TO DEFEAT IT QUICKLY!
OH WELL! CHANGE OF PLANS!
ROCK SLIDE!
SMASH

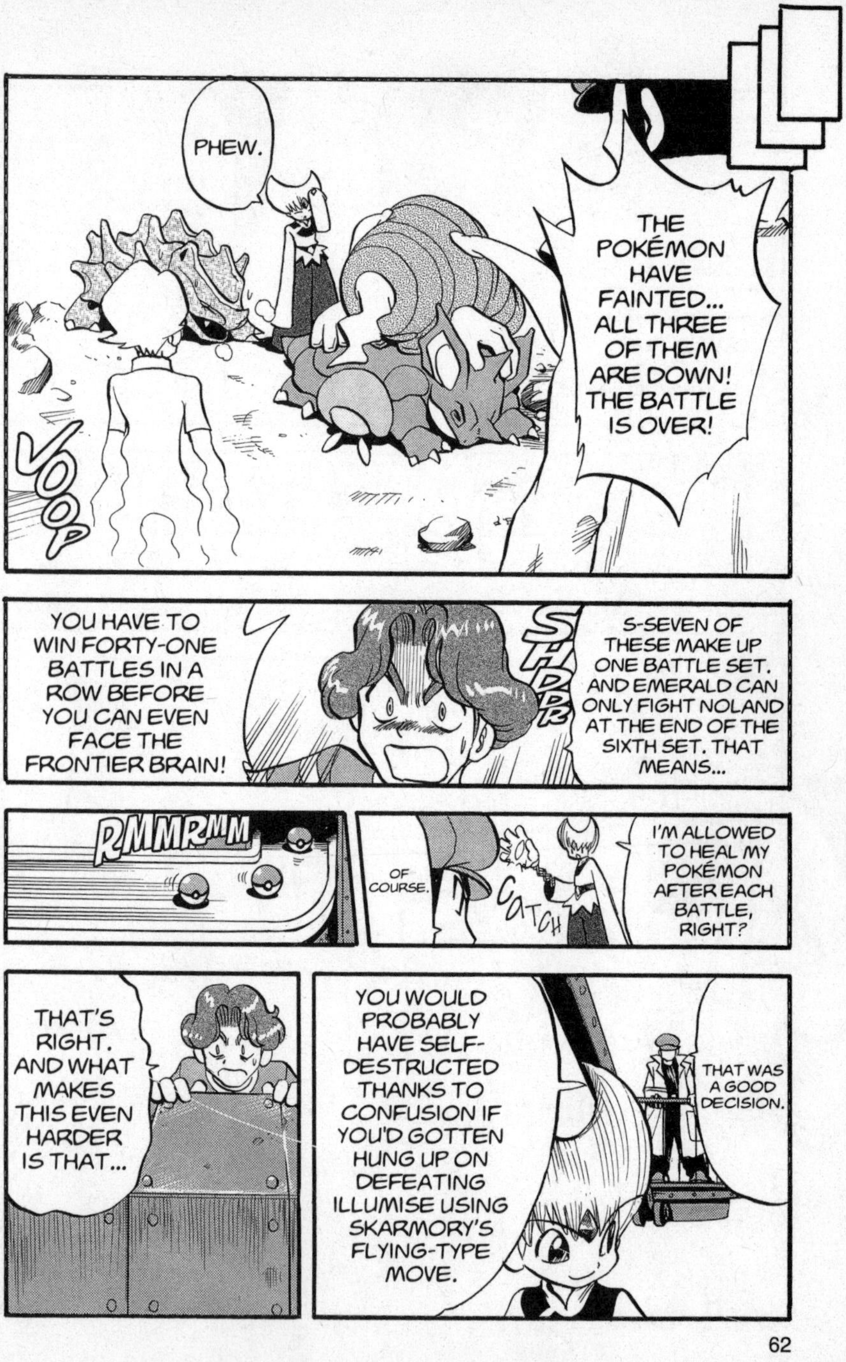
THE POKÉMON HAVE FAINTED... ALL THREE OF THEM ARE DOWN! THE BATTLE IS OVER!
PHEW.
VOOP
S-SEVEN OF THESE MAKE UP ONE BATTLE SET. AND EMERALD CAN ONLY FIGHT NOLAND AT THE END OF THE SIXTH SET. THAT MEANS...
SHDDR
YOU HAVE TO WIN FORTY-ONE BATTLES IN A ROW BEFORE YOU CAN EVEN FACE THE FRONTIER BRAIN!
I'M ALLOWED TO HEAL MY POKÉMON AFTER EACH BATTLE, RIGHT?
CATCH
OF COURSE.
RMMRMM
THAT WAS A GOOD DECISION.
YOU WOULD PROBABLY HAVE SELF-DESTRUCTED THANKS TO CONFUSION IF YOU'D GOTTEN HUNG UP ON DEFEATING ILLUMISE USING SKARMORY'S FLYING-TYPE MOVE.
THAT'S RIGHT. AND WHAT MAKES THIS EVEN HARDER IS THAT...

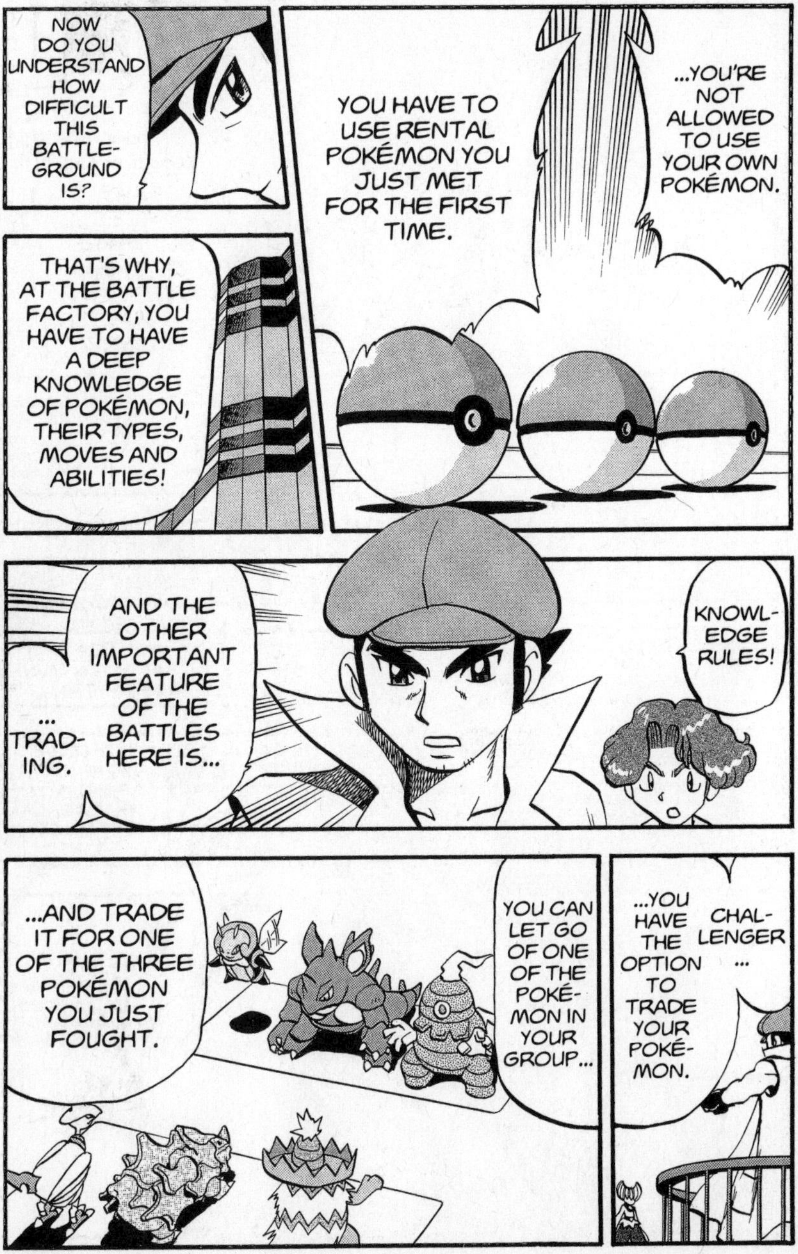
...YOU'RE NOT ALLOWED TO USE YOUR OWN POKÉMON.
YOU HAVE TO USE RENTAL POKÉMON YOU JUST MET FOR THE FIRST TIME.
NOW DO YOU UNDERSTAND HOW DIFFICULT THIS BATTLE-GROUND IS?
THAT'S WHY, AT THE BATTLE FACTORY, YOU HAVE TO HAVE A DEEP KNOWLEDGE OF POKÉMON, THEIR TYPES, MOVES AND ABILITIES!
KNOWL-EDGE RULES!
AND THE OTHER IMPORTANT FEATURE OF THE BATTLES HERE IS...
...TRAD-ING.
CHAL-LENGER...
...YOU HAVE THE OPTION TO TRADE YOUR POKÉ-MON.
YOU CAN LET GO OF ONE OF THE POKÉ-MON IN YOUR GROUP...
...AND TRADE IT FOR ONE OF THE THREE POKÉMON YOU JUST FOUGHT.

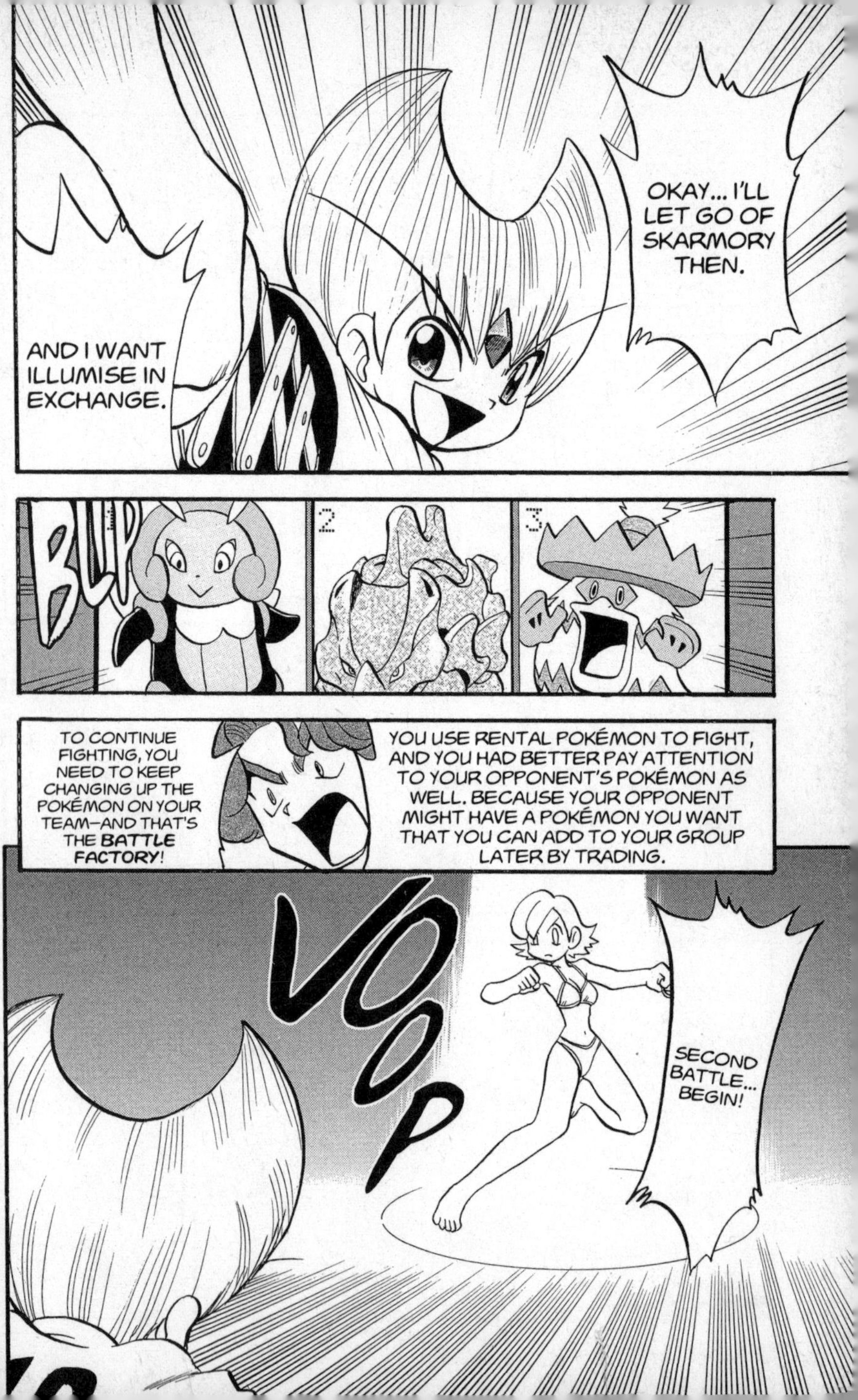
OKAY... I'LL LET GO OF SKARMORY THEN.
AND I WANT ILLUMISE IN EXCHANGE.
3
2
BLIP
1
YOU USE RENTAL POKÉMON TO FIGHT, AND YOU HAD BETTER PAY ATTENTION TO YOUR OPPONENT'S POKÉMON AS WELL. BECAUSE YOUR OPPONENT MIGHT HAVE A POKÉMON YOU WANT THAT YOU CAN ADD TO YOUR GROUP LATER BY TRADING.
TO CONTINUE FIGHTING, YOU NEED TO KEEP CHANGING UP THE POKÉMON ON YOUR TEAM—AND THAT'S THE BATTLE FACTORY!
SECOND BATTLE... BEGIN!
VOOP

DEAR MEMBERS OF THE PRESS...

Thank you for visiting my Battle Frontier today. Permit me to continue explaining the rules of this facility...

OWNER: SCOTT

FOR CONVENIENCE, WE USE NUMBERS TO REPRESENT A POKÉMON'S STRENGTH.

To ensure a fair battle, we represent the strengths of our Pokémon with numbers we call "levels." Challengers may use their PokéNav to check the level of their Pokémon before a battle.

CHALLENGERS MAY CHOOSE BETWEEN LEVEL 50 AND OPEN LEVEL.

You may choose between two courses. In the "Level 50" course, the highest level for your Pokémon is 50. But the "Open Level" course has no Pokémon level limits.

FUNCTIONS OF THE FRONTIER PASS

A Frontier Pass is handed out to challengers. This pass has many features, such as a map to check where each facility is located. Battle records are also recorded on the Frontier Pass. You may record any battle you wish and replay it later.

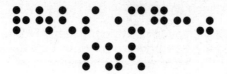

Pinsir Me, I Must Be Dreaming

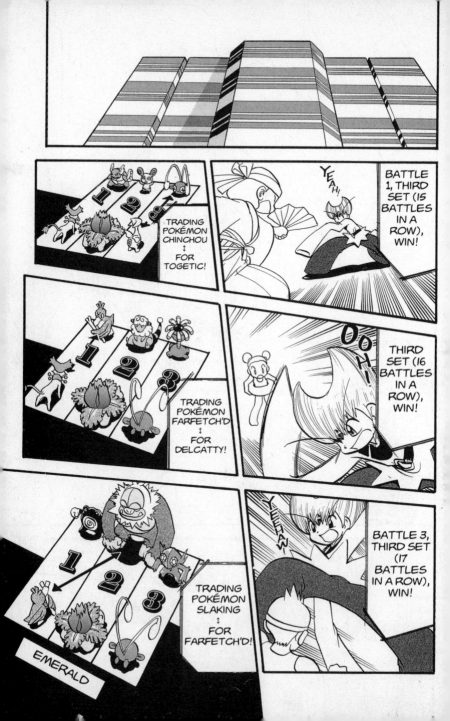

TRADING POKÉMON CHINCHOU ↕ FOR TOGETIC!

YEAH!

BATTLE 1, THIRD SET (15 BATTLES IN A ROW), WIN!

TRADING POKÉMON FARFETCH'D ↕ FOR DELCATTY!

OOH!

THIRD SET (16 BATTLES IN A ROW), WIN!

TRADING POKÉMON SLAKING ↕ FOR FARFETCH'D!

YEEHAW!

BATTLE 3, THIRD SET (17 BATTLES IN A ROW), WIN!

EMERALD

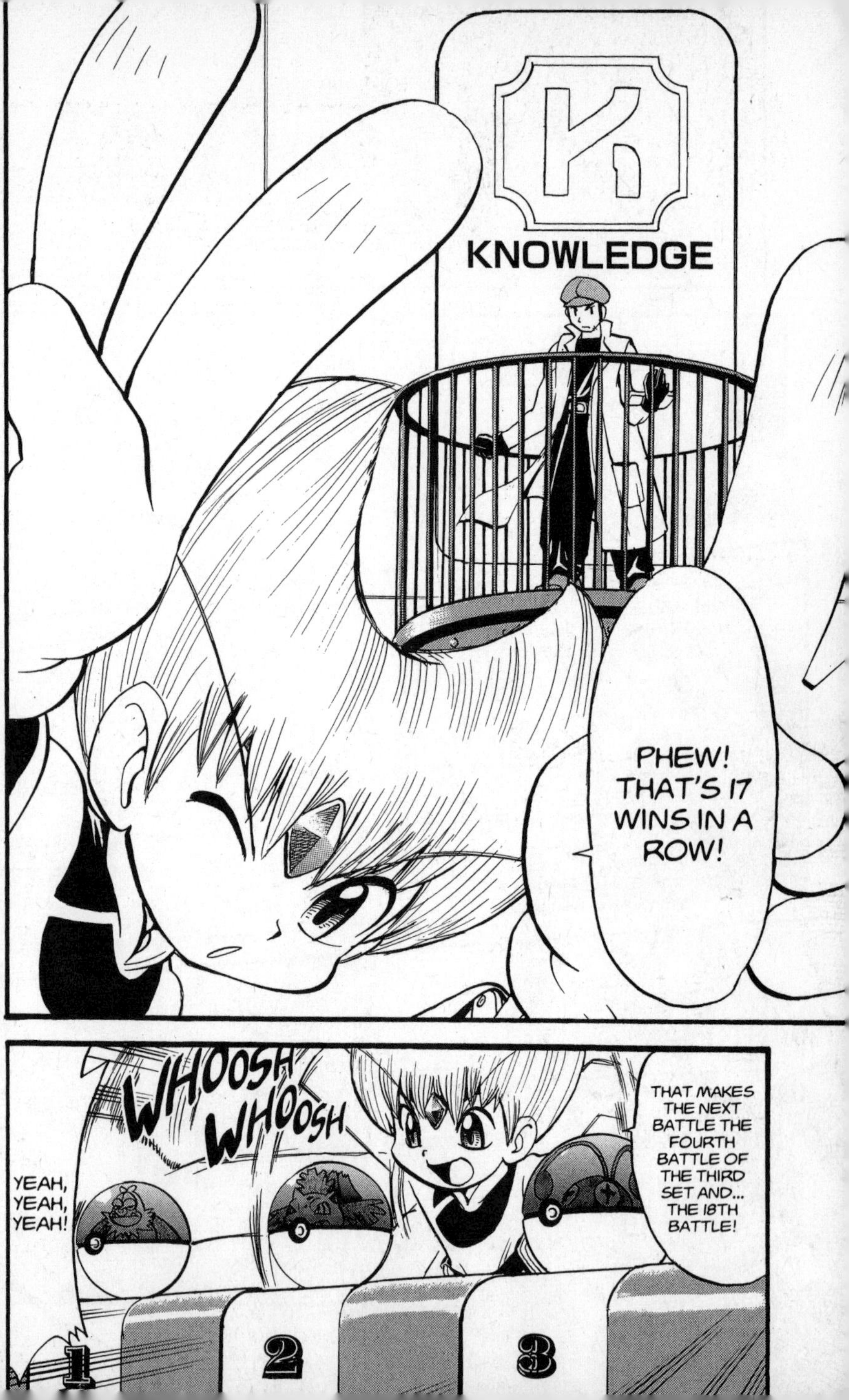
KNOWLEDGE
PHEW! THAT'S 17 WINS IN A ROW!
THAT MAKES THE NEXT BATTLE THE FOURTH BATTLE OF THE THIRD SET AND... THE 18TH BATTLE!
WHOOSH WHOOSH
YEAH, YEAH, YEAH!
1 2 3

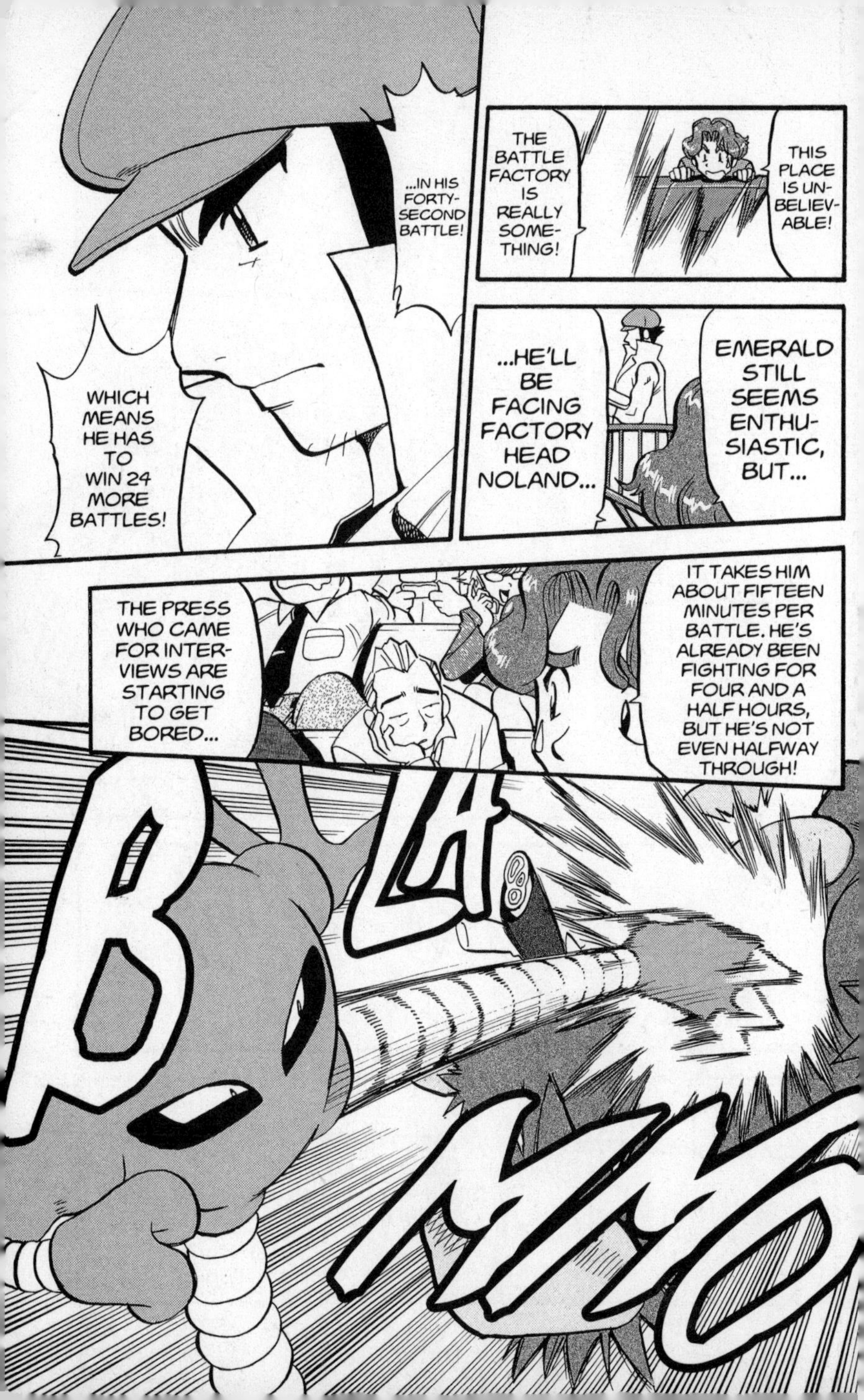
THIS PLACE IS UN-BELIEV-ABLE!
THE BATTLE FACTORY IS REALLY SOME-THING!
EMERALD STILL SEEMS ENTHU-SIASTIC, BUT...
...HE'LL BE FACING FACTORY HEAD NOLAND...
...IN HIS FORTY-SECOND BATTLE!
WHICH MEANS HE HAS TO WIN 24 MORE BATTLES!
IT TAKES HIM ABOUT FIFTEEN MINUTES PER BATTLE. HE'S ALREADY BEEN FIGHTING FOR FOUR AND A HALF HOURS, BUT HE'S NOT EVEN HALFWAY THROUGH!
THE PRESS WHO CAME FOR INTER-VIEWS ARE STARTING TO GET BORED...
BLAM

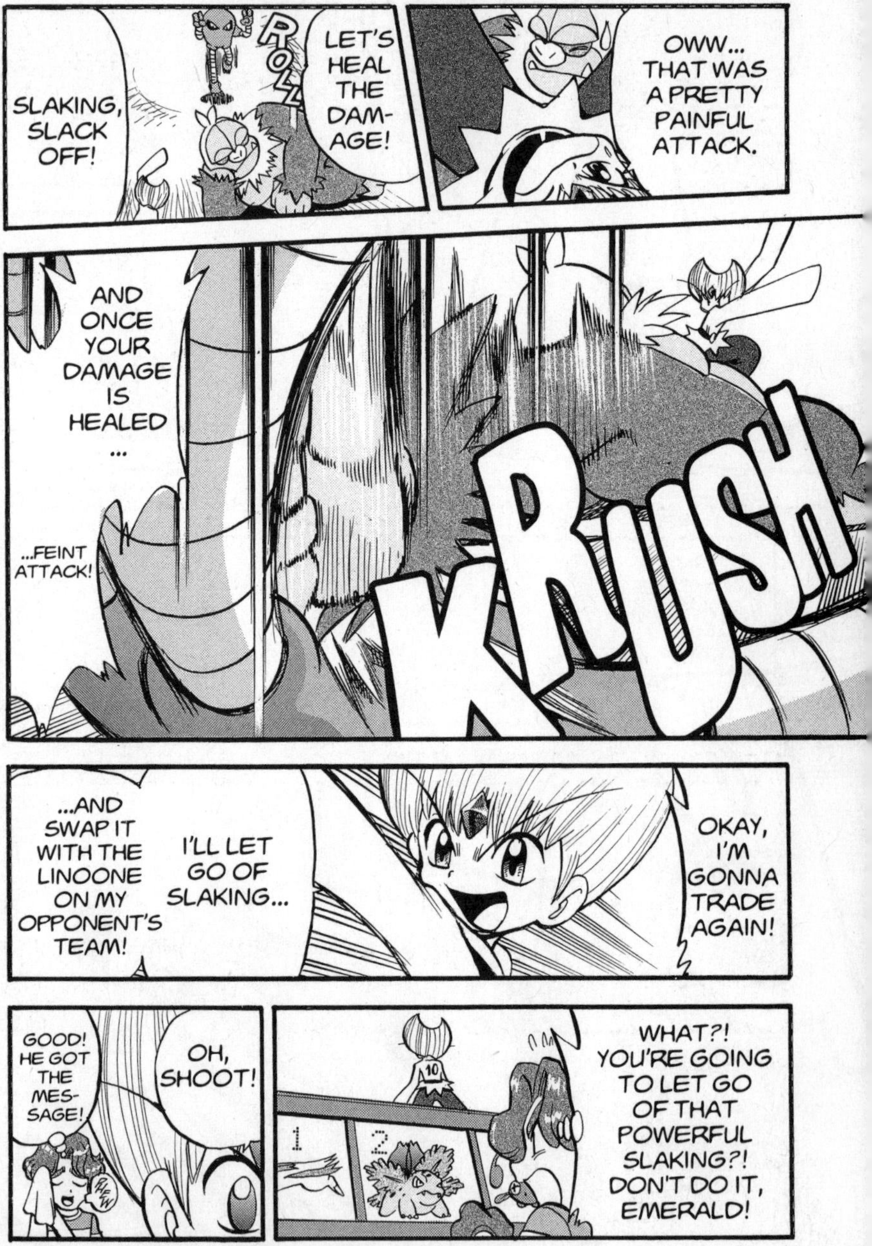
OWW... THAT WAS A PRETTY PAINFUL ATTACK.
LET'S HEAL THE DAMAGE!
ROLL
SLAKING, SLACK OFF!
AND ONCE YOUR DAMAGE IS HEALED ...
KRUSH
...FEINT ATTACK!
OKAY, I'M GONNA TRADE AGAIN!
I'LL LET GO OF SLAKING...
...AND SWAP IT WITH THE LINOONE ON MY OPPONENT'S TEAM!
WHAT?! YOU'RE GOING TO LET GO OF THAT POWERFUL SLAKING?! DON'T DO IT, EMERALD!
OH, SHOOT!
GOOD! HE GOT THE MES-SAGE!
PHEW

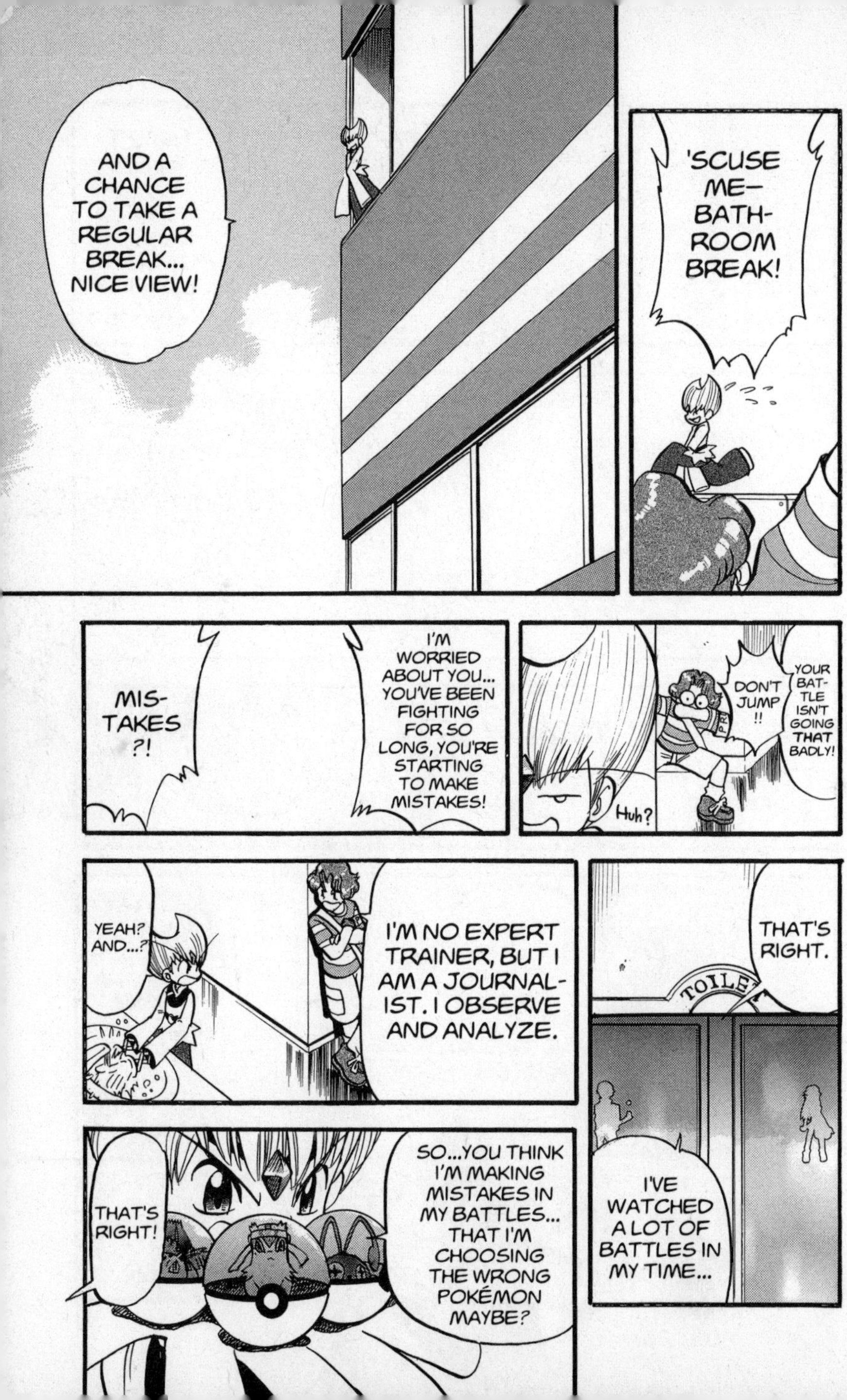
'SCUSE ME— BATH-ROOM BREAK!
AND A CHANCE TO TAKE A REGULAR BREAK... NICE VIEW!
YOUR BAT-TLE ISN'T GOING THAT BADLY!
DON'T JUMP !!
Huh?
I'M WORRIED ABOUT YOU... YOU'VE BEEN FIGHTING FOR SO LONG, YOU'RE STARTING TO MAKE MISTAKES!
MIS-TAKES ?!
THAT'S RIGHT.
TOILE
I'M NO EXPERT TRAINER, BUT I AM A JOURNAL-IST. I OBSERVE AND ANALYZE.
YEAH? AND...?
I'VE WATCHED A LOT OF BATTLES IN MY TIME...
SO...YOU THINK I'M MAKING MISTAKES IN MY BATTLES... THAT I'M CHOOSING THE WRONG POKÉMON MAYBE?
THAT'S RIGHT!

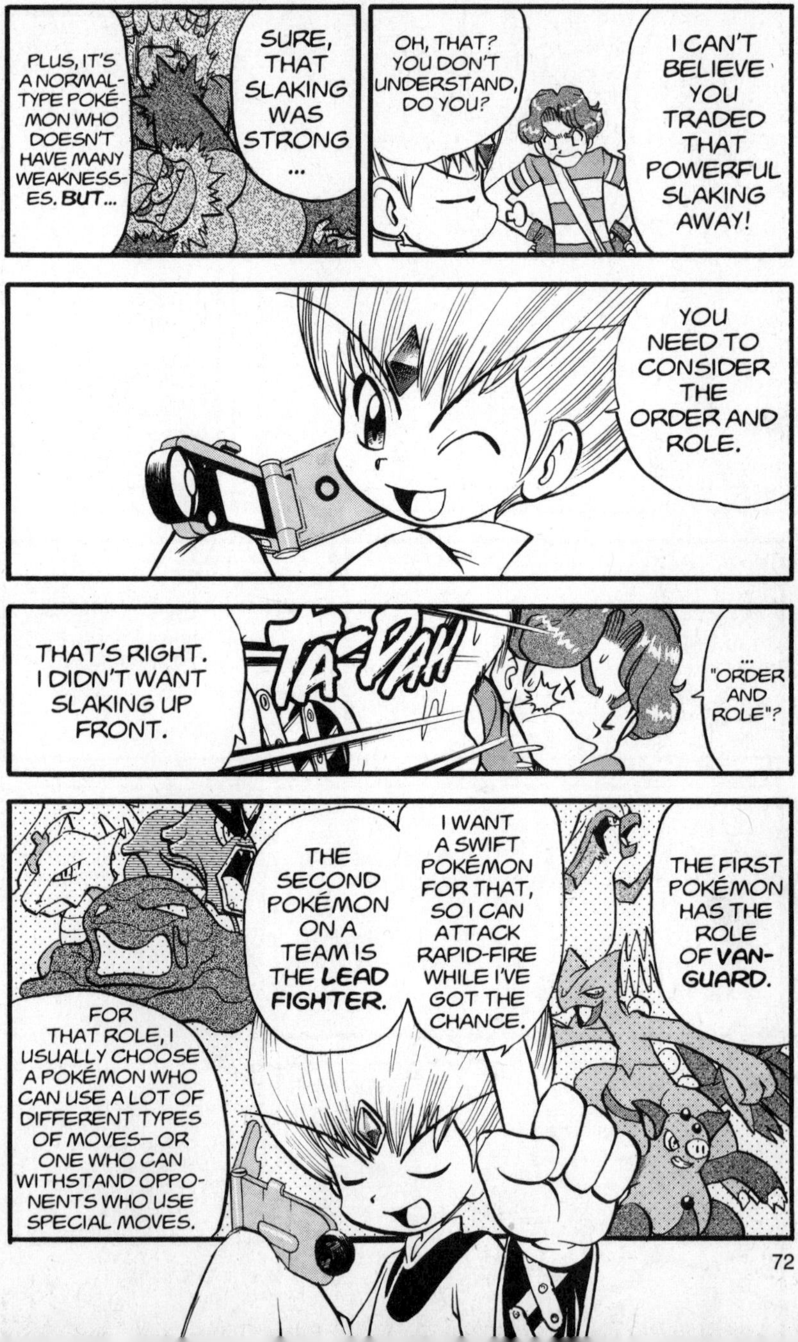
I CAN'T BELIEVE YOU TRADED THAT POWERFUL SLAKING AWAY!
OH, THAT? YOU DON'T UNDERSTAND, DO YOU?
SURE, THAT SLAKING WAS STRONG ...
PLUS, IT'S A NORMAL-TYPE POKÉMON WHO DOESN'T HAVE MANY WEAKNESSES. BUT...
YOU NEED TO CONSIDER THE ORDER AND ROLE.
... "ORDER AND ROLE"?
TA-DAH
THAT'S RIGHT. I DIDN'T WANT SLAKING UP FRONT.
THE FIRST POKÉMON HAS THE ROLE OF VANGUARD.
FOR THAT ROLE, I USUALLY CHOOSE A POKÉMON WHO CAN USE A LOT OF DIFFERENT TYPES OF MOVES—OR ONE WHO CAN WITHSTAND OPPONENTS WHO USE SPECIAL MOVES.
THE SECOND POKÉMON ON A TEAM IS THE LEAD FIGHTER.
I WANT A SWIFT POKÉMON FOR THAT, SO I CAN ATTACK RAPID-FIRE WHILE I'VE GOT THE CHANCE.

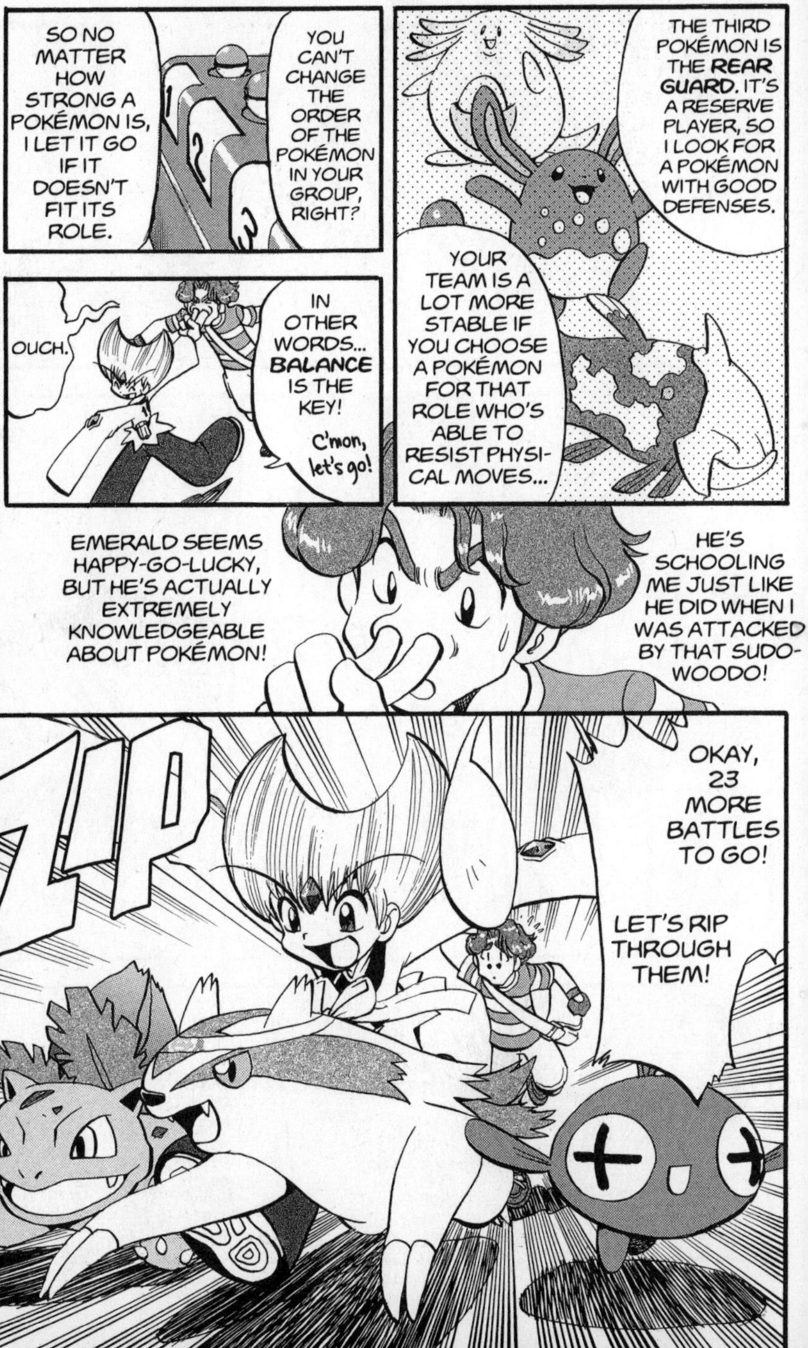
THE THIRD POKÉMON IS THE REAR GUARD. IT'S A RESERVE PLAYER, SO I LOOK FOR A POKÉMON WITH GOOD DEFENSES.
YOUR TEAM IS A LOT MORE STABLE IF YOU CHOOSE A POKÉMON FOR THAT ROLE WHO'S ABLE TO RESIST PHYSICAL MOVES...
YOU CAN'T CHANGE THE ORDER OF THE POKÉMON IN YOUR GROUP, RIGHT?
SO NO MATTER HOW STRONG A POKÉMON IS, I LET IT GO IF IT DOESN'T FIT ITS ROLE.
1
2
3
IN OTHER WORDS... BALANCE IS THE KEY!
C'mon, let's go!
OUCH.
HE'S SCHOOLING ME JUST LIKE HE DID WHEN I WAS ATTACKED BY THAT SUDOWOODO!
EMERALD SEEMS HAPPY-GO-LUCKY, BUT HE'S ACTUALLY EXTREMELY KNOWLEDGEABLE ABOUT POKÉMON!
OKAY, 23 MORE BATTLES TO GO!
LET'S RIP THROUGH THEM!
ZIP

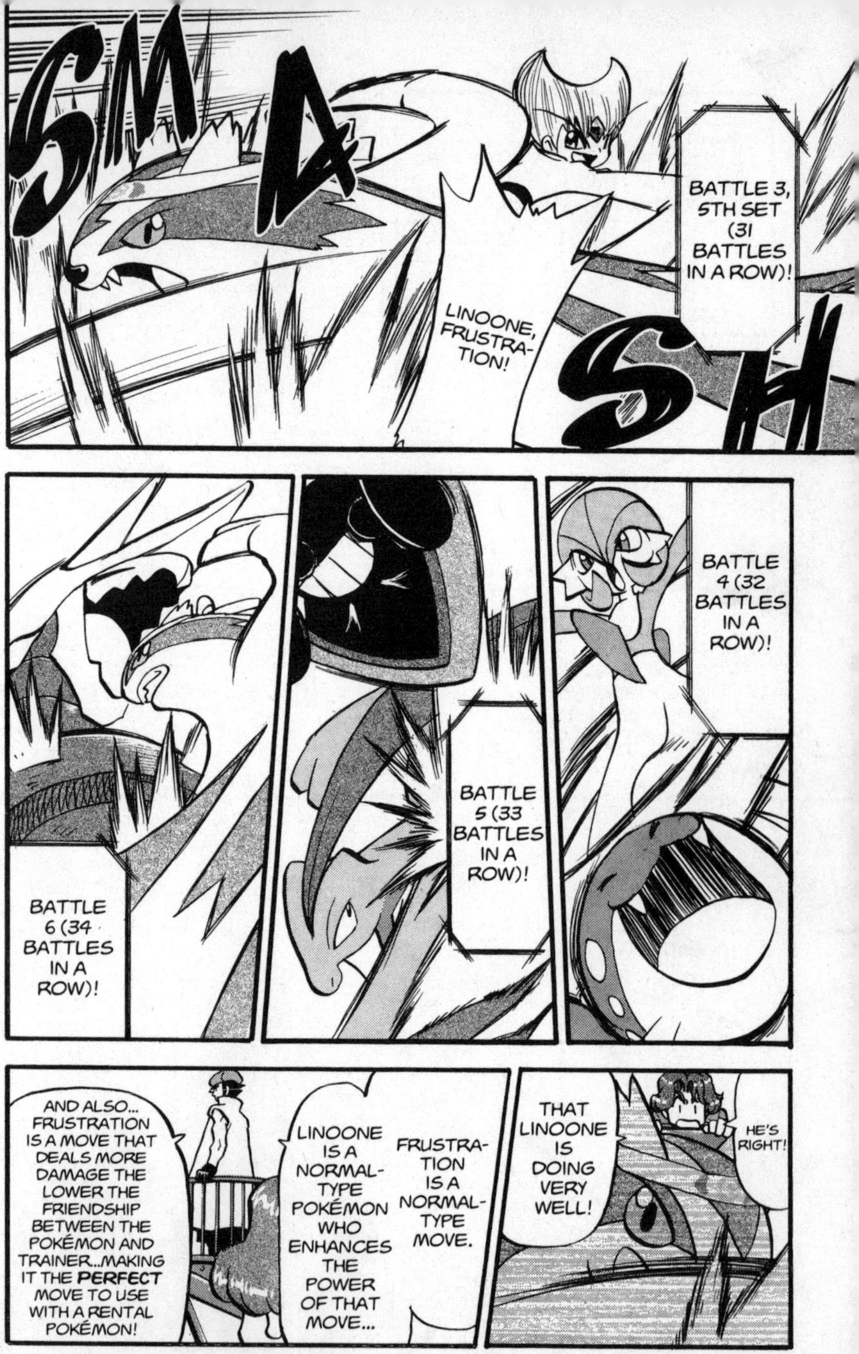
BATTLE 3, 5TH SET (31 BATTLES IN A ROW)!
SH
LINOONE, FRUSTRATION!
SMA
BATTLE 4 (32 BATTLES IN A ROW)!
BATTLE 5 (33 BATTLES IN A ROW)!
BATTLE 6 (34 BATTLES IN A ROW)!
HE'S RIGHT!
THAT LINOONE IS DOING VERY WELL!
FRUSTRATION IS A NORMAL-TYPE MOVE.
LINOONE IS A NORMAL-TYPE POKÉMON WHO ENHANCES THE POWER OF THAT MOVE...
AND ALSO... FRUSTRATION IS A MOVE THAT DEALS MORE DAMAGE THE LOWER THE FRIENDSHIP BETWEEN THE POKÉMON AND TRAINER...MAKING IT THE PERFECT MOVE TO USE WITH A RENTAL POKÉMON!

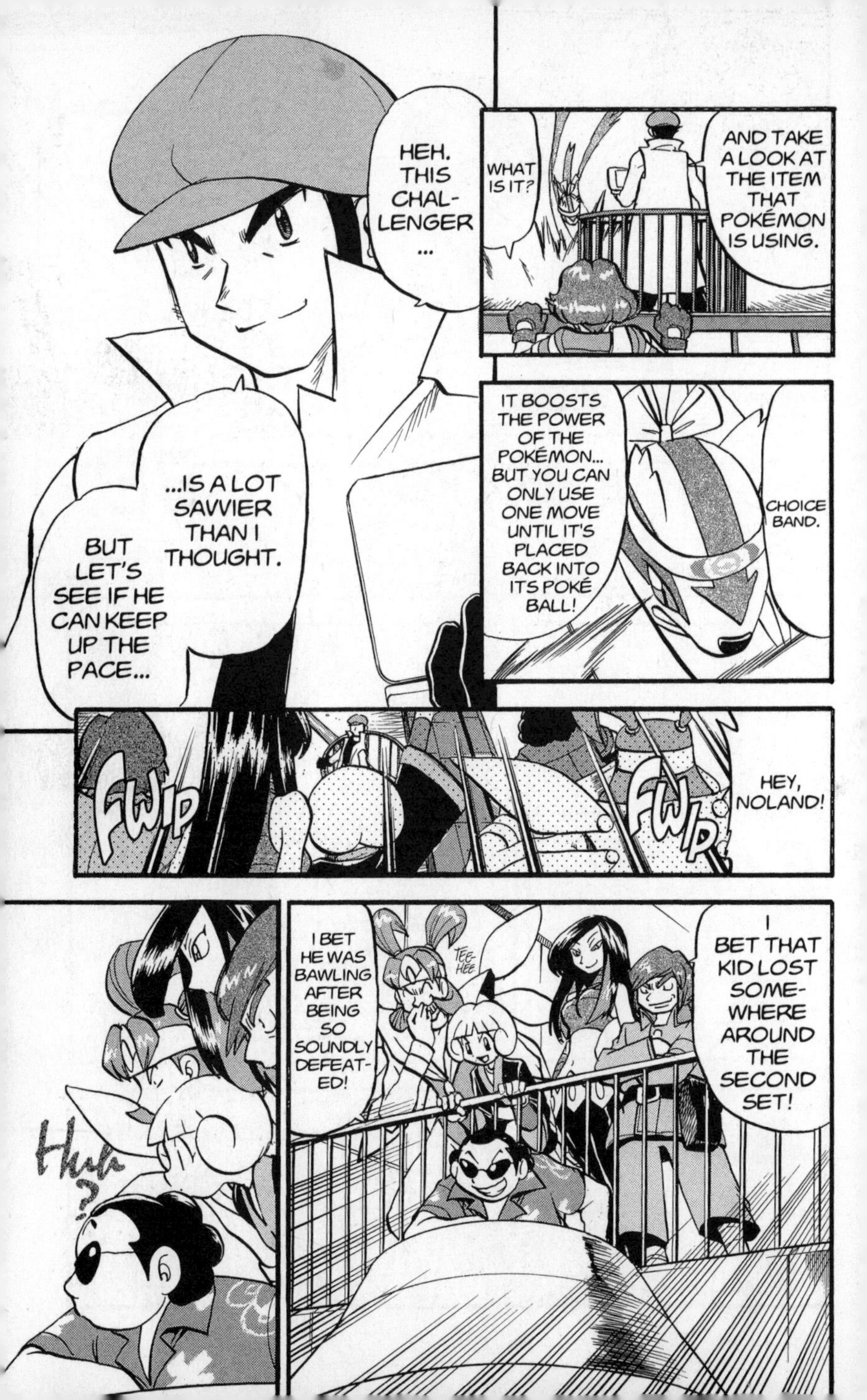
AND TAKE A LOOK AT THE ITEM THAT POKÉMON IS USING.
WHAT IS IT?
CHOICE BAND.
IT BOOSTS THE POWER OF THE POKÉMON... BUT YOU CAN ONLY USE ONE MOVE UNTIL IT'S PLACED BACK INTO ITS POKÉ BALL!
HEH. THIS CHAL-LENGER ...
...IS A LOT SAVVIER THAN I THOUGHT.
BUT LET'S SEE IF HE CAN KEEP UP THE PACE...
HEY, NOLAND!
FWIP
FWIP
I BET THAT KID LOST SOME-WHERE AROUND THE SECOND SET!
TEE-HEE
I BET HE WAS BAWLING AFTER BEING SO SOUNDLY DEFEAT-ED!
Huh?

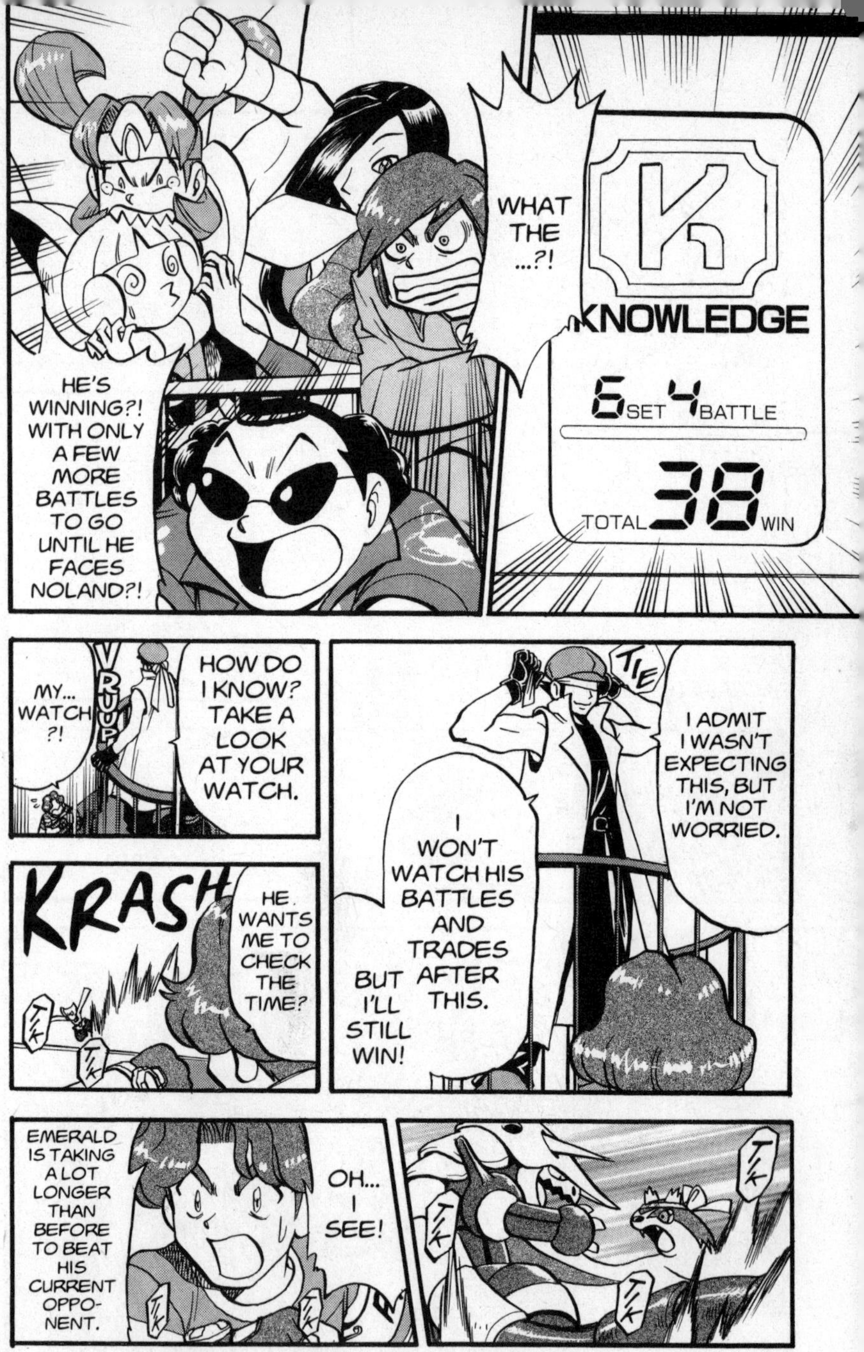

KNOWLEDGE
6 SET 4 BATTLE
TOTAL 38 WIN
WHAT THE ...?!
HE'S WINNING?! WITH ONLY A FEW MORE BATTLES TO GO UNTIL HE FACES NOLAND?!
TIE
I ADMIT I WASN'T EXPECTING THIS, BUT I'M NOT WORRIED.
I WON'T WATCH HIS BATTLES AND TRADES AFTER THIS.
BUT I'LL STILL WIN!
HOW DO I KNOW? TAKE A LOOK AT YOUR WATCH.
VRUUP
MY... WATCH ?!
HE. WANTS ME TO CHECK THE TIME?
KRASH
TIK
TIK
TIK
TIK
TIK
OH... I SEE!
EMERALD IS TAKING A LOT LONGER THAN BEFORE TO BEAT HIS CURRENT OPPO-NENT.
TIK
TIK

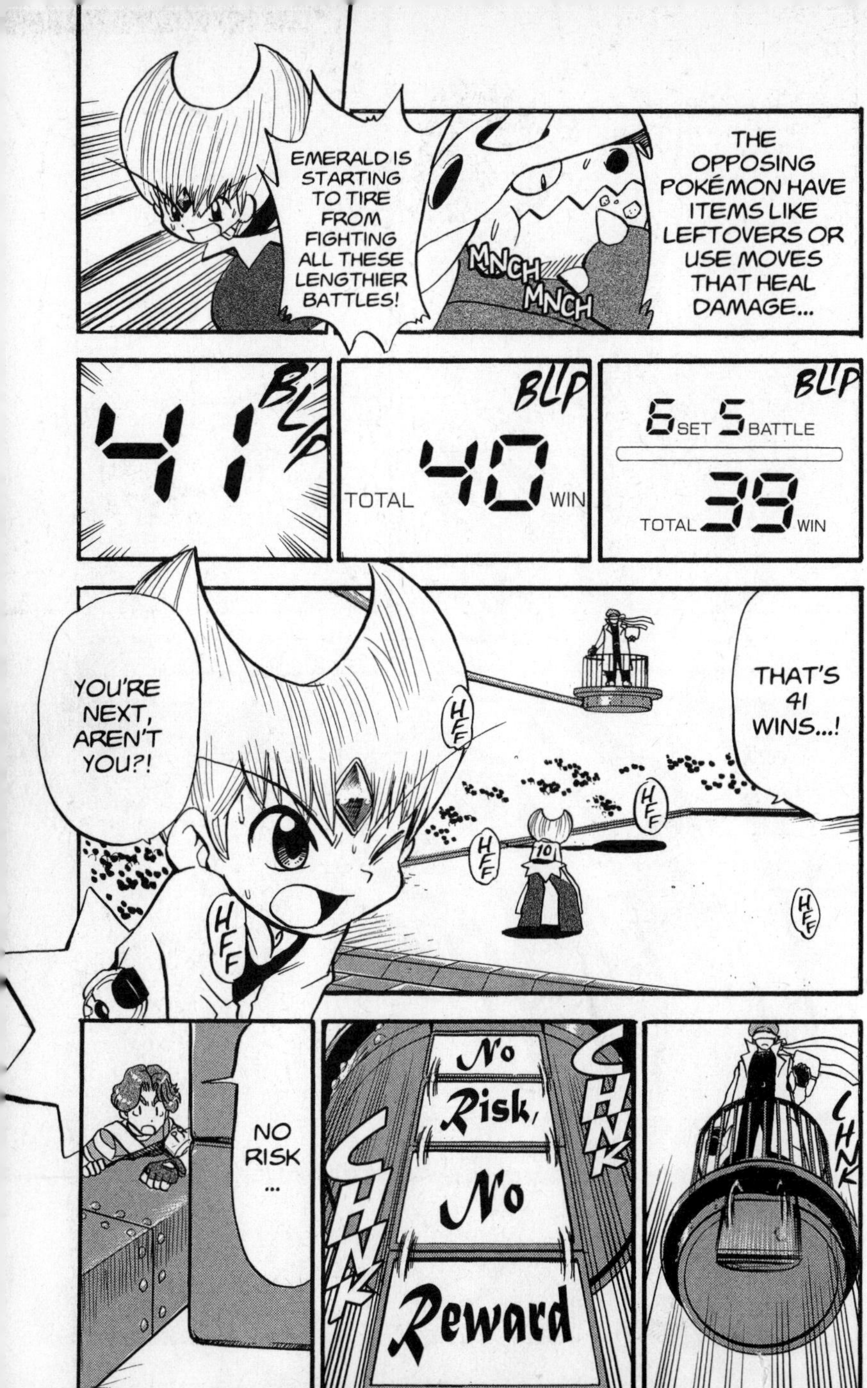
THE OPPOSING POKÉMON HAVE ITEMS LIKE LEFTOVERS OR USE MOVES THAT HEAL DAMAGE...
MNCH MNCH
EMERALD IS STARTING TO TIRE FROM FIGHTING ALL THESE LENGTHIER BATTLES!
BLIP
6 SET 5 BATTLE
TOTAL 39 WIN
BLIP
TOTAL 40 WIN
41
BLIP
THAT'S 41 WINS...!
HFF
HFF
HFF
HFF
HFF
YOU'RE NEXT, AREN'T YOU?!
CHNK
No Risk, No Reward
CHNK
CHNK
NO RISK ...

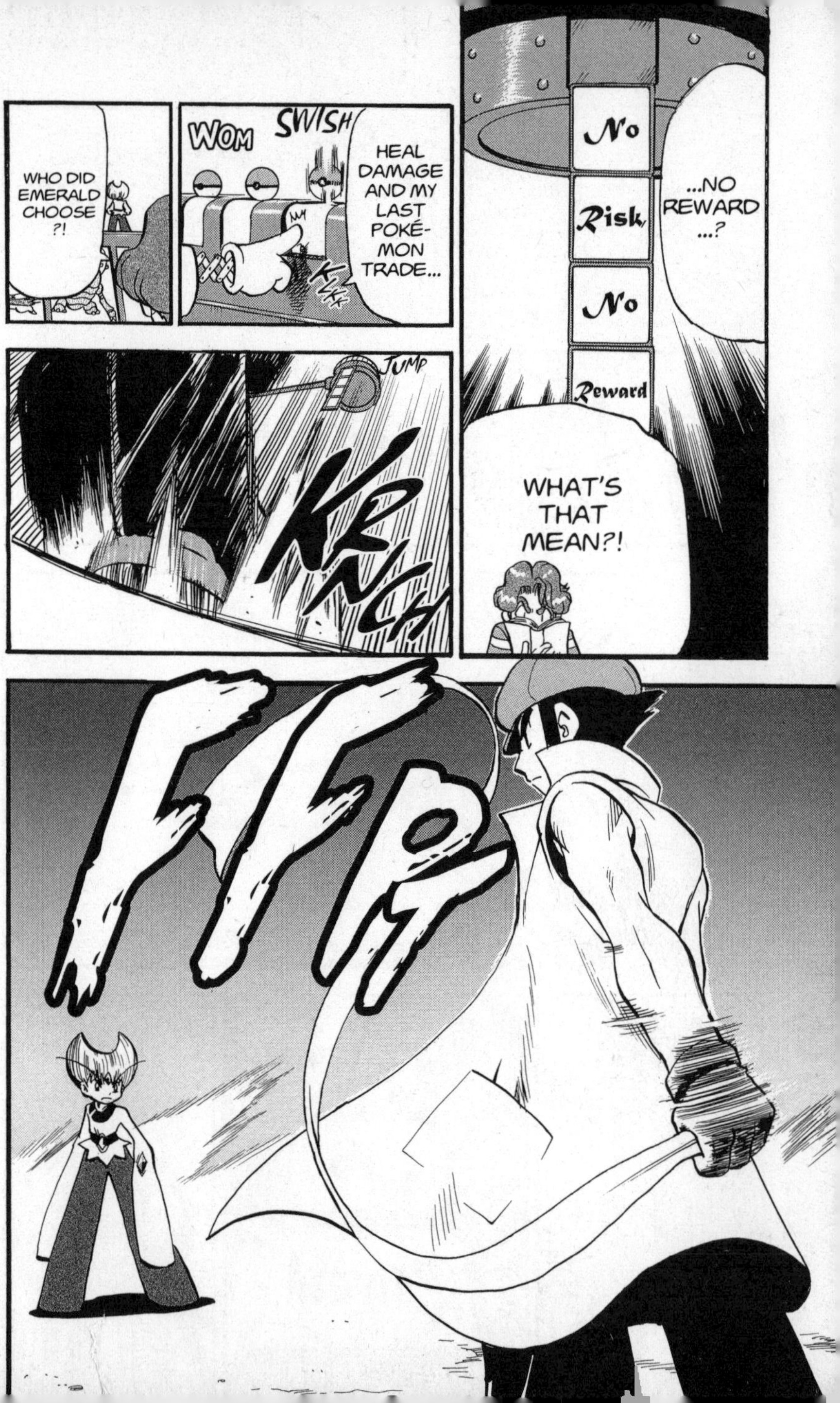

No Risk No Reward
...NO REWARD ...?
WHAT'S THAT MEAN?!
HEAL DAMAGE AND MY LAST POKÉMON TRADE...
SWISH
WOM
KLKK
WHO DID EMERALD CHOOSE ?!
JUMP
KRNCH
FLAP

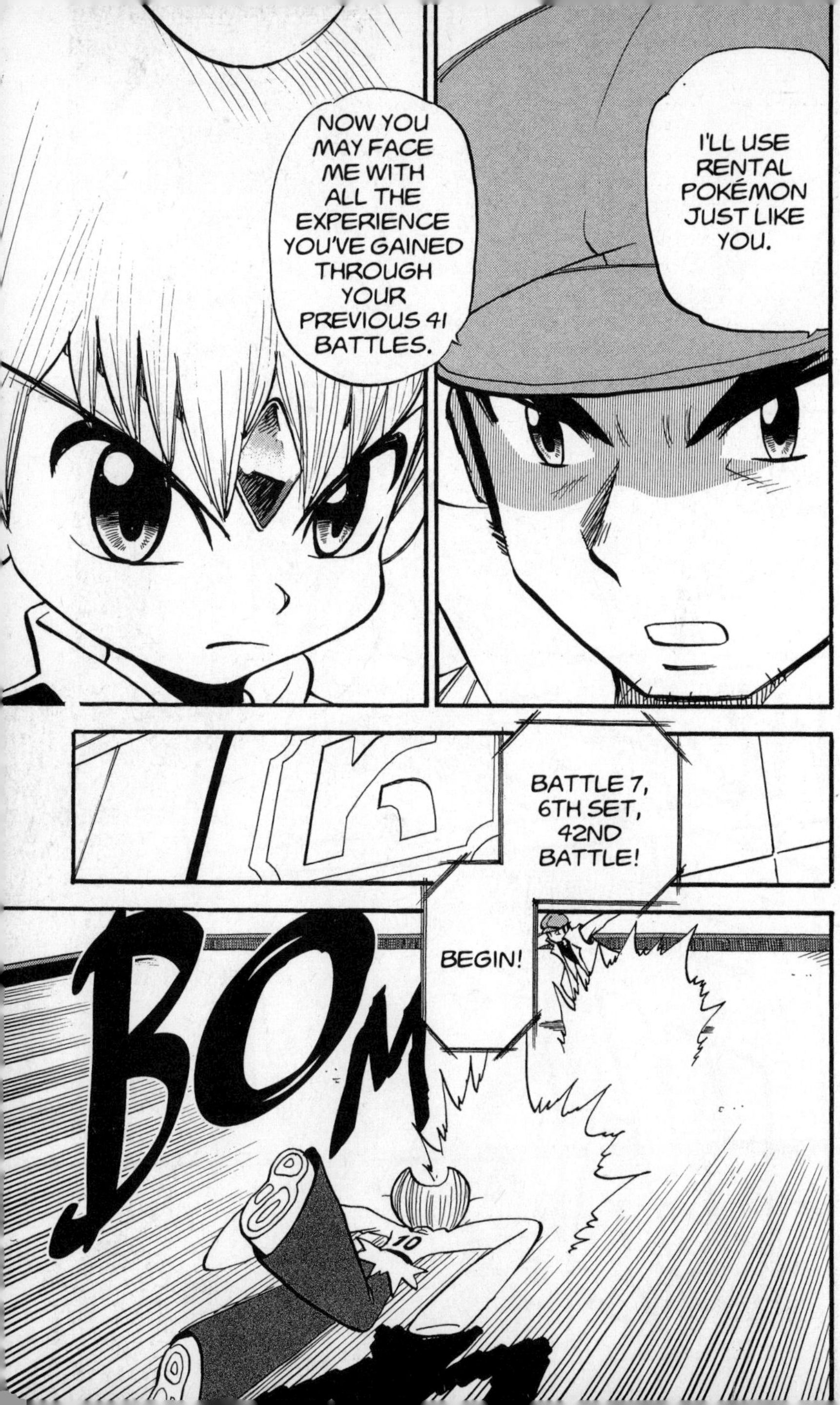
I'LL USE RENTAL POKÉMON JUST LIKE YOU.
NOW YOU MAY FACE ME WITH ALL THE EXPERIENCE YOU'VE GAINED THROUGH YOUR PREVIOUS 41 BATTLES.
BATTLE 7, 6TH SET, 42ND BATTLE!
BEGIN!
BOM

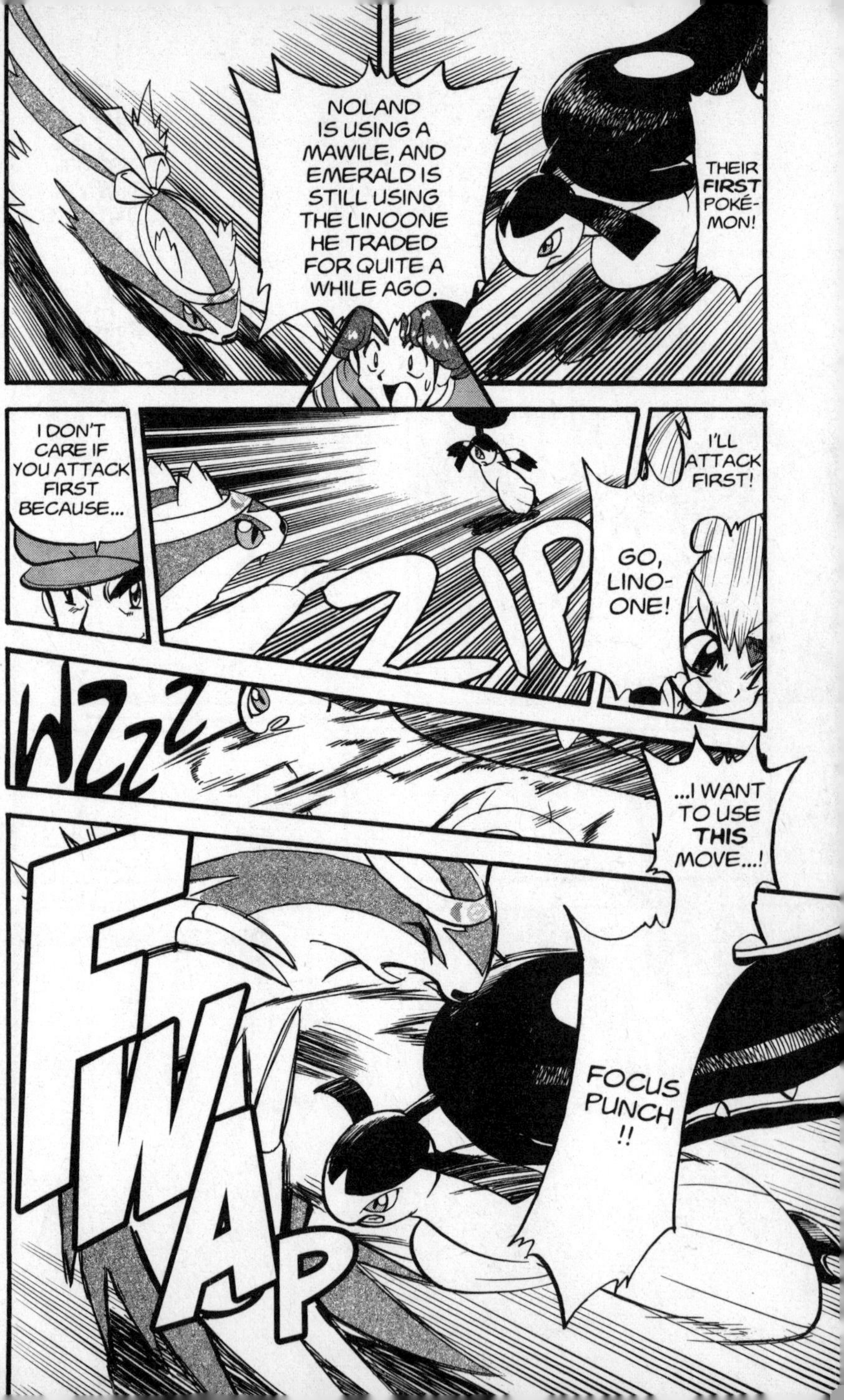
NOLAND IS USING A MAWILE, AND EMERALD IS STILL USING THE LINOONE HE TRADED FOR QUITE A WHILE AGO.
THEIR FIRST POKÉ-MON!
I'LL ATTACK FIRST!
GO, LINO-ONE!
ZIP
I DON'T CARE IF YOU ATTACK FIRST BECAUSE...
WZZZ
...I WANT TO USE THIS MOVE...!
FOCUS PUNCH!!
FWAP

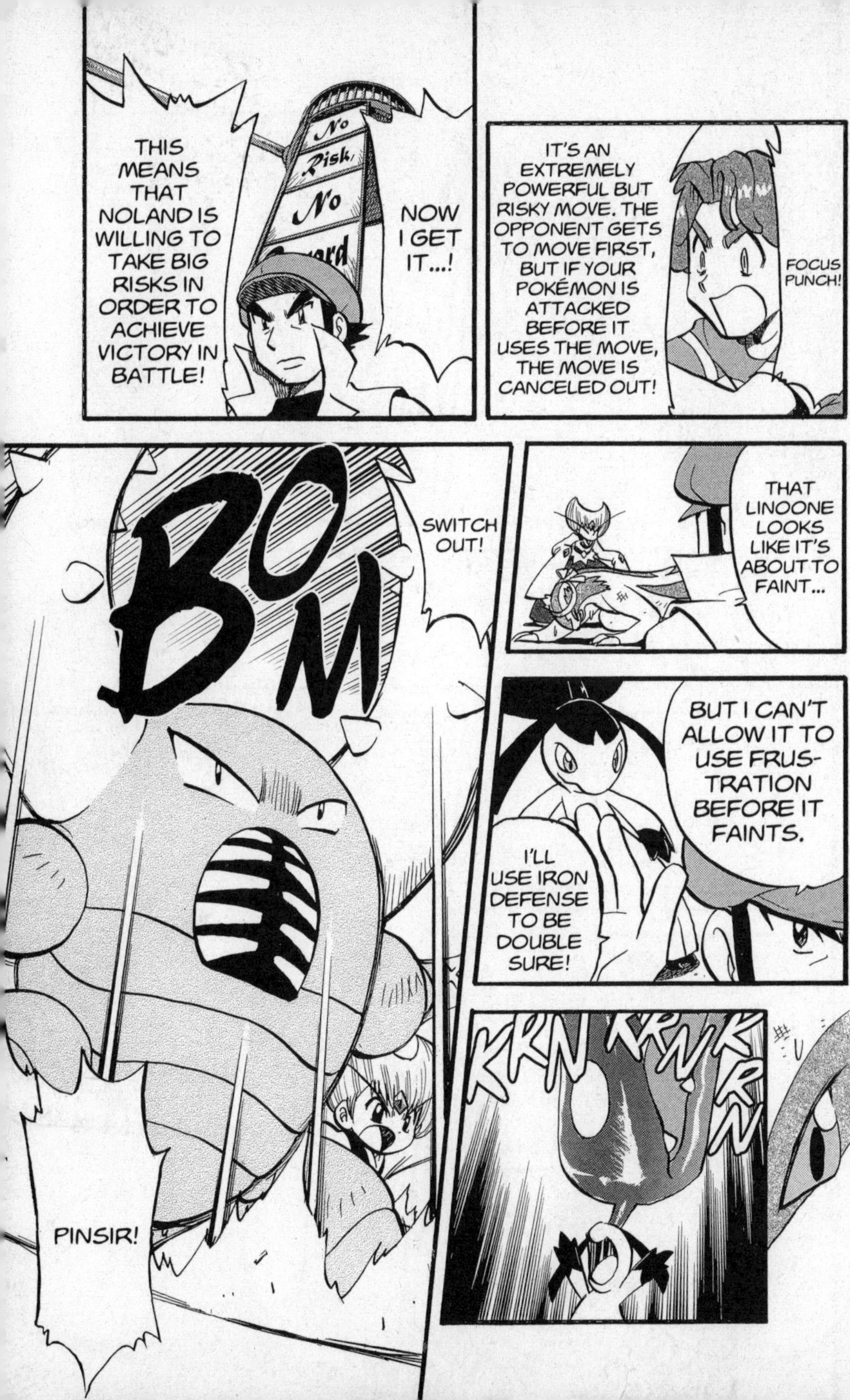
FOCUS PUNCH!
IT'S AN EXTREMELY POWERFUL BUT RISKY MOVE. THE OPPONENT GETS TO MOVE FIRST, BUT IF YOUR POKÉMON IS ATTACKED BEFORE IT USES THE MOVE, THE MOVE IS CANCELED OUT!
NOW I GET IT...!
THIS MEANS THAT NOLAND IS WILLING TO TAKE BIG RISKS IN ORDER TO ACHIEVE VICTORY IN BATTLE!
No Risk, No
THAT LINOONE LOOKS LIKE IT'S ABOUT TO FAINT...
BUT I CAN'T ALLOW IT TO USE FRUSTRATION BEFORE IT FAINTS.
I'LL USE IRON DEFENSE TO BE DOUBLE SURE!
KRN KRN KRN KRN
SWITCH OUT!
BOOM
PINSIR!

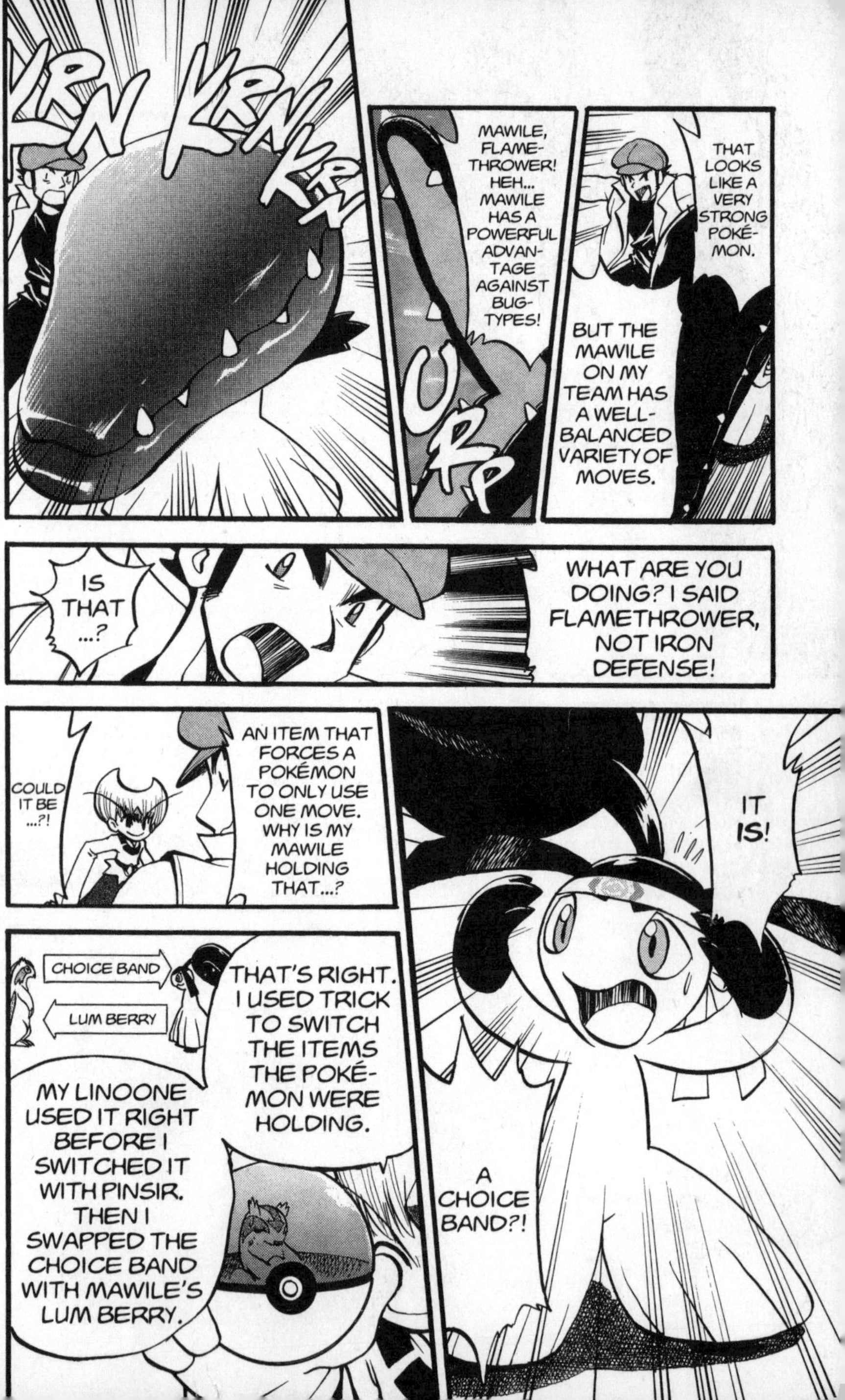
THAT LOOKS LIKE A VERY STRONG POKÉMON.
BUT THE MAWILE ON MY TEAM HAS A WELL-BALANCED VARIETY OF MOVES.
MAWILE, FLAMETHROWER! HEH... MAWILE HAS A POWERFUL ADVANTAGE AGAINST BUG-TYPES!
URP
KRN KRN KRN KRN
WHAT ARE YOU DOING? I SAID FLAMETHROWER, NOT IRON DEFENSE!
IS THAT ...?
IT IS!
A CHOICE BAND?!
AN ITEM THAT FORCES A POKÉMON TO ONLY USE ONE MOVE. WHY IS MY MAWILE HOLDING THAT...?
COULD IT BE ...?!
THAT'S RIGHT. I USED TRICK TO SWITCH THE ITEMS THE POKÉMON WERE HOLDING.
CHOICE BAND
LUM BERRY
MY LINOONE USED IT RIGHT BEFORE I SWITCHED IT WITH PINSIR. THEN I SWAPPED THE CHOICE BAND WITH MAWILE'S LUM BERRY.

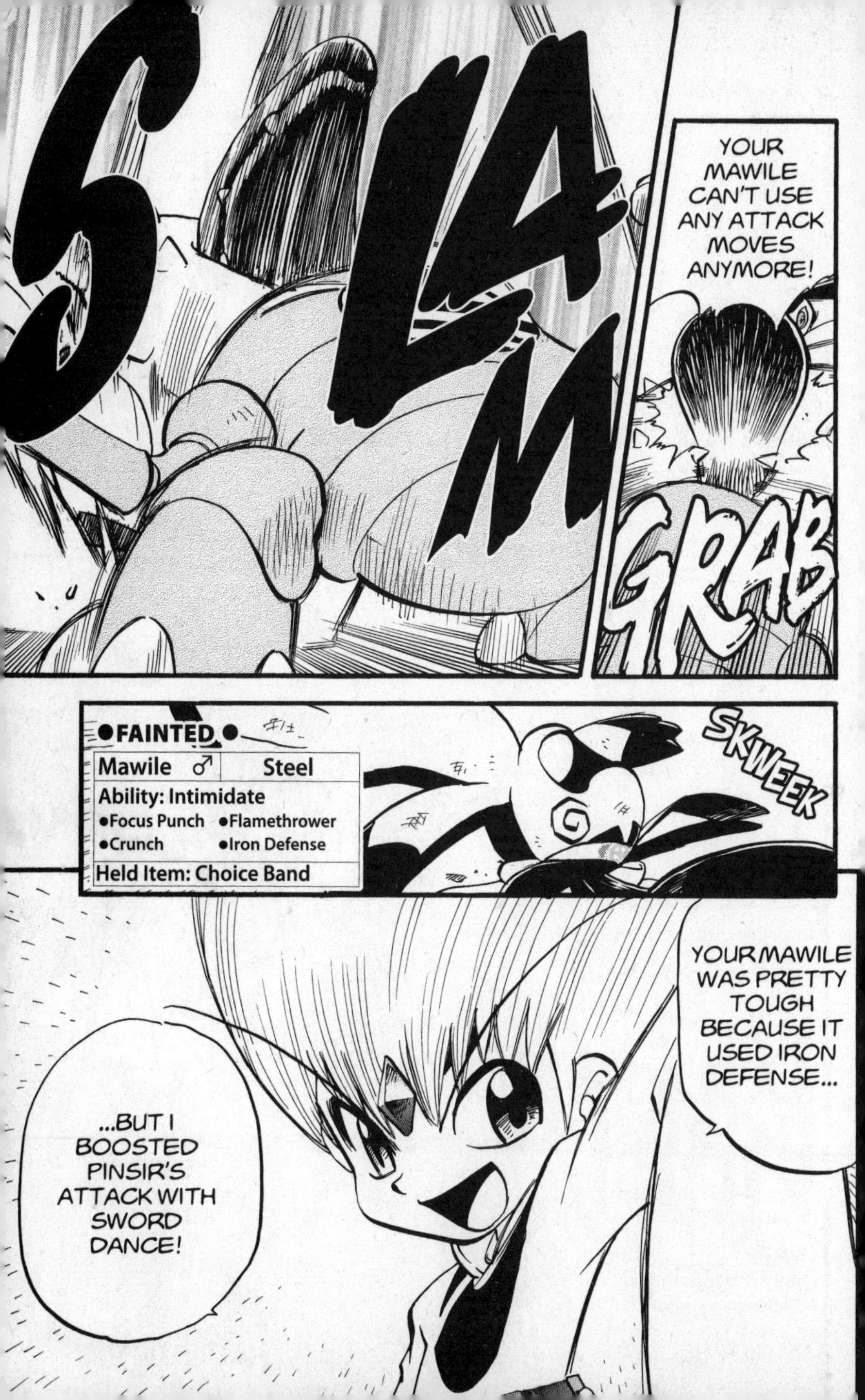
YOUR MAWILE CAN'T USE ANY ATTACK MOVES ANYMORE!
GRAB
SLAM
SKWEEK
●FAINTED●
Mawile ♂ Steel
Ability: Intimidate
●Focus Punch ●Flamethrower
●Crunch ●Iron Defense
Held Item: Choice Band
YOUR MAWILE WAS PRETTY TOUGH BECAUSE IT USED IRON DEFENSE...
...BUT I BOOSTED PINSIR'S ATTACK WITH SWORD DANCE!

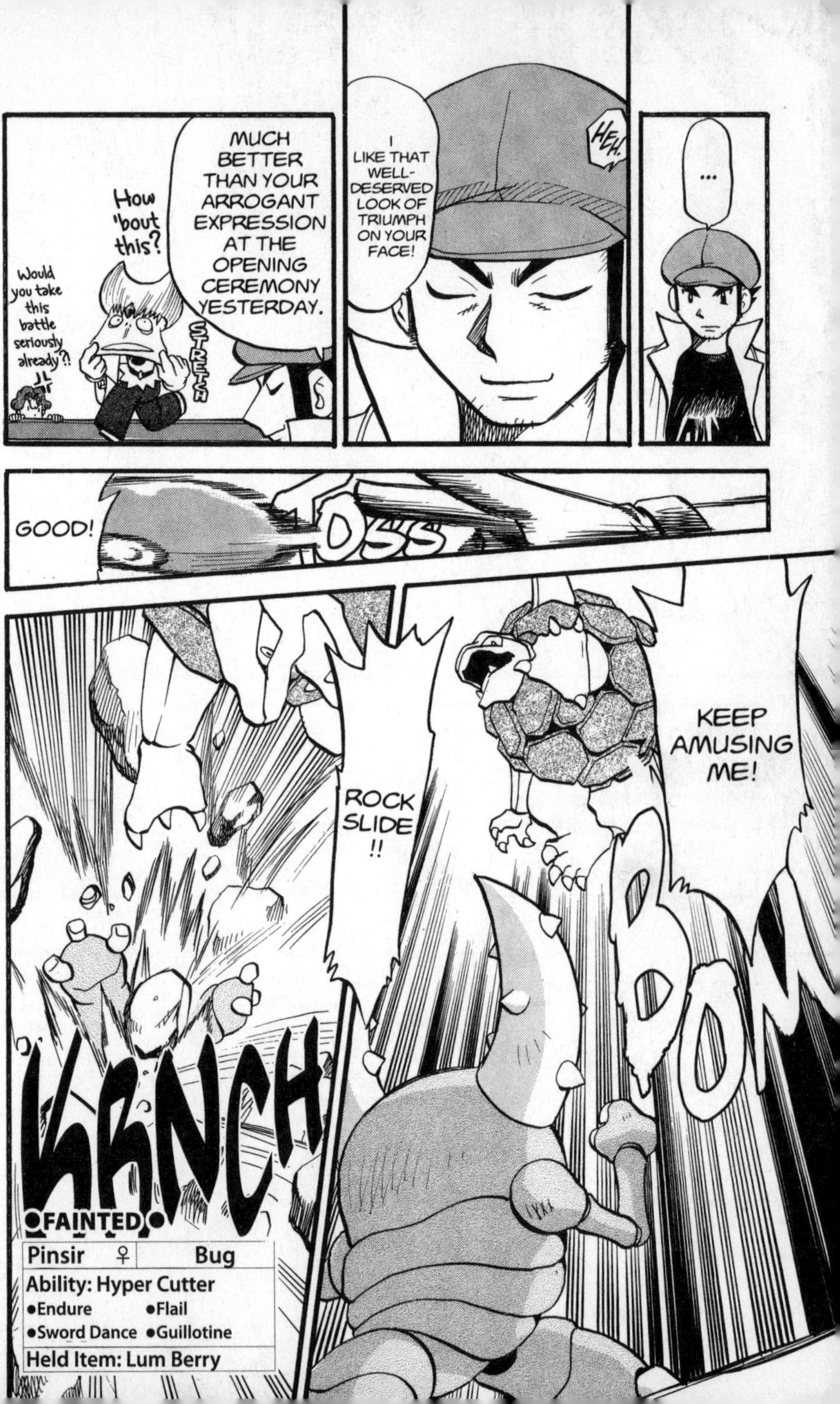
...
HEH.
I LIKE THAT WELL-DESERVED LOOK OF TRIUMPH ON YOUR FACE!
MUCH BETTER THAN YOUR ARROGANT EXPRESSION AT THE OPENING CEREMONY YESTERDAY.
STRETCH
How 'bout this?
Would you take this battle seriously already?!
GOOD!
DOSS
KEEP AMUSING ME!
ROCK SLIDE!!
BOOM
KRNCH
FAINTED
Pinsir ♀ Bug
Ability: Hyper Cutter
•Endure •Flail
•Sword Dance •Guillotine
Held Item: Lum Berry

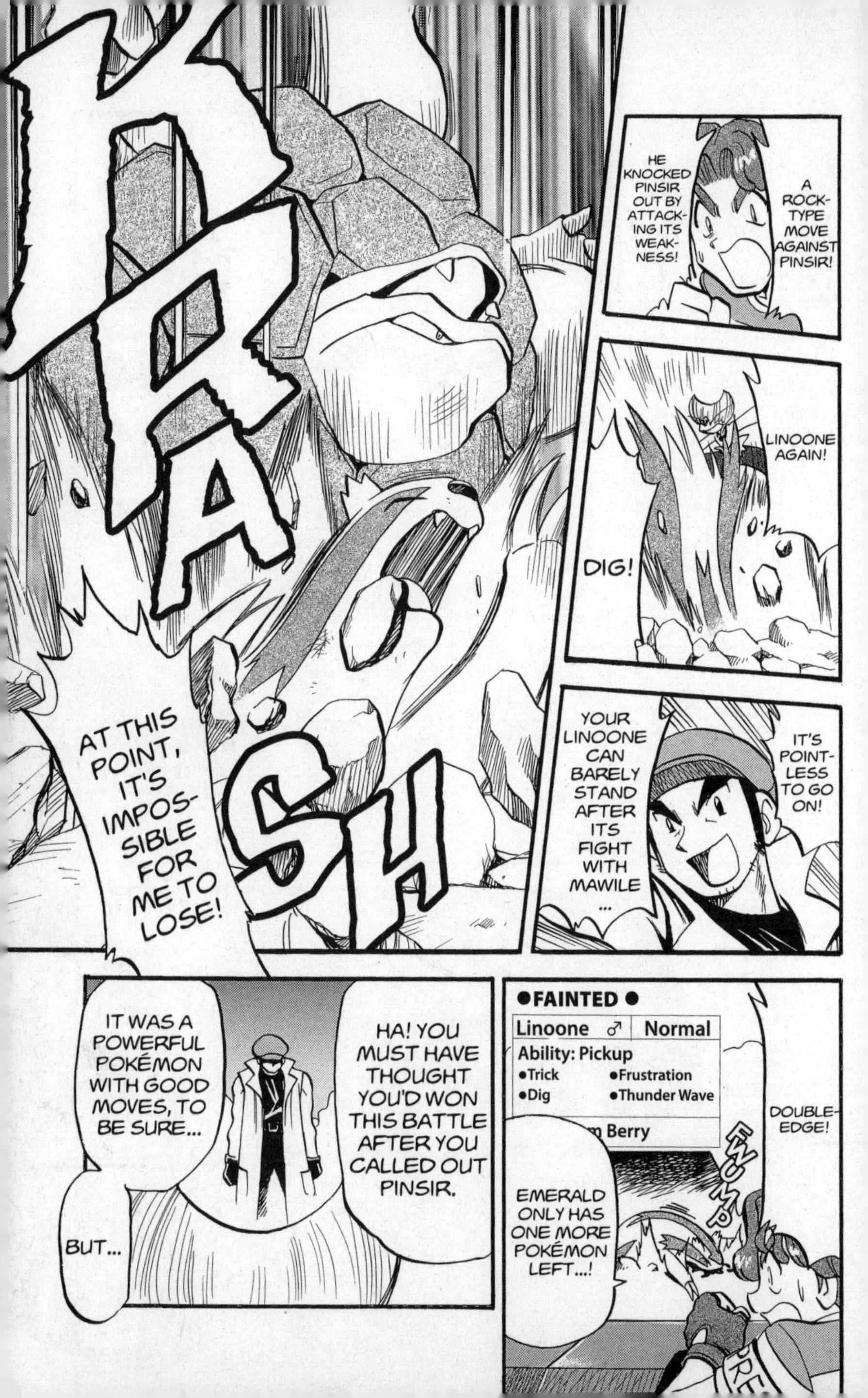
A ROCK-TYPE MOVE AGAINST PINSIR!
HE KNOCKED PINSIR OUT BY ATTACKING ITS WEAKNESS!
LINOONE AGAIN!
DIG!
IT'S POINTLESS TO GO ON!
YOUR LINOONE CAN BARELY STAND AFTER ITS FIGHT WITH MAWILE...
KA
SH
AT THIS POINT, IT'S IMPOSSIBLE FOR ME TO LOSE!
●FAINTED●
Linoone ♂ Normal
Ability: Pickup
●Trick ●Frustration
●Dig ●Thunder Wave
m Berry
DOUBLE-EDGE!
FWUMP
EMERALD ONLY HAS ONE MORE POKÉMON LEFT...!
HA! YOU MUST HAVE THOUGHT YOU'D WON THIS BATTLE AFTER YOU CALLED OUT PINSIR.
IT WAS A POWERFUL POKÉMON WITH GOOD MOVES, TO BE SURE...
BUT...

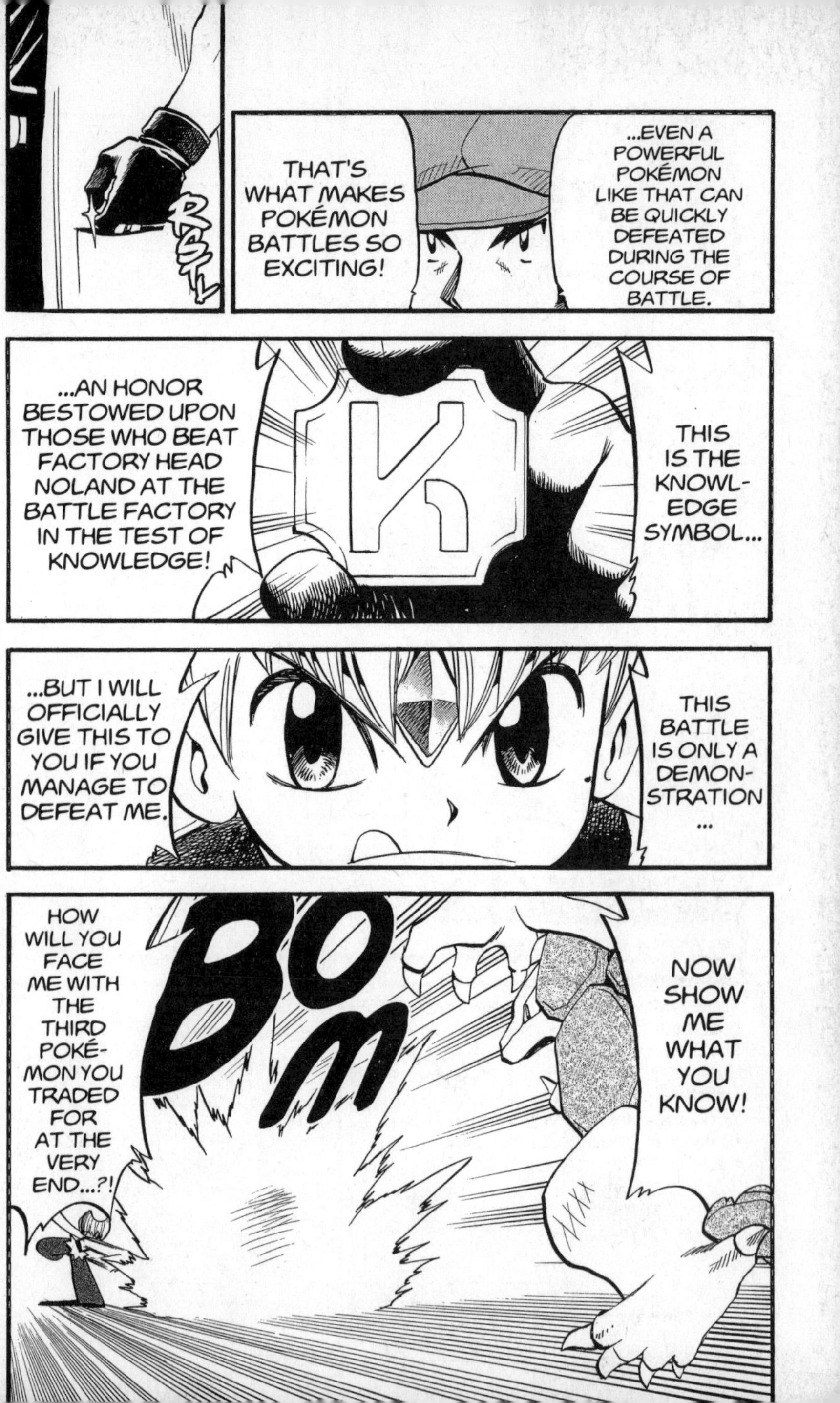

...EVEN A POWERFUL POKÉMON LIKE THAT CAN BE QUICKLY DEFEATED DURING THE COURSE OF BATTLE.
THAT'S WHAT MAKES POKÉMON BATTLES SO EXCITING!
RSTL
THIS IS THE KNOWL-EDGE SYMBOL...
...AN HONOR BESTOWED UPON THOSE WHO BEAT FACTORY HEAD NOLAND AT THE BATTLE FACTORY IN THE TEST OF KNOWLEDGE!
THIS BATTLE IS ONLY A DEMON-STRATION ...
...BUT I WILL OFFICIALLY GIVE THIS TO YOU IF YOU MANAGE TO DEFEAT ME.
NOW SHOW ME WHAT YOU KNOW!
BOOM
HOW WILL YOU FACE ME WITH THE THIRD POKÉ-MON YOU TRADED FOR AT THE VERY END...?!

DEAR MEMBERS OF THE PRESS...

Thank you for visiting my Battle Frontier today. Permit me to continue explaining the rules of this facility...

OWNER: SCOTT

■ IN CASE OF A DOUBLE KNOCKOUT ■

The result is a tie and a rematch will be arranged if the battle is between two regular Trainers. If the battle was against a Frontier Brain, the Brain is the winner.

■ BATTLE POINTS ■

The accumulation of Battle Points corresponds with your results at each facility. Collected Battle Points may be exchanged for items at the Battle Point Exchange Service Corner.

FACILITY RULES **BATTLE FACTORY**	Battle-type	Number of Pokémon	Type of Symbol	Wins needed to attain the Symbol
	Single	3 Pokémon	Knowledge	7 Battles × 6 Sets = 42 Consecutive Wins
	Double	3 Pokémon		

Battle Factory battles are fought using rental Pokémon. The challenger chooses three out of six randomly selected Pokémon. If the challenger wins, they have the option of exchanging one of their Pokémon for one of their opponent's Pokémon. The newly acquired Pokémon takes the same position in the group as the one that was traded away.

Factory Head Noland   Knowledge Symbol

◆307◆

Gotcha Where I Wantcha, Glalie

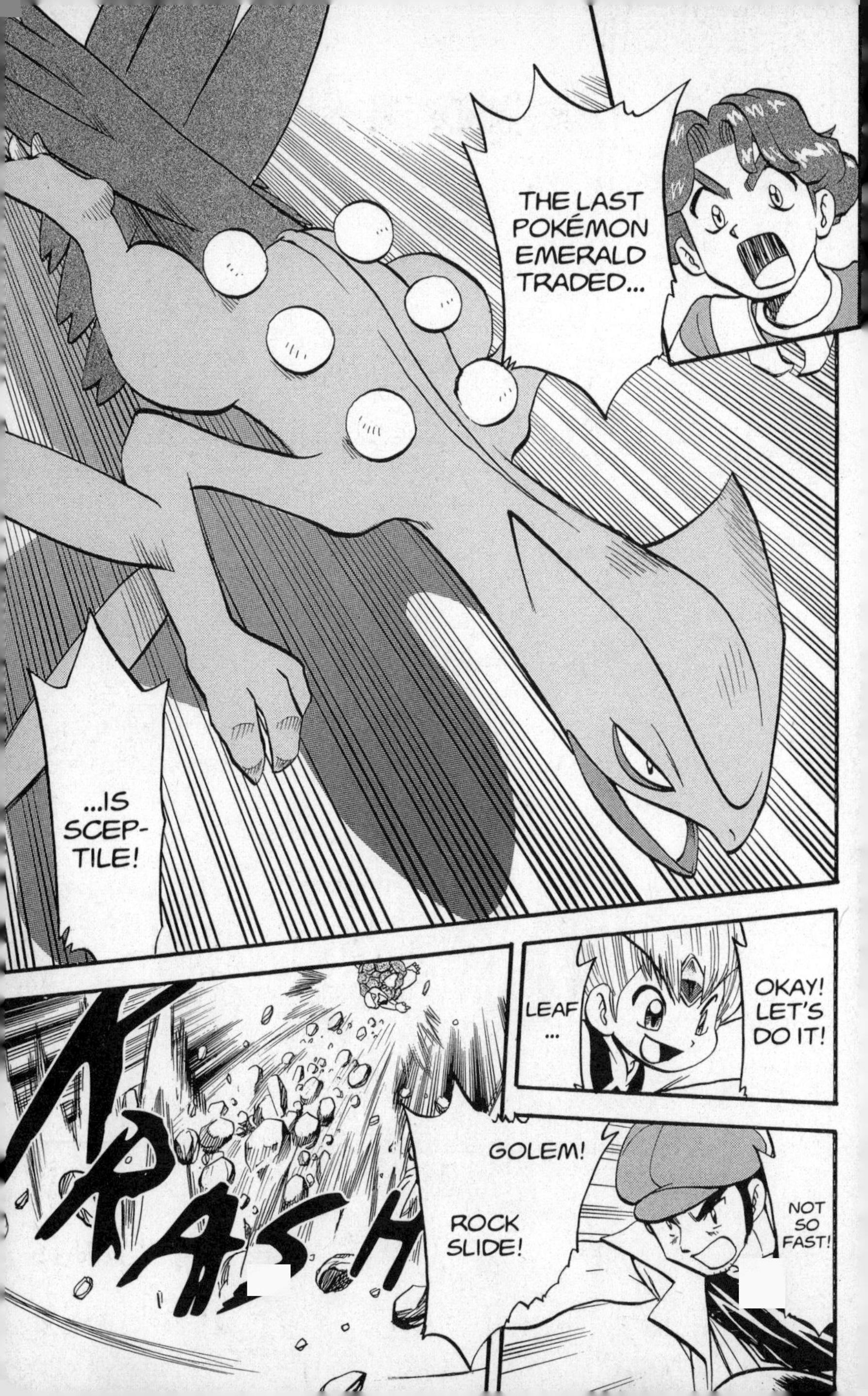
THE LAST POKÉMON EMERALD TRADED...
...IS SCEP-TILE!
OKAY! LET'S DO IT!
LEAF ...
NOT SO FAST!
GOLEM!
ROCK SLIDE!
KRASH

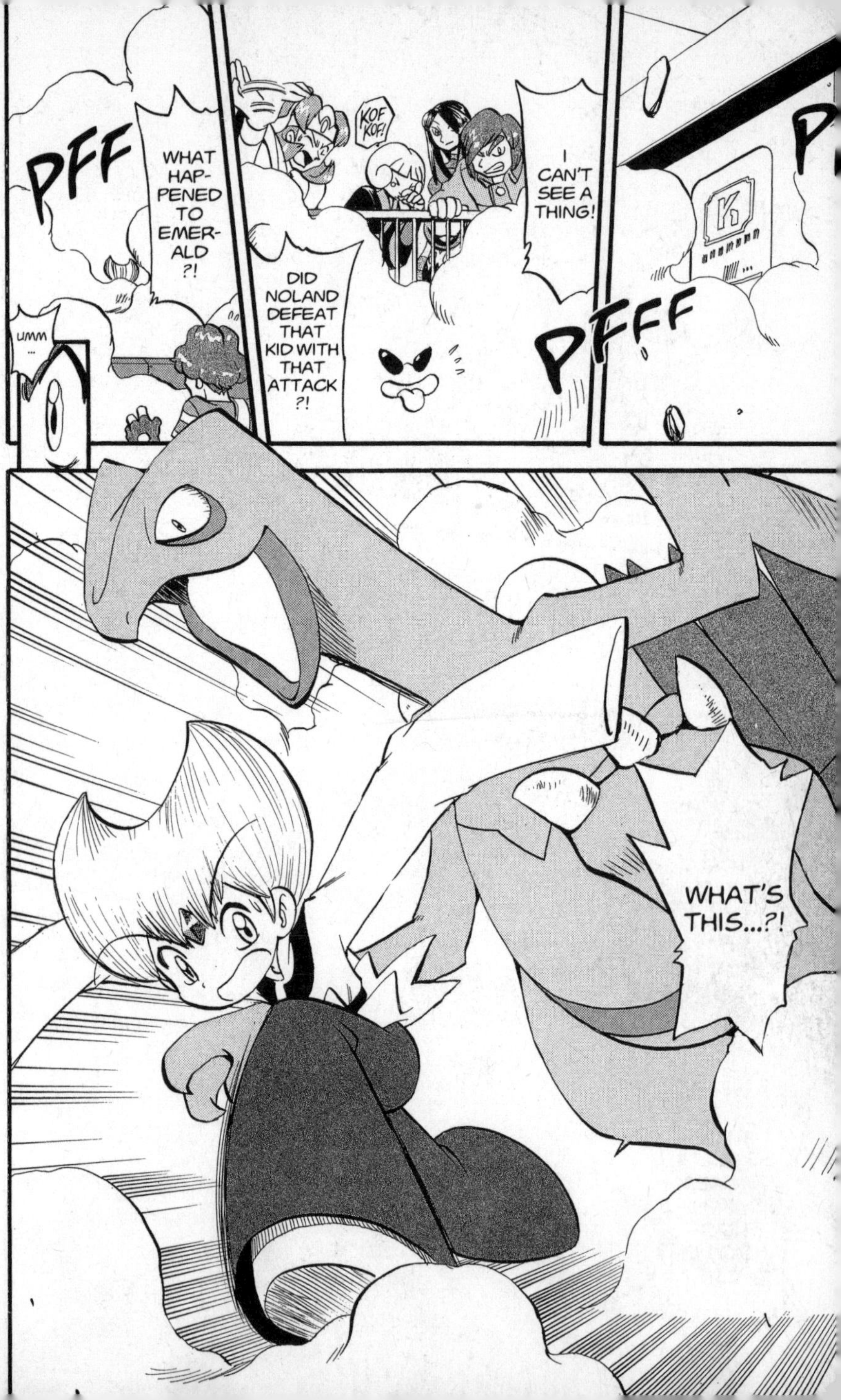
PFFF
I CAN'T SEE A THING!
KOF KOF!
DID NOLAND DEFEAT THAT KID WITH THAT ATTACK?!
WHAT HAPPENED TO EMERALD?!
PFF
UMM...
WHAT'S THIS...?!

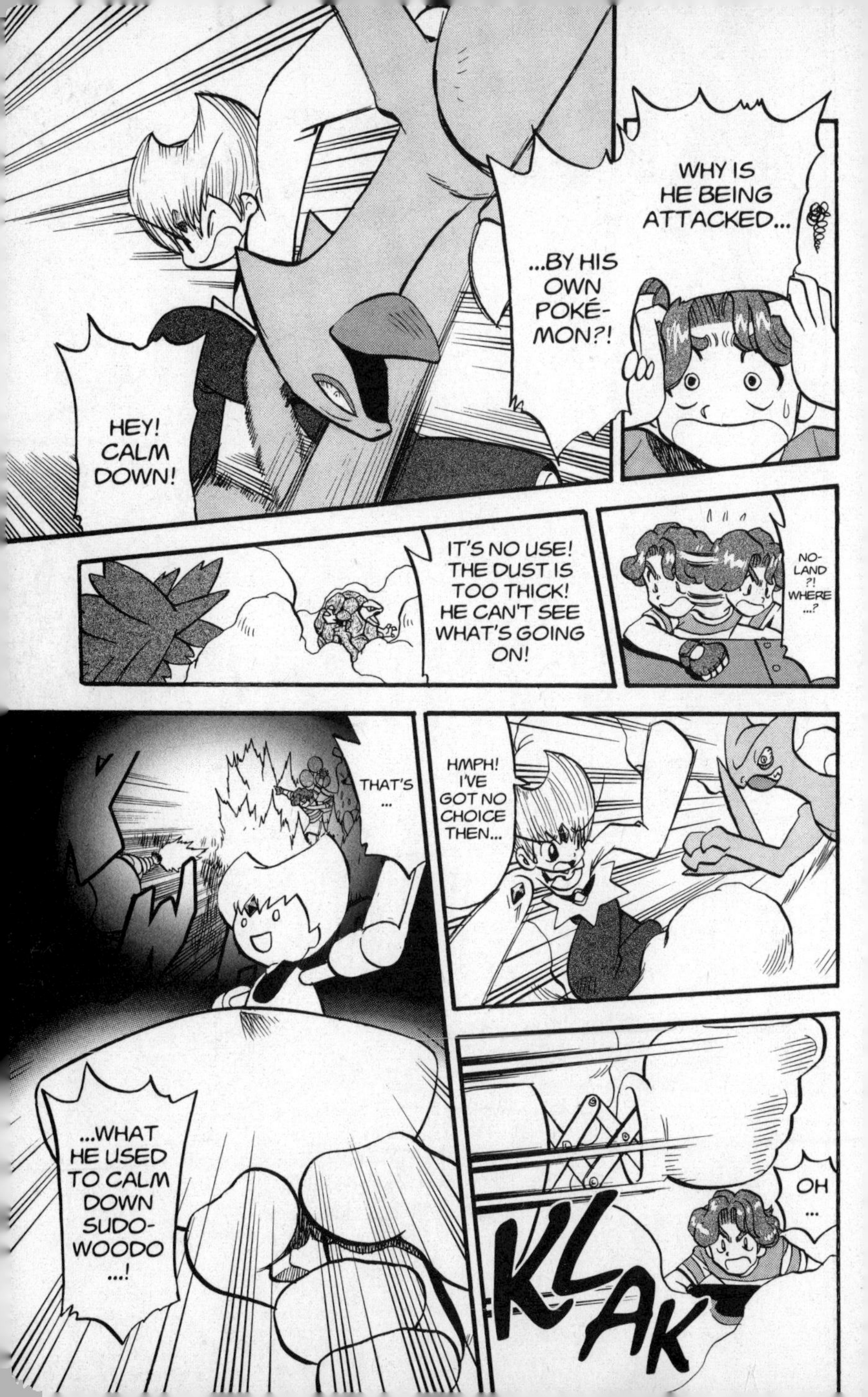
WHY IS HE BEING ATTACKED...
...BY HIS OWN POKÉMON?!
HEY! CALM DOWN!
NO-LAND ?! WHERE ...?
IT'S NO USE! THE DUST IS TOO THICK! HE CAN'T SEE WHAT'S GOING ON!
HMPH! I'VE GOT NO CHOICE THEN...
THAT'S ...
OH ...
KLAK
...WHAT HE USED TO CALM DOWN SUDO-WOODO ...!

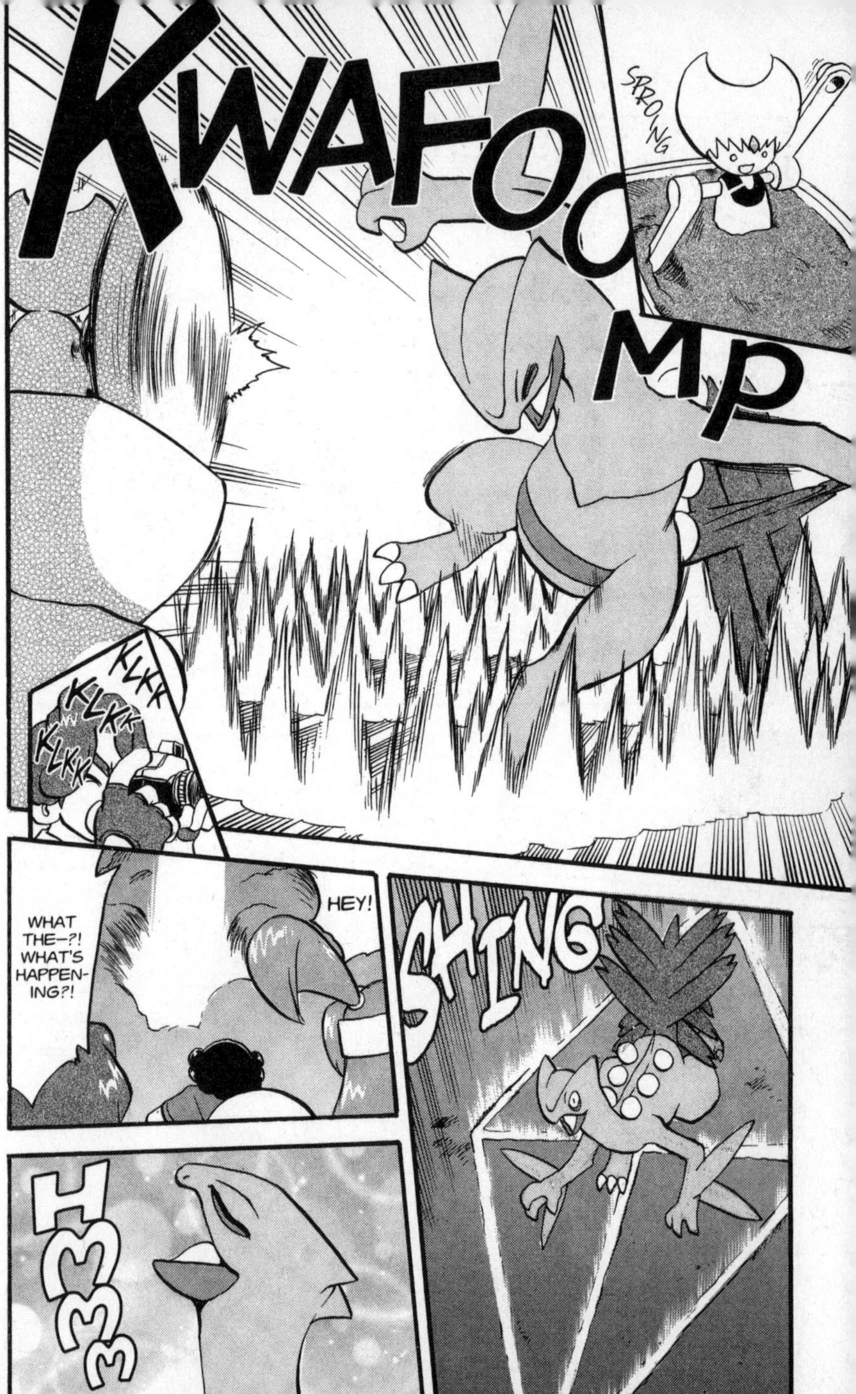
SPROING
KWAFOOMP
KLKK
KLKK
KLKK
SHING
HEY!
WHAT THE—?! WHAT'S HAPPEN-ING?!
HMMM

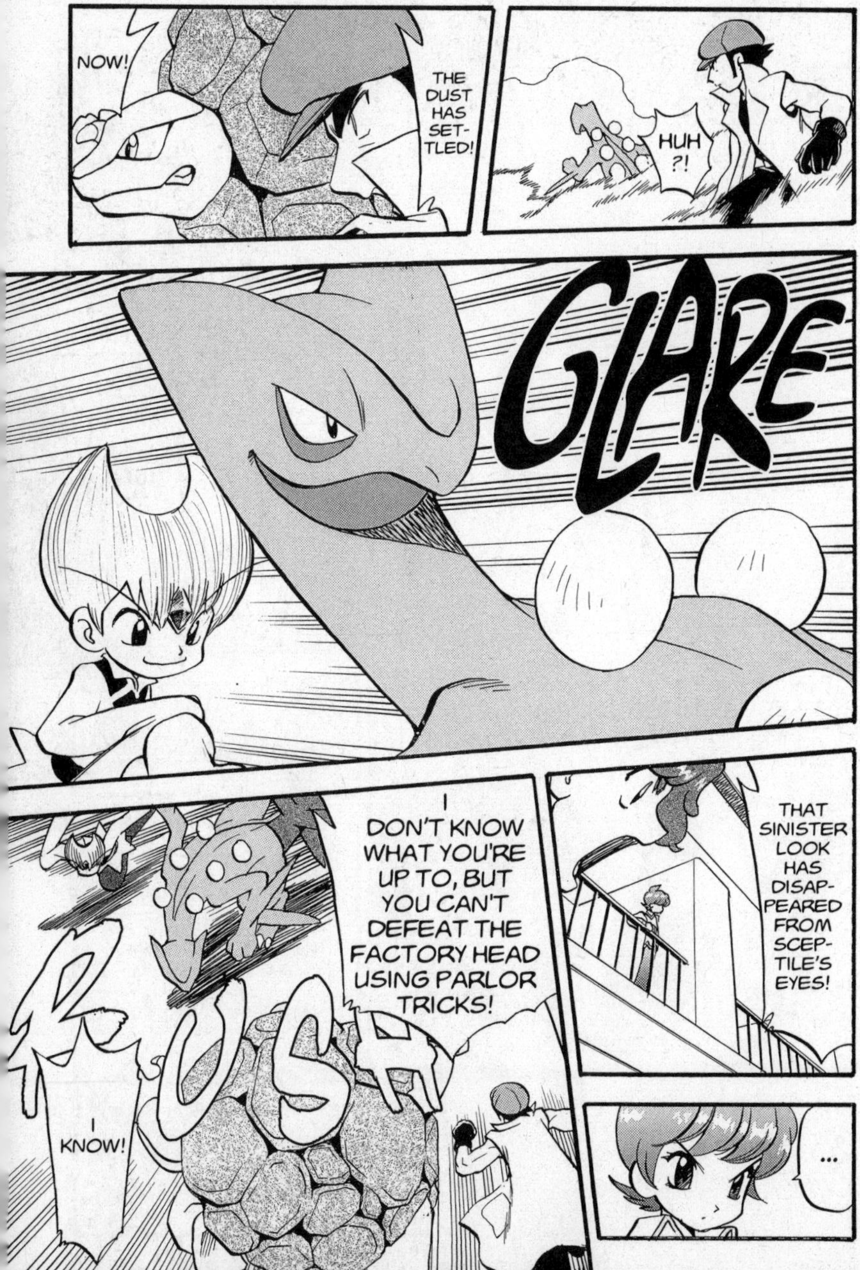
HUH ?!
THE DUST HAS SET-TLED!
NOW!
GLARE
THAT SINISTER LOOK HAS DISAP-PEARED FROM SCEP-TILE'S EYES!
...
I DON'T KNOW WHAT YOU'RE UP TO, BUT YOU CAN'T DEFEAT THE FACTORY HEAD USING PARLOR TRICKS!
RUSH
I KNOW!

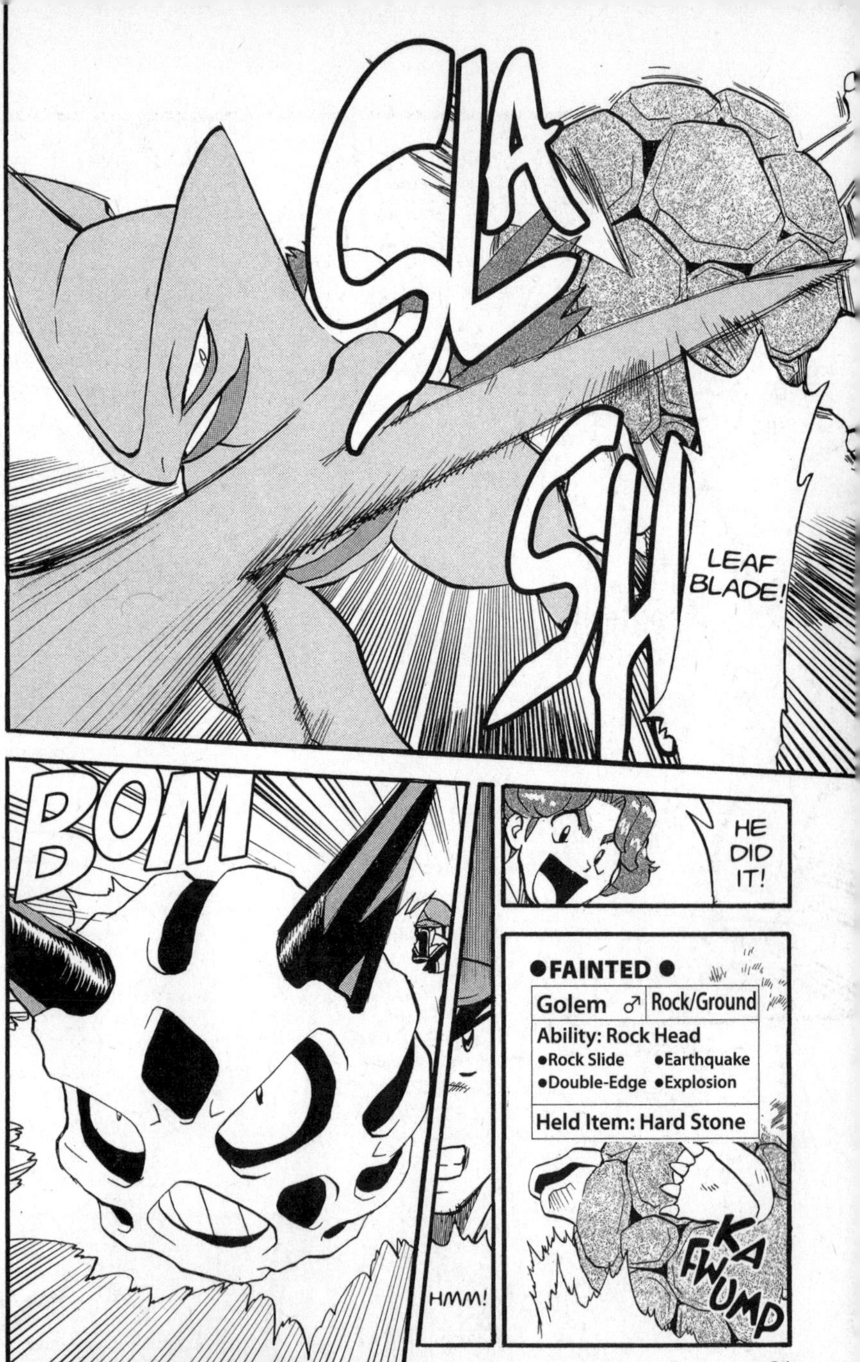
SLA
SH
LEAF BLADE!
HE DID IT!
●FAINTED●
Golem ♂ Rock/Ground
Ability: Rock Head
●Rock Slide ●Earthquake
●Double-Edge ●Explosion
Held Item: Hard Stone
KA FWUMP
HMM!
BOM

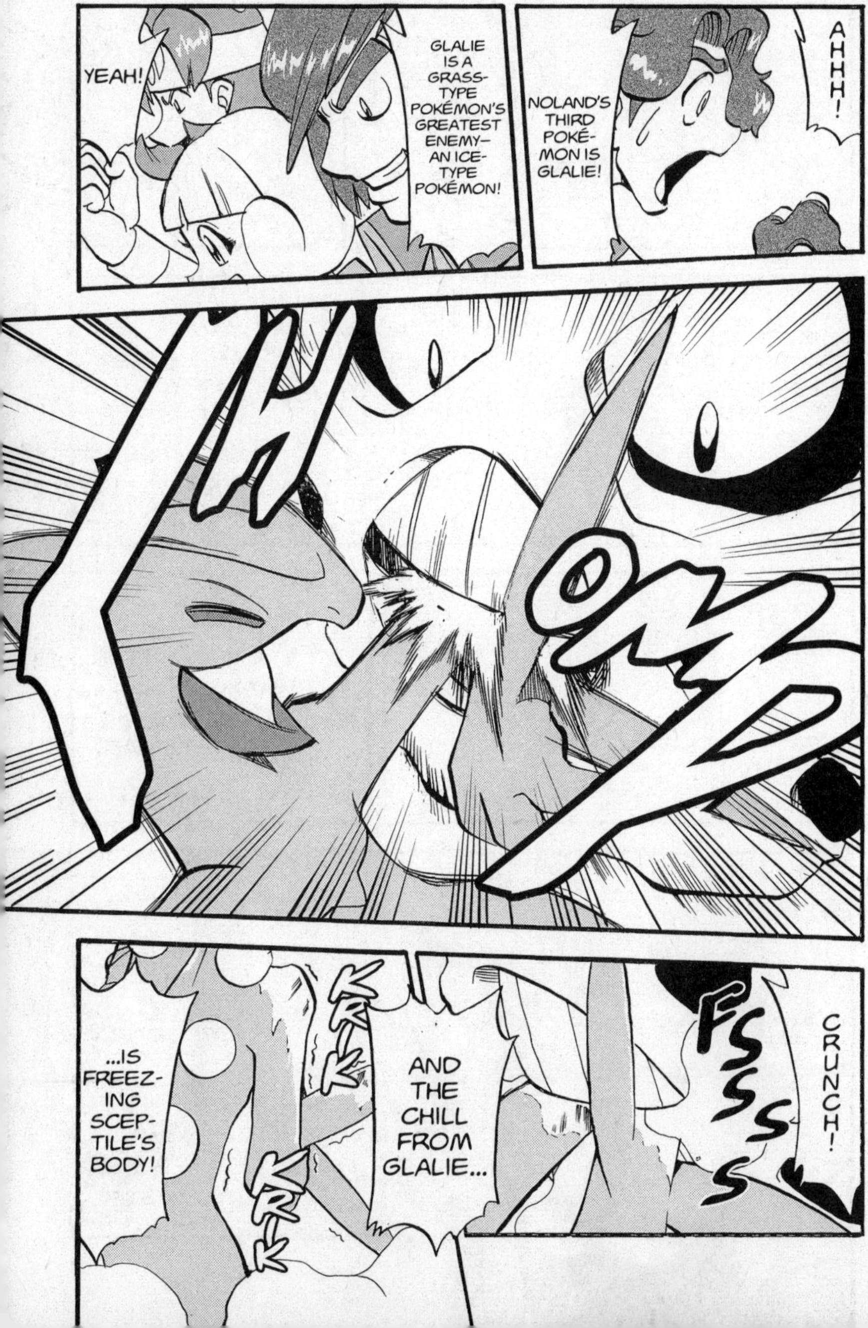
AHHHH!
NOLAND'S THIRD POKÉMON IS GLALIE!
GLALIE IS A GRASS-TYPE POKÉMON'S GREATEST ENEMY— AN ICE-TYPE POKÉMON!
YEAH!
CRUNCH!
FSSSS
AND THE CHILL FROM GLALIE...
...IS FREEZING SCEPTILE'S BODY!

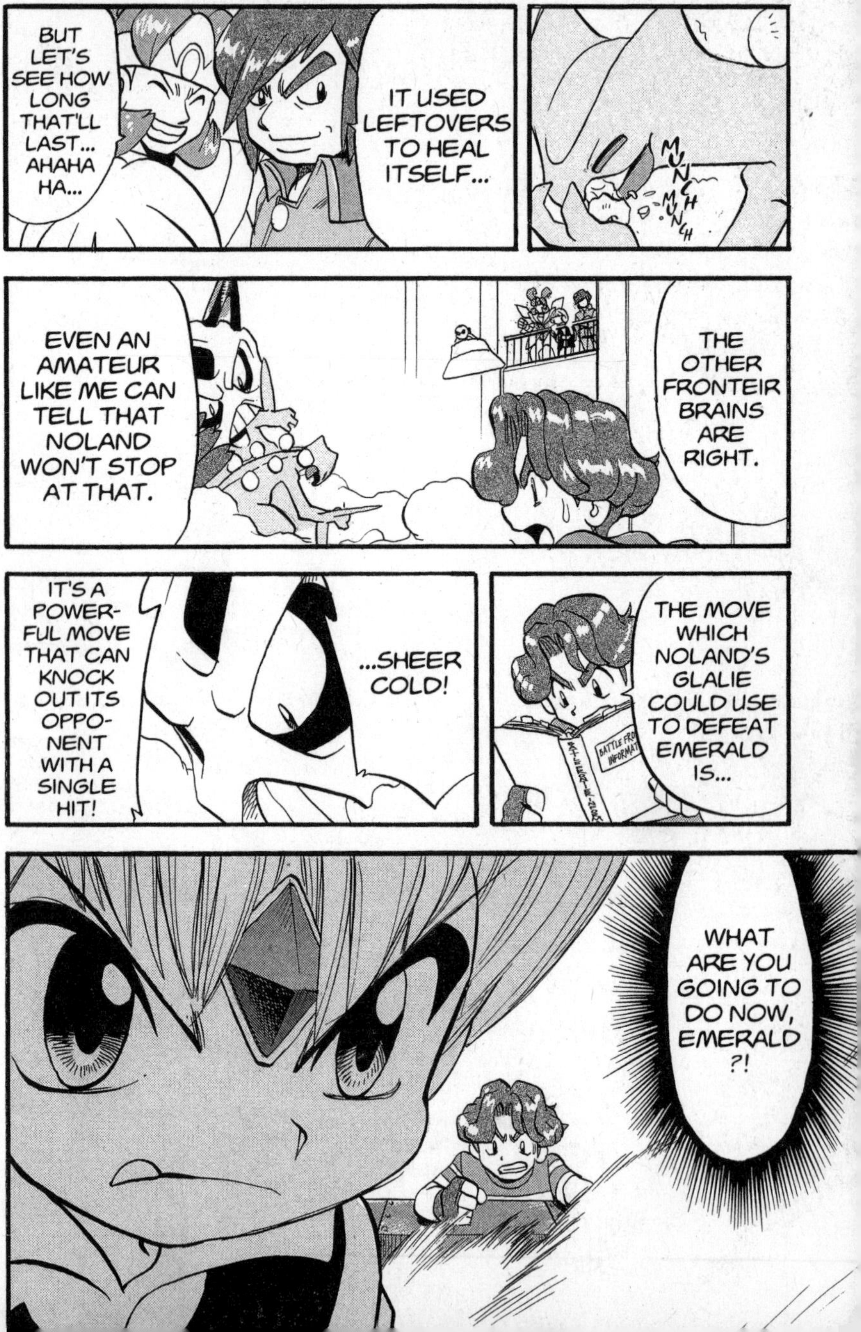
MUNCH MUNCH
IT USED LEFTOVERS TO HEAL ITSELF...
BUT LET'S SEE HOW LONG THAT'LL LAST... AHAHA HA...
THE OTHER FRONTEIR BRAINS ARE RIGHT.
EVEN AN AMATEUR LIKE ME CAN TELL THAT NOLAND WON'T STOP AT THAT.
THE MOVE WHICH NOLAND'S GLALIE COULD USE TO DEFEAT EMERALD IS...
...SHEER COLD!
IT'S A POWER-FUL MOVE THAT CAN KNOCK OUT ITS OPPO-NENT WITH A SINGLE HIT!
WHAT ARE YOU GOING TO DO NOW, EMERALD ?!

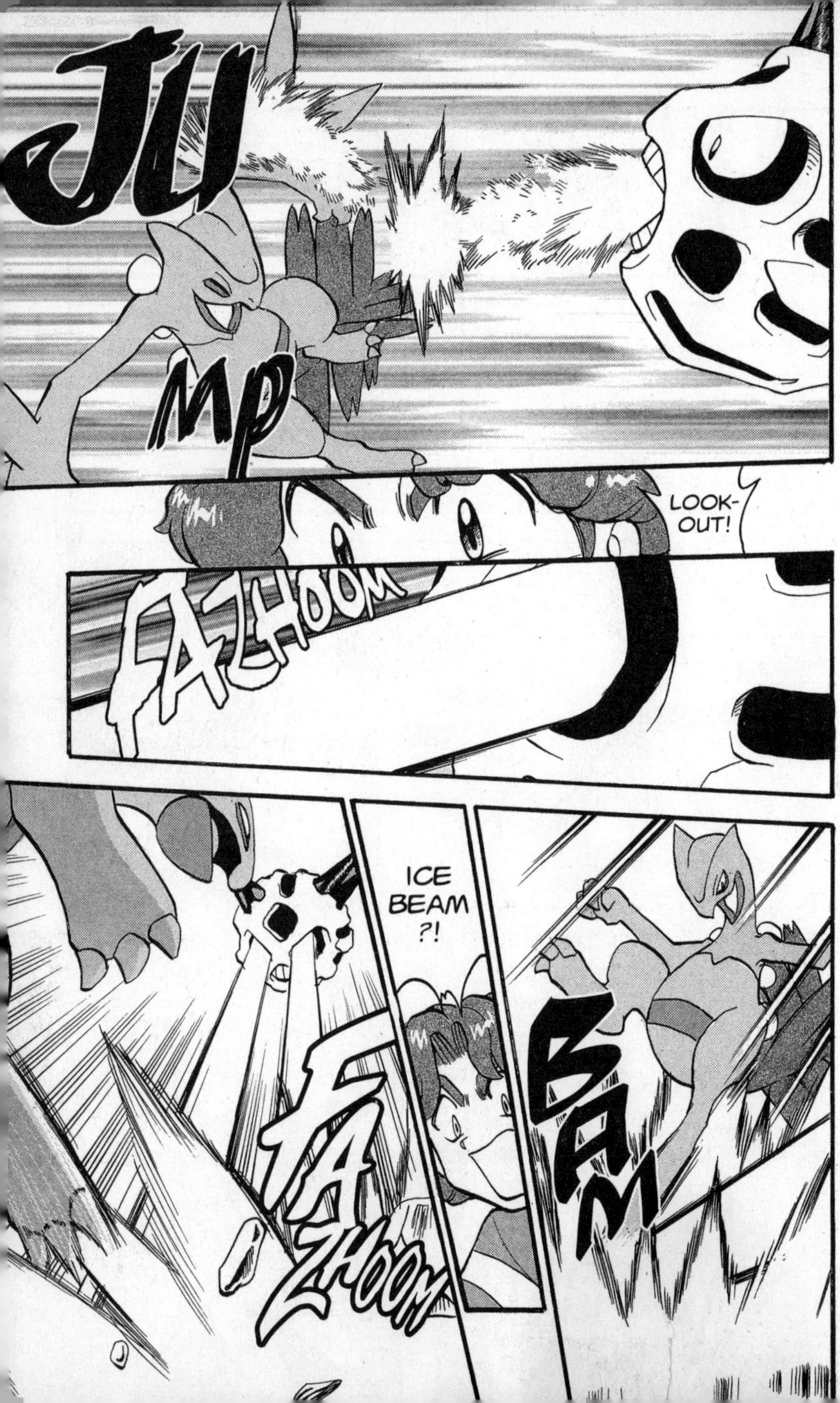
JUMP
LOOK-OUT!
FAZHOOM
BAM
ICE BEAM ?!
FAZHOOM

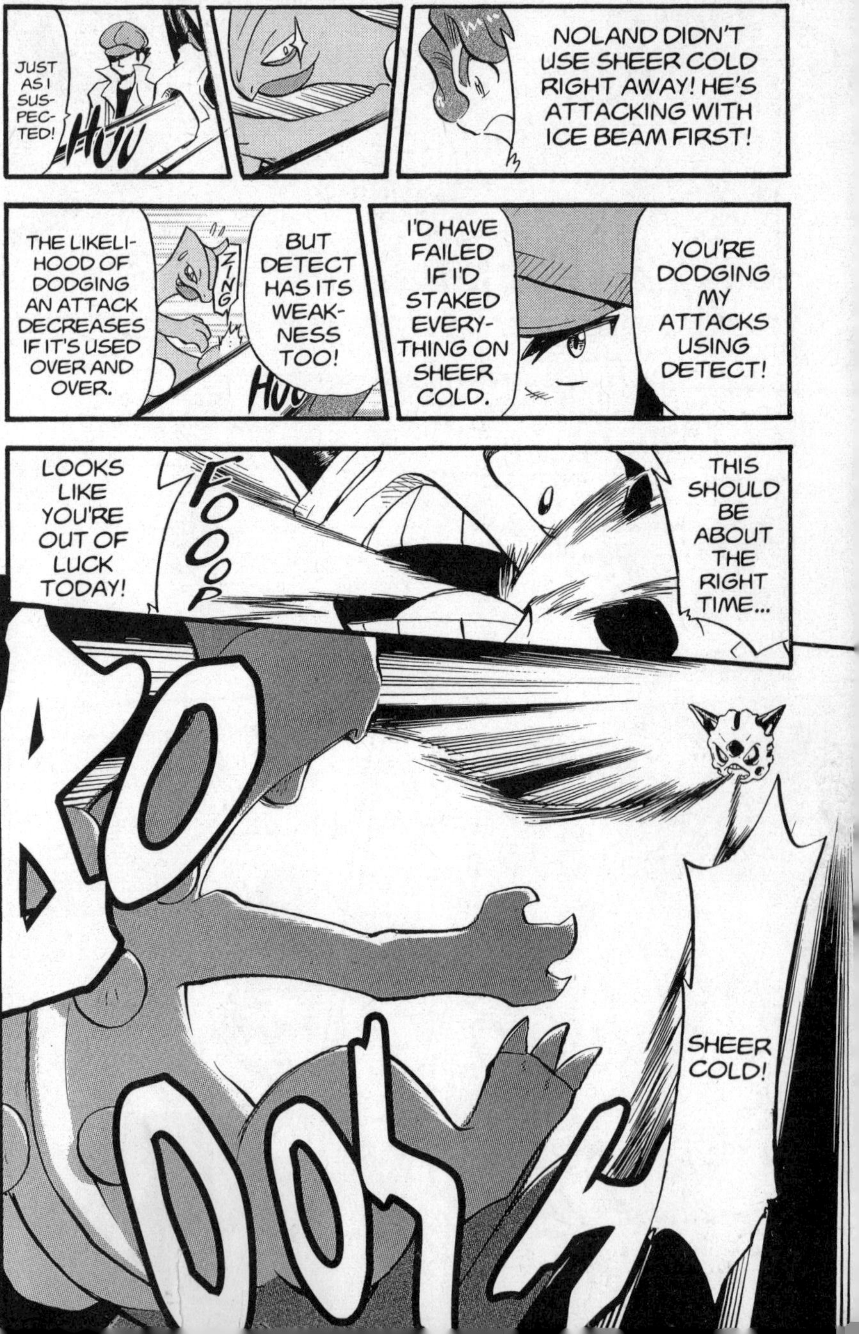
NOLAND DIDN'T USE SHEER COLD RIGHT AWAY! HE'S ATTACKING WITH ICE BEAM FIRST!
JUST AS I SUSPECTED!
YOU'RE DODGING MY ATTACKS USING DETECT!
I'D HAVE FAILED IF I'D STAKED EVERYTHING ON SHEER COLD.
BUT DETECT HAS ITS WEAKNESS TOO!
ZING
THE LIKELIHOOD OF DODGING AN ATTACK DECREASES IF IT'S USED OVER AND OVER.
THIS SHOULD BE ABOUT THE RIGHT TIME...
FOOOOP
LOOKS LIKE YOU'RE OUT OF LUCK TODAY!
SHEER COLD!

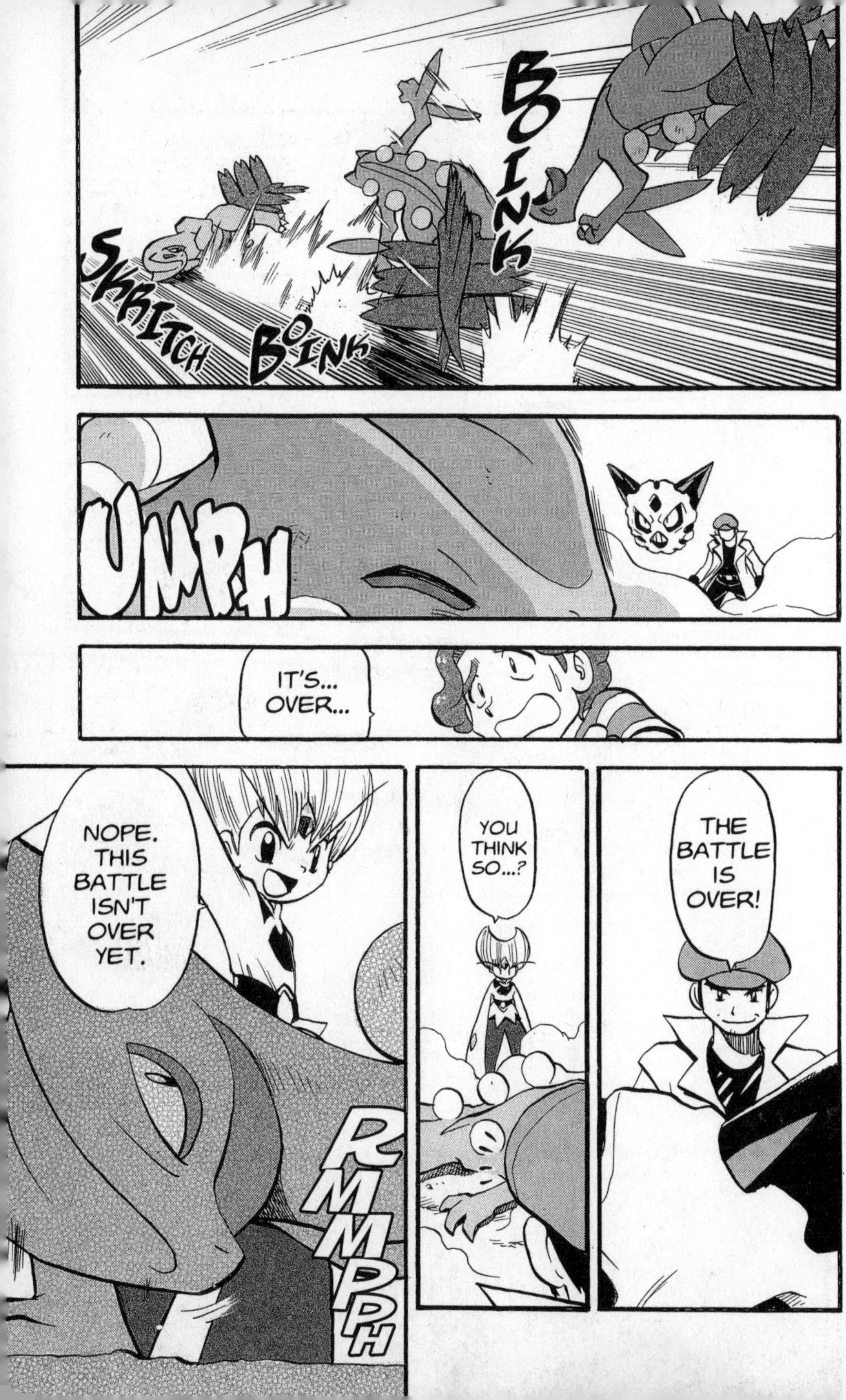
BOINK
BOINK
SKRITCH
UMPH
IT'S... OVER...
THE BATTLE IS OVER!
YOU THINK SO...?
NOPE. THIS BATTLE ISN'T OVER YET.
RMMPH

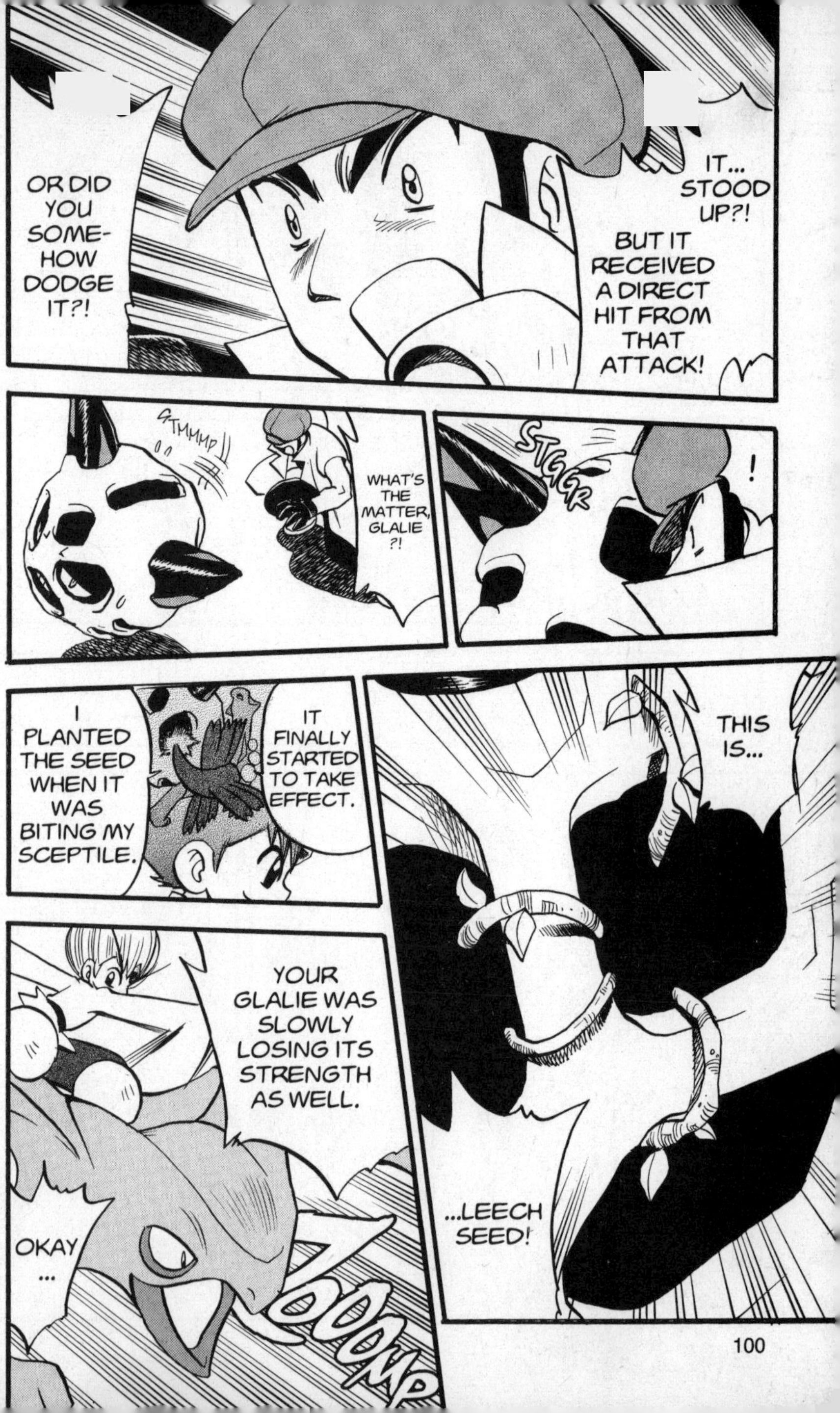
IT... STOOD UP?!
BUT IT RECEIVED A DIRECT HIT FROM THAT ATTACK!
OR DID YOU SOME-HOW DODGE IT?!
STGGR
!
WHAT'S THE MATTER, GLALIE?!
THIS IS...
...LEECH SEED!
IT FINALLY STARTED TO TAKE EFFECT.
I PLANTED THE SEED WHEN IT WAS BITING MY SCEPTILE.
YOUR GLALIE WAS SLOWLY LOSING ITS STRENGTH AS WELL.
OKAY...

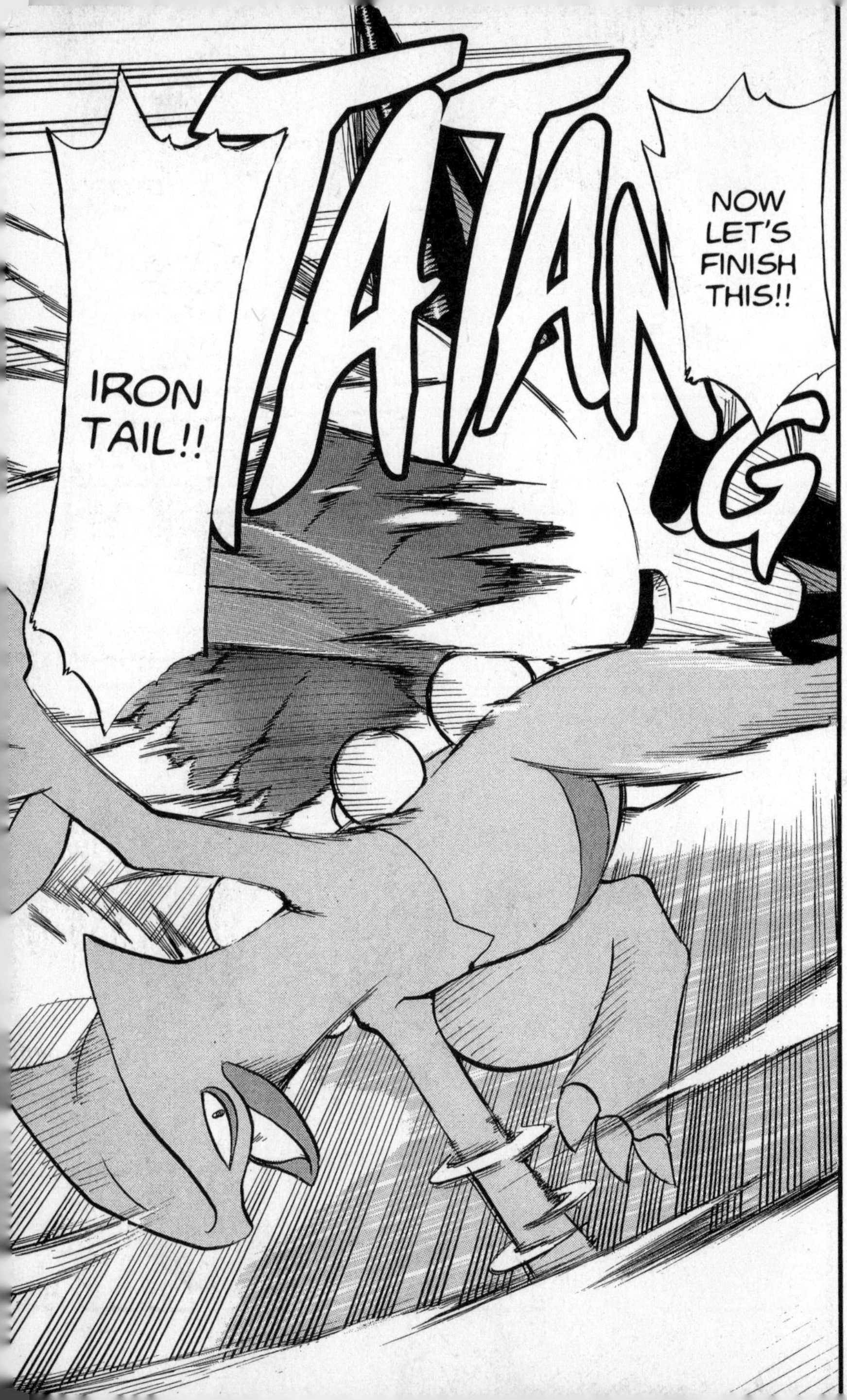
NOW LET'S FINISH THIS!!
TAAANG
IRON TAIL!!

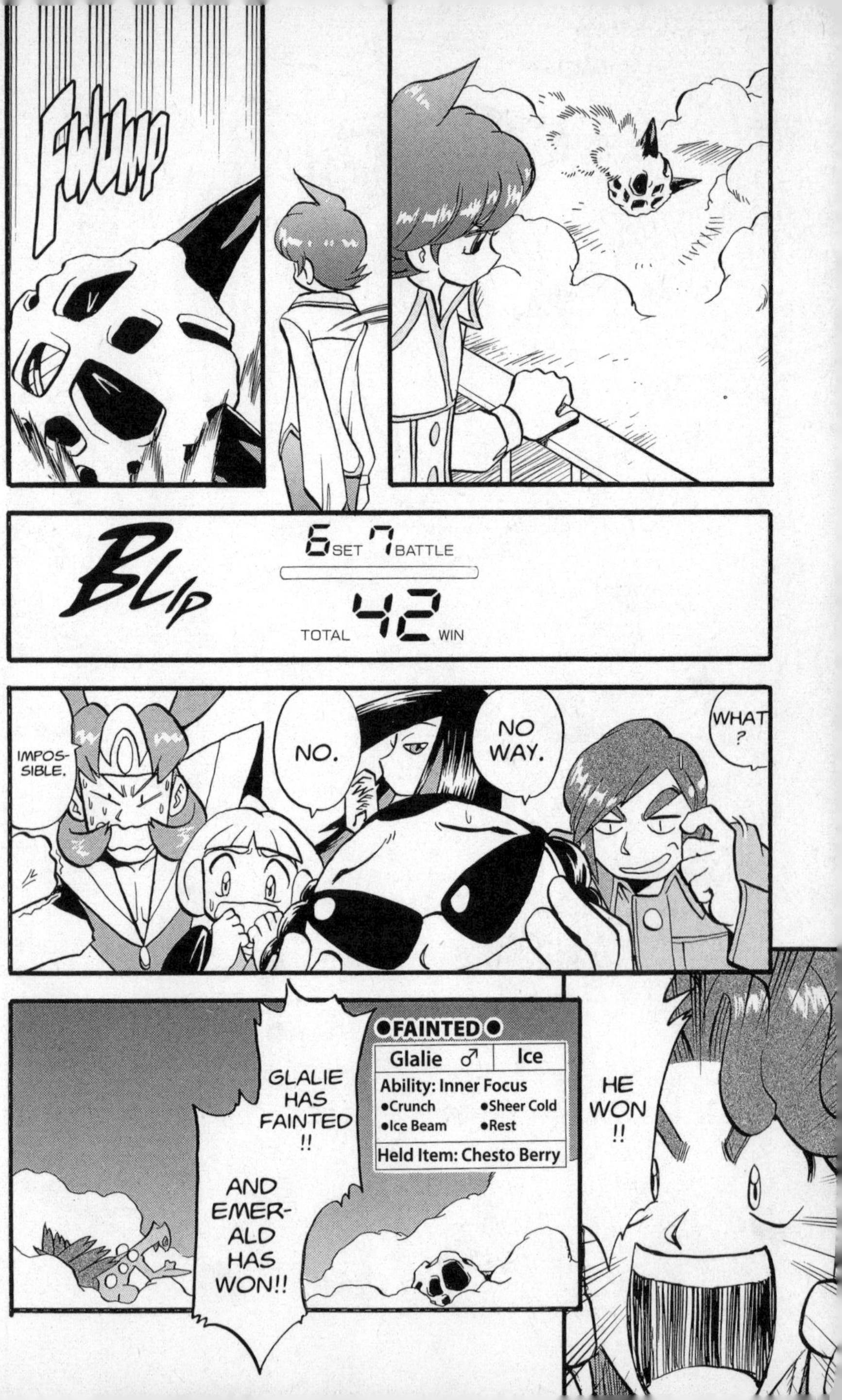
FWUMP
BLIP
6 SET 7 BATTLE
TOTAL 42 WIN
WHAT?
NO WAY.
NO.
IMPOSSIBLE.
HE WON!!
●FAINTED●
Glalie ♂ | Ice
Ability: Inner Focus
●Crunch ●Sheer Cold
●Ice Beam ●Rest
Held Item: Chesto Berry
GLALIE HAS FAINTED!!
AND EMERALD HAS WON!!

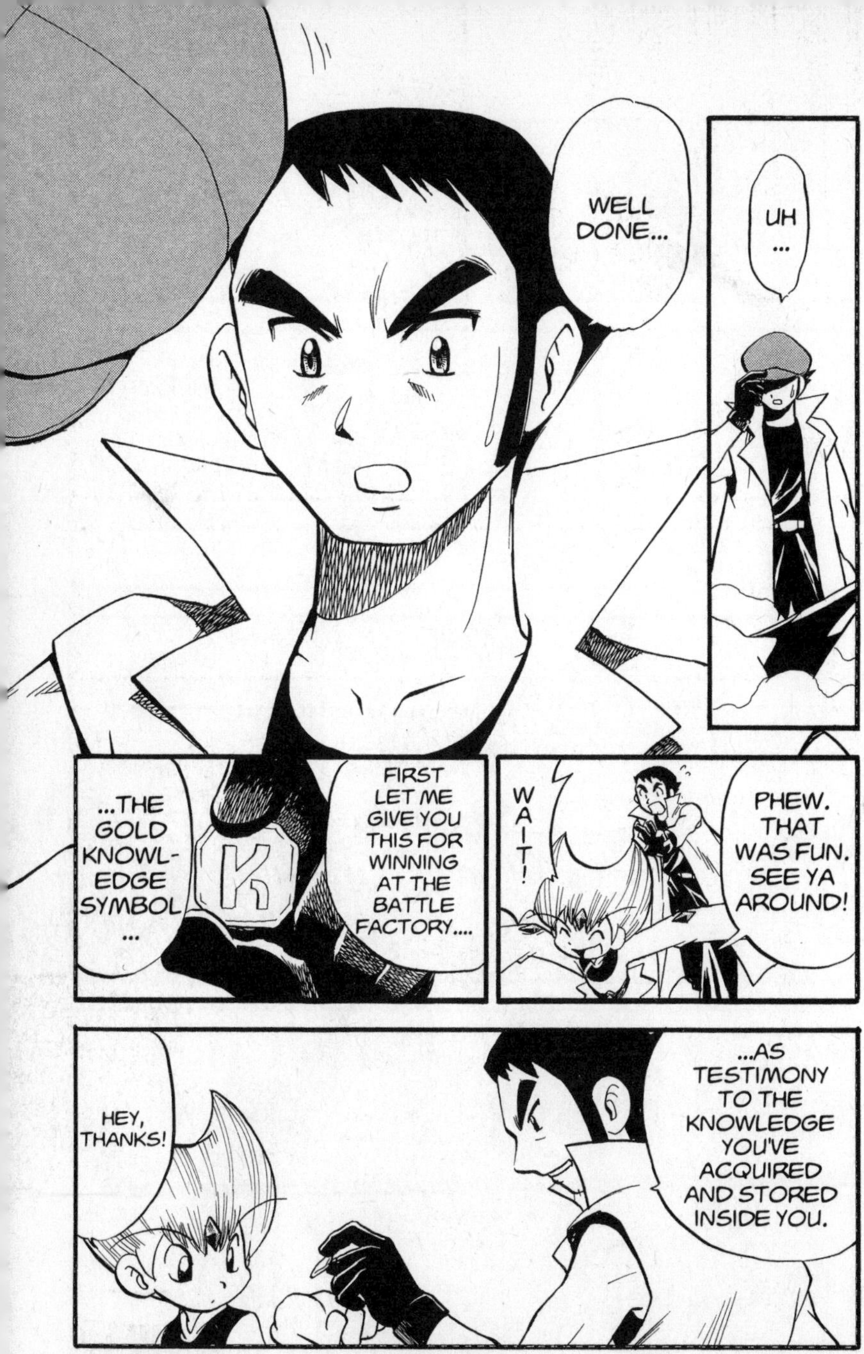
UH ...
WELL DONE...
PHEW. THAT WAS FUN. SEE YA AROUND!
WAIT!
FIRST LET ME GIVE YOU THIS FOR WINNING AT THE BATTLE FACTORY....
...THE GOLD KNOWL-EDGE SYMBOL ...
...AS TESTIMONY TO THE KNOWLEDGE YOU'VE ACQUIRED AND STORED INSIDE YOU.
HEY, THANKS!

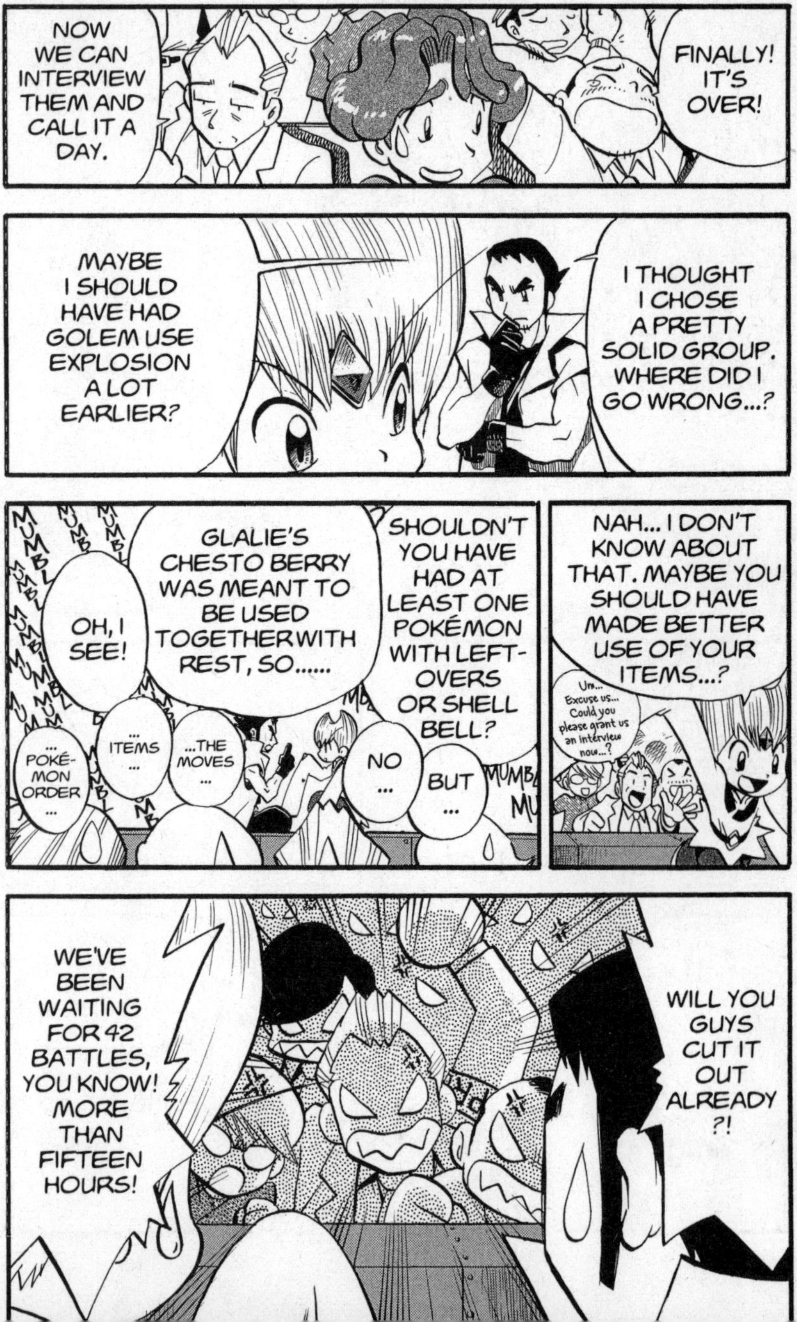
FINALLY! IT'S OVER!
NOW WE CAN INTERVIEW THEM AND CALL IT A DAY.
I THOUGHT I CHOSE A PRETTY SOLID GROUP. WHERE DID I GO WRONG...?
MAYBE I SHOULD HAVE HAD GOLEM USE EXPLOSION A LOT EARLIER?
NAH... I DON'T KNOW ABOUT THAT. MAYBE YOU SHOULD HAVE MADE BETTER USE OF YOUR ITEMS...?
Um... Excuse us... Could you please grant us an interview now...?
SHOULDN'T YOU HAVE HAD AT LEAST ONE POKÉMON WITH LEFT-OVERS OR SHELL BELL?
GLALIE'S CHESTO BERRY WAS MEANT TO BE USED TOGETHER WITH REST, SO......
OH, I SEE!
BUT ...
NO ...
...THE MOVES ...
... ITEMS ...
... POKÉ-MON ORDER ...
WILL YOU GUYS CUT IT OUT ALREADY ?!
WE'VE BEEN WAITING FOR 42 BATTLES, YOU KNOW! MORE THAN FIFTEEN HOURS!

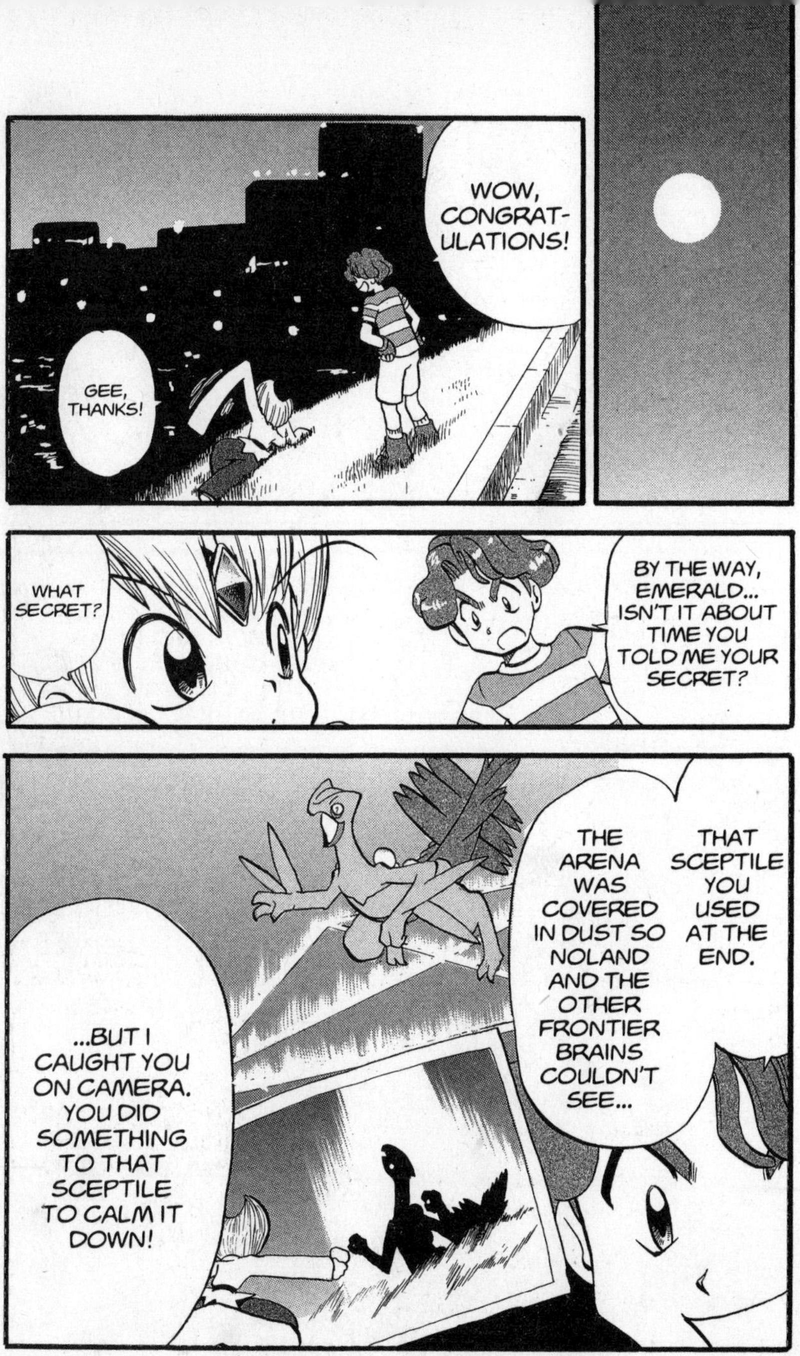
WOW, CONGRAT-ULATIONS!
GEE, THANKS!
BY THE WAY, EMERALD... ISN'T IT ABOUT TIME YOU TOLD ME YOUR SECRET?
WHAT SECRET?
THAT SCEPTILE YOU USED AT THE END.
THE ARENA WAS COVERED IN DUST SO NOLAND AND THE OTHER FRONTIER BRAINS COULDN'T SEE...
...BUT I CAUGHT YOU ON CAMERA. YOU DID SOMETHING TO THAT SCEPTILE TO CALM IT DOWN!

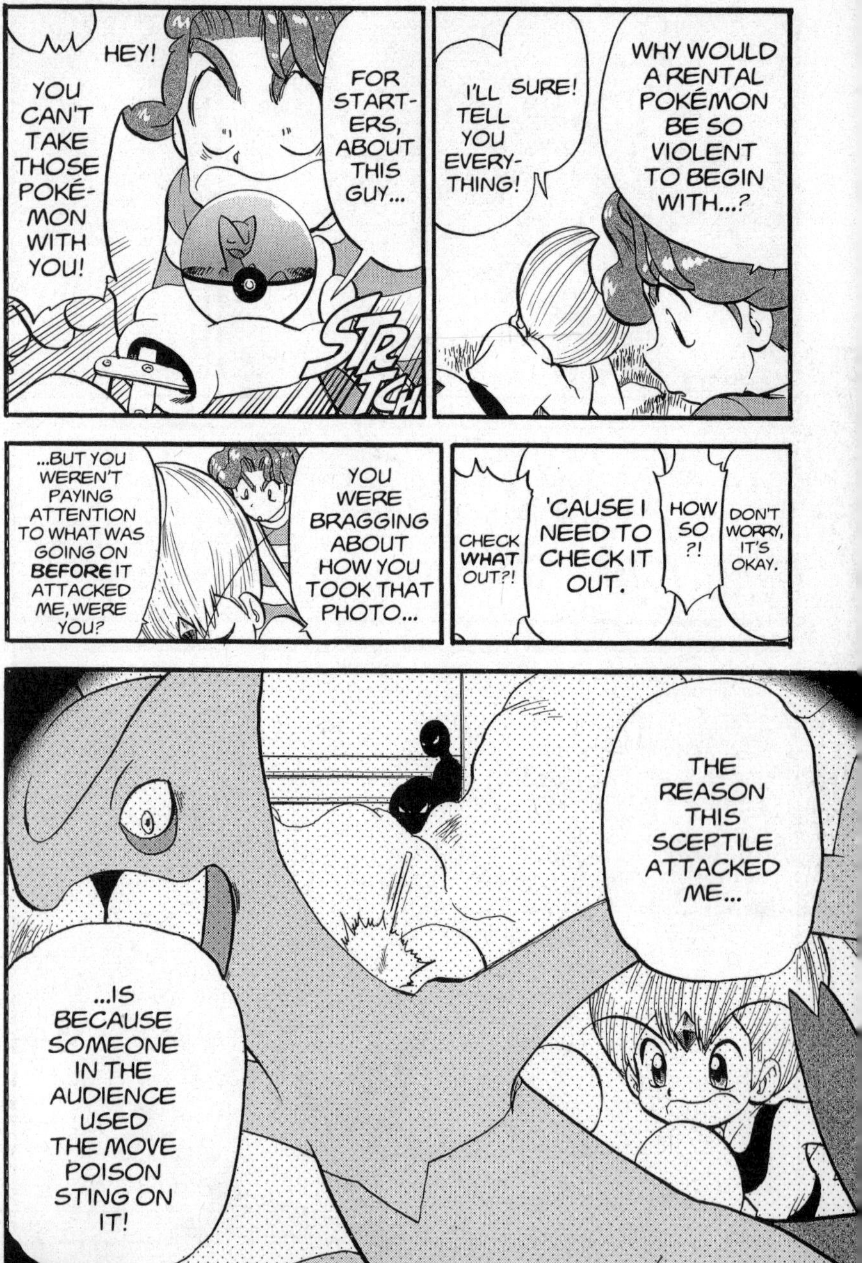
WHY WOULD A RENTAL POKÉMON BE SO VIOLENT TO BEGIN WITH...?
SURE!
I'LL TELL YOU EVERYTHING!
FOR STARTERS, ABOUT THIS GUY...
HEY!
YOU CAN'T TAKE THOSE POKÉMON WITH YOU!
STRTCH
DON'T WORRY, IT'S OKAY.
HOW SO?!
'CAUSE I NEED TO CHECK IT OUT.
CHECK WHAT OUT?!
YOU WERE BRAGGING ABOUT HOW YOU TOOK THAT PHOTO...
...BUT YOU WEREN'T PAYING ATTENTION TO WHAT WAS GOING ON BEFORE IT ATTACKED ME, WERE YOU?
THE REASON THIS SCEPTILE ATTACKED ME...
...IS BECAUSE SOMEONE IN THE AUDIENCE USED THE MOVE POISON STING ON IT!

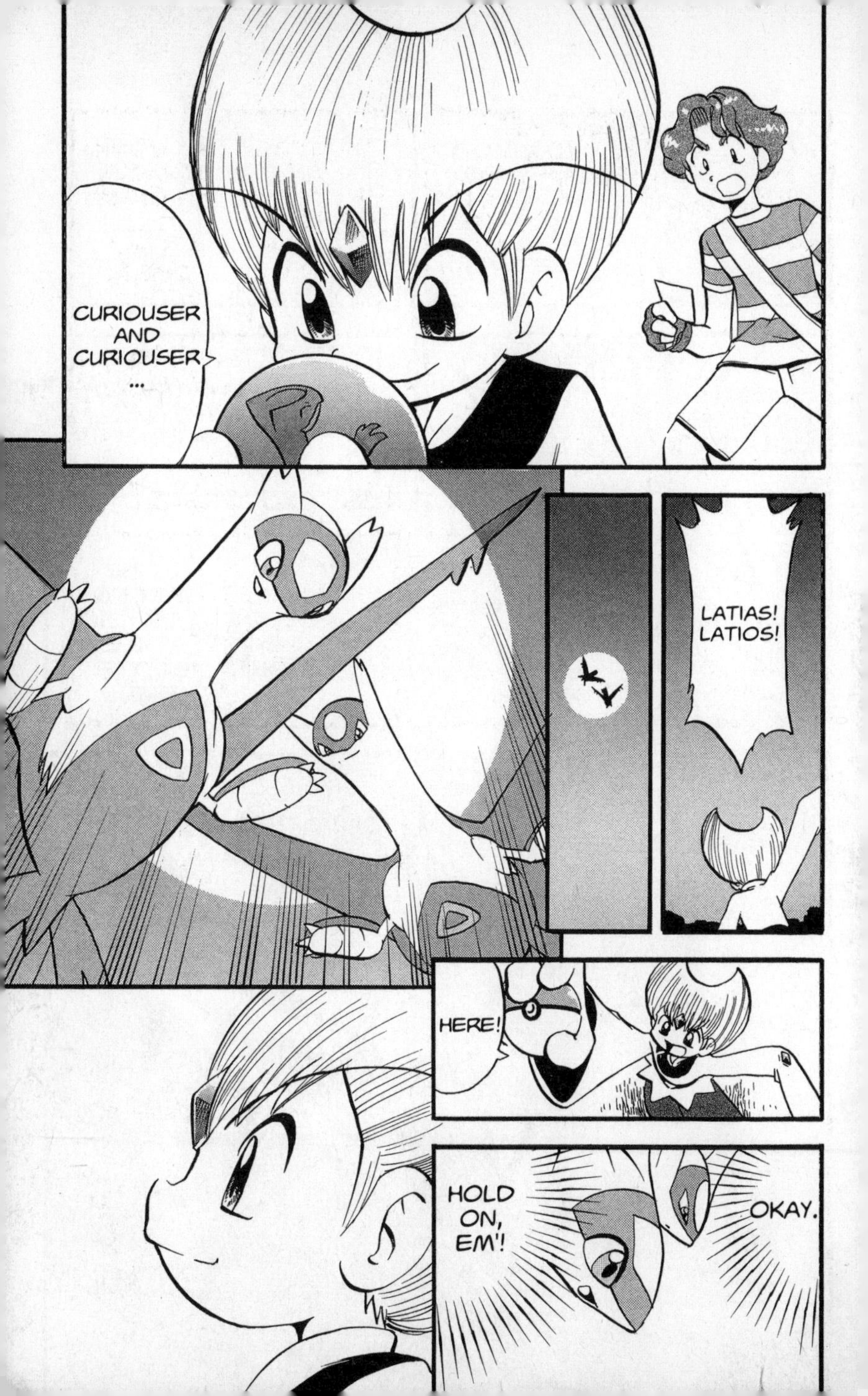
CURIOUSER AND CURIOUSER ...
LATIAS! LATIOS!
HERE!
OKAY.
HOLD ON, EM'!

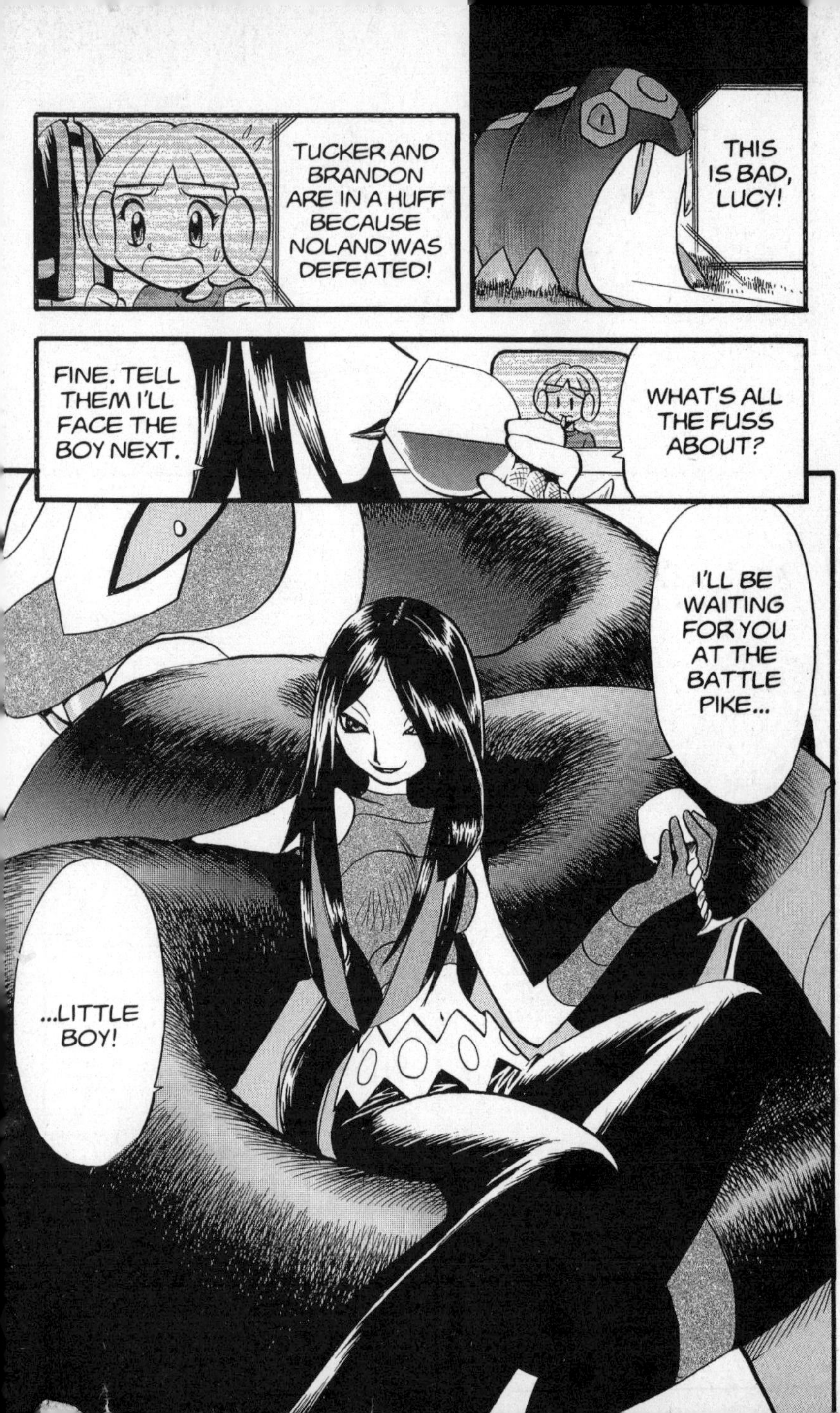
THIS IS BAD, LUCY!
TUCKER AND BRANDON ARE IN A HUFF BECAUSE NOLAND WAS DEFEATED!
WHAT'S ALL THE FUSS ABOUT?
FINE. TELL THEM I'LL FACE THE BOY NEXT.
I'LL BE WAITING FOR YOU AT THE BATTLE PIKE...
...LITTLE BOY!

DEAR MEMBERS OF THE PRESS...

Thank you for visiting the Battle Frontier today. Permit me to continue explaining the rules of this facility...

OWNER: SCOTT

FACILITY RULES	Battle-type	Number of Pokémon	Type of Symbol	Wins needed to attain the Symbol
BATTLE PIKE	• Single • Double • Wild Pokémon	3 Pokémon	Luck	14 Rooms × 10 Sets = 140 Rooms

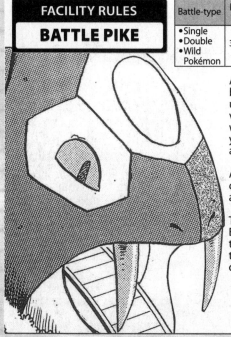

At this facility, you choose between three routes to travel until you reach the room at the very end. Eight possible events will occur inside each room. What you will encounter is determined at random.

A healing event, which heals the challenger's Pokémon, is included among the eight events.

There is also a Double Battle Event, but this will not occur if the challenger does not have two or more Pokémon capable of fighting.

Luck Symbol

Pike Queen Lucy

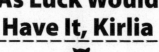

As Luck Would Have It, Kirlia

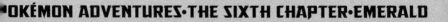

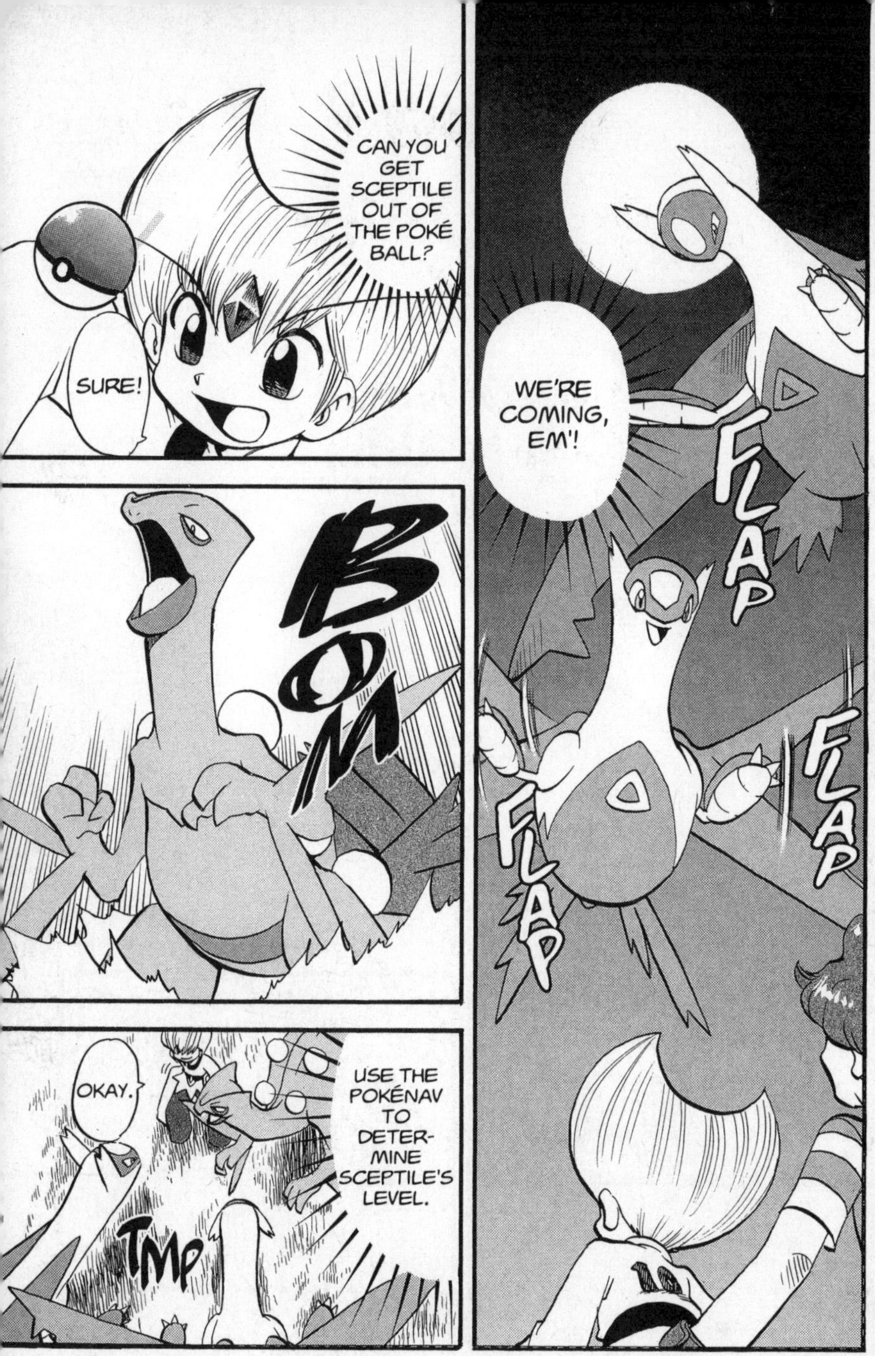
WE'RE COMING, EM'!
FLAP
FLAP
FLAP
CAN YOU GET SCEPTILE OUT OF THE POKÉ BALL?
SURE!
BOM
USE THE POKÉNAV TO DETER-MINE SCEPTILE'S LEVEL.
OKAY.
TMP

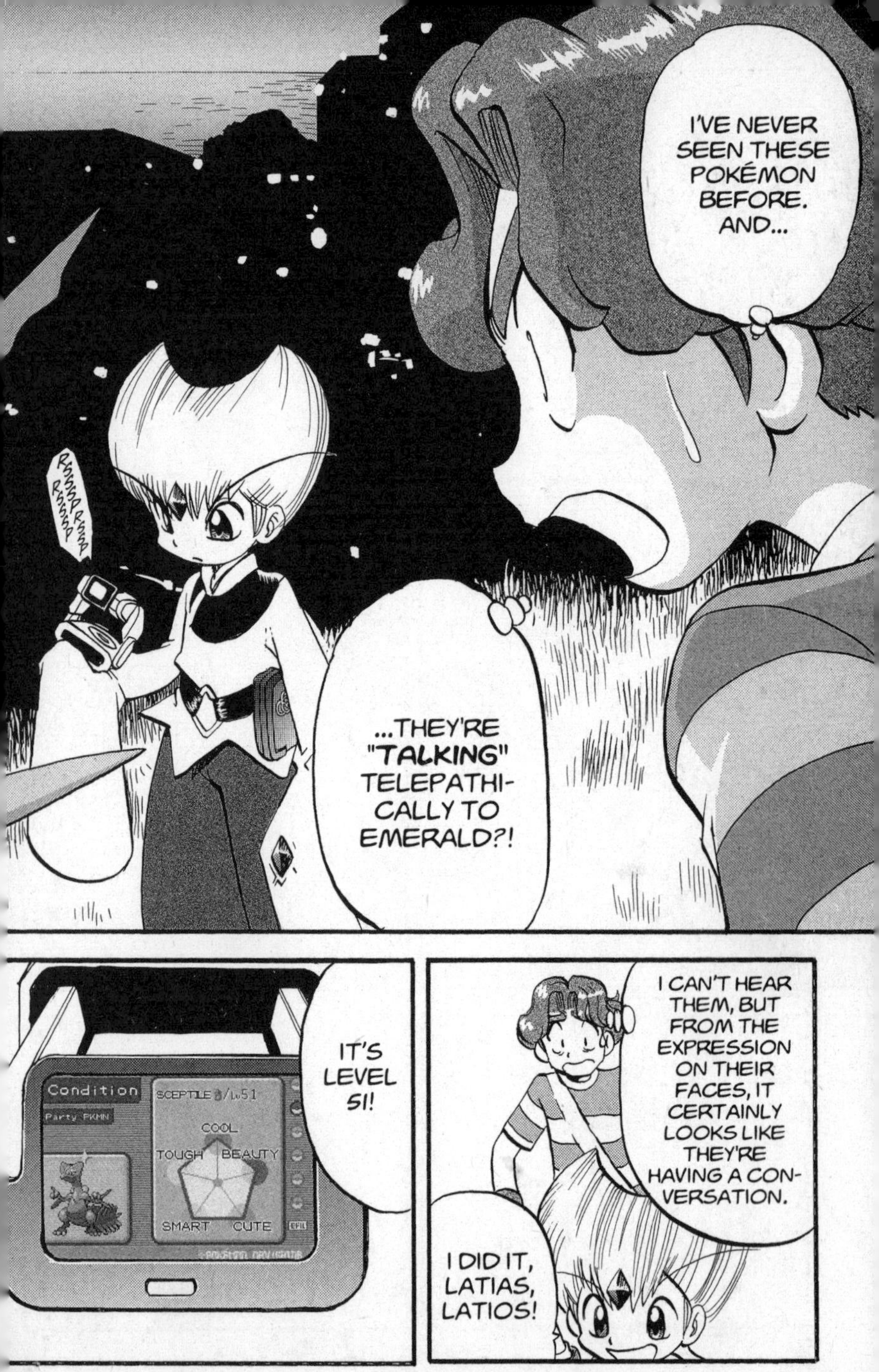
I'VE NEVER SEEN THESE POKÉMON BEFORE. AND...
RSSSP RSSSP RSSSP
...THEY'RE "**TALKING**" TELEPATHICALLY TO EMERALD?!
I CAN'T HEAR THEM, BUT FROM THE EXPRESSION ON THEIR FACES, IT CERTAINLY LOOKS LIKE THEY'RE HAVING A CONVERSATION.
I DID IT, LATIAS, LATIOS!
IT'S LEVEL 51!
Condition
Party PKMN
SCEPTILE
COOL
TOUGH
BEAUTY
SMART
CUTE

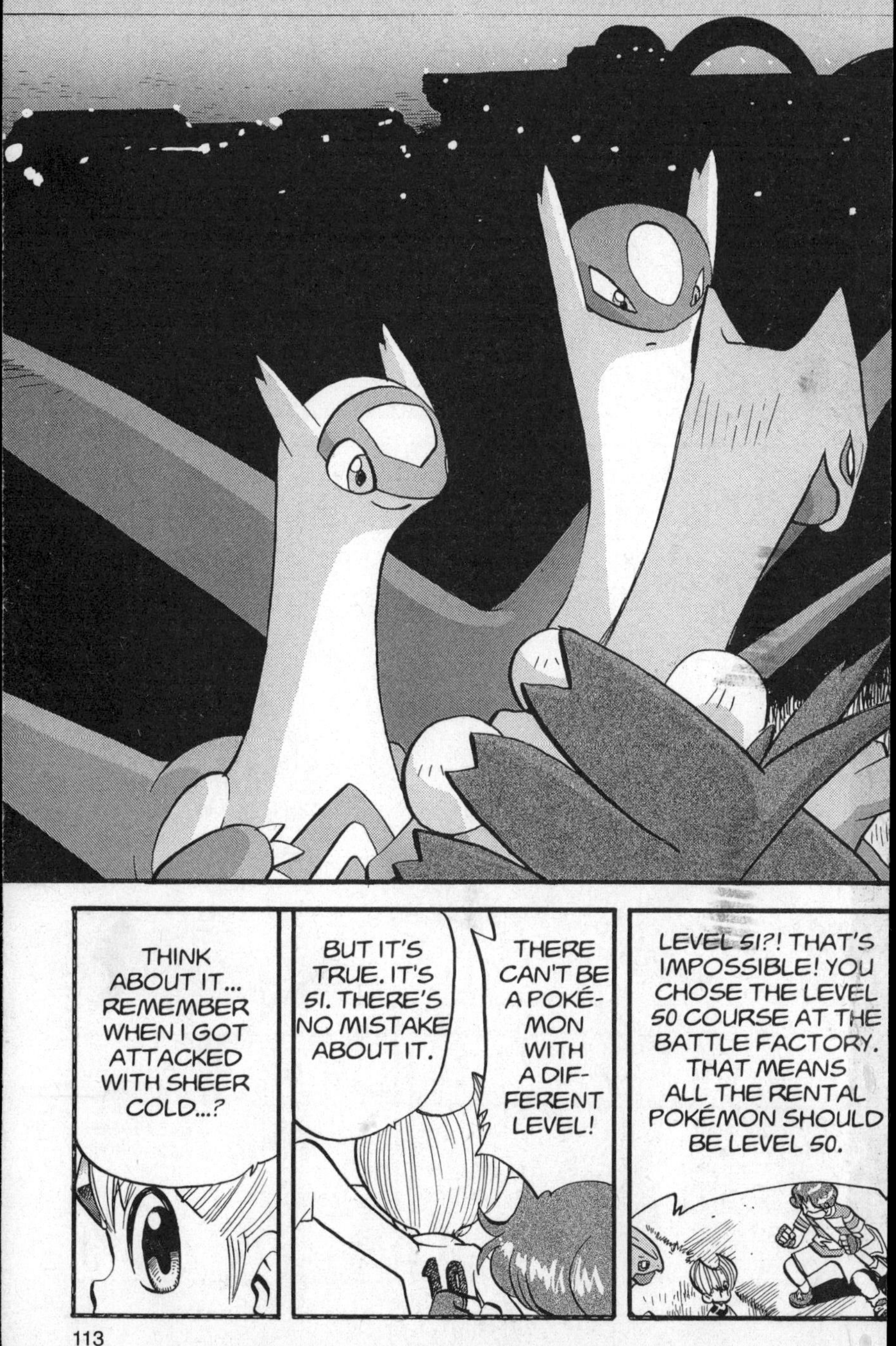
LEVEL 51?! THAT'S IMPOSSIBLE! YOU CHOSE THE LEVEL 50 COURSE AT THE BATTLE FACTORY. THAT MEANS ALL THE RENTAL POKÉMON SHOULD BE LEVEL 50.
THERE CAN'T BE A POKÉ-MON WITH A DIF-FERENT LEVEL!
BUT IT'S TRUE. IT'S 51. THERE'S NO MISTAKE ABOUT IT.
THINK ABOUT IT... REMEMBER WHEN I GOT ATTACKED WITH SHEER COLD...?

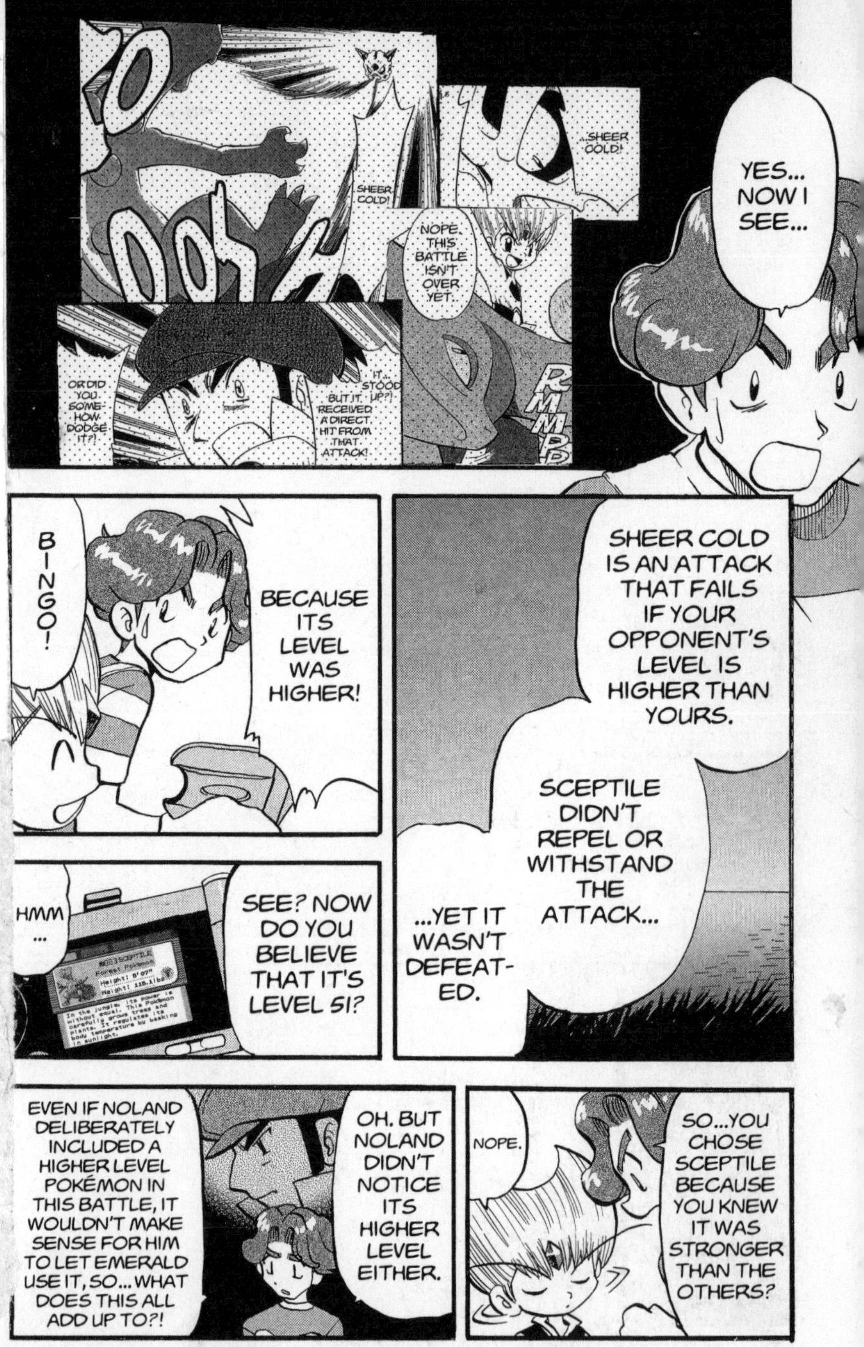
YES... NOW I SEE...
...SHEER COLD!
SHEER COLD!
NOPE. THIS BATTLE ISN'T OVER YET...
IT... STOOD UP?!
BUT IT RECEIVED A DIRECT HIT FROM THAT ATTACK!
OR DID YOU SOMEHOW DODGE IT?!
RMMB
SHEER COLD IS AN ATTACK THAT FAILS IF YOUR OPPONENT'S LEVEL IS HIGHER THAN YOURS.
SCEPTILE DIDN'T REPEL OR WITHSTAND THE ATTACK...
...YET IT WASN'T DEFEAT-ED.
BECAUSE ITS LEVEL WAS HIGHER!
BINGO!
SEE? NOW DO YOU BELIEVE THAT IT'S LEVEL 51?
HMM...
SO...YOU CHOSE SCEPTILE BECAUSE YOU KNEW IT WAS STRONGER THAN THE OTHERS?
NOPE.
OH. BUT NOLAND DIDN'T NOTICE ITS HIGHER LEVEL EITHER.
EVEN IF NOLAND DELIBERATELY INCLUDED A HIGHER LEVEL POKÉMON IN THIS BATTLE, IT WOULDN'T MAKE SENSE FOR HIM TO LET EMERALD USE IT, SO... WHAT DOES THIS ALL ADD UP TO?!

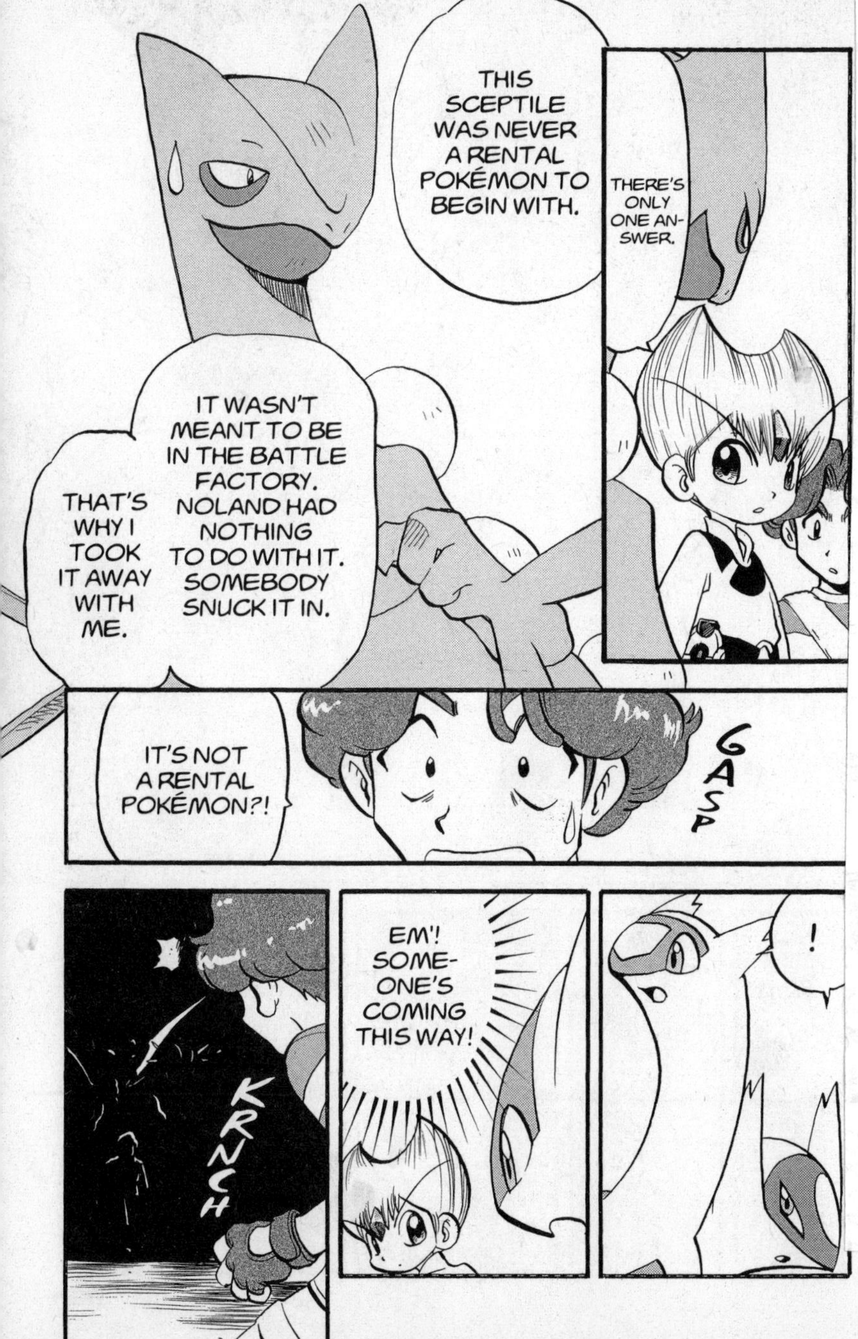
THERE'S ONLY ONE AN-SWER.
THIS SCEPTILE WAS NEVER A RENTAL POKÉMON TO BEGIN WITH.
IT WASN'T MEANT TO BE IN THE BATTLE FACTORY. NOLAND HAD NOTHING TO DO WITH IT. SOMEBODY SNUCK IT IN.
THAT'S WHY I TOOK IT AWAY WITH ME.
GASP
IT'S NOT A RENTAL POKÉMON?!
!
EM'! SOME-ONE'S COMING THIS WAY!
KRNCH

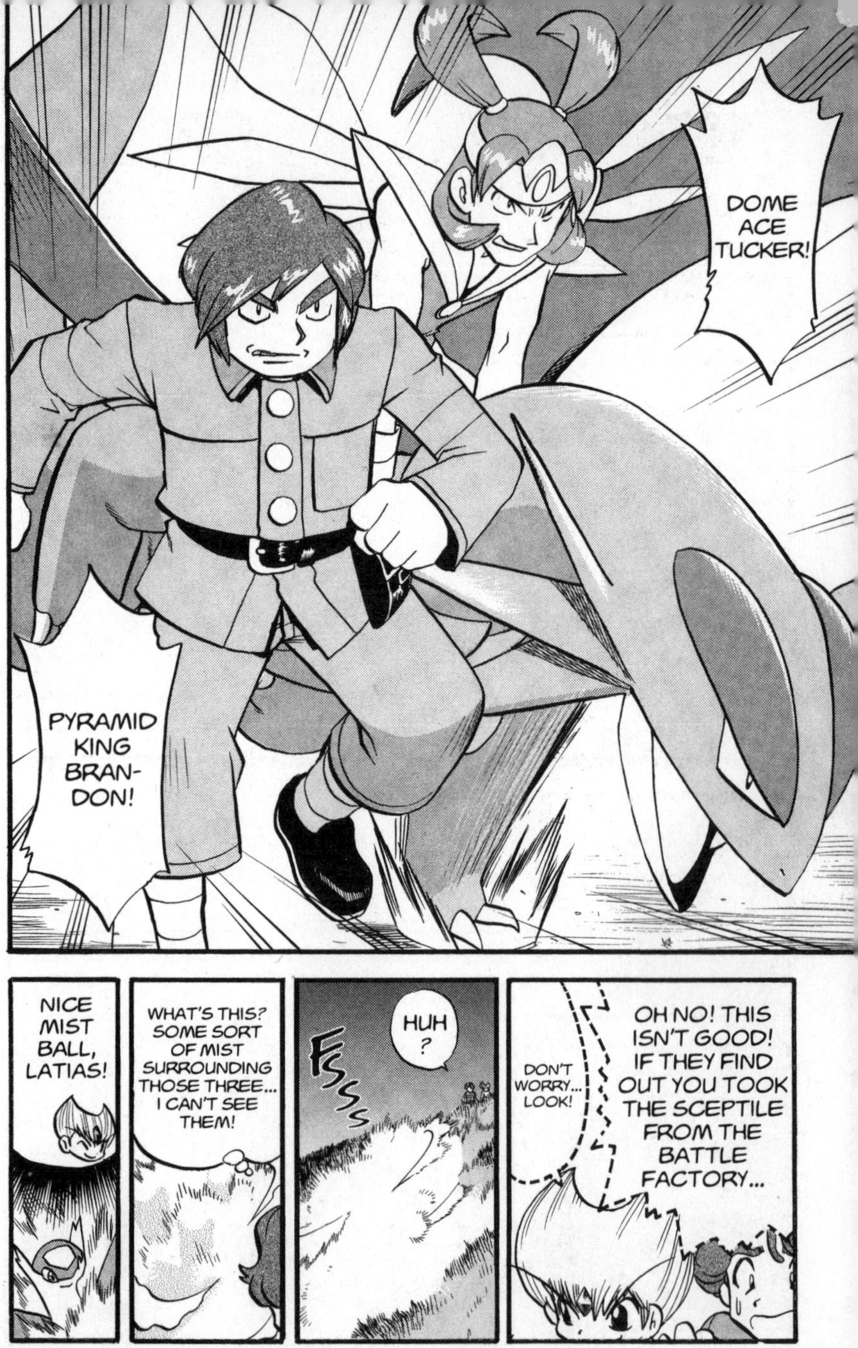
DOME ACE TUCKER!
PYRAMID KING BRAN-DON!
OH NO! THIS ISN'T GOOD! IF THEY FIND OUT YOU TOOK THE SCEPTILE FROM THE BATTLE FACTORY...
DON'T WORRY... LOOK!
HUH?
FSSS
WHAT'S THIS? SOME SORT OF MIST SURROUNDING THOSE THREE... I CAN'T SEE THEM!
NICE MIST BALL, LATIAS!

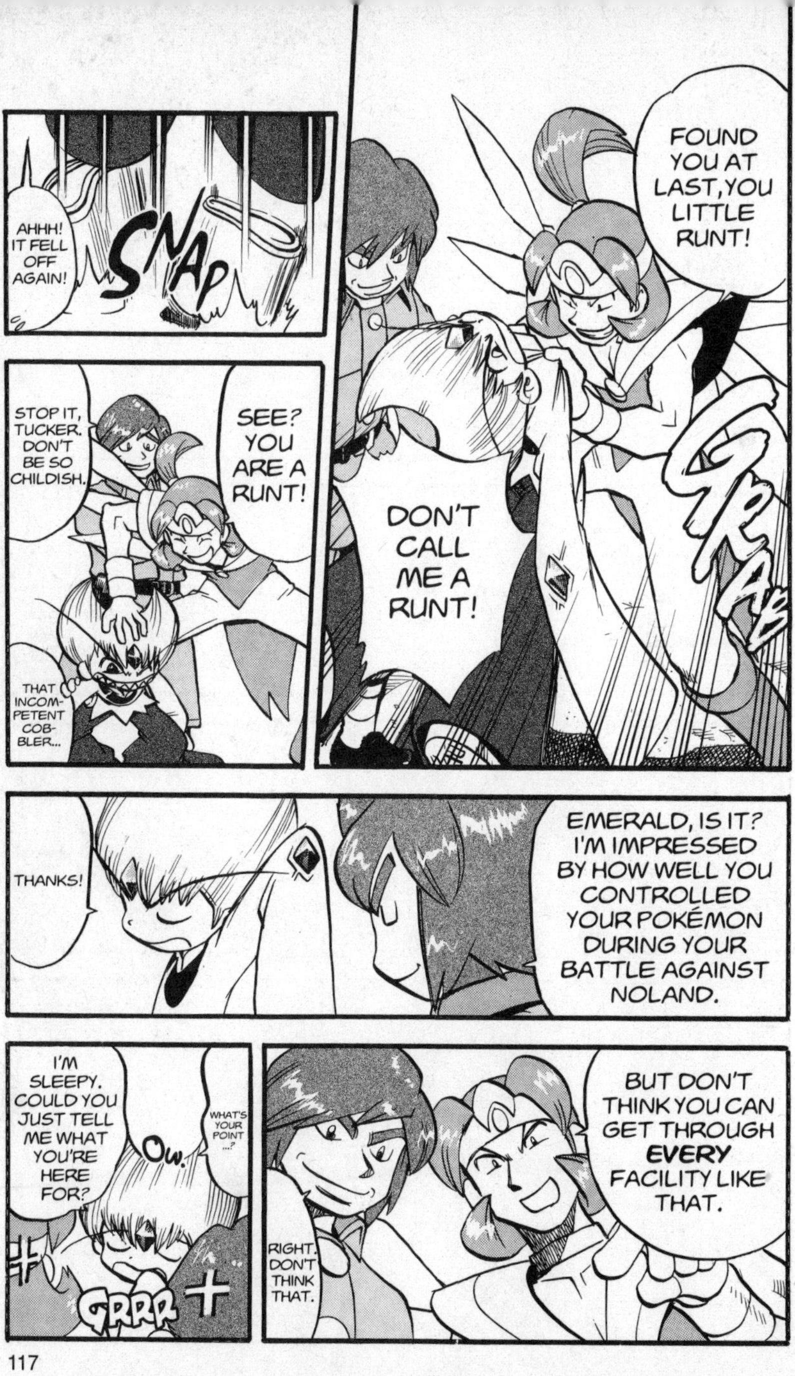

FOUND YOU AT LAST, YOU LITTLE RUNT!
DON'T CALL ME A RUNT!
AHHH! IT FELL OFF AGAIN!
SNAP
SEE? YOU ARE A RUNT!
STOP IT, TUCKER. DON'T BE SO CHILDISH.
THAT INCOMPETENT COBBLER...
EMERALD, IS IT? I'M IMPRESSED BY HOW WELL YOU CONTROLLED YOUR POKéMON DURING YOUR BATTLE AGAINST NOLAND.
THANKS!
BUT DON'T THINK YOU CAN GET THROUGH **EVERY** FACILITY LIKE THAT.
RIGHT. DON'T THINK THAT.
WHAT'S YOUR POINT ...?
OW.
I'M SLEEPY. COULD YOU JUST TELL ME WHAT YOU'RE HERE FOR?
GRRR

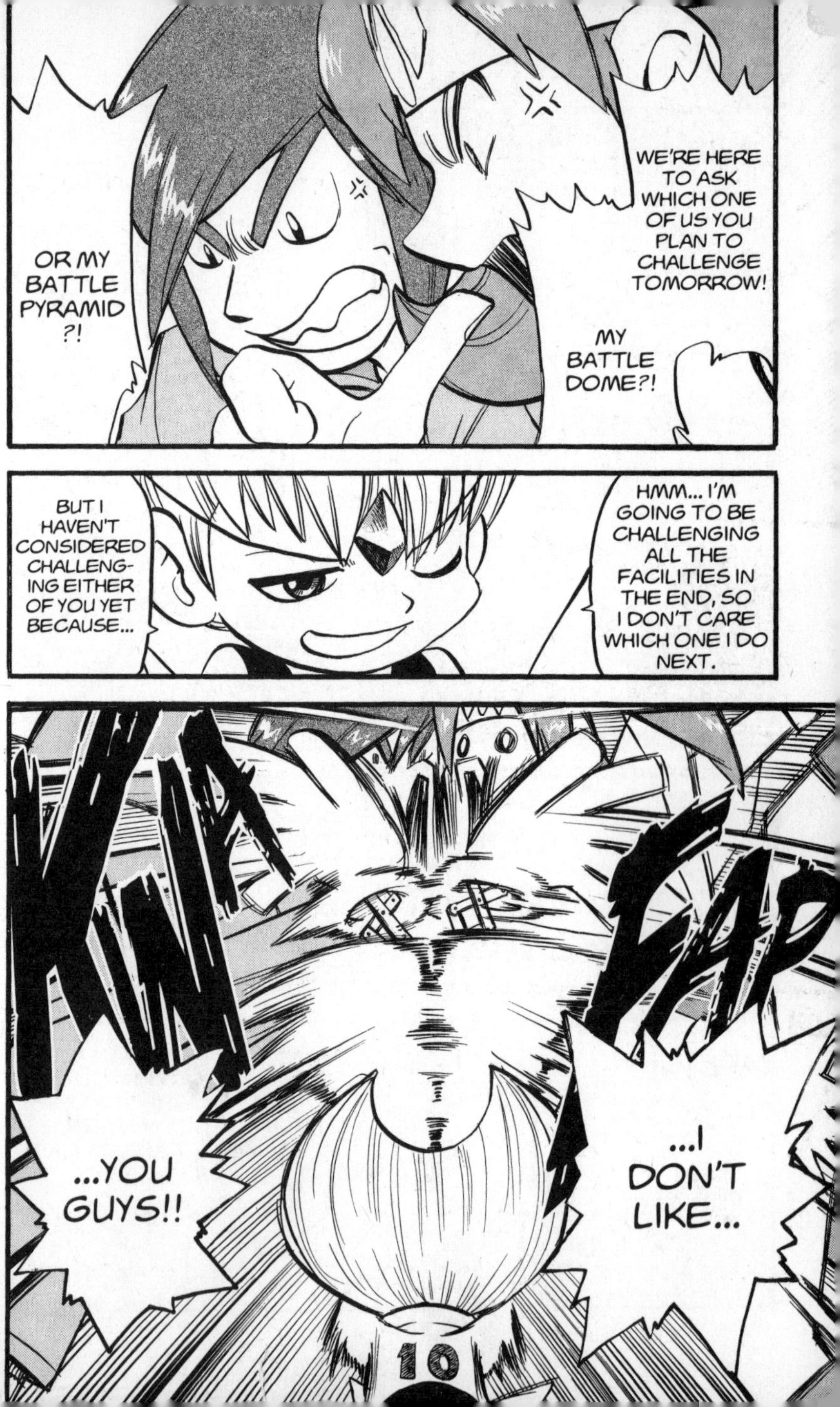
WE'RE HERE TO ASK WHICH ONE OF US YOU PLAN TO CHALLENGE TOMORROW!
MY BATTLE DOME?!
OR MY BATTLE PYRAMID ?!
HMM... I'M GOING TO BE CHALLENGING ALL THE FACILITIES IN THE END, SO I DON'T CARE WHICH ONE I DO NEXT.
BUT I HAVEN'T CONSIDERED CHALLENG-ING EITHER OF YOU YET BECAUSE...
...I DON'T LIKE...
...YOU GUYS!!
10

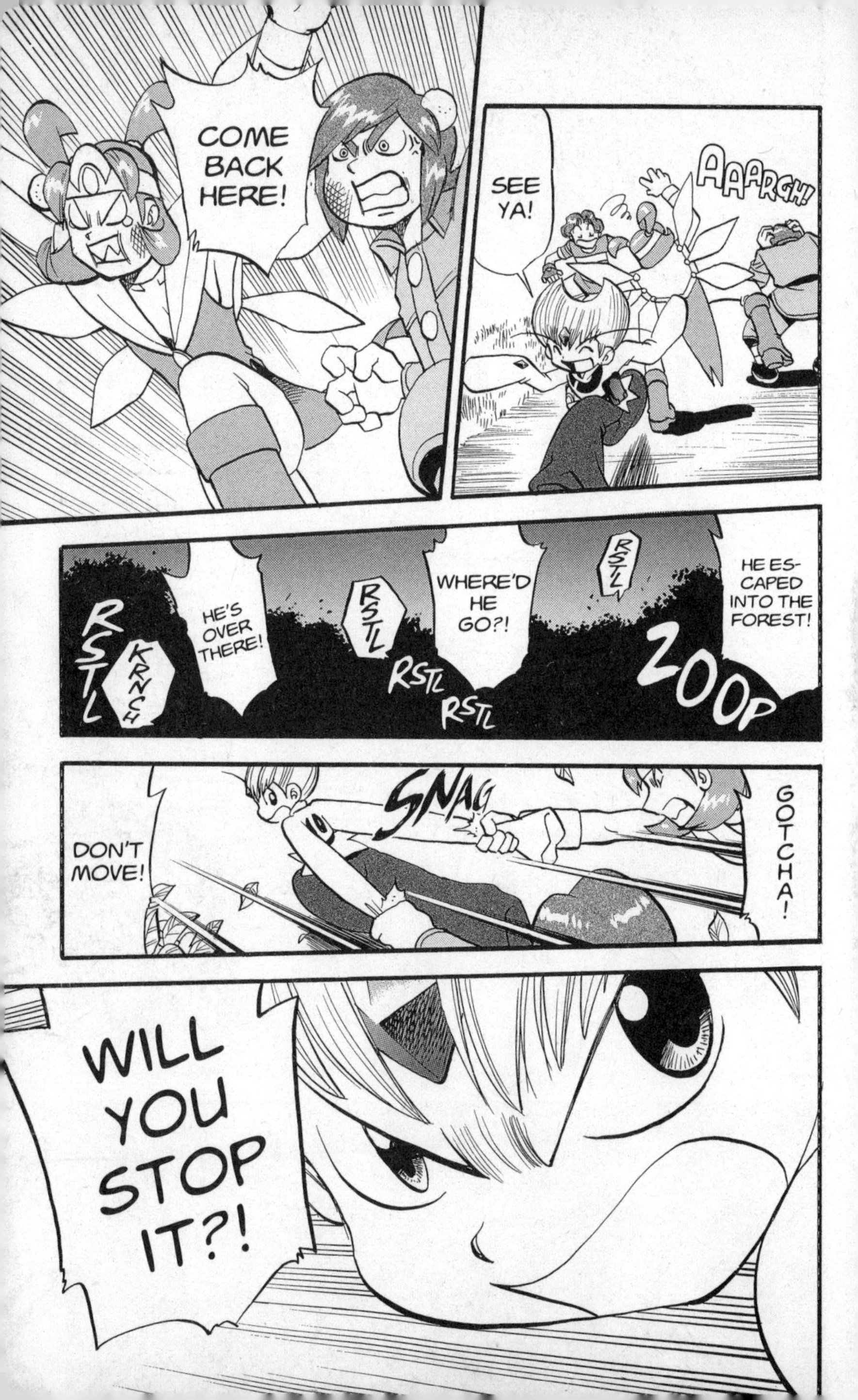
AAARGH!
SEE YA!
COME BACK HERE!
HE ES-CAPED INTO THE FOREST!
ZOOP
RSTL
WHERE'D HE GO?!
RSTL
RSTL
RSTL
HE'S OVER THERE!
RSTL
KRNCH
GOTCHA!
SNAG
DON'T MOVE!
WILL YOU STOP IT?!

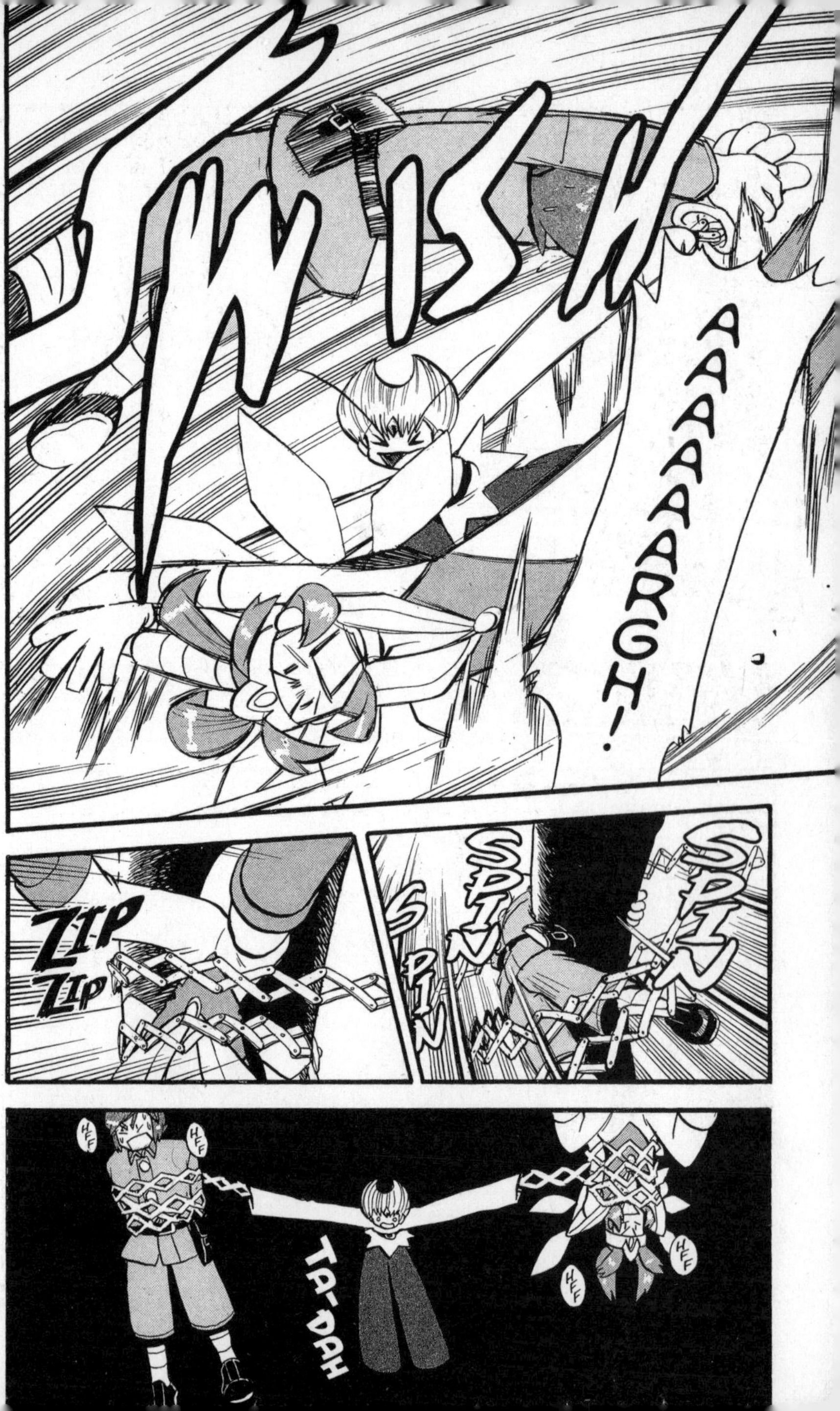
SWISH
AAAAAARGH!
SPIN SPIN
SPIN SPIN
ZIP ZIP
HFF HFF
TA-DAH
HFF HFF

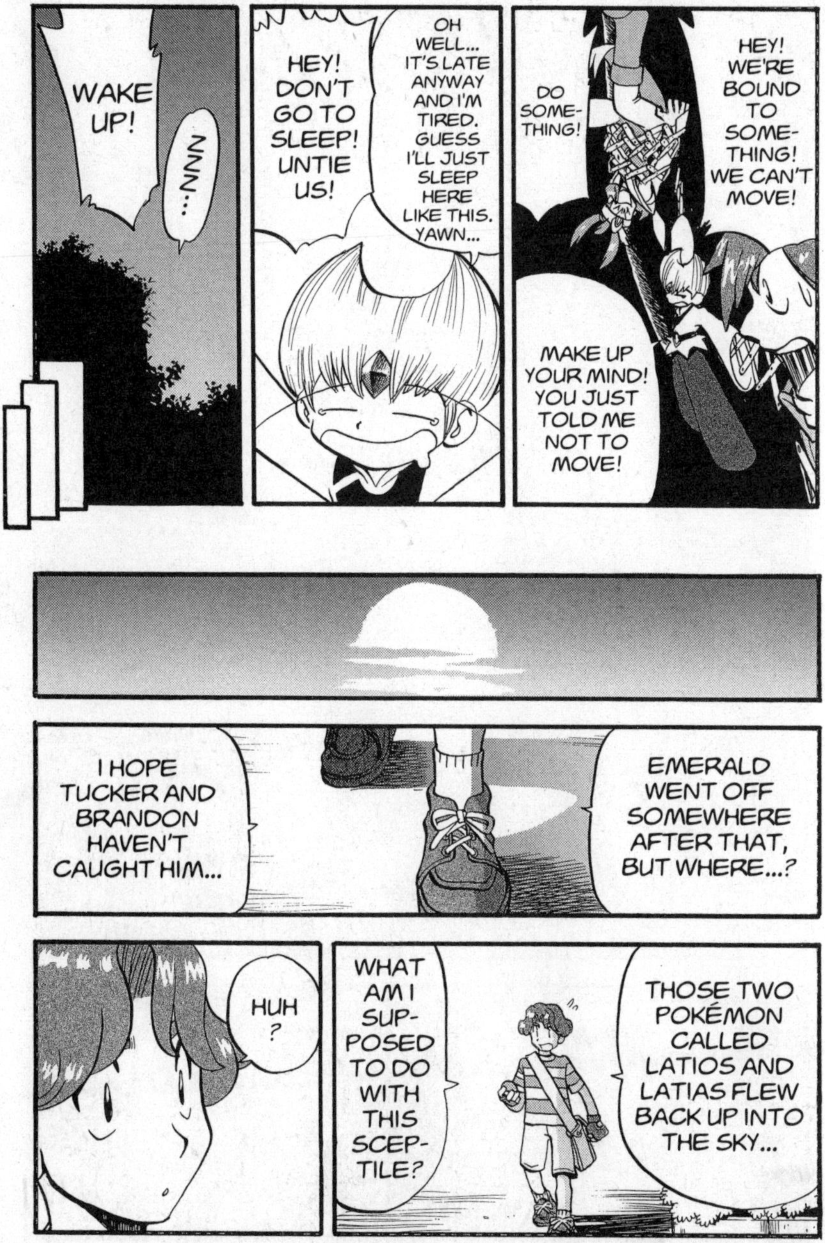
HEY! WE'RE BOUND TO SOME-THING! WE CAN'T MOVE!
DO SOME-THING!
MAKE UP YOUR MIND! YOU JUST TOLD ME NOT TO MOVE!
OH WELL... IT'S LATE ANYWAY AND I'M TIRED. GUESS I'LL JUST SLEEP HERE LIKE THIS. YAWN...
HEY! DON'T GO TO SLEEP! UNTIE US!
WAKE UP!
ZZZ...
EMERALD WENT OFF SOMEWHERE AFTER THAT, BUT WHERE...?
I HOPE TUCKER AND BRANDON HAVEN'T CAUGHT HIM...
THOSE TWO POKÉMON CALLED LATIOS AND LATIAS FLEW BACK UP INTO THE SKY...
WHAT AM I SUP-POSED TO DO WITH THIS SCEP-TILE?
HUH ?

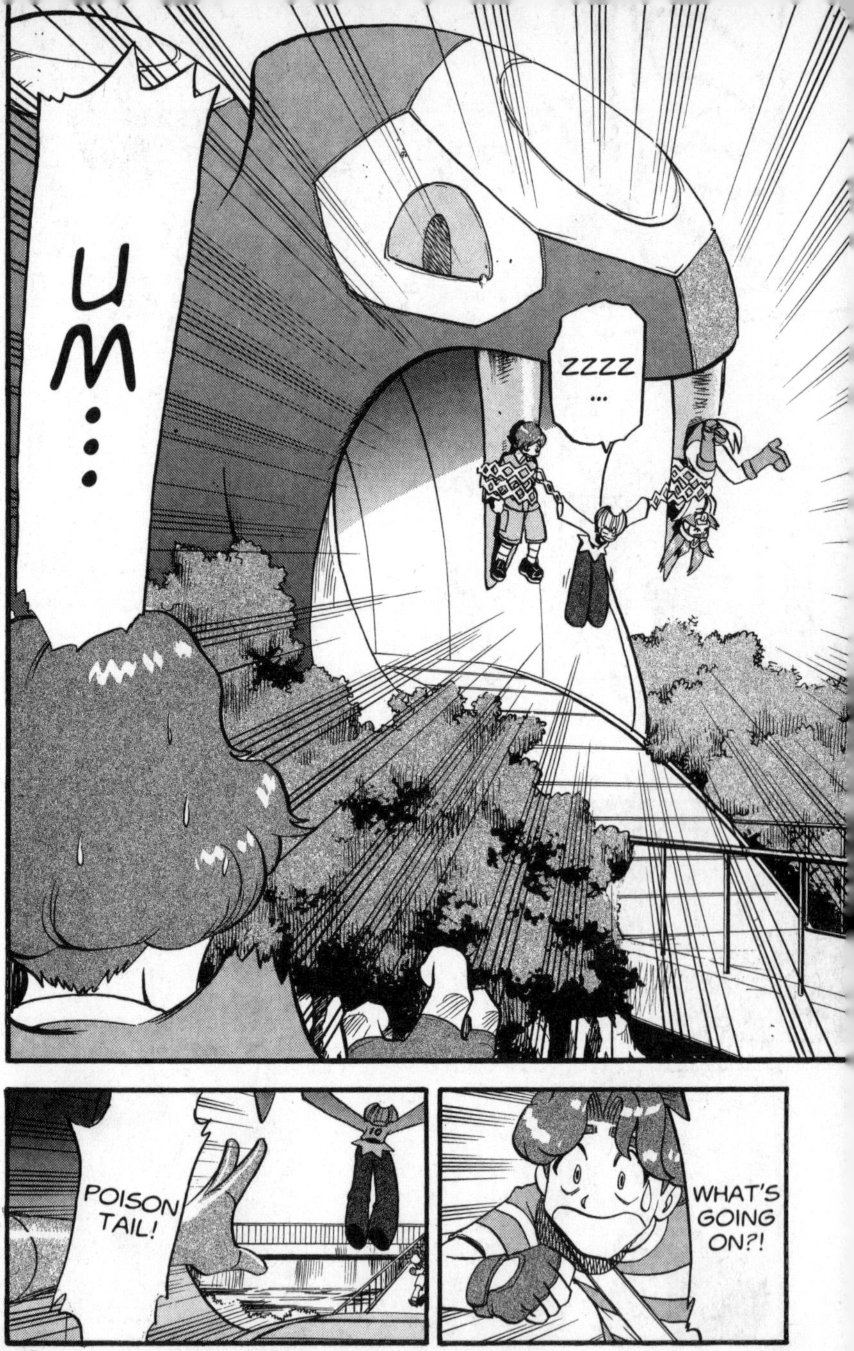
ZZZZ ...
UM...
WHAT'S GOING ON?!
POISON TAIL!

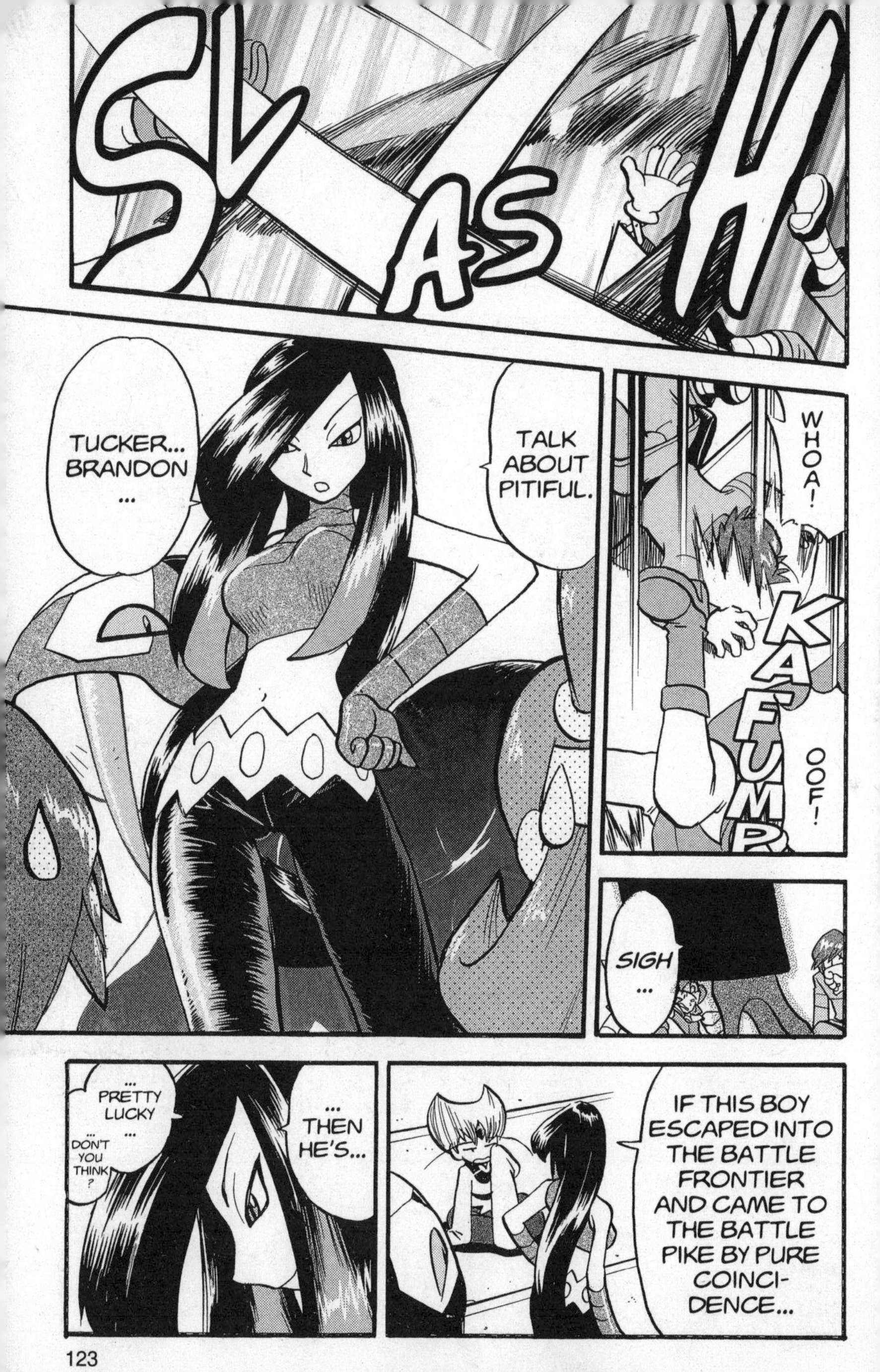
SLASH
WHOA!
OOF!
KAFUMP
SIGH...
TALK ABOUT PITIFUL.
TUCKER... BRANDON...
IF THIS BOY ESCAPED INTO THE BATTLE FRONTIER AND CAME TO THE BATTLE PIKE BY PURE COINCI-DENCE...
...THEN HE'S...
...PRETTY LUCKY...
...DON'T YOU THINK?

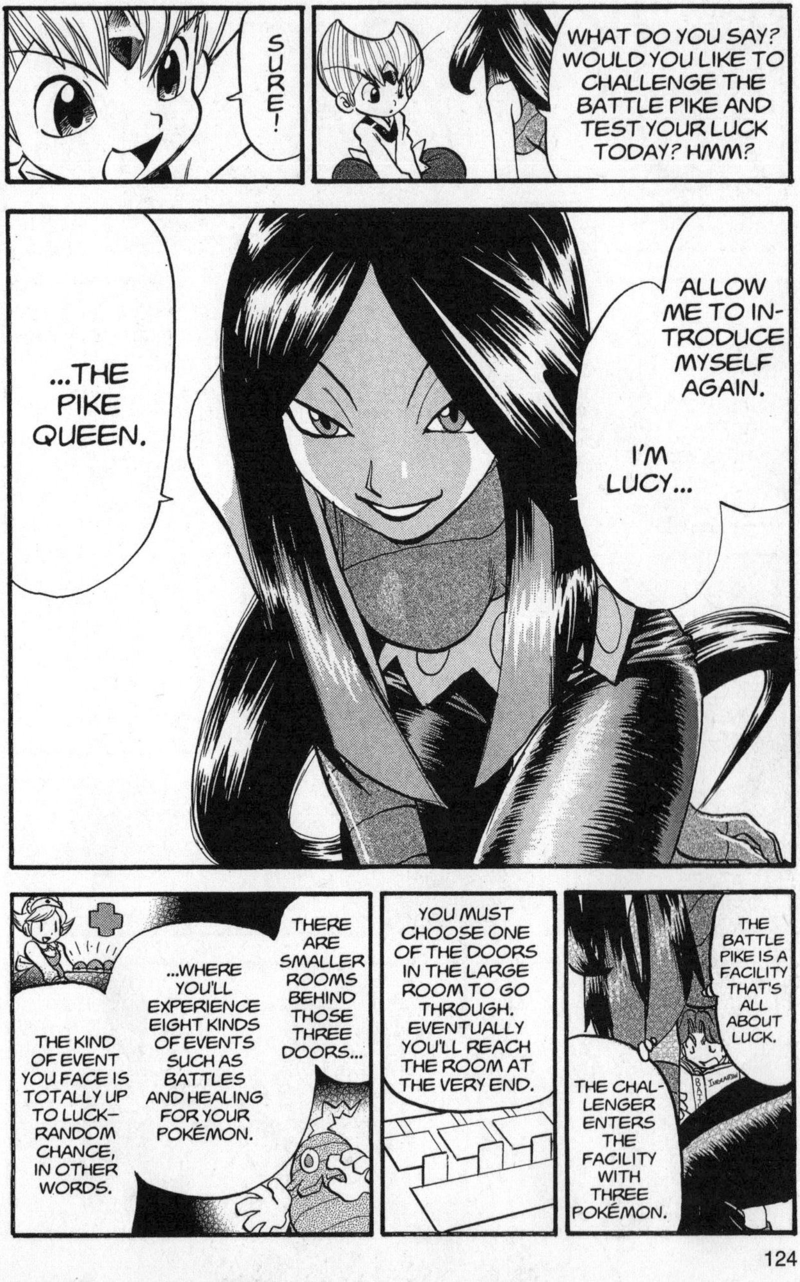
WHAT DO YOU SAY? WOULD YOU LIKE TO CHALLENGE THE BATTLE PIKE AND TEST YOUR LUCK TODAY? HMM?
SURE!
ALLOW ME TO INTRODUCE MYSELF AGAIN.
I'M LUCY...
...THE PIKE QUEEN.
THE BATTLE PIKE IS A FACILITY THAT'S ALL ABOUT LUCK.
THE CHALLENGER ENTERS THE FACILITY WITH THREE POKÉMON.
YOU MUST CHOOSE ONE OF THE DOORS IN THE LARGE ROOM TO GO THROUGH. EVENTUALLY YOU'LL REACH THE ROOM AT THE VERY END.
THERE ARE SMALLER ROOMS BEHIND THOSE THREE DOORS...
...WHERE YOU'LL EXPERIENCE EIGHT KINDS OF EVENTS SUCH AS BATTLES AND HEALING FOR YOUR POKÉMON.
THE KIND OF EVENT YOU FACE IS TOTALLY UP TO LUCK—RANDOM CHANCE, IN OTHER WORDS.

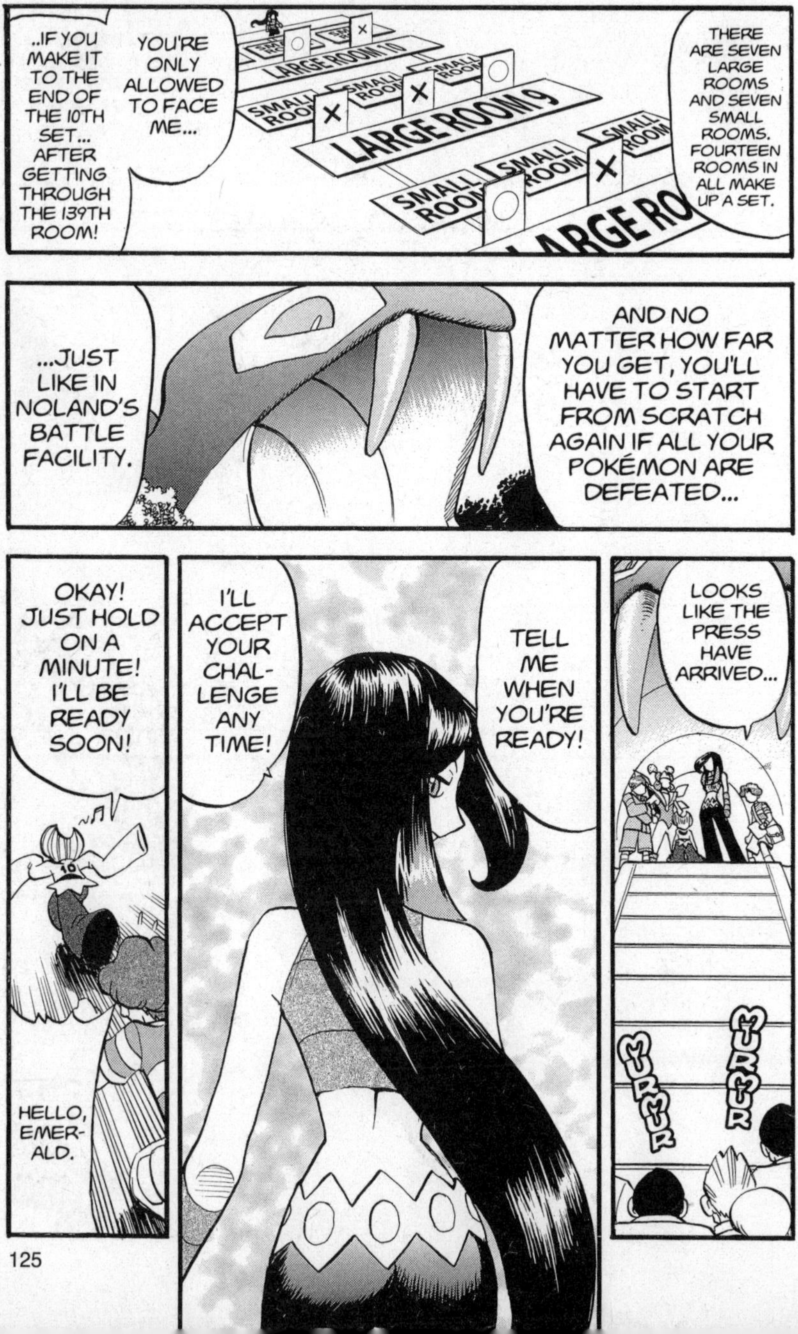
THERE ARE SEVEN LARGE ROOMS AND SEVEN SMALL ROOMS. FOURTEEN ROOMS IN ALL MAKE UP A SET.
LARGE ROOM 10
SMALL ROOM
LARGE ROOM 9
SMALL ROOM
SMALL ROOM
SMALL ROOM
YOU'RE ONLY ALLOWED TO FACE ME...
..IF YOU MAKE IT TO THE END OF THE 10TH SET... AFTER GETTING THROUGH THE 139TH ROOM!
AND NO MATTER HOW FAR YOU GET, YOU'LL HAVE TO START FROM SCRATCH AGAIN IF ALL YOUR POKÉMON ARE DEFEATED...
...JUST LIKE IN NOLAND'S BATTLE FACILITY.
LOOKS LIKE THE PRESS HAVE ARRIVED...
MURMUR
MURMUR
TELL ME WHEN YOU'RE READY!
I'LL ACCEPT YOUR CHAL-LENGE ANY TIME!
OKAY! JUST HOLD ON A MINUTE! I'LL BE READY SOON!
HELLO, EMER-ALD.

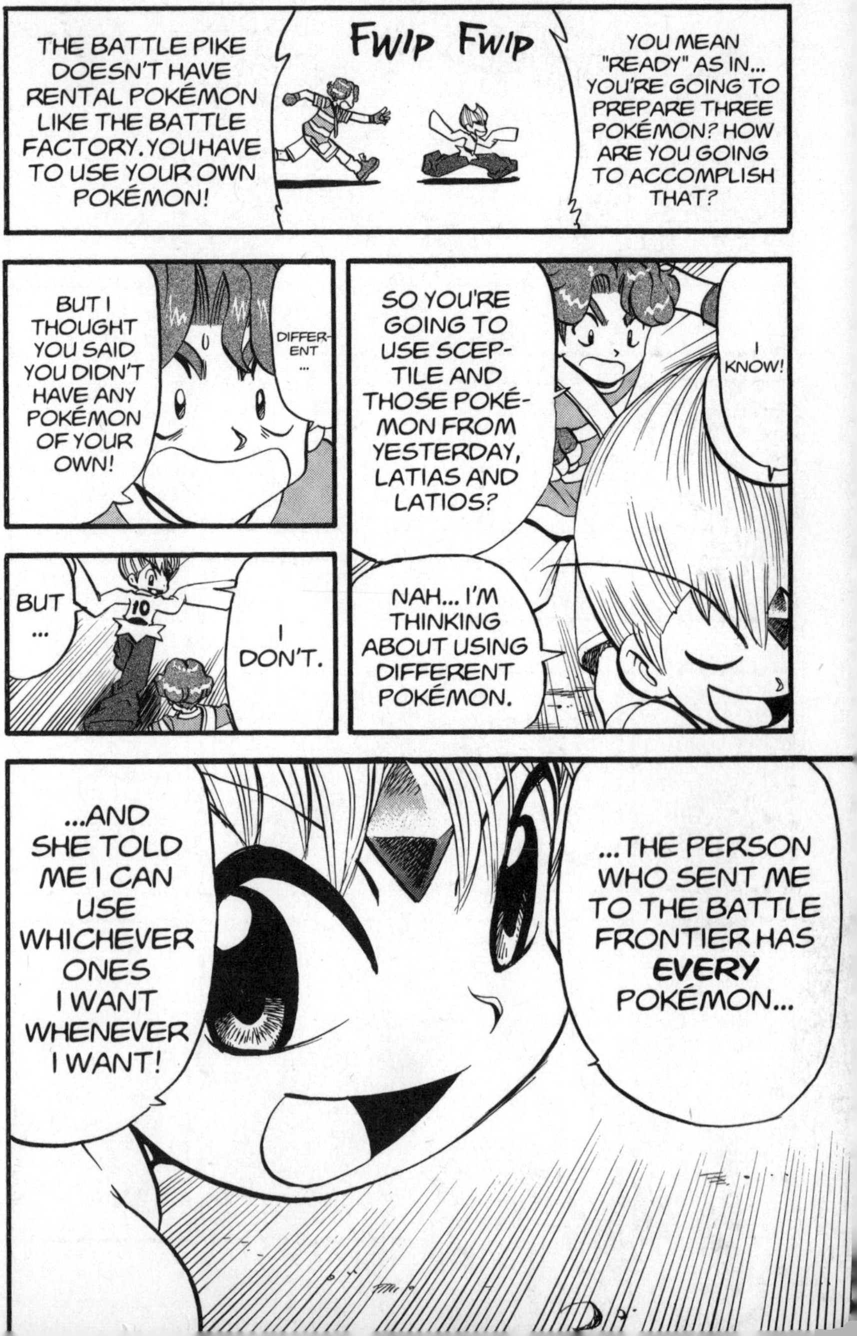
YOU MEAN "READY" AS IN... YOU'RE GOING TO PREPARE THREE POKÉMON? HOW ARE YOU GOING TO ACCOMPLISH THAT?
FWIP FWIP
THE BATTLE PIKE DOESN'T HAVE RENTAL POKÉMON LIKE THE BATTLE FACTORY. YOU HAVE TO USE YOUR OWN POKÉMON!
I KNOW!
SO YOU'RE GOING TO USE SCEP-TILE AND THOSE POKÉ-MON FROM YESTERDAY, LATIAS AND LATIOS?
NAH... I'M THINKING ABOUT USING DIFFERENT POKÉMON.
DIFFER-ENT ...
BUT I THOUGHT YOU SAID YOU DIDN'T HAVE ANY POKÉMON OF YOUR OWN!
I DON'T.
BUT ...
...THE PERSON WHO SENT ME TO THE BATTLE FRONTIER HAS **EVERY** POKÉMON...
...AND SHE TOLD ME I CAN USE WHICHEVER ONES I WANT WHENEVER I WANT!

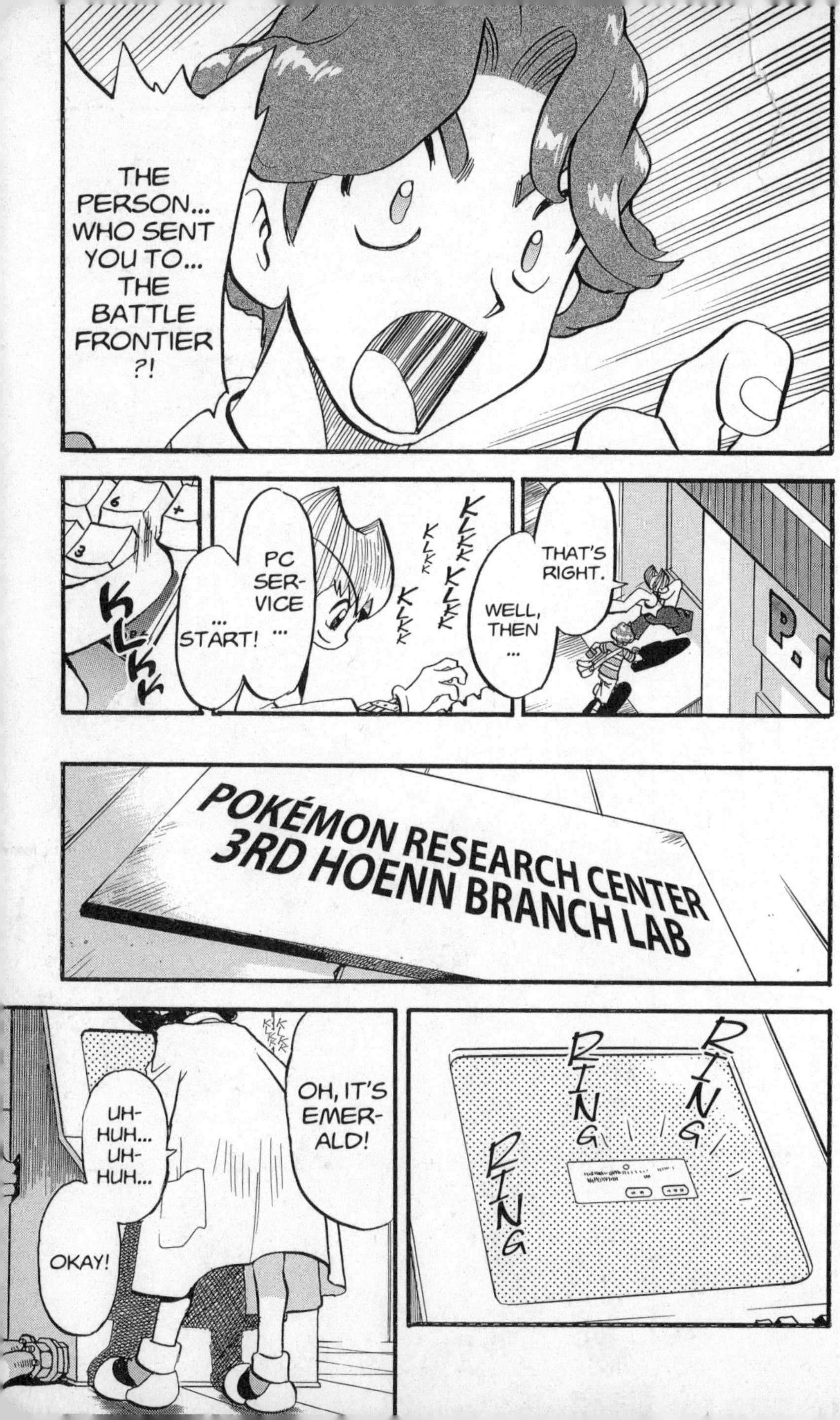
THE PERSON... WHO SENT YOU TO... THE BATTLE FRONTIER ?!
THAT'S RIGHT.
WELL, THEN ...
KLKK KLKK
KLKK KLKK
PC SER-VICE ... ... START!
KLKK
POKÉMON RESEARCH CENTER 3RD HOENN BRANCH LAB
RING
RING
RING
OH, IT'S EMER-ALD!
UH-HUH... UH-HUH...
OKAY!

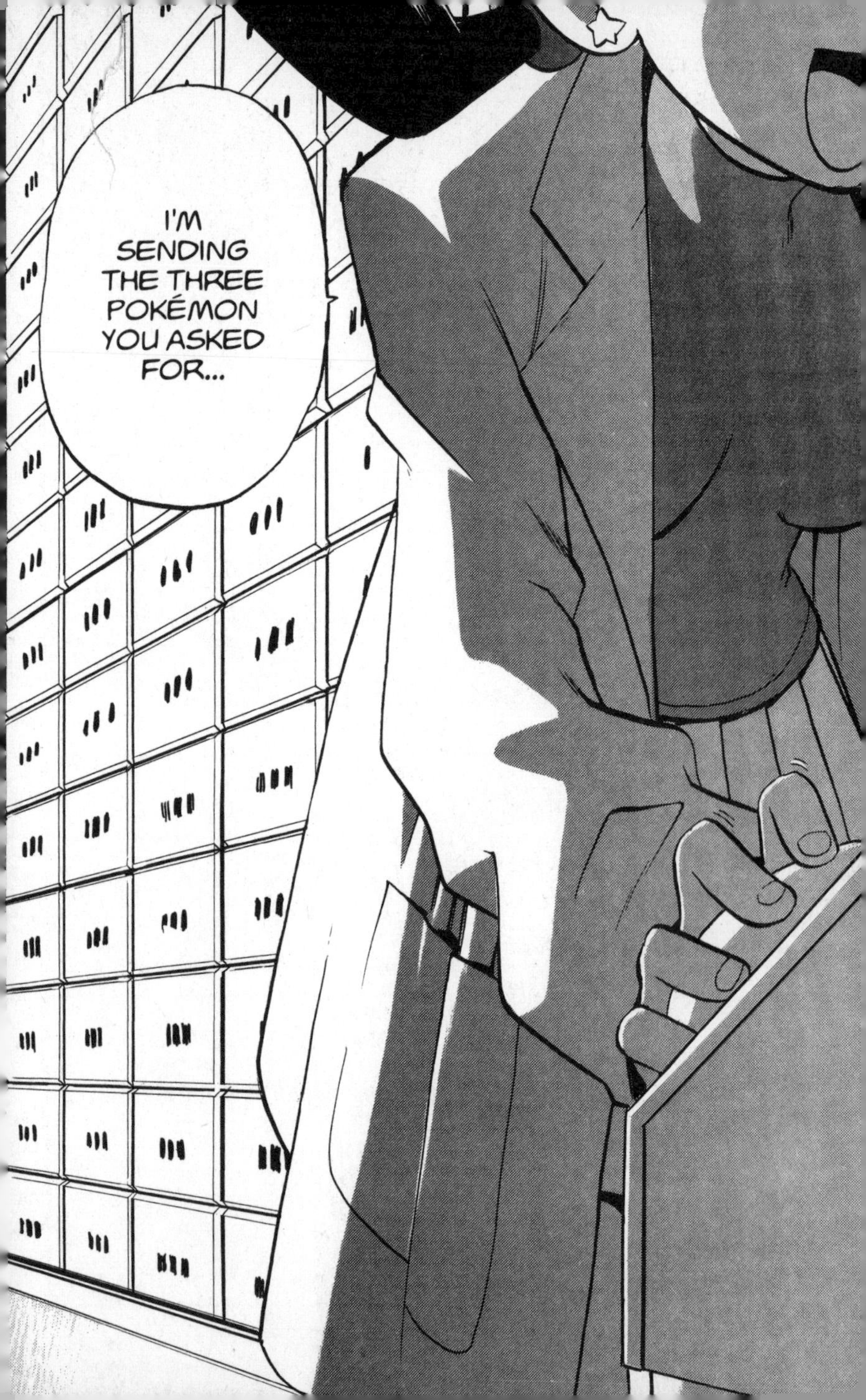
I'M SENDING THE THREE POKÉMON YOU ASKED FOR...

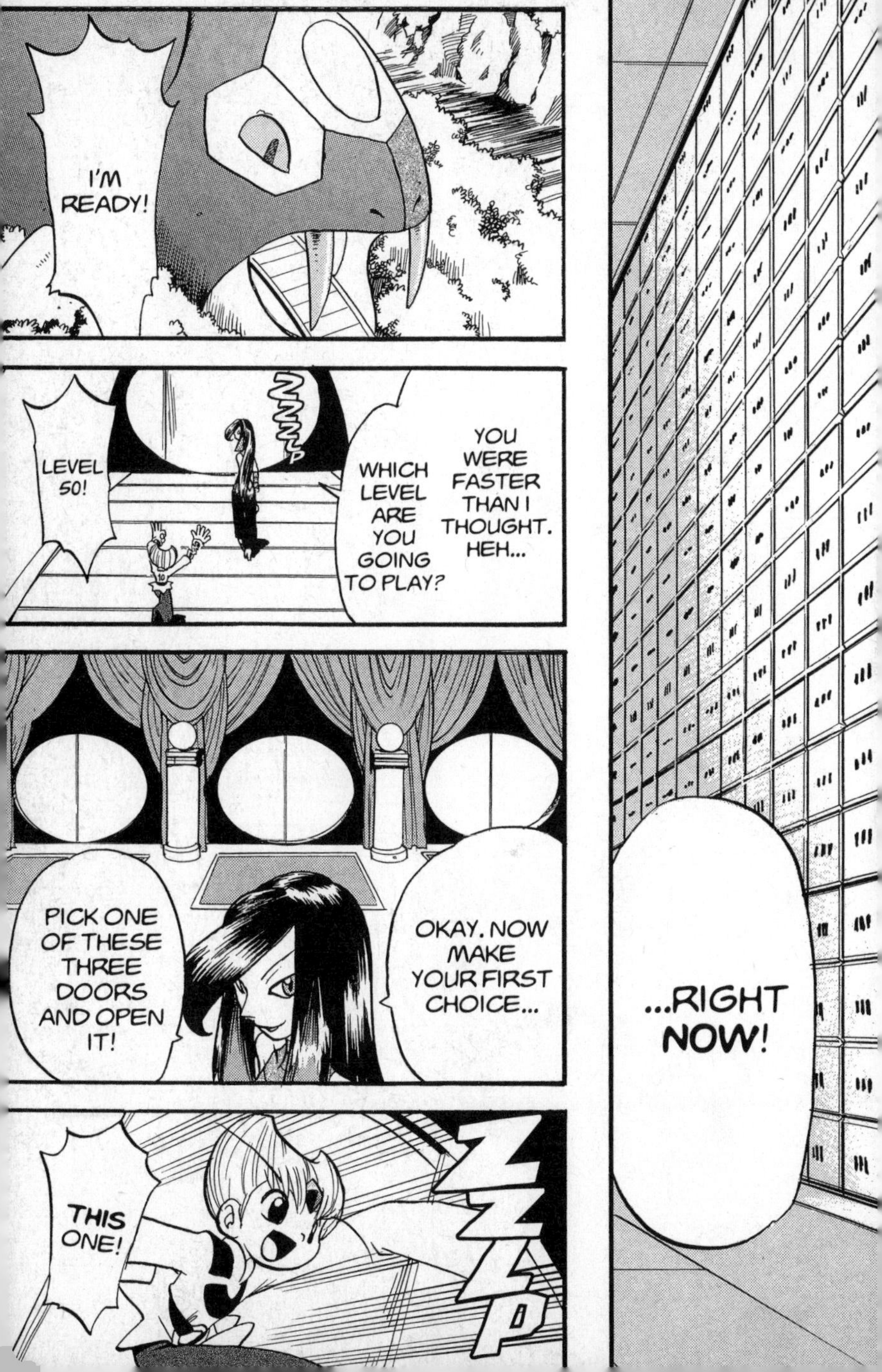
...RIGHT NOW!
I'M READY!
YOU WERE FASTER THAN I THOUGHT. HEH...
WHICH LEVEL ARE YOU GOING TO PLAY?
ZZZZP
LEVEL 50!
OKAY. NOW MAKE YOUR FIRST CHOICE...
PICK ONE OF THESE THREE DOORS AND OPEN IT!
ZZZP
THIS ONE!

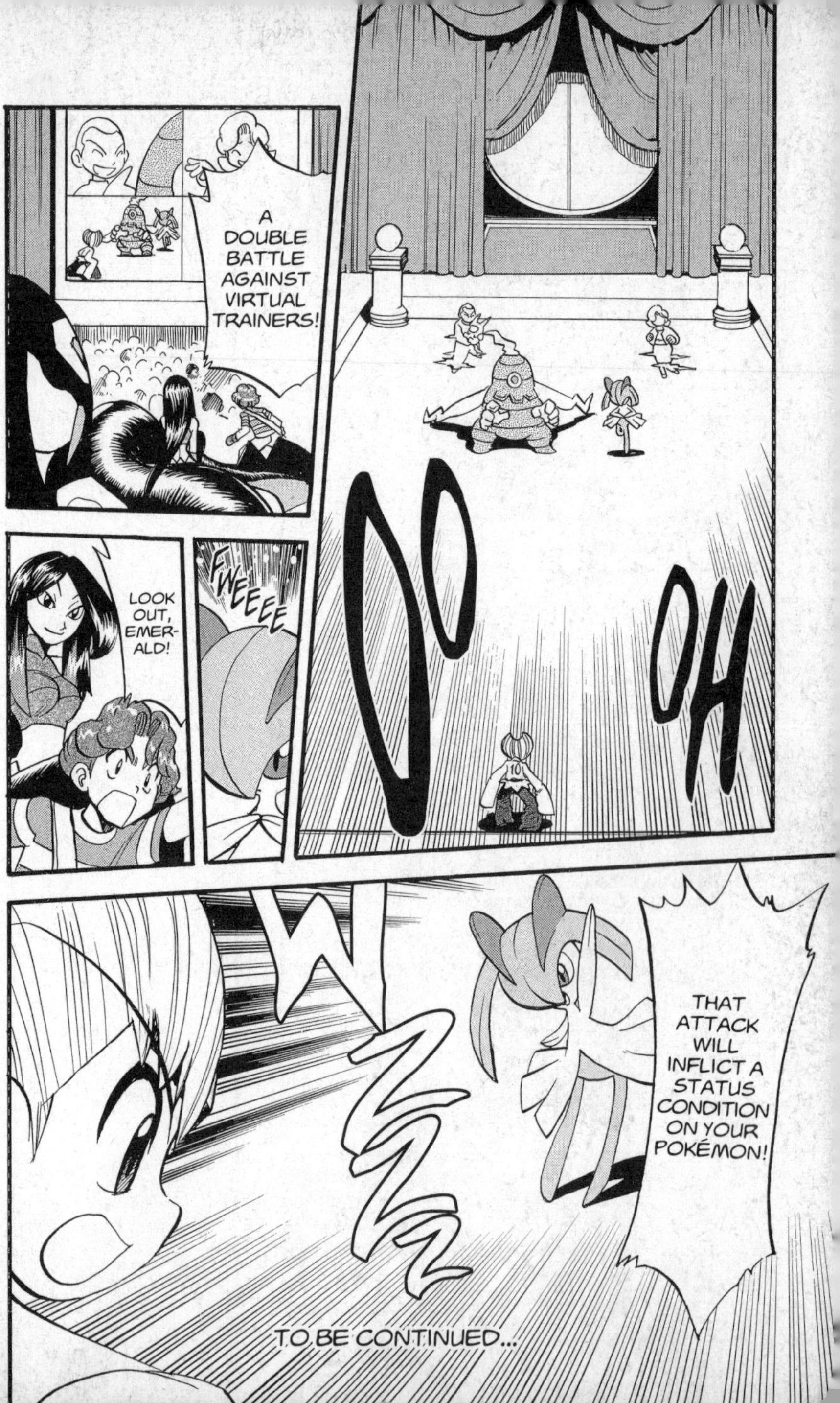
A DOUBLE BATTLE AGAINST VIRTUAL TRAINERS!
FWEEEE
LOOK OUT, EMER-ALD!
THAT ATTACK WILL INFLICT A STATUS CONDITION ON YOUR POKÉMON!
TO BE CONTINUED...

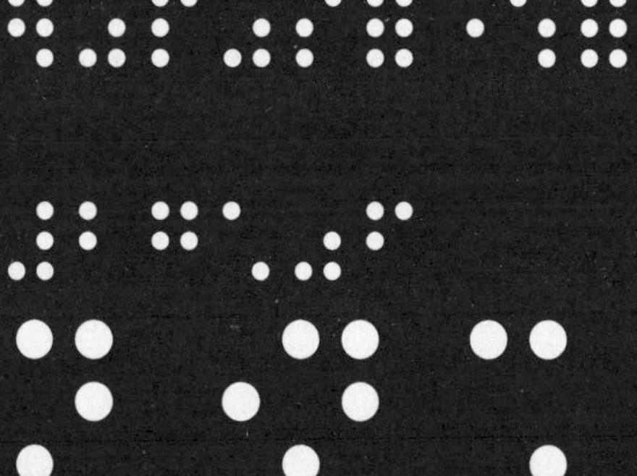

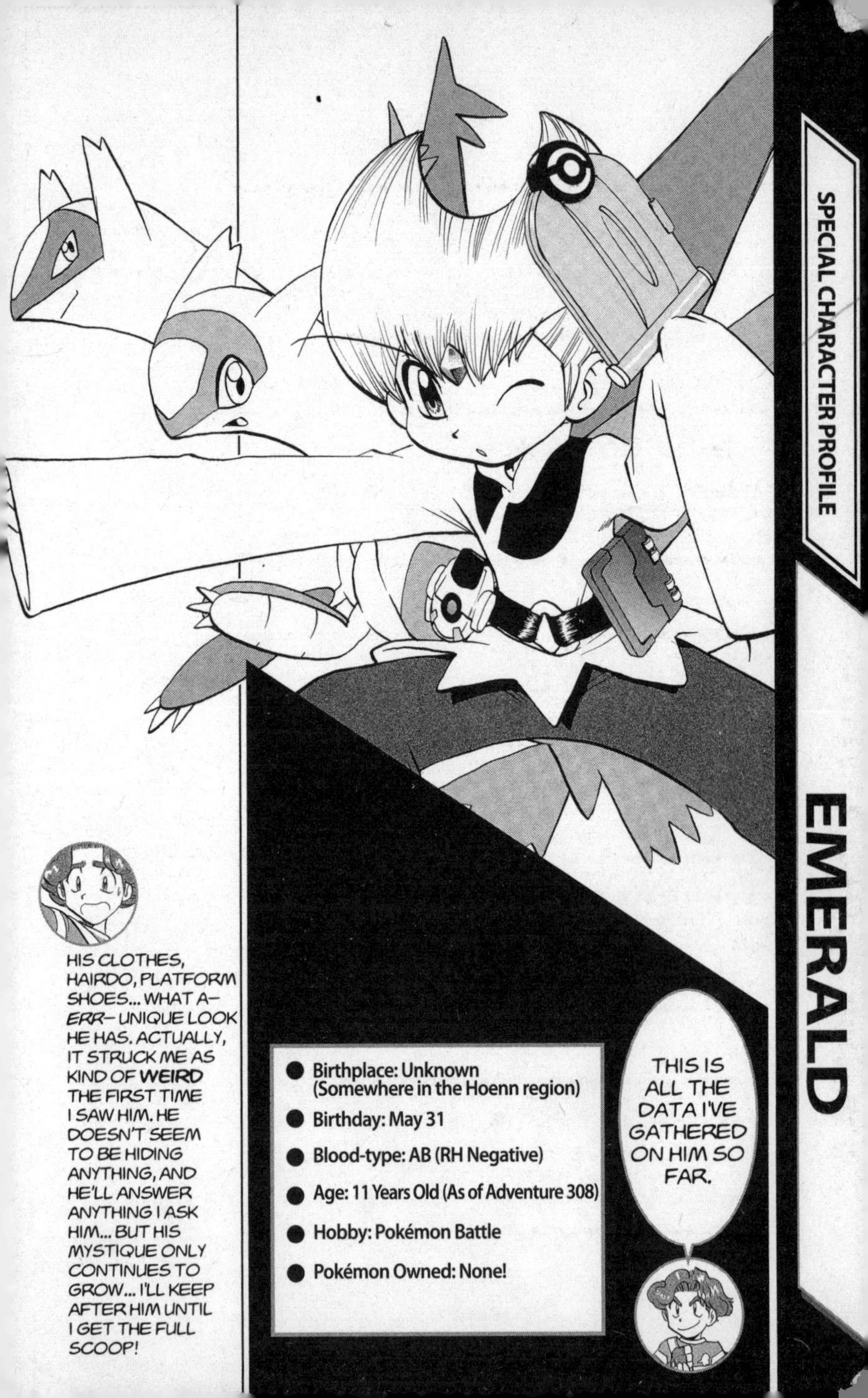
SPECIAL CHARACTER PROFILE
EMERALD
THIS IS ALL THE DATA I'VE GATHERED ON HIM SO FAR.
● Birthplace: Unknown (Somewhere in the Hoenn region)
● Birthday: May 31
● Blood-type: AB (RH Negative)
● Age: 11 Years Old (As of Adventure 308)
● Hobby: Pokémon Battle
● Pokémon Owned: None!
HIS CLOTHES, HAIRDO, PLATFORM SHOES... WHAT A– ERR– UNIQUE LOOK HE HAS. ACTUALLY, IT STRUCK ME AS KIND OF WEIRD THE FIRST TIME I SAW HIM. HE DOESN'T SEEM TO BE HIDING ANYTHING, AND HE'LL ANSWER ANYTHING I ASK HIM... BUT HIS MYSTIQUE ONLY CONTINUES TO GROW... I'LL KEEP AFTER HIM UNTIL I GET THE FULL SCOOP!

■POKÉDEX■

HE CHECKS POKÉMON DATA WITH THIS DEVICE. I'VE NEVER SEEN ONE BEFORE AND I DON'T KNOW WHO CREATED IT OR WHERE IT WAS MADE.

■E SHOOTER■

HE SHOOTS CALMING PELLETS OUT OF THIS DEVICE. THE POKÉMON TARGETED BY THE PELLETS CALMS DOWN RIGHT AWAY. BUT WHY?

■POKÉNAV■

A MUST-HAVE TOOL FOR ALL HOENN TRAINERS. THE TRAINERS PARTICIPATING IN THE BATTLE FRONTIER USE IT TO CHECK THEIR POKÉMON'S CONDITION, AMONG OTHER THINGS.

■FRONTIER PASS■

THIS CERTIFIES YOU AS A BATTLE FRONTIER CHALLENGER. EMERALD HAS ONE AND STORES THE SYMBOLS (THE BATTLE FRONTIER EQUIVA-LENT OF GYM BADGES) THAT HE WINS INSIDE IT.

■MECHANICAL HANDS■

MECHANICAL ARMS THAT STRETCH OUT FROM HIS SLEEVES. I HAVEN'T HAD A CHANCE TO LOOK UP HIS SLEEVES. WHERE ARE HIS REAL ARMS?

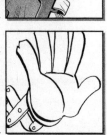

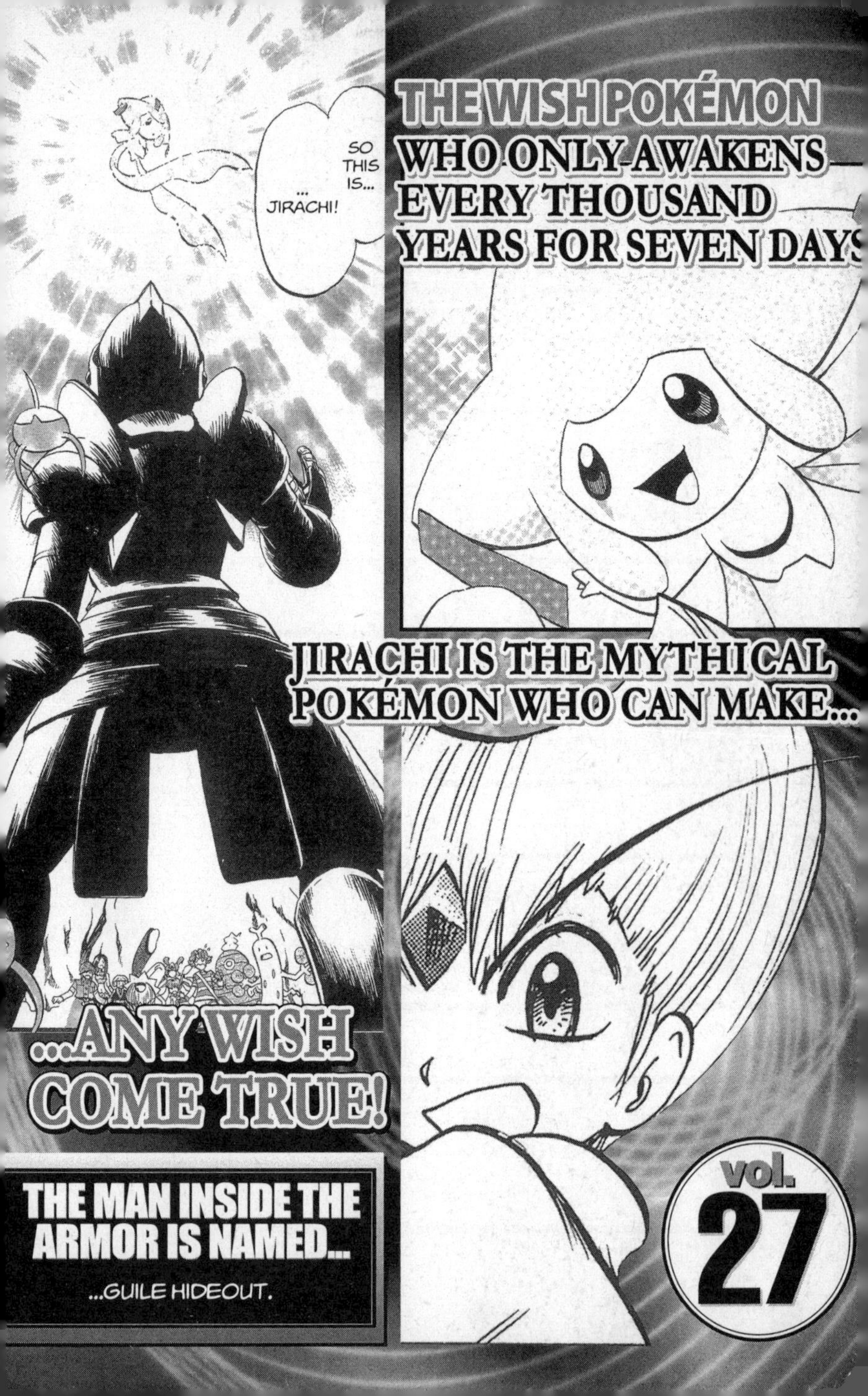
THE WISH POKÉMON
WHO ONLY AWAKENS—EVERY THOUSAND YEARS FOR SEVEN DAYS
JIRACHI IS THE MYTHICAL POKÉMON WHO CAN MAKE...
vol. 27
SO THIS IS...
...JIRACHI!
...ANY WISH COME TRUE!
THE MAN INSIDE THE ARMOR IS NAMED...
...GUILE HIDEOUT.

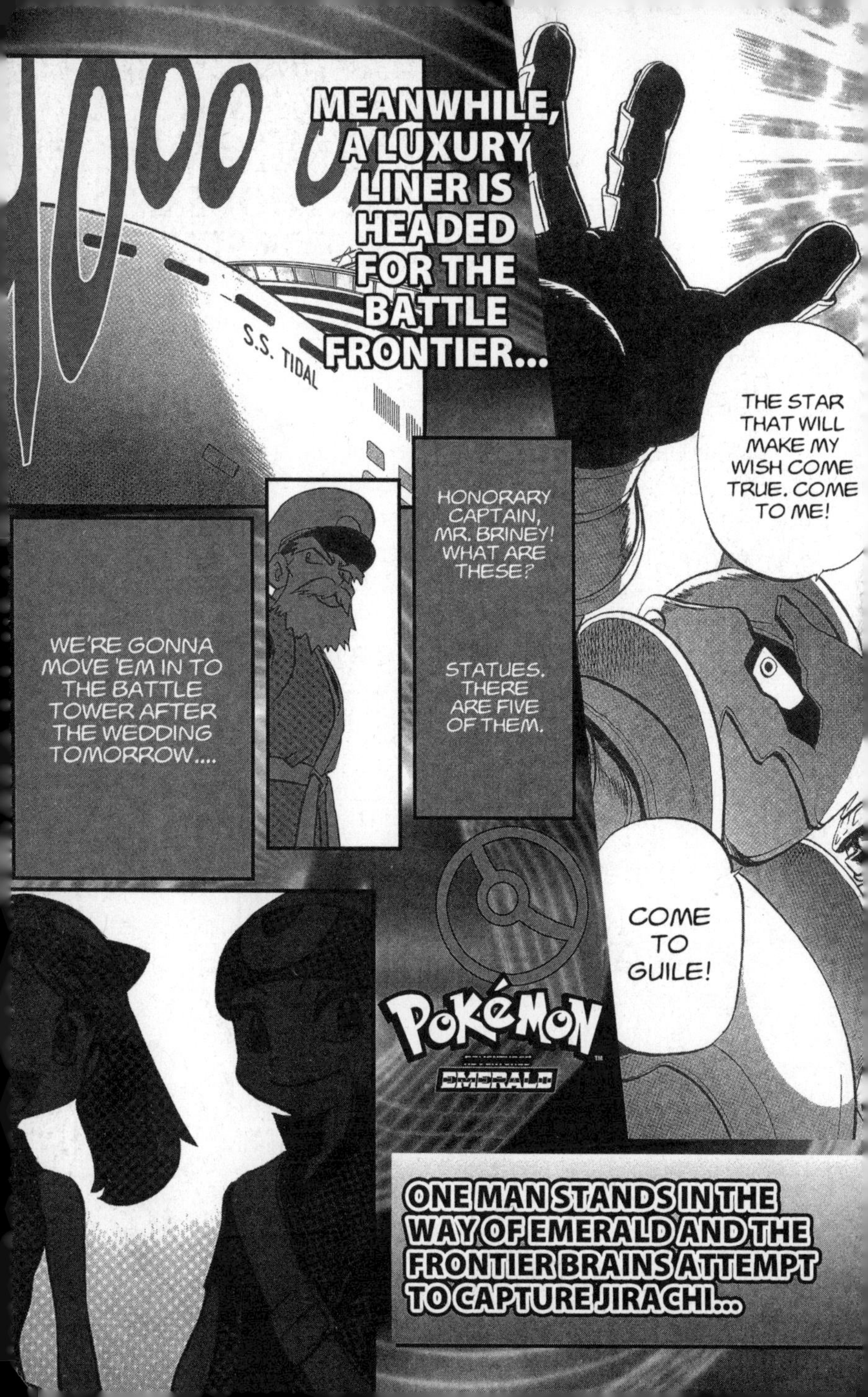
THE STAR THAT WILL MAKE MY WISH COME TRUE. COME TO ME!
COME TO GUILE!
MEANWHILE, A LUXURY LINER IS HEADED FOR THE BATTLE FRONTIER...
S.S. TIDAL
HONORARY CAPTAIN, MR. BRINEY! WHAT ARE THESE?
STATUES. THERE ARE FIVE OF THEM.
WE'RE GONNA MOVE 'EM IN TO THE BATTLE TOWER AFTER THE WEDDING TOMORROW....
POKéMON
EMERALD
ONE MAN STANDS IN THE WAY OF EMERALD AND THE FRONTIER BRAINS ATTEMPT TO CAPTURE JIRACHI...

Message from
Hidenori Kusaka

I've received the answers to a survey I placed in vol. 23.* This survey was designed so I could get to know more about you, our readers. I asked how old you are and how many volumes of the Pokémon Adventures series you own. I like to analyze things, so I really enjoyed crunching the data from the survey—such as the range of readers' ages, who reads the series in serialized form in magazines as opposed to who reads it after it's compiled into graphic novels, etc. I'm working hard to use this data to improve the comic. I'd like to thank everyone who helped out by taking the survey!

*In the original Japanese edition.

Message from
Satoshi Yamamoto

The main concept behind the new battleground called the Battle Frontier is to show how fun and complex a Pokémon Battle can be. How will Emerald defeat the Frontier Brains, who fight using a variety of strategies, unlike Gym Leaders, who mostly strategize along the lines of the Pokémon's type?

More Adventures Coming Soon...

When a mysterious armored person in search of the Wish Pokémon Jirachi attacks Nolan, Emerald is the prime suspect! Jirachi grants wishes, but only awakens every one thousand years for seven days.

How can Emerald and the Frontier Brains prevent Jirachi's power from falling into the wrong hands?!

AVAILABLE MARCH 2015!

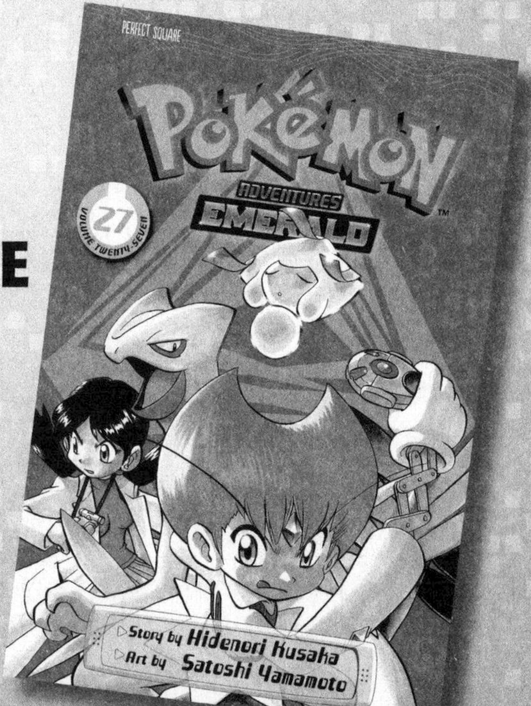
PERFECT SQUARE
POKéMON™
ADVENTURES
EMERALD
27 VOLUME TWENTY-SEVEN
Story by Hidenori Kusaka
Art by Satoshi Yamamoto

Pokémon

BLACK & WHITE™

STORY & ART BY SANTA HARUKAZE

YOUR FAVORITE POKÉMON FROM THE UNOVA REGION LIKE YOU'VE NEVER SEEN THEM BEFORE!

Available now!

A pocket-sized book brick jam-packed with four-panel comic strips featuring all the Pokémon Black and White characters, Pokémon vital statistics, trivia, puzzles, and fun quizzes!

PERFECT SQUARE

viz media
www.viz.com

RATED A ALL AGES
ratings.viz.com

© 2013 Pokémon.
©1995-2013 Nintendo/Creatures Inc./GAME FREAK inc. TM, ®, and character names are trademarks of Nintendo.
POKÉMON BW (Black • White) BAKUSHO 4KOMA MANGA ZENSHU © 2011 Santa HARUKAZE/SHOGAKUKAN

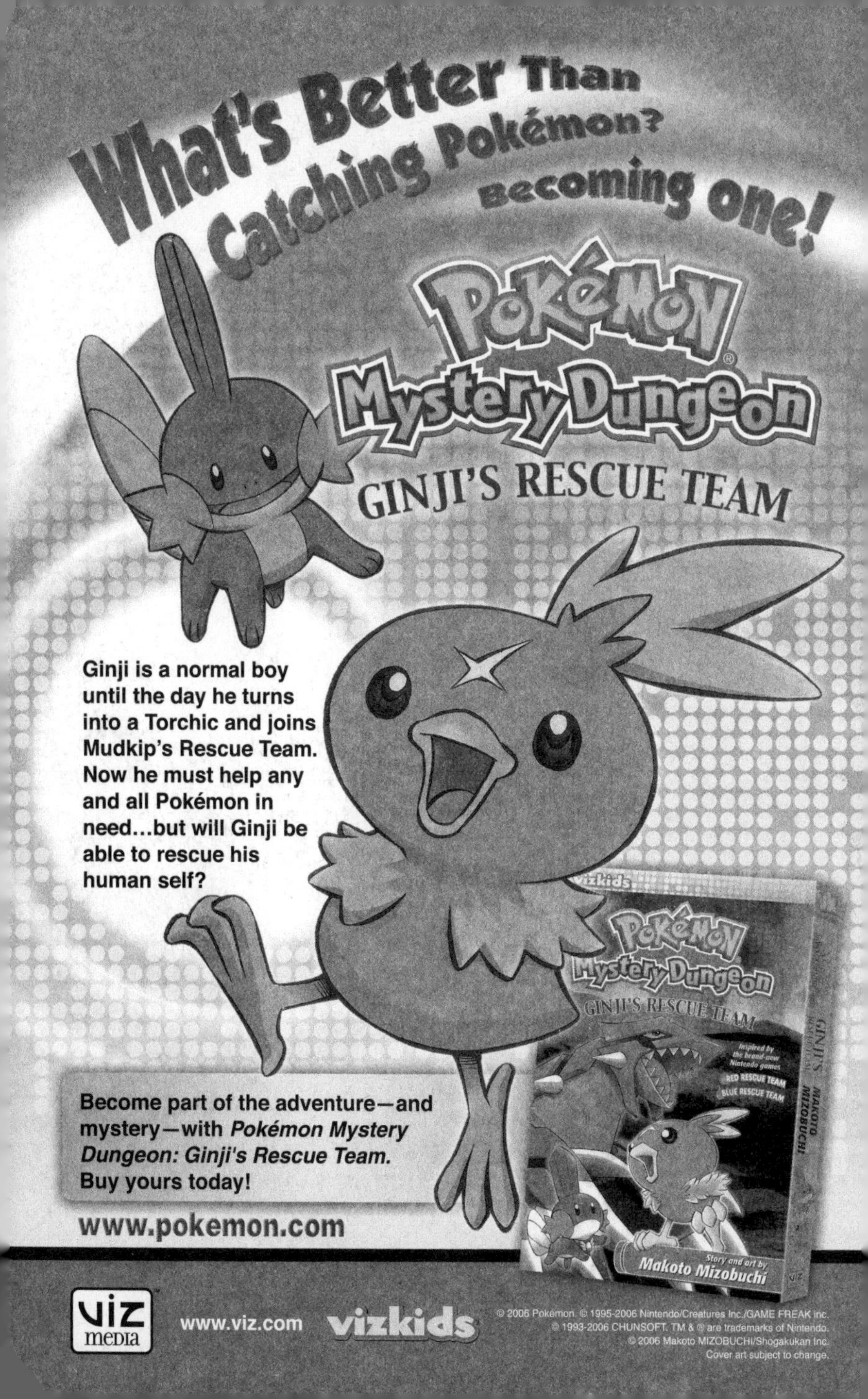
What's Better Than Catching Pokémon?
Becoming one!
Pokémon®
Mystery Dungeon
GINJI'S RESCUE TEAM
Ginji is a normal boy until the day he turns into a Torchic and joins Mudkip's Rescue Team. Now he must help any and all Pokémon in need...but will Ginji be able to rescue his human self?
Become part of the adventure—and mystery—with *Pokémon Mystery Dungeon: Ginji's Rescue Team.* Buy yours today!
www.pokemon.com
vizkids
Pokémon Mystery Dungeon
GINJI'S RESCUE TEAM
Inspired by the brand-new Nintendo games
RED RESCUE TEAM
BLUE RESCUE TEAM
Story and art by
Makoto Mizobuchi
MAKOTO MIZOBUCHI
viz media
www.viz.com
vizkids
© 2006 Pokémon. © 1995-2006 Nintendo/Creatures Inc./GAME FREAK inc.
© 1993-2006 CHUNSOFT. TM & ® are trademarks of Nintendo.
© 2006 Makoto MIZOBUCHI/Shogakukan Inc.
Cover art subject to change.

Take a trip with Pokémon

ALL THAT PIKACHU!

ANI-MANGA™

Meet Pikachu and all-star Pokémon! Two complete Pikachu stories taken from the Pokémon movies—all in a full color manga.

Buy yours today!

Pokémon

www.pokemon.com

© 2007 Pokémon. © 1997-2007 Nintendo, Creatures, GAME FREAK, TV Tokyo, ShoPro, JR Kikaku. © PIKACHU PROJECT 1998. Pokémon properties are trademarks of Nintendo. Cover art subject to change.

POKéMON MOVIE

Legend tells of The Sea Temple, which contains a treasure with the power to take over the world. But its location remains hidden and requires a mysterious key. Can Ash, Pikachu and their friends prevent the unveiling of these powerful secrets?

Pokémon Ranger and the Temple of the Sea

Own it on DVD today!

Pokémon USA, Inc.   www.pokemon.com

viz media
www.viz.com

© 2006 Pokémon. © 1997-2006 Nintendo, Creatures, GAME FREAK, TV Tokyo, ShoPro, JR Kikaku. © Pikachu Project 2005. Pokémon properties are trademarks of Nintendo.

The Struggle for Time and Space Begins Again!

Available at a DVD retailer near you!

Pokémon Trainer Ash and his Pikachu must find the Jewel of Life and stop Arceus from devastating all existence! The journey will be both dangerous and uncertain: even if Ash and his friends can set an old wrong right again, will there be time to return the Jewel of Life before Arceus destroys everything and everyone they've ever known?

Manga edition also available from VIZ Media

POKÉMON
ARCEUS
JEWEL OF LIFE
A TALE UNTOLD. A LEGEND UNLEASHED.

POKÉMON
ARCEUS
AND THE JEWEL OF LIFE

RATED
A
ALL AGES
rating.viz.com

www.vizkids.com   www.viz.com

© 2011 Pokémon. © 1997-2009 Nintendo, Creatures, GAME FREAK, TV Tokyo, ShoPro, JR Kikaku.
© Pikachu Project 2009. Pokémon properties are trademarks of Nintendo.

THIS IS THE END OF
THIS GRAPHIC NOVEL!

To properly enjoy this VIZ Media
graphic novel, please turn it around
and begin reading from right to left.

This book has been printed in the
original Japanese format in order
to preserve the orientation of the
original artwork.

Have fun with it!

3 1901 05315 3393

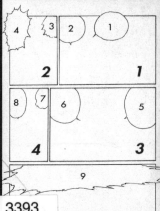

FOLLOW THE ACTION THIS WAY.

ARCEUS HAS BEEN BETRAYED—

NOW THE WORLD IS IN DANGER!

Long ago, the mighty Pokémon Arceus was betrayed by a human it trusted. Now Arceus is back for revenge! Dialga, Palkia and Giratina must join forces to help Ash, Dawn and their new friends Kevin and Sheena stop Arceus from destroying humankind. But it may already be too late!

Seen the movie? Read the manga!

MANGA PRICE: $7.99 usa $9.99 can
ISBN-13: 9781421538020 • IN STORES FEBUARY 2011

Check out the complete library of Pokémon books at VIZ.com

www.vizkids.com   www.viz.com

© 2011 Pokémon.
© 1997–2011 Nintendo, Creatures, GAME FREAK, TV Tokyo, ShoPro, JR Kikaku. © Pikachu Project 2009.
Pokémon properties are trademarks of Nintendo.
ARCEUS CHOUKOKU NO JIKUU E © 2009 Makoto MIZOBUCHI/Shogakukan.

Story and Art by Makoto Mizobuchi
Original Concept by Satoshi Tajiri
Supervised by Tsunekazu Ishihara
Script by Hideki Sonoda